THEY BUILT A CIVILIZATION AHEAD OF ITS TIME,
AND DOMINATED THE ANCIENT WORLD.

THEY WERE A PEOPLE OF MYSTERY WHOSE SECRETS
HAVE TURNED TO DUST—BUT WHO INSPIRE OUR AWE
AND WONDER EVEN TO THIS DAY. . . .

THE ANCIENT EGYPTIANS.
THEY SHOWED US HOW TO LIVE. AND HOW TO DIE.

Also by Christian Jacq

The Stone of Light

Volume I: Nefer the Silent

Volume II: The Wise Woman

Volume III: Paneb the Ardent

Ramses

Volume I: The Son of Light

Volume II: The Eternal Temple

Volume III: The Battle of Kadesh

Volume IV: The Lady of Abu Simbel

Volume V: Under the Western Acacia

The Living Wisdom of Ancient Egypt

About the translator

Sue Dyson is a prolific author of both fiction and nonfiction, including over thirty novels, both contemporary and historical. She has also translated a wide variety of French fiction.

THE STONE OF LIGHT

THE PLACE OF TRUTH

VOLUME IV

CHRISTIAN JACQ

Translated by Sue Dyson

POCKET BOOKS

New York London Toronto Sydney Singapore

An *Original* Publication of POCKET BOOKS

POCKET BOOKS, a division of Simon & Schuster, Inc.
1230 Avenue of the Americas, New York, NY 10020

Originally published in France in 2001 as *La Place de Verite*

Published by arrangement with XO S.A.

ISBN: 0-7434-0349-5

First Pocket Books trade paperback printing September 2001

10 9 8 7 6 5 4 3 2 1

Cover design by Rod Hernandez
Cover illustration by Gary Halsey

Printed in the U.S.A.

This story is dedicated to all the craftsmen of the Place of Truth, who were guardians of the secrets of the "House of Gold" and succeeded in passing them on in their works.

THE STONE OF LIGHT

THE PLACE OF TRUTH

VOLUME IV

1

The Place of Truth was in a state of near panic. Since the murder of Nefer the Silent, Master of the craftsmen's Brotherhood, all the inhabitants of the secret village—men, women, children, even animals—had come to dread the sunset. As soon as the sun sank behind the mountains to begin its nocturnal voyage to the heart of the underworld, all the villagers went to ground in their little white houses. Soon, a malevolent spirit would leave Nefer's tomb in search of prey.

One young girl had only just managed to escape from it, but no one dared trouble Ubekhet, the Wise Woman, who had withdrawn into mourning and despair since the death of her husband. She and Nefer had been initiated into the Brotherhood together; and they had become mother and father to the little community, which was centered around thirty craftsmen who had "heard the call," and their families.

"This can't go on any longer!" exploded Paneb the Ardent, a dark-eyed giant of a man. "We're skulking like rats and all the pleasure's gone out of life."

His wife, Uabet the Pure, was frozen to the spot by his anger. "Perhaps the ghost will eventually go away," she suggested timidly.

She turned to check on their children. All was well. Their two-year-old daughter, Iuwen, was peacefully asleep in bed, and Aapehti, their rebellious fifteen-year-old son, was drawing caricatures on a fragment of limestone in an attempt to forget his fear.

"No one but the Wise Woman can pacify her dead husband's soul," said Paneb, "and she no longer has the strength. They'll end up blaming me again—just you see if they don't!"

Paneb, leader of the starboard crew on the Brotherhood's symbolic ship, was the adopted son of Nefer the Silent and Ubekhet, and he adored them both. Yet a man who was beneath contempt, a traitor and a murderer hiding in the very bosom of the community, had tried to have Paneb accused of his spiritual father's murder. Although acquitted by the Wise Woman herself, the big man still felt suspicious glances following him around.

"I must resolve this matter myself," he decided.

Uabet, who was as frail as her husband was strong, threw herself into his arms. "Don't take such a risk," she begged. "Nefer's ghost is especially dangerous."

"Why should I be afraid of it? A father doesn't strike down his own son."

"This is more than a ghost hungry for vengeance. It can enter people's bodies and stop their blood circulating. No one, not even you, can defeat it."

At forty-one, Paneb had never been stronger and he had never yet met a foe who could match him. "I refuse to behave like a prisoner in my own village. We must be able to move about freely, at night as well as in the daytime."

"You have two children, Paneb, and a fine house worthy of a crew leader. Don't start a battle that is lost before it's begun."

Paneb took his wife by the hand and led her into the second room of their home, which was spotlessly clean, for Uabet was always on the lookout for the smallest speck of dust.

"Look at this stele, which I carved myself and set into the wall. It shows Nefer's radiant spirit, his immortal soul, which sails in the sun's ship and bestows its gifts upon us. The Master brought this Brotherhood to life. He could never bring death to it."

"But what about the ghost?"

"My father's secret name is Nefer-hotep, and 'hotep' means 'sunset, peace, plenty.' His ghost must be haunting us because one of the funerary rites wasn't performed correctly. We were all so overwhelmed by his murder that we must have made a serious mistake, and so Nefer's soul has appeared like this to demand the peace it yearns for."

"But what if the ghost's nothing but an evil spirit, greedy for blood?"

"That's impossible."

Paneb checked that he was wearing the two amulets vital for embarking on such a dangerous adventure: an eye of Horus and a scarab. The eye was a gift from Ched the Savior, the master artist who had revealed the secrets of drawing and painting to him. The precious talisman had been given life by the Wise Woman's celestial power; it enabled Paneb's eyes to see aspects of reality that eluded other men. The scarab had been hewn from the Stone of Light, the Place of Truth's greatest treasure, and it represented the righteous heart, the bodily organ that could perceive the invisible world and the eternal laws of harmony.

"Can you see my name?" he asked.

Uabet checked that the words PANEB THE ARDENT were correctly written in red ink on his right shoulder. "One last time," she pleaded, "I beg you not to do this."

"I intend to prove my innocence, and Nefer's, once and for all."

▲

A strange wind was blowing. Although the houses were tightly shuttered, it had found its way into them, and its mournful voice seemed full of menace.

Aapehti was scared and tried to hide in a laundry basket, but he was the sturdiest young lad in the village, and all he could hide of his stocky body was his chest.

Paneb caught him by the hips and set him roughly back on

his feet. "Aapehti, you're ridiculous! Follow your sister's example—she's sound asleep."

Iuwen chose that precise moment to wake up and burst into tears. Her mother rocked her to calm her sobs.

"I'll be back soon," Paneb promised.

The night of the new moon was dark, the Place of Truth silent. Sheltered behind its high walls, the village seemed asleep. But as he walked down the main street, which ran from north to south, Paneb heard snatches of conversations, whispers and laments.

The little settlement stood beyond the high-point of the annual Nile floods and occupied an entire desert valley, the former bed of a river, bordered by hills that screened it from view.

The Place of Truth lived apart from the outside world, isolated from the Nile valley, between Ramses' Temple of a Million Years and the mound of Djamet, where the primordial gods rested. The village had its own temple, shrines, workshops, wells, grain stores, a school, and two burial grounds where the craftsmen and their loved ones were buried.

Suddenly, Paneb halted. He thought he had seen someone slip into one of the smaller alleyways.

Unafraid, he gazed at the houses of eternity in the western burial ground. Most of them were topped with small pyramids made from white limestone, and when Ra was visible in the sky they glinted with a dazzling light. Brightly colored stelae, little gardens planted with flowers and shrubs, and welcoming white-fronted shrines prevented the place from feeling funereal; here the Brotherhood's ancestors watched over their successors.

Usually, all was peaceful. But tonight, on the path that led to Nefer the Silent's tomb, Paneb detected a hostile presence.

What if it was only the traitor, playing the ghost to lure him into an ambush and kill him? He rejoiced at the thought; nothing would give him more pleasure than cracking open the liar's skull!

Nefer's last home was as vast as it was splendid. In front of the entrance to the shrine, which the living were allowed to enter, Ubekhet had planted a persea tree. It had grown extraordinarily quickly, as if in a hurry to spread its benevolent shade over the open-air courtyard where banquets would be held in the dead man's honor.

Paneb walked through the pillared gateway, which was fashioned like the gateway to a temple, and halted again, in the middle of the courtyard. The hostile presence was stronger and closer. But where would the ghost emerge from? It must be from the slit in the chapel wall, made so that Nefer's living statue could look out over the earthly world.

The big man approached with measured step, as if exploring the place for the first time, although he knew it better than anyone, since he had decorated the whole of his spiritual father's tomb himself.

If he had rushed in, as he usually did, Paneb would not have seen the red shadow leap out of the funerary well, which had been filled with stones. The specter tried to strangle him. He managed to free himself just in time and struck it in the face. But his fist met empty air.

Twisting and turning like a snake, the red shadow tried to find the best angle of attack. Paneb ran to the shrine, where a torch was smoldering. He kindled it into flame, then strode toward his enemy, saying contemptuously, "I bet you don't like the light!"

The red shadow's face was not Nefer's—and it was distorted, as though in terrible pain.

As soon as the fire touched it, the ghost vanished back into the well.

"You won't hide from me in there!" roared Paneb.

He tore up two paving slabs, jammed the torch between them, and began to empty the well stone by stone. Whatever the danger, he was determined to reach the evil spirit's lair.

2

At the Celebration of the Mysteries, Ubekhet had assumed the symbolic office of Isis the widow, and this terrible ordeal had touched her very soul. Nefer had been her only love, and he always would be.

Since his death, she had lost the will to live. Fearing the worst, her big black dog, Ebony, never left her side, even for a moment, and always kept one eye open when he slept. He watched over his mistress constantly and shared her grief: he never asked for games or walks.

Ubekhet spent as little time as possible looking after the home where she had known such intense happiness with Nefer. The magnificent furnishings had been a gift from the craftsmen in honor of their Master, whose natural authority, firmness of character, and exceptional skills had always guided them to success.

At forty-eight, Ubekhet was still a beautiful woman, slender and graceful, with delicate features and silky hair streaked with gold. Her face radiated a gentle, reassuring light, her voice was melodious, and her blue eyes enchanting. The villagers worshipped her, all the more so because she had cared for all of them, at one time or another, with exemplary devotion.

But the Wise Woman no longer had the strength to carry on. The loss of Nefer was eating away at her, and she was allowing herself to slide toward death: all she wanted was to join him.

▲

The room was lit by a single lamp, a masterpiece that had been carved by the Brotherhood's carpenter, Didia the Generous. On a small column shaped like a papyrus stem, which emerged from a limestone base, lay a bronze dish containing oil. This fed a smokeless linen wick, like those used in the tombs.

During her sleepless nights, Ubekhet clung on to this last

glimmer of light; in the gentle light of the flame, she sometimes thought she glimpsed her husband's face, but the illusion was quickly dispelled, plunging her even deeper into despair.

Ebony laid his paw on the Wise Woman's arm, as though he knew the terrible decision she had taken. Ubekhet could go no further. She could not bear this state of shock any longer. By immersing herself in the world beyond, she could at last put an end to the torture.

The touch of the dog's paw, and the tenderness she saw in his hazel eyes, produced a kind of miracle: Nefer appeared in the light and spoke to her. "If I fail or die," he said, "don't let the flame of the Place of Truth go out. In the name of our love, Ubekhet, promise me you will carry on."

The Master had spoken those words when he was alive, but she had forgotten them. And Nefer had returned from the afterlife to remind her of her duty and her office, denying her the luxury of self-pity.

The sound of loud hammering echoed in her head. Anxiously, Ebony ran to the front door, barking. Someone was knocking.

"Open up, Ubekhet! Open the door, I beg you!"

The widow recognized Uabet's voice. Ebony stopped barking, and Ubekhet opened the door. Uabet the Pure stood there, with Aapehti's pet goose, Bad Girl, beside her.

"Come quickly—it's serious!" panted Uabet.

"What's the matter?"

"Paneb went to Nefer's tomb. If he keeps on fighting the ghost, he'll die. You're the only person who can persuade him to give up."

A faint smile appeared on Ubekhet's lips. "Do you think I'm still capable of helping anyone?"

"Paneb won't listen to anyone but you—and I don't want to lose him!"

"Wait just a moment."

The Master's widow went back into her bedroom and

opened a jewel box decorated with ivory. For the first time since her husband's death, she put on a necklace, earrings, and bracelets. Then she gazed at her reflection in the copper mirror, whose handle was shaped like a papyrus stem, the symbol of fulfillment and vital energy. She saw the face of a woman worn out by pain; a face she had to make up carefully to restore the appearance of youthful strength.

The transformation was so successful that it amazed Uabet. "You've never looked so beautiful. But come quickly."

With Ebony running ahead and Bad Girl following behind, the two women climbed up toward Nefer the Silent's tomb. The eastern sky was tinged with red; the breeze made Uabet shiver, and she began to climb more quickly.

▲

After several hours of uninterrupted toil, Paneb had managed to empty the funerary well. His strength undimmed, he had reached the wooden door of Nefer's chamber of resurrection, which was sealed with wax.

Looking up, he saw Uabet's face, silhouetted against the pink-tinged sky.

"Come back up here, Paneb," she ordered.

"Certainly not."

"You have no right to violate a tomb."

"The evil spirit is hiding. I'm going to find it."

"The Wise Woman forbids you to do so."

"The Wise Woman! But . . ."

"Yes, she's here."

Using the rough edges of the stone blocks as footholds, Paneb climbed back up as quickly as a cat. He did not believe Uabet, and wanted to check for himself.

Ubekhet was indeed there, wearing her most beautiful jewelry and dressed in the long red robe that denoted her position as mistress of the priestesses of Hathor.

"Do you really forbid me to go any further?" he asked.

"I must come down with you."

"No, it's too dangerous. I've seen the red ghost, and it's fearsome. And it isn't Nefer."

"It can only be an evil spirit caused by some mistake during the burial rites," said Ubekhet.

"Yes, that's what I think too; and I'm going to get rid of it. Make sure it doesn't get away if it escapes from me."

Paneb went back down to the bottom of the well. Without hesitation, he broke the seal and opened the door of the burial chamber. He moved aside the tools, linen chests, baskets containing embalmed food and statues of the dead man, and cleared a path to the sarcophagus. At any moment, the red demon might emerge from its hiding place and hurl itself upon him. All his senses on the alert, like a hunter on the track of a prey so formidable that he was not sure he could master it, Paneb moved every object slowly. Despite his huge size and strength, he could move as silently as a cat.

The sarcophagus had been covered with a very fine green winding-sheet, and laid upon a bed. Around the mummy's neck was a five-stranded necklace of white lotus flowers and willow leaves; on its chest lay a bouquet of persea and vine leaves.

A ray of light penetrated the cavern, but the rear portion remained in darkness. The ghost had gone to ground, and Paneb could not see it.

No doubt it would be better to leave and return with torches to light the room, thereby sapping the ghost's strength; but if Paneb withdrew, his adversary was bound to take advantage of that fact to strike.

Suddenly, Paneb noticed something wrong: the sun disk of celestial copper laid beneath the mummy's head was not giving off any light. It was covered in hieroglyphic texts, and ought to have surrounded the mummy with a golden radiance, driving away the demons of darkness.

He went close enough to touch it, and discovered that the precious symbol had been placed upside down. This was no mistake but an act of calculated malevolence. Not content with murdering Nefer, the traitor had also unleashed an evil spirit.

At the very moment Paneb laid his hand on the disk, the red specter sprang out of it. Its mouth twisted, its brow cleft from top to bottom, it tried again to strangle him. Its grip was so powerful that Paneb could not breathe.

Instead of trying to fight his intangible enemy, Paneb swiftly reversed the copper sun disk and placed it correctly under the nape of the mummy's neck. A flame darted from the disk and touched the red specter, whose eyes suddenly grew so large that they engulfed first its head, then its entire body.

Paneb could breathe again, but then he felt a terrible burning on his throat, and let out a cry of pain. Instinctively, he struck out at the specter, which dwindled to a little ball of fire before disappearing into the ground.

Fighting for breath, the big man tried to leave the burial chamber and regain the free air. But the walls of the well began to close in on him, and he knew he was going to die.

"Climb back up, Paneb," screamed Uabet. "Climb back up, quickly!"

3

General Mehy sniffed the dish of lamb cutlets his cook had presented to him, then threw it in the man's face. "They're overcooked, you fool."

"But I did exactly as you said, my lord, and—"

"The cucumber salad was vile, and you dared serve me a wine that smelt of cork! Get out of this house at once, and don't ever set foot in it again."

Mehy's anger was not feigned, and the cook beat a hasty retreat. It was unwise to argue with the most powerful man in the rich province of Thebes.

The general had begun his career in the corps of charioteers. He was rather short, with a round face, dark-brown eyes, fleshy lips, very black hair slicked to his scalp, a broad, powerful chest, and plump hands and feet. Self-confident and ambitious, he had risen to become commander in chief of the Theban troops and governor of the city's west bank—and one of his duties was to ensure the safety and well-being of the Place of Truth.

The Place of Truth! That damned Brotherhood had dared reject him as a candidate when he was a youth. Worse still, it possessed a priceless treasure, the Stone of Light, which he must seize if he was to become master of Egypt. One night Mehy had glimpsed the Stone, from the top of a hill overlooking the Valley of the Kings where the craftsmen were celebrating a ritual; but he had been spotted by a Nubian guard and had had to get rid of him by smashing his skull.

That was his first crime, but it had been followed by several others, which he had either committed himself or delegated. All were intended to throw opponents off his trail and ensure that they did not prevent him acquiring the supreme treasure.

"Rinse your fingers, my tender lion," suggested his wife, Serketa, and she held out to him a long-spouted silver vessel containing perfumed water.

Serketa had dyed blond hair, light-blue eyes, and an opulent bosom, and was permanently preoccupied with her weight. She was also a born killer, whose talents Mehy had developed by involving her in his progressive conquest of power. She had agreed to the murder of her own father so that Mehy could inherit his fortune, and later she had become a murderess herself, deriving intense pleasure from the act of killing.

Because Serketa had given him only two daughters, whose fate did not interest him in the least, the general had intended to divorce her; but she had guessed what was in his mind, so, knowing she might well become dangerous, he had instead decided to make an ally of her. From that moment on, they had hidden nothing from each other and acted in perfect harmony.

Mehy drank a cup of palm wine. The drink was far too potent for most people, but the general could hold his alcohol and enjoyed excellent health, with the exception of an irritating skin rash which appeared on his left leg whenever he was angry.

And right now it was beginning to itch. . . .

Serketa knelt before him and kissed his thighs. "Why fret so, my sweet crocodile?" she lisped, in her little-girl voice.

"Because Nefer's murder hasn't produced the results we expected."

"Have a little patience. First, our main enemy is well and truly dead; second, the traitor we ordered to kill him is completely in our power; lastly, the traitor's latest message confirmed that the Brotherhood is in utter disarray."

"That may be so, but it still exists," said Mehy bitterly.

"Yes, but in what state? By reversing the disk under the mummy's head, the traitor unleashed the specter that's terrorizing the Place of Truth. The villagers are convinced that Nefer's bent on revenge, and they'll end up hating one another."

"Let's hope you're right. But I'd be much happier if the villagers had announced they were leaving the Place of Truth and handing it over to me. Then we could have searched it perfectly legally and discovered the Stone's hiding place."

"Wouldn't the craftsmen have taken it with them?"

"If they had, they'd have been attacked and killed—which naturally I'd have deplored in the most moving terms. But they didn't make that mistake. Instead, they've gone to ground behind their high walls—walls which I, their sworn enemy, must ensure are sturdy and sound."

"Nefer's murder was essential," said Serketa. "Without him, the Brotherhood no longer has a soul. There's no one good enough to succeed him. The leader of the port crew is merely a skilled craftsman without a trace of brilliance, the Scribe of the Tomb is too old, and the Wise Woman will never recover from her husband's death."

"You're forgetting Paneb, the new leader of the starboard crew."

"No, I'm not. Our informant says he's much too impulsive to be appointed Master. The loss of his spiritual father will drive him to madness, I'm sure of it. Just as we planned, the Place of Truth will destroy itself from the inside, and all we'll have to do is harvest its wealth and its secrets."

The general led Serketa out into the luxuriant garden of his sumptuous west-bank house; like all the many properties he owned, it was cared for by an army of servants. The pair sat down in a small pavilion shaded by sycamores and carob trees. Mehy loathed the country, the heat, and the sun, whose savage bite he feared.

A servant immediately brought them cool beer, which Serketa declined with disdain.

"I met this Paneb fellow a long time ago, when he was working in a tannery," Mehy recalled. "He was young then, insolent, and already as strong as a wild bull. The very model of a soldier, yet he refused to join the army and serve under my command. No one could have dreamt he'd become one of the pillars of the Place of Truth."

"No, the only pillar was Nefer the Silent. He planned and directed the work and resolved the craftsmen's quarrels, and he can never be replaced. The specter will drive away several families, and other disasters will soon strike the Brotherhood."

One of the house guards ran up. "General, a message from Pi-Ramses." He handed Mehy a sealed papyrus, then returned to his post.

"A letter from Tjaty Bay," said Mehy. "King Saptah and Queen Tausert have summoned me to report on the state of

Thebes's treasury and present the results of my inquiries into Nefer's murder."

"But they know you aren't allowed to enter the village."

"Of course, but they want to check that I'm doing everything possible to identify the murderer and make sure the Brotherhood's safe."

"Be careful," warned Serketa. "Tausert might be setting a trap for you."

"She's certainly capable of doing that. But her main preoccupation is to hold on to power by controlling her henchman, Tjaty Bay, who succeeded in putting that cripple Saptah on the throne. The court at Pi-Ramses has become nothing but a nest of vipers. Since the death of Ramses the Great, pharaonic authority has grown weaker and weaker—and that, my sweet, is our good fortune. Once we have the Stone of Light, the country will belong to us. What a pity I can't send my soldiers to raze that village to the ground and kill its inhabitants."

Serketa quivered with pleasure at the thought of such carnage. "Yes, isn't it? But what are you going to do?"

"First, I shall go to the lay workers' camp, to meet the Scribe of the Tomb and ask him if his internal inquiries have made any progress. Then I shall sail for Pi-Ramses—you'll come with me, of course."

Serketa had been waiting for him to say those last words. She would never let her dear husband play his games unless she was an integral part of them. And if he so much as glanced at some young beauty, she would strangle the slut before punishing Mehy.

But her husband was a realist. He knew he would not succeed without Serketa's active involvement, for his delightful wife lacked all humanity and moral sense, and was more than willing to carry out his evil plans. And, since she was not only deadlier than a horned viper but every bit as ambitious as himself, the future looked decidedly rosy.

"Shouldn't you stop deliveries of food to the village?" she asked.

"I considered it," admitted Mehy, "and I could have blamed an underling and then replaced him with a more zealous scribe. But I have already eliminated the obstacles in our path. Besides, while we are away the old Scribe of the Tomb would cause such a fuss that the echoes would reach Pi-Ramses. Don't forget that I am the official protector of the Place of Truth, and that the central government must perceive my conduct to be above reproach. Up to now, this strategy has won me praise and promotions."

Serketa began to touch up her luxurious green eye makeup, which repelled insects and protected her from dust.

Mehy thought she looked anxious. "Is it Queen Tausert who worries you?"

"She is formidable, it's true, and I hope young Saptah's supporters succeed in killing her as soon as possible. But no, it was Paneb I was thinking about. You're right. That fiery-tempered giant will probably be tempted to take control and rule over the Brotherhood like a tyrant."

"Bearing in mind what we know about the craftsmen's rule, that's impossible," objected Mehy.

"Paneb isn't afraid of being hated, and he'd trample all over the village laws, whatever they might be."

The general's throat tightened with sudden anxiety. "But if that happened, the traitor would have killed Nefer for nothing."

"Not at all. If Paneb did seize power he wouldn't use it wisely, as Nefer did. And if he dared do so, we'd make sure his rise to power came to an abrupt halt."

"You have a plan already?"

"Of course I have," she replied, with a fierce smile.

4

The starboard crew's stonecutters were refilling the funerary well at Nefer the Silent's tomb.

"Paneb must be dead," declared Karo the Impatient, a stocky fellow with thick eyebrows, a broken nose and short, powerful arms.

"No, he isn't," retorted an equally burly colleague, Casa the Rope. "He's lying in the shrine, and I'm sure the Wise Woman will bring him back to life."

"When it's the end, it's the end," said Fened the Nose.

"When I pulled him out of the well," Nakht the Strong reminded them, "he was still breathing."

Elegant Ched the Savior, a painter with immaculately groomed hair and mustache, was not taking part in the heavy work, but was casting a critical eye over his colleagues. Userhat the Lion, the broad-chested head sculptor, was making sure that the well was completely filled. Renupe the Jovial, another sculptor, who had a fat belly and the face of a malicious spirit, was getting ready to re-cover it with paving stones, aided by his rather edgy colleague, Ipuy the Examiner.

"The goldsmith's coming out of the shrine," exclaimed Renupe.

Thuty the Learned, a man who looked so fragile that he might break, ran toward them, shouting, "Paneb's alive!"

"Alive? In what way?" demanded Fened. "Like a stone, a vegetable, or a man?"

"No one's sure yet."

"Let's go and see."

They all headed for the shrine. Three craftsmen guarded its entrance: Pai the Good Bread, whose chubby face had for once lost its jollity; Gau the Precise, with his unattractive, long-nosed face and heavy, slightly flabby body; and Unesh the Jackal, who was built just like the predator he was named for.

Inside the shrine, the starboard crew's carpenter, Didia the Generous, a tall, slow-moving fellow, was helping Hay, leader of the port crew, to hold Paneb in a sitting position so that Ubekhet could sound his chest.

Userhat ran up to Unesh and Pai, and panted, "Can he speak?"

"Be quiet," Gau told him. "The Wise Woman is listening to the voice of his heart."

Paneb's eyes were open, but he was completely inert; he looked just like a statue. His skin was red, as if he had just been scalded.

Fortunately, he had not lost his amulets; and Ubekhet rubbed the eye and the heart between her thumbs to restore their full effectiveness. She had said not a single word, and there was no glimmer of hope in her eyes. Although she had already used her magnetic energy on the giant's neck and back, she had failed to make his life force flow again.

Suddenly, an enormous cat jumped up onto Paneb's knees. It was so big that it looked more like a lynx than a house cat. Curling itself up into a ball, it began to purr. Immediately, Paneb's eyes lost their glazed expression. Ubekhet let out a sigh of relief. The cat was the embodiment of the sun's victory over the darkness, and it had absorbed the last traces of the harmful fluids that the evil spirit had forced into the painter's flesh.

At last the big man awoke. "The specter . . ." he said uncertainly. "The walls . . . the walls were suffocating me. Where are they?"

"It was only an illusion," said Ubekhet gently, "and here you are, back among us."

"I knew he was indestructible!" exclaimed Renupe. "Don't they say that a part of Ramses the Great's *ka* has passed into Paneb's? Thanks to that energy, he has saved the Brotherhood. We must praise Paneb!"

The sculptor's enthusiasm was infectious, and the lucky patient got to his feet to the accompaniment of his colleagues' cheers.

"Let me through," ordered a hoarse, authoritarian voice. It was Kenhir, the seventy-seven-year-old Scribe of the Tomb. He was the central government's representative in the Place of Truth, and had given up a brilliant career in Karnak to devote himself to this village and its inhabitants. Although he never stopped criticizing their countless faults, he loved them more than anything in the world, so much so that the government had been unable to force him to retire.

Kenhir was corpulent and clumsy, and could now only walk with the aid of a stick—except when he was in a hurry and forgot to walk like a pain-racked old man. It was Kenhir's job to keep the Journal of the Tomb, in which he wrote down everything that happened in the community, whether large or small. To the craftsmen, he was a veritable slave driver, who tolerated no sloppiness. He meticulously checked every reason for absence, and, if a man was sick, consulted the Wise Woman to make sure that the craftsman really was ill and unable to do his work.

It was also his task to ensure that the tools—which belonged to Pharaoh—were in good condition, to distribute them, collect them in, and have them repaired. Nevertheless, each member of the Brotherhood was allowed to make tools for his own personal use, and Kenhir could be relied upon to make sure there was no confusion.

"People are saying the ghost has killed Paneb," he said anxiously.

Rat-faced Assistant Scribe Imuni was ready to take notes.

"Actually, it's just the opposite," declared Paneb.

Kenhir looked Paneb up and down. "I must say, you do look alive."

"Paneb has saved the village," said Nakht the Strong. "If the ghost had gone on terrorizing us, several families would have left."

"He risked his life for us," said Fened the Nose. "A deed like that not only clears him of all charges but also marks him out as our next Master."

The Scribe of the Tomb turned to the Wise Woman and Hay, leader of the port crew. They indicated their approval.

The traitor was devastated. He had recoiled when he saw Charmer, the cat, because that animal had clawed him once, when he was looking for the Stone of Light—which was so well hidden that he had still not managed to discover its hiding place. And now Paneb, after his victory over the red specter, had become not only the hero of the Brotherhood but also its future Master.

But the most important thing was still to destroy Nefer the Silent, who had been loved by all and whose authority no one had questioned. By reversing the disk beneath the mummy's head, the traitor had tried to kill Nefer a second time; had he succeeded, even if Paneb had managed to destroy the evil spirit Nefer would never have returned.

Still, all was not lost. The village court might not yield to the enthusiasm of the moment and choose Paneb the Ardent; after mature reflection, they'd surely reject him. But if they did elect him Master they'd be making a disastrous mistake. He'd be an appalling Master. He'd cause divisions among the craftsmen and create endless dissent in the village. And then the traitor could take advantage of the chaos. It was he, and he alone, who should have been leading the Place of Truth for all these years. But his worth had been ignored, so his vengeance was fully justified.

General Mehy and his wife had enabled him to amass wealth outside the village, in exchange for the information he gave them. He was already a rich man. All that remained was for him to acquire the Stone of Light and use it to bargain with.

Ubekhet had composed herself. "Thanks to Paneb, Nefer is at last at peace. The Light shines beneath his head, his body of resurrection welcomes the sun's secret power, and his name of Nefer-hotep is complete. He has become one of our

Brotherhood's benevolent ancestors, a powerful, radiant spirit whom we shall worship every morning in all our houses. For him, all trials are at an end; and to honor him and carry on his teachings, we shall go on fighting to keep the Place of Truth alive."

Everyone sensed that sadness would never again leave Ubekhet's eyes; but the Wise Woman was once more at work, and she would overcome her despair to take care of the little community. With the aid of her magic, no obstacle would be insurmountable.

"I've got a bad cold," complained Fened the Nose. "Will you give me some medicine for it?"

"My workshop is open again," said Ubekhet with a broad smile.

"I've got a cut on my foot that won't heal," piped up Casa the Rope, "and that's much worse than a mere cold."

Ubekhet looked at the cut. "This is a problem I know and can cure."

Thuty the Learned turned to Paneb. "What do you intend to do?"

"I am now the servant of the *ka* of Nefer the Silent, my spiritual father, and I forbid anyone to approach his tomb. It is I, and I alone, who shall bring the offerings and look after his House of Eternity."

"As you wish," nodded Unesh the Jackal. "But do you want to take on all Nefer's offices?"

"Being leader of the starboard crew is quite enough for me. Now, go away. I want to be alone with the Wise Woman to worship the memory of the man whom we love and who can never be replaced."

No one protested, and the craftsmen moved off.

"Paneb will make an excellent Master," suggested the traitor to the Scribe of the Tomb.

"That's for the court to decide," replied Kenhir.

Kenhir had scarcely crossed the threshold of his house

when his young wife, Niut the Lively, whom he had married in order to make her his heir, came running up to him.

"General Mehy is at the main gate of the village," she said, "and is asking to see you urgently."

5

Mehy had to give his name and titles at every one of the five forts along the road to the village. Commander Sobek had instructed his Nubian guards to be rigorous, and all visitors, no matter what their rank, must respect the rules.

At the Fifth Fort, Mehy was greeted by Sobek himself.

The big, muscular Nubian was completely incorruptible. He was also a driven man, haunted by a question that had remained unanswered for the last twenty years: who had killed one of his men on a hill overlooking the Valley of the Kings? His investigations into the incident had ground to a halt; and the murder of Nefer the Silent had pushed the crime into the background for the moment, but Sobek was still convinced that someone had long been plotting against the Brotherhood and that the two matters were linked.

The Nubian did not like Mehy, whom he thought pretentious, self-important, and overambitious. However, he had no reason to refuse him access to the lay workers' camp, where the "men of the outside" worked for the Brotherhood's well-being, under the direction of Beken the Potter.

"Any problems to report, Sobek?" asked Mehy.

"No, none to do with my work."

"Make sure you keep me fully informed. I set great store by my excellent administration."

"The outside workers are well paid, they are happy with

their working conditions, and the village seems to have all it needs."

"Inform the Scribe of the Tomb that I wish to see him urgently."

While he waited for Kenhir to arrive, Mehy gazed around the lay workers' workshops. At sunset they would return to their homes, on the fringes of the cultivated area. Their work was strictly organized, so as to relieve the craftsmen of as many humdrum tasks as possible and allow them to concentrate on their life's work: to enable the Stone of Light to shine forth in all their works and give substance to the mysteries of the House of Gold.

Soon, thought Mehy, this place would belong to him, and he alone would give the orders.

Kenhir hobbled toward the visitor. When he reached Mehy, he halted and leant heavily on his walking stick.

"How are you, Kenhir?" asked the general.

"Not well, not at all well. My age weighs on me more heavily with every day that passes."

"Shouldn't you think about taking a well-deserved retirement?"

"There's still too much for me to do, especially after recent tragic events."

"It is precisely because of Nefer's murder that I'm here. The king has summoned me to the capital and he wants to know the results of my inquiries; but you're the only person with the authority to carry out an investigation inside the village."

"Indeed, General."

"Have you identified the murderer?"

"I'm afraid not," said Kenhir.

"Have you any suspects?"

Kenhir looked embarrassed. "I shall tell you the truth, General, on condition that you promise me not to repeat it."

Mehy stiffened. Had the old scribe unmasked the traitor? "You're asking a lot. I can't keep anything from His Majesty."

"King Saptah is a young man, and Pi-Ramses is a long way from the Place of Truth, which you and I both have a duty to protect. I shall write the king a detailed report on my investigation, and you can reassure him by telling him that the Brotherhood will continue to work as if nothing had happened."

The general's muscles tensed, and his left leg began to itch furiously. So Nefer's death had not succeeded in breaking the craftsmen's spirit! He said, "Very well, Kenhir. I promise I won't say anything."

"We're almost certain the guilty party is a member of the Brotherhood."

"But . . . Are you saying there's a traitor among you?"

"I fear so," admitted the old man wearily.

"I find that hard to believe. My own theory is much more plausible."

"May I know what it is?" asked Kenhir, intrigued.

"I think the Master's murderer must be a lay worker."

"A lay worker? But they're forbidden to enter the village."

"The murderer must have managed to sneak inside without being spotted by the gatekeeper, no doubt intending to steal valuables from Nefer's house. Nefer surprised him, and the thief killed him."

"A lay worker," murmured the Scribe of the Tomb, a glimmer of hope lighting up his eyes.

"I advise you to question them. If the results are disappointing, I'll question them again, in their homes, away from the lands belonging to the Place of Truth. My skilled men will make them talk—if the murderer is indeed one of them, you can be sure he'll confess."

"I'll put your plan to the village court."

"Good," said Mehy. "Then I'll tell the king we're joining forces to seek out the truth."

"Above all, tell him we await his orders to construct his House of Eternity and his Temple of a Million Years."

"As soon as I return, we'll meet and talk again; I hope that by then you will have caught the murderer."

"I hope so too," said Kenhir.

Just managing to contain his rage, Mehy climbed back into his chariot without having asked the most important question: who had succeeded Nefer the Silent, if not Paneb the Ardent, who alone could save the Brotherhood from disaster? The traitor would soon confirm the craftsmen's decision, and Serketa was right to have already thought up a plan for getting rid of the inconvenient painter.

▲

Commander Sobek listened carefully to what the Scribe of the Tomb had to say.

"A lay worker?" he exclaimed in astonishment.

"Why not?"

"The guard would have seen him slipping into the village."

"Even the best guard can't be watchful every second. And the murderer must have found a way of climbing a wall without being seen."

"Yes, but once inside the village he'd soon have been spotted," objected Sobek.

"That was what he feared, so he took special precautions."

"And a lay worker would have to be mad to kill the Master."

"He acted in a moment of panic."

"I'd be glad if Mehy were right and all the craftsmen were innocent," admitted Sobek, "but I'm not sure he is right."

"Question the lay workers," said Kenhir. "Gather their statements and try to discover the truth."

"You can rely on me."

As the old scribe left to return to the village, the big Nubian pondered a puzzling question. Mehy knew Sobek would have to carry out the inquiry, so why hadn't he told Sobek about his theories?

▲

Paneb had just finished making an alabaster offertory table for the shrine in Nefer's tomb. It would stand at the foot of the hieroglyph-adorned stone door that gave access to the otherworld. On the rectangular top, he had carved a leg and ribs of beef, a duck, onions, cucumbers, cabbages, figs, grapes, dates, pomegranates, cakes, loaves of bread, and jugs of milk, wine, and water.

Magically brought to life by the Wise Woman, the table would work without human intervention, providing Nefer's *ka* with the subtle essences of the foods embodied in the alabaster. In this way, even after the deaths of the Master's close family, the living stone would continue to feed him.

But Paneb was not content with this act of homage, which was paid to all the dead. Guided by the Wise Woman's advice, he had decided to carve a statue of Nefer with exceptionally beautiful eyes, corresponding closely to the anatomical reality that Egyptian medicine had discovered. The cornea would be formed from rock crystal, to emphasize the clarity of the eye's perception, and the white of the eye from magnesium carbonate, containing iron oxides which looked like tiny capillaries. The pierced pupil would again be carved from rock crystal, and the iris created from brown resin, incorporating the necessary asymmetry between pupil and cornea.[1]

▲

Dawn was breaking and Paneb had just laid down his tools, when Ubekhet entered the workshop. A ray of sunlight lit up the statue, whose eyes gazed out upon eternity. Ubekhet could not hold back her tears.

Through his spiritual son's genius, Nefer was alive, beyond the reach of decay and death. Standing with his right foot forward and his arms hanging down by his sides, he seemed to be walking along the beautiful paths of the West, and continuing to guide the Brotherhood toward the East.

Ubekhet wanted to kneel before the statue, but Paneb stopped her.

"His *ka* will dwell within the stone," he told her, "but it is in you that he lives, and you are the bearer of his wisdom. You're the leader of the Place of Truth now: don't abandon us."

6

Neither Mehy nor Serketa paid the slightest heed to the splendors of Pi-Ramses, the capital city built by Ramses the Great in the Nile Delta. He had chosen this location because it was close to the northeastern invasion corridor, enabling him to act swiftly in an emergency. Served by a port where cargo boats could load and unload, the "Turquoise City" was crisscrossed by canals lined with orchards, gardens, and luxurious houses. It was a delightful city to live in, but it also housed a garrison of picked troops and an arsenal that produced weapons for the soldiers who guarded the frontier.

The general and his wife were taken to the palace, whose walls bore the names of Ramses, written in ovals symbolizing the universe through which the royal soul traveled for all time.

Tjaty Bay received them immediately in his office, whose papyrus cupboards groaned under the weight of documents. Short, edgy, and nervous, with dark eyes that were forever darting back and forth, and a little pointed beard, the tjaty was a shadowy figure; but he kept a firm grip on the reins of government. He had devoted himself to the service of Queen Tausert, whom he admired, and young King Saptah, whom he had put on the throne in order to end all the disputes and intrigues.

"I am glad to see you again, General," said Bay. "And how delightful to meet your charming wife. I hope the journey wasn't too tiring?"

"No indeed," said Mehy. "It was a peaceful interlude."

"Good, good. You'll be housed in an apartment at the palace, and I've given orders that your stay in the capital is to be a most agreeable one. I would imagine your wife feels the need to refresh herself and rest?"

Two servingwomen appeared, and Serketa was invited to follow them—much to her displeasure.

As soon as the door of the office closed, the tjaty's forced amiability vanished and Mehy found himself facing a stern, incisive head of government, who demanded, "What exactly is happening in Thebes?"

"Don't worry, Tjaty. The situation is completely normal, and I predict fabulous harvests and excellent revenues from taxation."

"No one doubts your remarkable qualities as an administrator, my dear Mehy, but what are we to think of the murder of Nefer the Silent?"

"This appalling tragedy completely astounds me. The Scribe of the Tomb and myself have joined forces to identify the guilty party."

"I am glad to hear it. But have you any promising leads?"

"Only Kenhir can make inquiries inside the village, Tjaty. If he needs my assistance on the outside, I'll provide him with as many men as he needs."

"It seems to me that you have your own suspicions, General."

"Nothing very specific. But I'm convinced that the criminal is one of the lay workers."

Bay consulted a papyrus. "That is what Kenhir has written to me, indeed, and he is rather inclined to share your opinion."

Mehy was mortified. So the scribe had sent a message to the Tjaty by special boat, continuing to communicate directly with central government without informing the general.

"Kenhir assures me that the Brotherhood will go on working with its customary dedication, and that Pharaoh can count on it to fulfill all its duties.

"He also says that an evil spirit tried to disrupt the serenity of the village, but was thwarted by the courage of Paneb, the starboard crew's new leader. Master Nefer now rests in peace, and the craftsmen are preparing to create the monuments needed to give Saptah's reign its full radiance."

"The whole country will rejoice," declared Mehy with as much conviction as he could muster.

"The murderer has yet to be punished, though, and the craftsmen must be reassured about their safety."

"That is one of my missions, Tjaty, and I fully intend to succeed."

"Let us understand each other, General. You and I have already managed to avert a civil war, and we must now consolidate the authority of King Saptah and Queen Tausert."

"Are you insinuating . . . that they are in danger?"

"Don't play the innocent with me, Mehy. Saptah is exceptionally intelligent, but he has no experience of government, and his health is fragile; without Tausert's support he would be unable to bear the weight of his office. The queen herself has fearsome adversaries to contend with—half the court cannot forgive her for being a woman, and the other half hates her for being the widow of Seti II."

"Her Majesty has a fascinating personality," said Mehy, "and she made a great impression on the Theban people. To my mind, she also has the bearing of a pharaoh."

"That's very true, but senior army officers in Pi-Ramses wish to see a strong man at the head of Egypt, a man who can resist any invaders, or even take action to prevent an invasion."

"And has this strong man made himself known?"

"Yes. He's called Setnakhte. He's somewhat elderly, but he knows Syria and Canaan well, and he has the confidence of the best troops."

"To the extent that he might take power by force?"

"Not yet, General, not yet. I hope he will adhere to the rule of law and that he won't dare embark on such a destructive adventure. But unfortunately the possibility can't be ruled out. . . . It would be foolish to be too optimistic, don't you think?"

Mehy thought for a moment. The tjaty had not passed on such important information by chance; which meant he had not summoned Mehy to Pi-Ramses solely to discuss Thebes's prosperity and Nefer's death.

Faced with such a skilled strategist, the general was obliged to take a risk. "Your trust and your confidences do me honor, but what is it that you want from me?"

"An excellent question," said Bay. "My words are indeed among the state's greatest secrets. The fact that you are now party to those secrets makes you one of the best-informed officials in Egypt. What I want from you is your unquestioning support. Of course, you might consider pledging your allegiance to Setnakhte, in the hope of becoming his first minister."

"Tjaty, I assure you I—"

"I am well acquainted with human nature, General, and I prefer to be safe than sorry. If you try to betray the rightful pharaoh, I shall show you no mercy."

▲

Mehy and Serketa were among the guests at a lavish banquet which Queen Tausert had honored with her presence. They agreed that she was more beautiful and more dangerous than ever, and Serketa was jealous of her regal bearing.

From the gleam in his wife's eyes, Mehy realized that she harbored murderous longings. "Calm yourself, my sweet," he whispered in her ear. "In her own territory, the queen is out of reach."

Serketa smiled at an old dignitary who had not said a word since the start of the meal. "Were you born here? she asked, in an attempt to cheer him up.

"I had that good fortune, beautiful lady, and I have enjoyed an unblemished career. Since I made no mistakes, I have had the privilege of serving true leaders."

"Is King Saptah not a true leader?" asked Mehy in surprise.

"Naturally we all respect the rightful pharaoh, but we are wary of his youth and inexperience. Let us hope that time will be his ally and that he will learn to govern."

"Doesn't he ever attend celebrations like this one?" asked Serketa.

"Never. After celebrating the dawn ritual, he spends most of his day in the temple, studying the writings of the Ancients. Such fervor is laudable, but it might prove inappropriate in the present situation."

"I'm from Thebes," Serketa told him, simpering like a little girl, "and I don't know much about the court at Pi-Ramses. Are you saying that Queen Tausert is the true ruler of the country?"

"No one has any doubt at all about that."

"You don't seem to approve," commented Mehy. "Why is that?"

"Don't be too curious, General," said the old man, "and be content with what you have. Thebes is a pleasant city, you rule it with an iron fist, and the value of your results is recognized. Wanting more than that would lead you into dangerous realms, where you'd find no allies."

"Are you aware that Tjaty Bay honors me with his trust?"

"I'm aware of everything that goes on in Pi-Ramses, and I advise you to leave as soon as possible."

Mehy said furiously, "Who do you think you are? How dare you speak to me like that?"

The man stood up, and the couple saw that he was surprisingly fit and strong for someone of his age.

"I have many duties, and I do not ordinarily attend official banquets; but this one gave me the chance to meet you. Before I leave, I should stress that Setnakhte has no need of you and that a general's first duty is to obey his king."

7

Beken the Potter, leader of the outside workers, had no sooner arrived at their camp than he was intercepted by Sobek.

"Assemble your people at Obed's forge," ordered the commander.

The cantankerous potter instantly demanded, "What's going on?"

"You'll soon see."

"I want to know now."

Sobek scratched the scar under his left eye, a reminder of a struggle to the death with a leopard in the Nubian grasslands. Anyone who knew Sobek knew this gesture meant he was getting angry and might explode into furious rage at any moment.

"Don't lose your temper," urged Beken, his voice rather less confident. "I only wanted to know—"

"Assemble your workers."

Beken decided it was wisest to obey, but he had great difficulty in gathering together all the "men of the outside," who included washermen, butchers, bakers, brewers, cauldron makers, tanners, weavers, woodcutters, fishermen, and gardeners. They all argued and protested, in ever-louder voices.

Obed the Blacksmith, a stocky, bearded Syrian, was the first to protest. "You treat us worse than bullocks on their way to the slaughterhouse! What's got into you, Beken?"

"Commander Sobek's orders—nothing to do with me."

"Aren't you supposed to plead our cause when someone abuses their authority?"

"Go and complain to the man responsible."

Obed was a man to be reckoned with. He had no hesitation in confronting Sobek, who was observing the chaos with impatience.

"We're free workers," declared the blacksmith, "and you have no rights over us."

"You'd better remember," retorted Sobek, "that if any lay worker commits a crime it's my duty to arrest him."

Obed scowled. "So we're all criminals, are we? You treat us like dirt, Sobek, and I'm going straight to Kenhir to tell him so."

"I'm acting on his orders," snapped Sobek. "You're all under suspicion of having murdered Nefer the Silent."

The blacksmith's mouth dropped open. As if by a miracle, the noise stopped, giving way to a heavy silence.

"Form a line," Sobek ordered, "and stand still. I shall use Obed's forge as an office, and I'm going to question you one by one."

"I want Beken with me to defend me," said the cauldron maker. "We all know your methods—you'd make anybody confess!"

Sobek turned to him. "Can you give a single example?"

The cauldron maker looked down. "Well, no . . ."

"I must have clear answers, and I shall take the time necessary to obtain them. Innocent men with clean hands have nothing to fear and will be swiftly released. But whatever you do, don't try to lie to me: my nose is as keen as a hunting dog's."

Beken came up to him, and said quietly, "May I talk to you alone, man to man?"

"Actually that would suit me well—I was planning to question you first."

The two men went into the forge. It suited Sobek's purposes admirably, for it was a perfect symbol of the antechamber of hell where the murderer would burn.

"So, Beken, what is it you want to tell me?"

"One of my men's missing."

"Are you sure?"

"Yes, it's Libu, one of the washermen, son of a Libyan woman and a Theban man. He is fifty and has to work hard to feed his family. He steals small pieces of cheap cloth from time to time, but I turn a blind eye to it."

"Perhaps he's ill?" suggested Sobek.

"If so, his wife would have told me. It's not at all like him to be missing, I assure you."

"I'll go to his house. While you wait, get back to work."

▲

Libu thought he must be dreaming. A slow-witted fellow, he could scarcely understand what had happened to him. When a peasant woman had hailed him, on the road leading to the Place of Truth, he thought she had mistaken him for someone else. But it was indeed his name that she had spoken, and she knew everything about him, including his petty thefts.

Anxiously, Libu had defended himself by explaining about his modest job and his family's needs.

The woman had reassured him. She had been sent by his fellow washermen, who had just received a consignment of new linen from the workshops at Ramses' temple and were planning to share out the best pieces before returning to work. An unexpected bounty not to be missed!

"I don't know you," said Libu. "Where are you from?"

"I'm Beken the Potter's new niece," replied Serketa winningly.

"Oh . . . oh, I see. But do you really find him attractive?"

"He's so kind! It's thanks to him that these linens are being shared out."

Serketa left the path and headed toward a thicket of tamarisks, on the edge of the desert.

"This is where the meeting will be," she explained. "It's a nice, quiet place."

"That's just as well. If Commander Sobek caught us, we'd lose our jobs and be sent to prison for a long time."

"Don't worry. Beken has taken care of everything."

Libu was already dreaming of the profit his wife would make when she sold the fine linen he'd take her. His trade might be a poor one, but it did have certain advantages.

His eyes lit on the peasant woman's ample curves. "He chooses his nieces well, does Beken," he said admiringly. "But he's only just taken a new one. He usually keeps them longer than that."

"At the moment he's feeling particularly vigorous."

"What an old ram! If I'd known, I wouldn't have married and I'd have lived like him."

"You know, I'm not so fierce. And where there's enough for one, there's enough for two."

Libu laid his calloused hand between Serketa's breasts. "If my wife knew . . ."

"Who's going to tell her?"

He bent and kissed her nipples, then ran his lips down toward her belly. His position was perfect. From her wig, Serketa extracted a long needle coated with poison, which she drove with a doctor's precision into the back of Libu's neck. His body arched and stiffened. She pushed him violently away and watched his horrible death throes with excitement and delight.

Then she retrieved the murder weapon, stripped her victim, and dressed him in a fine kilt that she had hidden under her loose-fitting tunic. It had belonged to Nefer the Silent, and had been stolen by the traitor.

Once she was certain that there was no one about, the peasant woman set off back toward the fields.

▲

There was no longer any doubt: Libu had run away. His wife was in tears, and Sobek had ordered his men to search every cubit of the Place of Truth and the surrounding areas. If they found nothing, he'd have to ask Mehy for help.

"Libu must have committed a pretty serious crime if it made him run off and abandon his family," said Beken.

"There's no proof that he murdered Nefer," objected Sobek. "Did he ever show any hostility to the Master?"

"No, but there is some circumstantial evidence. Libu was a

petty thief, as I told you, and he must have broken into Nefer's house to steal, and been caught red-handed."

"Yet nobody saw him? And there's no trace of the stolen items in his house?"

Sobek's questions troubled the potter. He was still searching for answers when a guard burst into the forge.

"We've found him, sir! The only trouble is, he's dead."

The Nubian went immediately to the scene.

"Sir, look at the kilt he's wearing," said one of his men. "The highest quality! There's even a mark, in hieroglyphics."

Sobek peered at it. It was the heart and the windpipe: the sign for the word *Nefer.*

"No witnesses, of course?" he asked.

"None, sir. Early in the morning, this place is deserted."

▲

Ubekhet examined the kilt. "Yes, it belonged to Nefer. He had two brand-new kilts, and I've just checked: one is missing."

"The mystery is solved," said Kenhir. "Libu did indeed murder the Master. When he found out that Sobek was going to question the lay workers, he ran away. But destiny did not allow him to remain unpunished, and death struck him before he could profit from his crime."

"Is that what you'll say in your report?" asked Sobek.

"In *our* report," Kenhir corrected him.

"I won't sign it."

"Why not?" asked Ubekhet.

"Because I don't believe Libu died a natural death."

"But the kilt . . . Surely that proves he was guilty?" persisted Kenhir.

Sobek shook his head. "Someone's trying to deceive us."

"In that case, sign the report," advised Ubekhet. "The monster hiding behind this new crime will be convinced he's succeeded in fooling us."

8

Thanks to Niut's incessant cleaning, Kenhir's official home shone like a jewel. There was not a single speck of dust to spoil the elegant furniture, and she had even managed to clean his office without disturbing his files. As she was also an excellent cook, Kenhir ought to have been the happiest of husbands, with plenty of spare time in which to write his beloved *Key of Dreams.*

But her behavior was troubling him. "Sit down for a moment, please," he said.

"Idleness is the worst of all vices," she retorted.

"You're making me dizzy, and I want to have a serious talk with you."

Niut sat down on a straw-seated chair. "I'm listening."

"I am an old man, you are a young woman. I married you only so that I could leave you all my possessions, and I made it clear that you're free to live your life as you wish. Why do you devote all your time to this house and my comfort? Why don't you pursue your own happiness?"

"Because I'm happy doing this, and I don't want anything else." She stood up. "I've laid out clean clothes for you for the meeting of the village court. I do hope you'll reach the right decision. The Place of Truth needs a true leader like Paneb."

▲

The Place of Truth's court, "The Assembly of the Set-square and the Right-angle," convened in the open-air courtyard of the Temple of Ma'at and Hathor. It consisted of the Wise Woman, the leader of the port crew, the Scribe of the Tomb, Turquoise, senior priestess of Hathor, and four others chosen by lot: Ched the Savior, Nakht the Powerful, Gau the Precise, and another priestess of Hathor.

The court made decisions relating to the life of the

Brotherhood, ranging from declarations of succession to the resolution of disputes between villagers. Its judgments could not be challenged by any outside authority, and its task was to distinguish truth from falsehood and to protect the weak from the strong.

"Several craftsmen," announced Kenhir, "have submitted an official proposal that Paneb the Ardent be named Master and successor to Nefer the Silent. I don't need to emphasize the importance of our decision, which must be unanimous."

"Paneb risked his life to save the Brotherhood," said Nakht. "I don't much care for his manner—everyone knows that—but facts are facts. When we need to defend ourselves once again, he will be our strongest bulwark."

"If a spiritual son is faithful to his father," said the Wise Woman, "shouldn't he succeed him?"

"It isn't only that Paneb is an exceptional craftsman," said Hay. "He also has a leader's temperament. His leadership would be very different from Nefer's, and there'd be bound to be some friction, but we have no choice: I believe we should place our trust in him."

"Such an attitude is unusual, coming from you," remarked Kenhir.

"All that matters is the Brotherhood. And I'm convinced Paneb will serve it with all his strength."

"I agree with Hay," nodded Gau. "I agree his lack of tact will probably cause trouble, but we need his courage and his energy."

Turquoise and the other priestess of Hathor remained silent.

"Unless I'm mistaken," observed Kenhir, "no one opposes the appointment of Paneb the Ardent as Master of the Place of Truth."

"You're forgetting me," cut in Ched the Savior.

Kenhir looked at him in surprise. "Paneb was your pupil, and you've always supported him."

"Exactly."

"What do you mean?"

"From the very first moment, I knew Paneb would be a great painter; but it took many years to train him and to enable his hand to express itself freely while still respecting the rules of harmony. It's right that he should have become a crew leader. He has already learnt to rein in his temper and has already shown that he can lead his crew without betraying the spirit of the Brotherhood. But if we take things too quickly, Paneb will be consumed by his own fire. We must give him time to settle into his new office and judge him on his actions."

"But we haven't got any time!" exclaimed Nakht.

"Our Scribe of the Tomb is in excellent health and perfectly capable of representing us to the authorities while the two crew leaders devote themselves to their tasks. Let's wait a little before we take a final decision."

"If yours is the only vote against Paneb, will you change your mind?" asked Kenhir.

"No," said Ched firmly. "That would be unforgivable cowardice. A flame akin to the fire of Set burns in Paneb's heart, a fire as terrifying as a lightning bolt. It destroys any obstacle in its path, but it would destroy Paneb, too, if we asked too much of him."

The Wise Woman said nothing more, so Kenhir was obliged to announce the court's decision: Paneb would not be appointed Master of the Place of Truth.

▲

Turquoise removed the linen cover from the squat vessel, which contained a precious eye balm made from galenite, pyrite, vegetable ash, copper and arsenic. The superb redhead wore her forty years as though they weighed no more than a feather. As Ubekhet's assistant, and senior priestess of Hathor, she took care of the ritual objects used in the temple and supervised the preparation of the makeup that transformed simple housewives into servants of the goddess.

In this unique village everyone held a sacred office. The craftsmen and their womenfolk were their own priests and priestesses, and no celebrants were brought in from the outside to officiate at their ceremonies. The only supreme authority they recognized was that of Pharaoh and the Great Royal Wife.

Turquoise counted the vases of ointment to make sure none was missing. These vases were squat, stable, and waterproof, and covered with linen caps; they were little works of art, carved from limestone, alabaster, or serpentine.

Once she had finished her inventory, the priestess laid bunches of flowers on the altar of the temple where the Wise Woman would soon officiate. In happier days, Ubekhet and the Master had entered the temple together to celebrate the dawn rite. At this time of day, in every home, the villagers offered fire to the statues of the ancestors and poured water onto the flowers laid out in their honor, in order to bring out the scent to please their *ka*s. Without this offertory ritual, the Brotherhood would not have survived.

Today Ubekhet would officiate alone, since the court had not appointed a new Master. She would be at once king and queen, high priestess, and Master of the craftsmen.

Wearing a garnet necklace Paneb had given her, Turquoise crossed the open-air courtyard, pondering the strange bond that linked her to the big man. True, the intensity of their love was undiminished, and no darkness had tarnished their passion. Paneb knew Turquoise would keep her vow to remain unmarried and that he would never be permitted to spend a night at her house. What he did not know was that Turquoise was supplying him with a magical strength that Uabet the Pure did not possess.

Since their first meeting, Turquoise had sensed that Paneb the Ardent would play a decisive role in the history of the Brotherhood and that she would help him to become a true leader, capable of going beyond himself and his own faults.

Paneb burned with a fire that only the Great Work could calm. While Uabet provided him with a necessary balance,

Turquoise fed the flame of desire within him. Unlike his spiritual father, he sought not wisdom or serenity but a creative power that was not of this world. It was up to Turquoise, the sorceress, to guide him toward a love of work and the Brotherhood, and so prevent him from becoming mired in ambition. Ched the Savior was right to reject his appointment; had it been necessary, Turquoise would have supported Ched.

The village was still slumbering as she stepped into the main street. To her surprise, Paneb came to meet her.

"You're up early," she said.

"It's such a lovely morning . . . And I wanted to see you."

Tuquoise frowned. "It's time for the sacred rites, not for pleasure."

"Exactly—and we must always try to make those rites more and more beautiful. Because a crew leader must know every craft, I've been working with Thuty the goldsmith recently. And it occurred to me that, as you're a priestess of Hathor, this jewel might be of some use to you."

The first rays of the rising sun glinted off a fine gold band. It was incredibly light, decorated with colored rosettes and with two tiny gazelles' heads, crafted to perfection.

Astonished, Turquoise allowed Paneb to place the band upon her head like a crown. Then, just as the villagers were beginning the morning ritual, he turned and walked away.

9

The grain storage jars were one and a half cubits tall, egg-shaped, and perfectly watertight. Made with clay from Middle Egypt, these essential objects were at once light and easy to handle, and were marked with the names of their owners.

Under instructions from his wife to fill two jars, the head sculptor, Userhat the Lion, made his way slowly toward the grain stores to the northwest of the village. His predecessors had dug vertical walls out of the marl, with well-defined corners, carefully covering the rocky soil with mortar. The grain was stored in several different compartments, according to its quality and date of delivery.

Thanks to the Scribe of the Tomb's careful management, the grain stores were always full and, even in a time of crisis, the Place of Truth ran no risk of running out of bread.

To Userhat's immense surprise, he found Hay standing by the first store, in a heated argument with the furious wives of Pai the Good Bread and Gau the Precise. Although the women hurled all manner of insults at him, Hay calmly refused to allow them access to the grain reserves.

"What's the matter?" asked Userhat.

"The tjaty has requisitioned the silos," replied Hay. "We are forbidden to touch them until we receive further orders."

▲

"This requisition is illegal!" thundered Paneb.

"Yes, it is," agreed Kenhir, "but kindly don't take it out on my walls or my furniture. I'm not the one who signed this letter, it was one of the tjaty's scribes."

"Yes, but you're the one who appointed Hay."

"While we wait for the situation to be clarified, we must be careful not to do anything that might endanger the village. We have enough grain to make bread and beer for several days before we have to touch our reserves."

"But you have arthritis and your gout's bad at the moment and you can't walk properly."

"I shall increase the usual treatment," said Ubekhet, who had just finished examining her patient, "but it will be at least two days before Kenhir's back on his feet."

"Then I shall go to see General Mehy on my own," decided

Paneb. "It's up to him to sort out the mistake and prevent this sort of nonsense happening again in future."

Ubekhet sighed. "Do try to be tactful—it's simply an administrative mistake."

"When we're creating a painting or a statue," retorted Paneb, "we're not allowed to make mistakes."

Paneb walked along swiftly. He was determined to shake Mehy up—and no excuses would be tolerated. He'd tear up the requisition in front of him and demand damages and compensation in the form of an immediate delivery of top-quality cosmetics.

A gentle tongue licked his leg. "Ebony! I didn't say you could come with me."

There was a look of pleading in the dog's large hazel eyes.

▲

Halfway between the Place of Truth and the government offices, a rough-looking, unshaven man of about fifty barred Paneb's way.

"Morning, friend," said the man. "Fine day, isn't it?"

"That depends who for."

"I'd like to have a little talk with you."

"We don't know each other, and I'm in a hurry."

"You're not very friendly."

"Get out of my way. I've told you, I'm in a hurry."

"To be honest, my friends would like to join in our conversation."

Several men sprang out of the wheat fields and surrounded the craftsman. Paneb counted nine and noticed that they all looked the same: same body shape, same gait, same low forehead. And they were all brandishing clubs.

"You see," said the unshaven man, "we should all keep quiet and not annoy other people. But you're getting on my nerves. So my friends and I, we're going to teach you to keep quiet—permanently."

"Suppose I were to say a word, one single word, that would sort out the situation?"

The man stared at him in surprise. “A word? What word?”

“Attack!”

Ebony leapt forward and sank his teeth into the unshaven man’s forearm, producing a shout of pain. Head down, Paneb charged at the nearest attacker and butted him in the chest. Then, throwing himself sideways, he dodged a blow from a club and brought both fists down hard on his attacker’s neck.

A savage blow to his ribs almost knocked Paneb down, but he ignored the pain, kept his feet, and broke the attacker’s jaw with his knee. But another club crashed down on his left shoulder, and he realized that this band was made up of vicious fighters, trained in hand-to-hand combat. Despite his bruised ribs, Paneb threw himself to the ground, lifted up a heavy fellow by the testicles, and threw him at two of his comrades, who toppled backward. Paneb lashed out with his heel and broke one man’s nose, but then another man clubbed him from behind.

Paneb was almost finished. Fortunately, though, Ebony came to his aid by biting the leg of the man who had just clubbed him and who was preparing to finish the big man off. The dog bit the attacker viciously in the leg. The man howled in surprise and pain, and dropped his club. Paneb instantly grabbed it. Still dazed, his eyes misted, and covered in blood, he hauled himself to his feet and whirled the club round his head.

“Let’s get out of here!” shouted the unshaven attacker.

Those of his men who were still able-bodied picked up their unconscious comrades, and the band fled like a flock of sparrows. Ebony would happily have chased after them, but he chose instead to stay with Paneb, who lavished caresses upon him as he got his breath back.

▲

The offices of the government of Thebes’s west bank were clustered around a central courtyard. The soldiers guarding it unsheathed their short swords as the monstrous, blood-soaked creature staggered in, and one of the scribes was so terrified that he dropped his papyrus scrolls and took refuge behind his superior.

Ebony growled and bared his teeth, in preparation for another fight.

"I am Paneb the Ardent, a craftsman from the Place of Truth, and I wish to see General Mehy immediately."

The big man's reputation had traveled far beyond the walls of the village, and everyone knew that with his bare hands he could take on and beat a considerable number of armed men.

"I'll tell him," promised an officer. "Wait here—and keep your dog under control."

The wait was a brief one. Mehy himself, dressed in the latest fashion, came out to receive his visitor.

"Paneb! What on earth . . . ?"

"I was attacked. Nine men with clubs. And they weren't just peasants, either."

"What do you mean?"

"Professionals—they knew how to fight."

Mehy's face darkened. "This is exactly what I was afraid of."

Paneb flew into a rage. "You knew someone was going to try to kill me?"

"No, of course not, but alarming reports have been coming in of bands of Libyan mercenaries crossing the desert to enter the region and rob travelers. I'll double the number of patrols so that these bandits can be arrested as soon as possible. Nine men, you say; and you beat them?"

"They ran away, and some of them have broken bones."

"Come, I'll take you to the hospital."

"No, thank you. The Wise Woman will treat me. But that's not why I'm here. As leader of the starboard crew, I must lay a serious problem before you. And, given the importance of my office, you ought to speak to me more respectfully."

"Yes, yes, of course. Let's go into my office."

As Ebony began to follow them, Mehy halted. "Shouldn't the dog stay outside?"

"Ebony is a brave and valiant fighter. He's coming with me."

"Very well."

Paneb hated Mehy's office, which he thought overloaded with pretentious vases and second-rate paintings.

Mehy sat down behind his desk and said, "Take a seat, Paneb."

"There's no point."

"Surely you must be thirsty?"

"Yes. Thirsty for justice."

The general's eyes widened in surprise. "Justice? Why? What injustice are you complaining about?"

"The requisitioning of the Place of Truth's grain stores."

"But . . . that's completely illegal."

"Maybe so, but we received this document, signed by one of the tjaty's assistants." Paneb slapped down the blood- and sweat-stained papyrus on the desk.

Mehy read it attentively. "This is a forgery," he said when he had finished. "This assistant doesn't exist."

10

That morning, Mehy hunted for over five hours in the papyrus reedbeds, and carried out a veritable massacre of kingfishers, hoopoes, and ducks. But even this ferocious slaughter was not enough to calm his temper, which he had scarcely been able to contain as he listened to Paneb.

Nine soldiers, exorbitantly paid in gold to keep their mouths shut, nine veterans who had already left for the Libyan frontier . . . How had Paneb managed to beat them, even if he was nearly twice their size?

Serketa's plan had worked perfectly: drawn out of the village by the forged document, Paneb had fallen into the trap laid by the soldiers, who had been ordered to intercept a dangerous miscreant and kill him if he resisted. One against nine: Paneb should have had absolutely no chance. There was only one explanation: Paneb must derive supernatural power from the Stone of Light. He fed on its energy, which gave him a strength no one could combat.

That made Mehy even more determined to get his hands on the Stone. It enabled the Brotherhood to resist adversity and face up to appalling trials without losing heart. So long as they had it, even the fiercest attack would cause only minimal damage.

Naturally, Mehy had already done more than Paneb was asking: he had made an official apology to the Scribe of the Tomb and had given the Brotherhood pots of ointments and jars of wine to ensure that the government's regrettable error was forgotten.

▲

Queen Tausert's beauty and elegance had completely enslaved Tjaty Bay. Whatever the time of day, she was dazzling, skillfully made up, and adorned with discreet gold jewelry produced by the talented Thuty. Faithful to Seti II's memory, Tausert had not remarried; she governed Egypt with authority but without ostentation, and avoided conflict with Saptah's supporters.

"Has Pharaoh's health improved?" she asked.

"Unfortunately not, Majesty," Bay answered, "but the king never complains, for he is happy to read the writings of the Ancients and converse with the wise men in the temple."

"Is he no longer at all interested in affairs of state?"

"He has full and complete trust in you."

"You foresaw that this would happen, didn't you?"

Bay lowered his eyes.

"Setnakhte has been making a great stir recently," the queen went on. "His name, 'Set is Victorious,' is rather worrying. Are we in control of the situation?"

"Not completely, Majesty. His words carry a lot of weight,

and he believes it necessary to continue Seti's bloodline, which was interrupted by your husband's death."

"Why does he think that?"

"He thinks that Egypt is growing weak and that you don't pay enough attention to the army. As he sees it, a show of force in Syria and Canaan is essential."

"I strongly disagree. Do you think he's bold enough to try to seize power?"

"Setnakhte's a man who thinks before he acts, but he's also strong-willed; so we ought to take him very seriously."

"So I have as many enemies as ever," sighed the queen.

"Unfortunately, that's so, Majesty, and the present composition of the court doesn't make me feel very hopeful. But I shall make sure they have no room to maneuver, and I'm constantly strengthening my defensive system to enable you to govern in peace."

The queen smiled in a way that made the tjaty blush. She said, "I promised you a surprise, do you remember? This world is only an unworthy portion of reality, Bay, and we must think about our Houses of Eternity. The Wise Woman has not yet found a location for mine in the Valley of the Queens, but I have taken a decision regarding yours."

A lump rose in Bay's throat. All he wanted was to remain with Tausert, until death and beyond.

"You shall dwell in the Valley of the Queens, not far from Seti II, whom you served so faithfully."

The tjaty almost fainted. "Me, in the Valley of the Queens? But . . ."

"Because of your devoted service to the country, you deserve this exceptional honor. Tomorrow, you shall leave for the Place of Truth and you shall entrust the Brotherhood with its new mission: to construct Saptah's Temple of a Million Years and two tombs, the king's and your own."

"Majesty, how . . . how can I thank you?"

"By continuing to be yourself, Bay."

Shaking with emotion, the tjaty dared to whisper the request that haunted him. "Majesty, when the gods crown you Pharaoh, may my House of Eternity be close to your own?"

The tjaty, Ubekhet, Kenhir, and Paneb were all gathered round, listening to Hay.

"The temple is to be built between those of Thutmose III and Ramses," he said. "As for Saptah's tomb, we've found a good site, a little to the north of Seti's."

Bay nodded his approval.

"Since you're the servant of both those kings," continued Hay, "yours will be excavated close to Saptah's, in the same part of the Valley."

"I assume it will be a simple chamber, without decoration?" asked Bay.

"That is usually so for nonroyal persons, but it's not Queen Tausert's wish, nor King Saptah's," replied Kenhir. "Here's the plan we have drawn up."

Several successive passageways, a sarcophagus chamber, decorated walls . . . Bay was dumbfounded. "But this is like a royal tomb."

"That is the queen's wish," confirmed the Wise Woman. "This House of Eternity will not be consecrated in the same way as a pharaoh's, but it will reflect the great work carried out by its occupant."

For the first time since he had begun serving Egypt, Bay found himself lost for words.

▲

Fened carried out a final check on the chosen location, then Ubekhet approached respectfully, bearing Nefer's gold hammer and chisel. When she struck the rock for the first time, she did not wound it but revealed its secret life, preserved in the silence. And this life would take form in King Saptah's House of Eternity.

Sobek was apprehensive. He had doubled the guard at the

entrance to the Valley of the Kings and had himself searched the hills overlooking "the Great Meadow," where, day after day and night after night, the souls of kings were transmuted. The attack on Paneb worried him greatly. If the men were indeed Libyan mercenaries, they wouldn't think twice about attacking the burial grounds in the hope of finding gold. He must take specially rigorous precautions to safeguard the valley.

And yet, could he believe what Mehy had said? Sobek was not about to take any risks with the valley's safety, but he couldn't help suspecting that that overambitious general had not told the truth.

▲

Thanks to the Wise Woman's ointments, Paneb's wounds were no more than a bad memory. With renewed vigor he swung up his great pickax, on which the fire of heaven had drawn the muzzle and two ears of the beast of Set.

By this simple act, he filled his crew with enthusiasm and the desire to carry a new masterpiece through to its conclusion. The stonecutters assisted him, and the other craftsmen constructed a workshop where the sculptors, painters, and goldsmith would be able to work.

The miracle happened again. The tools sang, thoughts and efforts were united, and the atmosphere on the site was joyous. To everyone's surprise, Paneb was not at all high-handed; he supervised the work calmly, resolved difficulties patiently, and always led by example.

"Nefer was right to choose Paneb as his spiritual son," admitted Karo the Impatient.

"Let's not get excited too soon," advised Unesh the Jackal. "For the moment, he's controlling himself, but his true nature will soon come to the fore again."

"You're wrong," said Gau the Precise. "He's well aware of what a crew leader's duties are."

"You're deceiving yourself," said Fened the Nose.

"No, he isn't," cut in Nakht the Strong. "I was Paneb's sworn enemy, but I truly believe his new responsibilities have transformed him, and that we were right to appoint him crew leader."

▲

Kenhir lowered himself onto the seat that had been carved for him out of the rock, to watch the work unfolding. He was in a dreadful mood. Tormented by a nightmare, he had spent a disturbed night and feared that the day would produce one mishap after another.

The first occurred midmorning, when Casa the Rope found he could not stand upright. "It's my back," he moaned, with a grimace of pain.

Paneb didn't hesitate. Using the method the Wise Woman had taught him, he manipulated the stonecutter's back so as to realign it correctly and enable the energy to circulate properly along the spine, which was regarded as the tree of life.

"He'll need to rest for several days," Paneb told Kenhir.

A few minutes later, it was Pai the Good Bread's turn to stop work. "I've sprained my wrist," he announced. "I need a bandage."

Kenhir saw that the injury was a real one, for the wrist was swelling up. Just at that moment, Ipuy the Examiner let out a dreadful howl; Nakht's pickax had flown out of his hands and crushed Ipuy's right foot.

His colleagues gathered round and lifted him onto a stretcher.

"I'm beginning to wonder if this site is cursed," growled Karo.

— 11 —

At the starboard crew leader's official home, in the southeastern corner of the village, Paneb had just finished painting the woodwork with cedar oil. In some places he had used a translucent oil, and in others a blackish one to imitate ebony.

Now he was tenderly cradling Iuwen, his green-eyed daughter, who looked incredibly fragile in the arms of her giant of a father.

At last, Paneb felt reassured. Userhat's injury hadn't been the last: Fened had been wounded on the face by a flying sliver of stone. Paneb had turned to the Wise Woman for help. She spent the whole night chanting incantations against the evil eye, and had eventually driven it away.

The craftsmen had agreed to return to work, although they were still uneasy. But nothing bad had happened; and when Renupe the Jovial began singing a song glorifying the Brotherhood's founder, the Servants of the Place of Truth rediscovered the joy of their work.

Without explaining why, the Wise Woman had told Paneb to complete Saptah's House of Eternity as quickly as possible. They had also begun excavating Bay's tomb, so he would have to ask a great deal of his crew if he was not to harm the quality of the work or cancel rest days. So he had asked for volunteers: men who were willing to give up their days off in return for bonuses. Despite protests from their wives, Nakht the Strong, Userhat the Lion, Casa the Rope, and Unesh the Jackal had put themselves forward.

▲

For the first time in several months, Paneb was enjoying a few hours' rest at home. But his peace was short-lived: Uabet came out of the bedroom, and it was obvious that she was angry.

"Two of my hair-sticks are missing," she complained. "You haven't taken them, have you?"

She set great store by these little wood and bone pins, which were pointed at one end and very useful for dressing the hair. Moreover, Paneb had decorated these particular sticks with falcons' heads, carved in such minute detail that most of her friends were green with envy.

"You know I never touch your things," said Paneb.

"Then it must be Aapehti."

"Where is he?"

"I don't know. Every since he learnt how to make plaster, he thinks he's a master craftsman. I can't control him any more."

Iuwen smiled up at her father, who kissed her gently on the forehead. She asked, "Will you stay with me forever?"

"Of course I will. But just now I must go and find your brother."

"Has he done something silly again?"

"Let's hope not."

▲

"Aapehti? He left more than an hour ago," said Pai the Good Bread's wife. "He's working hard, and the front of our house will soon be as good as new, but what a dreadful manner he has. If you say one word to him, he takes offense and starts making threats. You'd better show him who's master, or there'll be some fine fun and games, I promise you."

Paneb asked several of the other women, but no one knew where Aapehti had gone. Userhat's wife was very worried about her eldest son, who had quarreled with him that very morning.

In vain, Paneb scoured the village and the outlying areas. If Aapehti had left the lands owned by the Place of Truth, ought he to tell Sobek's men? But he had yet to take a look at the rubbish pit, which lay to the south of the village. It was there that assorted rubbish was burnt, reduced into a compact mass which was purified by the sun, and then buried in a stone-lined pit.

When he got there, Paneb couldn't believe his eyes. On top of the heap of rubbish, Aapehti was torturing Userhat's boy, threatening to drive the stolen hair-sticks into his hands.

"Come away from there!" roared Paneb.

Aapehti stood frozen to the spot for a long moment, and his victim took the opportunity to run away.

"That piece of filth insulted me," explained Aapehti.

"Why did you steal those hair-sticks?"

The question caught the lad unprepared. "For . . . for my own amusement."

"You're nothing but a cruel little thief, Aapehti, and you misuse abominably the strength the gods have given you."

The youth emerged nervously from the rubbish pit. "You're not going to punish me, are you?"

"First, give me back the sticks."

Aapehti knelt down. "Here they are. But don't hit me. Mother'd be angry with you and—"

The slap was so violent that Aapehti was thrown to the ground.

"This village has its laws, boy, and you will respect them. There will be no further warnings. Either you are at work first thing tomorrow morning, or you will leave the Place of Truth."

"Can I come home?"

"Tonight you will sleep on the doorstep, and you will have no supper. An empty stomach helps people to think about the error of their ways."

▲

Kenhir's gout attack had been cured, and his arthritis was less severe, but he now had pain in the middle of his back and could no longer spend part of the night writing his *Key of Dreams.* Following Niut's advice, he had found a position that enabled him to forget the pain: sitting on a cushion, with one leg stretched in front of him, his wooden writing tablet attached by a nail to his study wall. His hieroglyphs were becoming more and more illegible, but the old scribe had lost none of his mental agility and would not allow anyone else to keep the Journal of the Tomb.

"You should keep a wary eye on your assistant," warned Niut.

"Imuni is a competent, serious-minded scribe. Thanks to him, the lists of tools and supplies are absolutely accurate."

"That's good," she said, "but he covets your position, you know, and he isn't a good-hearted man."

"Has he hurt you?"

"Just let him try! No, it's you I'm thinking of."

"Don't worry, Imuni isn't ready to succeed me yet. And he may never be."

"Won't that make him bitter?"

"If it does, I shall send him away to continue his career in some quiet province. Either Imuni realizes how immensely fortunate he is to live here, or he'll become a mere petty functionary."

Niut smiled in satisfaction. "Your breakfast is ready."

Perfectly grilled grains, honey-sweet figs, and a cake stuffed with dates: Kenhir found each breakfast—and lunch and dinner—a feast. Imuni, though, did not appreciate the finer things in life, a serious flaw, which was probably why he felt unfulfilled.

At that moment, the little rat-faced scribe knocked at the door and asked to see Kenhir. Niut made him wait until her husband had finished his meal.

"A report from Commander Sobek," Imuni said excitedly.

"Why are you squeaking like that?" asked Kenhir.

"Because the reputation of the Place of Truth is at stake. We must act immediately."

"About what?"

"A cow has disappeared."

"What's that to do with us?"

"She belonged to Ramses' Temple of a Million Years and was to be the incarnation of Hathor at the next festival of the goddess in the temple at Deir el-Bahri."

"That's certainly annoying, but what can we do about it?"

"It was a craftsman's fault that the cow ran away, so the Brotherhood is responsible. Sobek's report states clearly that there were witnesses and that our keeping silent won't be enough to dispel the scandal."

"Which craftsman is responsible for this?"

"The report doesn't say."

Another disaster—right in the middle of excavating a royal tomb! Kenhir said wearily, "Hand me my walking stick."

▲

Sobek was sitting on a stool in his office at the Fifth Fort. He looked tired.

"Is this really serious?" asked Kenhir.

"Unfortunately it is. That's why I had to write that report and ask you to shed any light you can on the matter."

"You forgot to include the name of the alleged culprit."

"I hate slander," said Sobek gruffly.

"You mentioned witnesses . . . ?"

"Witnesses can be bought—particularly when the accused is a crew leader by the name of Paneb the Ardent."

12

Kenhir and Ubekhet looked worriedly at Paneb.

"So long as you stay on land owned by the Place of Truth, you're safe," said Kenhir. "I shall begin legal proceedings at once, and try to prove the witnesses' statements are false."

"I won't have my movements restricted because of something I didn't do," said Paneb angrily. "Limiting my movements will only weaken the Brotherhood."

"That's true, I'm afraid, but your first duty is to finish King Saptah's House of Eternity."

"Can't we just find the cow?"

"I doubt she ever existed."

"That's not what Sobek thinks," retorted Paneb, "and he's investigated the matter thoroughly."

"You were attacked by no fewer than nine men," Kenhir reminded him. "You escaped from them, but you mustn't take too many chances with your luck."

"I won't live like a prisoner, but I will do what the Wise Woman advises."

"Come with me to the temple," said Ubekhet.

The villagers already knew Paneb had been attacked again,

and he was happy to receive signs of encouragement from them. From his determined gait, everyone realized he was preparing to fight, though he was intelligent enough to allow the Wise Woman to guide him.

"Whenever Nefer had to make a decision that was vital for the Brotherhood's future he came here," she revealed as she walked through the pillared gateway of the temple. Its facade was decorated with large stelae dedicated to Pharaoh's *ka,* as well as scenes showing offerings being made to Ma'at and to Sekhmet, goddess of the Peak of the West, who was depicted as a lion-headed serpent.

Ubekhet and Paneb purified themselves, anointed themselves with myrrh, and put on fine linen robes and white sandals. Then they entered the temple, where the atmosphere was one of matchless peace.

"You are the temple and you live," chanted the Wise Woman in the half-light. "You calm the southern wind, you replace the burning sun with benevolent shade, your two walls are the Peaks of the West and the East, your vault is the sky, and we are nourished by your Light."

In this place, which the Brotherhood had created as a dwelling for the Divine power, sacred acts took place by themselves, without the need for human intervention.

"The incident is much more serious than it seems," said the Wise Woman. "If the cow did run away, it means that Hathor's protection is leaving us. And without it our magic will not work."

"Don't you think this may be just another trap? Nefer was murdered, and now someone wants to kill me."

"You're in danger, certainly, but the cow is giving us a warning. If we ignore it, our defenses will be weakened, and the worst will happen. We must find her and lead her to Hathor."

"Right," said Paneb. "Then I shall find her myself."

▲

Leaning on his walking stick, Kenhir stared into the eyes of a young official fresh from the scribes' school. So this specimen, he thought, was the man in charge of all the animals belonging to Ramses' Temple of a Million Years.

The scribe had received him in a high-ceilinged office which was pleasantly cool, thanks to a clever arrangement of small windows, allowing the air to circulate. The papyrus scrolls were all impeccably arranged, and the chairs were comfortable.

"This is a very great honor," said the scribe. "I wasn't expecting you."

"You make accusations against a Servant of the Place of Truth and you don't expect me to come and see you? Have you forgotten that I am the state's representative inside the village and that if you attack one of its inhabitants, you are attacking me?"

"Wouldn't you . . . er . . . like to sit down?"

"Certainly not, my boy. My legs have carried me this far and I hope they will carry me for a long time to come."

Several colleagues had warned the scribe that Kenhir was not easy to handle, but they had suggested that age might have mellowed him. It seemed they were mistaken.

"So," Kenhir went on, "what about these witnesses of yours?"

"The term is perhaps a little too strong."

" 'Too strong?' What does that mean?"

" 'Witness' implies a precise legal term, and I didn't wish to—"

"Will you or will you not show me these witnesses?"

"They are simple, uneducated peasants, and they don't find it easy to express themselves. A judge might consider their observations imprecise and—"

"Did they see Paneb the Ardent steal a cow dedicated to Hathor? Yes or no?"

"I wouldn't be quite as dogmatic as that, particularly since there is a rather large herdsman who might be confused with Paneb."

Kenhir's eyes narrowed. "Are you trying to tell me that you have no evidence whatsoever?"

"Indeed, there . . . er . . . isn't a great deal, and you must believe that I hadn't really envisaged a court case."

"Yet you've caused all this fuss. Why?"

The scribe looked away. "A certain kind of opportunity. You, an experienced scribe, will understand that it's difficult to climb the ladder of promotion. So, I assumed that—"

"You belong to that class of young predators who will do anything to make people talk about them and gain their superiors' approval, without caring one jot for the law of Ma'at!"

"But indeed, Kenhir, the cow really has disappeared, and—"

"That's your own fault, by all accounts! And you're using slander to try to exonerate yourself and make someone else pay for your mistake."

"Perhaps we could . . . er . . . come to an understanding, between scribes. After all, the Place of Truth isn't your family."

"Understand this, my boy. The Scribe of the Tomb isn't an official like all the others. He lives according to a spirit of brotherhood which you'll never even begin to understand. Hand in your resignation at once and leave the west bank as fast as you can. Otherwise, I shall take personal charge of your case."

Broken, the official collapsed heavily on to a low chair. "What about my cow?"

"Find her yourself!"

▲

Much relieved, Kenhir headed back to the village. The walk had tired him a little, but he felt positively jaunty at the thought of bringing back such excellent news.

When Ubekhet emerged from her workshop, the old scribe felt much as he had done the first time they met: despite her grief, she was still as radiant as a gentle spring sun, and her presence alone was enough to make a man believe in happiness.

"Everything is sorted out," he told her. "It was an overambitious official picking a quarrel in order to have us blamed for his own mistake. He even thought he could involve me in his tawdry scheme! Paneb can sleep peacefully."

"He's gone," said Ubekhet.

"Gone? Gone where?"

"To find Hathor's cow."

"But that's no longer anything to do with us."

"I think it is, Kenhir. The scribe at Ramses' temple was only the instrument of destiny. In thinking he could incriminate us, he was voicing the goddess's call."

"An attempt has already been made to kill Paneb, Ubekhet! Surely sending him into the unknown like this is making him take unnecessary risks?"

"The priestesses of Hathor believe his mission is essential."

Kenhir leant more heavily on his stick. "I'm beginning to understand. You're setting him one of the trials that may lead him to the summit, aren't you?"

Ubekhet gave a small smile. "The sacred cow really is in danger."

"And if Paneb can't bring her back, he won't come back, either."

"That's for the goddess to decide."

"The office of Scribe of the Tomb is no easy one," mused Kenhir, "but it's still preferable to being a crew leader in the Place of Truth."

▲

"I've had a message from the traitor," announced Serketa, licking her greedy lips. "The Brotherhood is continuing to excavate tombs for Bay and King Saptah, and is building Saptah's temple on the west bank. But without Paneb—"

"What? Are you joking?" Mehy stared at her.

"Paneb has left the village, and no one knows where he's gone."

"We mustn't rejoice too soon."

"The traitor says it's definitely not an official journey. Perhaps Paneb's nerve has broken. He was nearly killed in that last attack, so perhaps he's decided to leave the village for good—after all, it's brought him nothing but trouble."

"It would be understandable. But that fellow doesn't seem the type to give up so easily."

"Every man has his weaknesses, my tender lion," whispered Serketa.

13

A herdsman gave Paneb directions, and he was able to track the cow as far as the edge of the papyrus reedbeds, where the stems grew over twelve cubits high.

A fisherman was sitting on a straw chair on the bank, munching a flat cake.

"Has a cow passed this way?" asked Paneb.

"I'll say! She was magnificent, with big soft eyes and a hide like gold."

"Why didn't you stop her?"

"First of all, it's not my job; second, that cow doesn't look like an ordinary cow. People round here say Hathor is protecting her and that nobody ought to touch her. If you take my advice, you won't venture in there. A fair few experienced hunters haven't come out alive."

▲

Paneb pushed aside the first papyrus stalks, and entered a hostile world where every step brought danger. But the mission the Wise Woman had entrusted to him was vital for the Brotherhood's future, and he would rather die than fail.

He came under constant attack from leeches, and from

mosquitoes and other insects, while a multitude of birds and small animals, disturbed by the intruder, set up a clamor that made the papyrus quiver. A water snake brushed past Paneb's legs, but he did not slow down.

If a trap had been set for him, his attackers would be no better off than he was. Fear had no hold on him, and he plunged deeper and deeper into this shadowy world where life and death were locked in a pitiless struggle.

Just as he was beginning to lose hope, he saw her: an incredibly beautiful cow, with a delicate face and eyes that radiated infinite tenderness. She was standing on a grassy islet surrounded by murky water. As he approached, she did not run away; but Paneb sensed that she was anxious, and that only imminent danger was preventing her from rushing off into a papyrus thicket. Something dark and sinister, shaped like a tree trunk, was making its way through the water toward the island. In a few seconds, the crocodile's jaws would close on the cow's hind legs.

At the very moment the crocodile attacked, Paneb leapt on to its back. The creature reared up so violently that he was sure it had broken his ribs, but he did not loosen his grip. The monster's strength was ten times that of Paneb, who was pleased to have met a worthy adversary at last. Letting out a mighty roar, he marshaled all his reserves of strength and managed to pry open the crocodile's jaws hard enough to rip them apart.

▲

The cow entered the courtyard of the Temple of Hathor, wearing a headdress made from a gold disk flanked by two feathers. She had been purified with incense smoke and her eyes accentuated with black and green kohl.

After abandoning the Place of Truth, Hathor had returned. She had come back to her temple, and before she returned to the enclosure at Deir el-Bahri she would reveal to her servants the harmony that had existed since the beginning of time.

When the Wise Woman anointed the cow's forehead with holy oil, the animal seemed to smile at her. And, despite his painful ribs, Paneb also had a smile on his lips.

▲

At Hay's request all the craftsmen were working together, putting the final touches to King Saptah's Temple of a Million Years. The building was of modest size, and stood close to the temple of Thutmose III, the illustrious pharaoh who had written the *Book of the Stars' Creation,* which the Brotherhood's artists used to help them decorate Houses of Eternity in the Valley of the Kings. Saptah's temple also enjoyed the protection of the immense temple built by Ramses the Great.

"Little King Saptah is a lucky man," commented Fened the Nose. "What a wonderful location."

"Let's hope that the next world will be kinder to him than this one," grunted Karo the Impatient. "If the rumors are true, he's constantly ill and won't live long."

"It was Queen Tausert who insisted his temple should be built here, and as quickly as possible," pointed out Userhat the Lion. "She has true greatness of spirit."

"Oh, you think so, do you?" scoffed Unesh the Jackal. "She's just following one of her schemes, that's all. By manipulating that feeble, incompetent youth, she's making his followers look on her more favorably."

"Let's forget politics," urged Pai the Good Bread. "I'd have liked King Saptah to come and visit our village."

"No chance of that," said Nakht the Strong. "He never leaves the Temple of Amon at Pi-Ramses, and the only thing he enjoys is reading the writings of the Ancients."

"How do you know all this?" asked Gau the Precise.

"From our wives," replied Renupe the Jovial. "They chatter to the guards, who talk to the messenger and the lay workers, and we're as well-informed as the people who live in the capital."

"Let's have a drink and get back to work," advised Thuty the Learned.

Although there were still a few details requiring attention, the shrine was ready to function, and the priests could come to live there in two days' time.

▲

As the traitor carried out his duties alongside his colleagues, he watched every movement on the site with minute attention. The previous evening, the Servants of the Place of Truth had brought lapis lazuli, turquoises, myrrh, fresh incense, fine linen, cornelian, red jasper, alabaster, and other materials necessary for the life of the temple. The traitor was sure that when the Scribe of the Tomb had opened the storeroom, he had also taken out the Stone of Light, hidden in the heavy wooden chest that Paneb had stubbornly carried on his shoulders, despite his wounds.

Hiding the Stone in Saptah's temple: what an excellent idea! If it had not dawned on him, the traitor would have gone on fruitlessly searching the village. But Hay had made a mistake by asking Paneb and the starboard crew to help with a task he ought to have carried out on his own; and that mistake had attracted the traitor's attention. The big man had come to this place for only one reason: to hide the priceless treasure.

But where exactly? Until the work was finished, the craftsmen could move about as they wished within the building, and the traitor took advantage of this freedom to enter the crypt. It had been dug underneath the paved floor, and was where statues and ritual objects were stored. He opened the chests, but found nothing, and soon rejoined his colleagues.

"The shallow grooves the sculptors have carved in the stone walls of the shrine," explained Hay, "show where we are to fix the gold plates, which will be molded to the shape of the relief carvings and held in place with gold-headed pegs."

Kenhir handed out the plates. The traitor played his part in installing them, convinced he had seen through the trick the Wise Woman and the two crew leaders had devised. One of the plates would conceal a deep cavity, in which the Stone of Light would be placed; the light that radiated from it would be lost in the glimmer from the gold. But how was he to find the right place?

Fortune smiled on him: he spotted Paneb and Hay heading toward the rear of the temple, carrying a sheet of gold which was wider and heavier than the others. Moreover, the two crew leaders had taken care to avoid prying eyes.

▲

When they finished work, the craftsmen gathered under an old acacia tree to share a meal brought by peasant women who worked for Ramses' temple. The fresh onions were delightfully crisp, and the beer was agreeably cool.

"This little temple is splendid," said Casa the Rope, "and the tomb will be equally splendid. King Saptah should be pleased."

"How lucky we are," commented Didia the Generous. "As we build, we experience the mystery of creation, and mirror the work of the Great Architect upon this earth."

"Provided we offer up this dwelling—which is his, not ours," Unesh reminded him.

"When the light of the setting sun turns the stonework to gold," murmured Ipuy the Examiner, "even our smallest deeds take on their full meaning."

As the sun set behind the Peak of the West, the countryside fell silent and so did the craftsmen. Some wandered away from the group to be alone and meditate.

The traitor went to the rear of the temple. He sat down close to the wall, just beneath the great gold plate. No one could see him, but he waited for a long time so as to be absolutely sure he hadn't been followed. Then, with a copper chisel, he removed the plate.

No light sprang forth from the cavity. What the two crew leaders had placed inside was not the Stone but a statuette of the goddess Ma'at, the embodiment of righteousness.

14

The late April heat was stifling. The Scribe of the Tomb had ordered the water deliveries to be doubled, and in order to create a little coolness, the craftsmen had canopied the narrow streets with palm branches.

Karo the Impatient knocked at Paneb's door. Little Iuwen opened it. "Do you want to see my daddy?" she asked.

The stonecutter's natural aggression melted away. "Is he here?"

"He's getting dressed, with Mummy. Do you want to come in?"

"Well, yes."

"Then you can tell me a story about good and evil spirits."

The little girl took Karo by the hand and led him over to a sturdy, rush-seated chair.

"I'm not much good at stories, you know," he said.

"You must know some, because you work in the forbidden places, like my daddy. Is that really where the spirits hide?"

Karo rubbed his broken nose to give himself time to think. "There are some, that's true."

The arrival of a freshly washed and scented Paneb extricated Karo from a sticky situation.

"Is there an emergency, Karo?"

"Have you been outside this morning?"

"Not yet."

"Last night it didn't get any cooler at all. And today seems likely to be unbearably hot."

"I don't doubt it, but why rail against nature?"

"The peasants aren't working in the fields anymore, no one is traveling on foot, the only thing anyone is thinking about is saving themselves from this appalling heat. But we have to ruin our health in the Valley of the Kings, which is just like an oven! My comrades have asked me to be their spokesman: let the crew stay in the village until the end of this heat wave."

Karo was expecting a furious reaction, and he was quite ready to refer the dispute to the village court.

"Very well," said Paneb.

Karo gaped at him. "What do you mean, 'very well'?"

"I mean I grant your request. Anything else?"

"Er, no, nothing. Nothing at all."

"Prepare the burial goods in the village workshops. Ched and Userhat will supervise."

"Of course, of course. But what about you?"

"I shall be doing my duty."

▲

Heavily laden with sacks containing his brushes and his cakes of color, Paneb left the village.

The gatekeeper, who was sitting in the shade provided by a thick cloth stretched between poles, asked in amazement, "Surely you're not going to the Valley?"

"Of course I am," replied Paneb. "I've got work to do."

"The donkey drivers were complaining of the heat just after sunrise, and they aren't coming back until sunset. You'll die, up there in the mountains."

"Don't worry, the sun's my natural element."

Paneb went to the stable, where his donkey was munching some fodder. North Wind would obey no one but him. The previous evening, Paneb had trimmed the animal's exceptionally hard hooves and, as he always did, the donkey lay down whimpering, pretending he was in unbearable pain. After his torturer had given him a large helping of willow bark, his favorite treat, North Wind had allowed him to get on with it.

The donkey had a white muzzle and belly. He had grown into an enormous creature, immensely strong. Despite his size, he loved it when Paneb kissed him gently on the nose and stroked his head.

"Will you come with me to the Valley of the Kings?"

A glint appeared in the almond-shaped eyes, and the donkey's ears sprang to attention.

"I have a lot of materials to carry, and it'll be a hard journey."

The donkey walked out of the stable, sniffed the burning air, and halted facing the path that led to the Great Meadow. Paneb loaded him with two baskets, which he half filled, not forgetting to add some waterskins. North Wind led the way and set the pace.

North Wind and Ebony: the crew leader had at least two faithful friends, not to mention Bad Girl, the evil-tempered goose who delighted in guarding her master, and Charmer, the monstrous cat who drove evil spirits from his home.

The craftsmen were right: it was much too hot to work. And Paneb had accepted all the reasons for absence which the craftsmen had submitted over the last few months: sickness, tiredness, family problems, and all sorts of other temporary difficulties.

But he was the crew leader; and as such he must put the work first, whatever the circumstances.

As he climbed the slope leading to the pass, from where he would descend into the Valley of the Kings, solitude hung heavy on Paneb. And yet the bond of brotherhood he felt was deep and sincere. He loved them all, from Ched to Karo: all the chosen men who had devoted their lives to the Place of Truth. But none of them was at his side now, and no doubt it was better this way. It was up to him to do his duty, not complain about his lot or other people's inadequacies.

▲

The two Nubians who guarded the Valley of the Kings were astonished to see a donkey and a man approaching, both of them scarcely out of breath. Another chapter was sure to be added to the legend of Paneb's inexhaustible strength.

Stepping into the furnace, Paneb and his companion walked past the entrance to Ramses the Great's tomb and headed for the site of Saptah's and Bay's tombs. Once there, the craftsman quickly unloaded North Wind, then gave him water to drink, and laid out a mat in the shade, so that the donkey could lie down.

Paneb began with Bay's tomb, where the temperature was noticeably cooler than outside. The crew had completed only the pillared chamber; the portion beyond, which would have formed the House of Gold, was to remain rough-hewn. Nevertheless, Pharaoh's faithful servant would rest there in peace.

In the first passageway, Paneb completed the scene depicting the tjaty standing behind King Saptah, then he drew Bay worshipping a sun god with a falcon's head. Bay was not a ruler, but he had seen the Light that dwelt within the symbolic person of the king, and that Light would guide him along the beautiful paths of eternity.

In the grip of a creative fever, Paneb felt no tiredness. Next, he went to Saptah's tomb, where he lit ten torches, whose triple wicks gave off no smoke. He prepared pigments: a dazzling white and an ocher that shone like gold, conjuring up the purity of the royal soul and the magic of its transmutation.

Like Ched, he made pigments that could not be harmed by the air and were insoluble in water and resistant to damage by fire. His palette, which Gau had given him, had become his third eye, on which the different shades were mixed and then fixed with linen and poppy seed oils, and an essence derived from the pistachio tree.

Remembering the rule Ched had taught him, he set himself several different viewpoints simultaneously as he painted, and was careful to avoid deceptive perspectives. His brushes expressed both grace and stillness, and brought out the hidden reality within the harmony of form.

Paneb's paintings would ensure that Saptah remained eternally young, his serene face illuminated forever by the creative forces at work in his tomb. On the ceiling, red vultures carrying a white crown bore away his spirit into the bosom of its celestial mother, safe from all decay. Through color, the figures came to life and the hieroglyphs spoke; whatever fate lay in store for the little lame king, here he would find a fulfillment worthy of the greatest pharaohs.

Adding a final touch of white to the robe of a protective Isis, Paneb left the tomb just as the sun was setting.

To his astonishment, there, sitting on a stool, hands folded and resting on his walking stick, was Kenhir, savoring the last moments of the day.

"Whatever are you doing here?" asked Paneb.

"Like you, my work. Tell me how many wicks and cakes of color you've used."

"I didn't count."

"I thought as much—yet another job I must do myself. Do you at least know how long you spent in the tomb?"

"No, I've no idea."

"Three days! If I hadn't come to feed your donkey and give him a drink, the poor creature would be dead. Sometimes, your negligence is unforgivable."

"You came all this way, in this terrible heat . . . ?"

"At my age, people like the heat. Besides, it's unthinkable for a craftsman to work in the Valley of the Kings without my being here to exercise the proper controls. Aren't you thirsty?"

"A bit."

Kenhir handed him a gourd of water.

When Paneb had quenched his thirst, Kenhir said, "Show me your paintings."

As soon as they went into the tomb, he saw that Paneb had forgotten to put out the torches. But how could he scold him when his paintbrush gave life to such marvels?

15

It was a miracle that Mehy's galloping horse did not knock over a little girl who was playing beside the road. Maddened with rage, the general spurred the beast onward, toward his house.

He left his exhausted mount to a groom and hurtled into the reception chamber. There, Serketa was exchanging polite conversation with some rich Theban women. They were heaping insults on King Saptah and lavishing praise on Setnakhte.

Mehy muttered a few pleasantries, then withdrew to his rooms.

"We'll leave you now, my dear," said one of the guests.

"There's no hurry," said Serketa.

"Your husband looks as if he has a lot on his mind."

"Refurbishing the barracks is proving much less easy than he expected. He's met all kinds of problems and obstacles."

The ladies exchanged understanding smiles.

"Tomorrow evening there's to be a banquet in honor of the new year of the king's reign," said the mayor's wife. "You'll be in our party, of course."

"I'd be delighted," replied Serketa, preening herself like a cat.

As soon as the ladies had gone, she ran to the bedchamber, where Mehy was taking out his anger on the linen sheets, tearing them to ribbons with his teeth.

"Stop it," ordered Serketa. "Behavior like that is unworthy of a future master of Egypt."

"Would you rather I vented my anger on you?"

"If it will bring you to your senses, by all means do so."

The general trampled on the tattered remnants of a sheet, and threw himself down on his bed. "I'm beginning to think murdering Nefer was a waste of time. His death has made Paneb invincible, and the Brotherhood has emerged from this trial stronger than ever. The Place of Truth has announced that

Saptah's temple is finished, and that both his tomb and the tjaty's are almost ready. It's a triumph for the craftsmen. And that damned traitor still hasn't discovered where the Stone of Light is hidden."

"Don't give up hope," said Serketa, massaging his shoulders. "I agree that Paneb looks victorious, but he'd be nothing without his community's magic. And who provides that magic? A widow who has been weakened by the death of her husband."

"You know perfectly well the Wise Woman is beyond our reach."

"I'm not so sure of that, my tender jackal."

▲

Ubekhet had treated the fluttering in Fened's chest, and the grumbling in Pai the Good Bread's belly. Then it seemed that every single person in the village was having trouble with their teeth. First, there was a serious abscess, which had had to be drained, then a mouth ulcer, which she had treated with a paste made from cow's milk, dried carob fruit and fresh dates, which had to be chewed for nine days. Then fillings, which were made with spelt flour, honey, and grit from the millstones. There had even been a case of a rotting tooth, a rare affliction in the land of the pharaohs. None of these problems required the involvement of a more highly qualified tooth doctor, and Ubekhet advised all the villagers to clean their mouths and teeth thoroughly, using water purified with natron and a paste that removed grease and stains. Chewing papyrus shoots was also good.

"There's a letter for you," announced Renupe's wife, handing out the post brought by the messenger, Uputy.

Ubekhet's head was spinning, so she sat down and closed her eyes. Carrying out so many delicate treatments had tired her, and she did not recover as easily as in the days when she and Nefer had discussed their day's work and shared the burden of their respective duties. The memory of their happiness brought a lump to her throat, and she wished she could abandon herself to a dream that would take her to him. But she must stay here in the village, to which Nefer had devoted his life, until her strength was exhausted.

As she read the letter from the head doctor of the province of Thebes, Ubekhet felt as if the world had collapsed around her ears.

▲

"Are you sure?" asked Kenhir in astonishment.

"Read it yourself: the head doctor is refusing me deliveries of balm, including styrax. Without them, there are many illnesses I can no longer treat."

"This is the first time anything like this has ever happened. Who on earth does this idiot think he is?"

"He says that his decision is dictated 'by serious reasons which cannot be disputed.' What on earth can it mean?"

"I'm going straight to the palace to ensure that the deliveries are reinstated," declared the Scribe of the Tomb.

▲

Daktair was fat, with short legs, small dark eyes which often gleamed with malice, and a red beard which he smoothed and perfumed every morning. The son of a Greek mathematician and a Persian alchemist, he had become head of the central workshop and head doctor of Thebes with Mehy's secret support. For a long time, he had believed he could force people to accept his vision of pure knowledge, but tradition had prevented him from putting his plans into practice.

Daktair had dreamt of an Egypt freed from its useless beliefs and firmly committed to progress, but he had had to give up his dream, and had gradually yielded to a life of ease and respectability. He had long since ceased to believe in the existence of the Stone of Light, though General Mehy was still obsessed with the idea of owning it. And what had become of Mehy, the conqueror who was willing to do anything to gain power? He had become merely master of the rich Theban province, without realizing his ambitions.

Embittered, Daktair amused himself by contriving disputes among the various doctors attached to the palace, and ate more and more gluttonously, preferring his cook's fine dishes to the prostitutes he now seldom visited.

When Serketa suggested dealing a death blow to the Place of Truth by attacking the Wise Woman, Daktair felt a glow of pleasure he had thought lost forever. Egypt and the whole world ought to be hailing him as a genius, instead of which he was confined to a mundane administrative post. Well, now he had a chance for revenge, and he would seize it greedily.

As he had expected, the Scribe of the Tomb himself came to demand an explanation.

The two men loathed each other on sight. To Kenhir, Daktair was a perfect example of an overambitious man who had become a useless, incompetent, and arrogant senior official. To Daktair, Kenhir was the hateful embodiment of an old-fashioned scribe, clinging tenaciously to outdated learning.

"What is the meaning of this stupid letter?" demanded Kenhir.

"You forget whom you are speaking to!"

"Unfortunately not: I am speaking to an obnoxious little man who flaunts a title he doesn't deserve, and who must have lost his mind if he thinks he can infringe the laws governing the Place of Truth."

The fierceness of the attack left Daktair speechless for a few seconds, but anger fueled a counterattack. "I know those precious laws as well as you do!"

"Then you know that you are forbidden to interrupt deliveries of medicinal substances to the Place of Truth."

Daktair smiled gloatingly. "Except when my duty obliges me to do so."

The Scribe of the Tomb found such smugness worrying. "Explain yourself."

"You think me worthless, don't you? Well, you're wrong, my dear Kenhir. As the palace's most senior doctor, I keep a close eye on my subordinates at all times, and I permit no laxity in their conduct, let alone any serious lapses."

"The only thing you're expert in is administration. You couldn't cure even the simplest ailment."

Daktair turned purple. "I forbid you to speak to me like that!"

It was Kenhir's turn to smile. "If you had any dignity left, you would resign here and now, but you're too cowardly and too fond of your privileges. I shall therefore send His Majesty a report, informing him that you are abusing your authority."

"I wouldn't do that if I were you," said Daktair menacingly.

"I'm not in the least impressed by threats."

"You're wrong to take my letter so lightly, Kenhir. If you had any intelligence left, you'd stop supporting the Wise Woman."

"And why, pray, should I do that?"

"Is it true that Ubekhet has been appointed by the Brotherhood to care for the sick within the village?"

The Scribe of the Tomb nodded.

"When she identifies a serious case which she cannot treat, should she not call in a specialist from outside?"

"That is indeed the Wise Woman's duty."

Daktair's small eyes glittered with triumphant malice. "Well, my dear Kenhir, she did not fulfill it. She placed a sick person in danger of death and will therefore be punished with the utmost severity. Given her incompetence, I have suspended the deliveries of medicinal items to a person who cannot use them correctly."

"You're making this up!"

"The importance of my office does not permit me to do so," replied Daktair with irony. "I don't act without proof."

"What proof?"

"A complaint from the sick craftsman who was so badly treated."

16

Kenhir's back was hurting, so he lowered himself slowly onto a high-backed chair. To his right stood the Wise Woman; to his left was Paneb. In front of them stood Casa the Rope, whose square face seemed frozen in an expression of despair.

"We want the whole truth," said Kenhir sternly.

"All right, all right," agreed the stonecutter, "but it's not what you're thinking."

"Did you or did you not go to the east bank last week?"

"Yes, I did, to meet a customer who wanted some funerary statuettes."

"And did you spend a long time in the alehouse on the quayside?"

"It was hot and I was thirsty," said Casa defensively.

"You drank a lot, didn't you?"

"I was very thirsty."

"You spent a long time talking to several people about your painful abscess."

"That's quite possible," admitted Casa.

"And you omitted to mention that the Wise Woman was going to treat you."

"To be frank, I'm not too sure what I did say."

"According to witness statements gathered by Daktair, you complained that you were in horrible pain and that no one was showing any interest in your case."

"I can't remember . . ."

"The witnesses realized you were in danger and alerted the health authorities."

"I didn't ask them to do anything like that."

"Are you sure?" asked Paneb.

"As sure as anybody can be."

"Who was your customer?"

"When I got to the address I'd been given, there was no one there. All right, I'd drunk too much, but I'm sure I went to the right place."

"You have committed a grave error," said Kenhir, "for you should not have left the village without telling the Wise Woman about that abscess."

"She was busy treating a little girl, and I didn't want to wait."

"Today, because of you, she has been accused of negligence and there's a danger that she may no longer be able to practice her craft."

Casa hung his head. "I'll explain to the judges, and the misunderstanding will soon be cleared up."

"Daktair has already begun court proceedings to have the Wise Woman declared unfit to practice medicine."

The stonecutter clenched his fists. "I'll break his head!"

"Don't do anything idiotic like that, whatever you do," advised Kenhir.

"There's only one thing to do," said Ubekhet. "I must prove my abilities to the head doctor and the specialists at the palace."

▲

General Mehy emptied his cup of white wine in a single draught. "I know you drink nothing but water, my dear Daktair, but you should make an exception occasionally. A fine victory deserves a suitable celebration."

"The Wise Woman hasn't been dismissed yet."

"Ah, but she has chosen the worst of all solutions. She should have fought in the courts. Her arrogance will be her downfall."

"I haven't managed to bribe all the doctors," confessed Daktair. "Some are hostile to me, others are fundamentally honest. And, so as not to damage my own credibility, I can't pick the patient they'll watch the Wise Woman treat—the selection must be made by one of them, who'll be chosen by lot."

"A difficult case, I hope?"

"You can be sure of that! The Wise Woman's reputation

annoys most of the doctors, but she might succeed if I don't take decisive action."

"What do you plan to do?"

"As soon as I know who the patient is, I shall poison his or her food or drink. Whatever the Wise Woman's talents may be, she won't manage a cure. And she will present her colleagues with a corpse."

Mehy drew a long, comfortable breath. "You're a remarkable scholar, my friend."

"And yet I'm stuck in a boring post where my mind and learning are going to waste. Why have you abandoned your grand plans?"

Suddenly sobering up, the general rose to his feet. "What makes you think I have?"

"The Place of Truth is triumphant, the entire country is sinking into crisis, and you, you are content to rule Thebes. As for the old traditions stifling Egypt, no one is fighting against them. What can I hope for now, except the death of my illusions?"

"I haven't given up anything," said Mehy, "and I haven't forgotten you. Thanks to me, you're in a frontline position; and the only one resting on his laurels is you! I've been waging a war for several years, and I've dealt some formidable blows to an enemy who's more fearsome than any army, for that enemy possesses the Stone of Light."

"That's nothing but an illusion, General."

"I remind you that I've seen it and I know its power. The Brotherhood survives only because of it, though they dare not use the Stone's true powers. To seize it, I must first destroy the defenses that surround it, beginning with the Wise Woman. That's why I need your help."

▲

The midday May heat would be unbearable, so Daktair and the doctors set off very early for the Place of Truth, in army chariots driven by Mehy's men. They were only a little way behind the caravan of donkeys delivering water to the village.

Commander Sobek himself greeted the visitors at the First Fort. Although extensive inquiries had enabled him to verify Casa's story, the Nubian was still skeptical; if the stonecutter was the traitor, he had succeeded in deceiving everyone.

Daktair said haughtily, "Bring the Wise Woman here."

"You have permission to enter the lay workers' encampment," said Sobek. "She's waiting for you there."

Dressed in a short-sleeved red dress and a fine gold necklace, Ubekhet made an immediate impression on her fellow doctors, especially their leader, a specialist in digestion problems, who bowed before her.

"I hope you will emerge victorious from this trial," he declared with feeling.

"No gossiping," cut in Daktair. "Wise Woman, are you ready to examine the patient?"

"Take him into the Scribe of the Tomb's office."

The patient was a stooping fifty-year-old man with a gray face and eyes sunk deep into their sockets. Visibly exhausted, he allowed himself to be led without a word.

"I require a witness to be present to watch what you do," said Daktair.

"I have no objection to that."

A doctor volunteered. He was present at the lengthy medical examination, during which Ubekhet listened to the voices of the different organs, examined the skin closely, studied the back of the eyes and felt the abdomen. Lost in her work, she analyzed the patient's urine and then a sample of blood, taken from the earlobe.

"Have you finished?" asked the doctor at last.

Ubekhet threw him a look signifying that she did not wish to answer in front of the sick man.

Sensing her concern, the patient dared to speak. "At Thebes, they said you'd help me."

"And I shall. I shall prescribe remedies for you."

"I'm worn out. I'd like to lie down."

After entrusting the patient to Obed the Blacksmith, who lent him his bed, the Wise Woman appeared before her judges.

"Anything irregular to report?" Daktair asked the doctor.

"Nothing. The examination was carried out with admirable thoroughness."

"What is your diagnosis, Wise Woman?"

"He has a serious heart problem, but that's an illness I know and I can cure. Unfortunately, there's something else, too, something much more serious."

The doctors' leader was astonished. "What do you mean?"

"There's poison flowing through the patient's veins."

"That's impossible," protested a heart doctor. "I examined him this morning and I'd have noticed it."

"Examine him again," insisted Ubekhet, "and you'll come to the same conclusion as I've done."

The doctors were very concerned, and fell into deep discussion.

"This is just a feeble attempt to divert attention from the real issue," commented Daktair.

Calmly, the Wise Woman listed the remedies she considered necessary.

"I have nothing to add," said the heart doctor. "It's obvious that our colleague's skills are remarkable."

"I, alas, feel they're inadequate," said Ubekhet. "The patient you brought here is dying, and I cannot save him."

"Note what she says!" exclaimed Daktair. "The Wise Woman of the Place of Truth acknowledges in front of you all that she does not have the necessary skills to cure sickness! The charges brought against her are therefore proven, and I propose that she be stripped of her office immediately."

17

The doctors Daktair had bribed agreed vigorously with what he had said, but the senior doctor and the heart doctor opposed him resolutely. The Wise Woman stayed calm throughout, and waited for the fuss to die down.

"Follow us to the palace," ordered Daktair. "Because of your dangerous practices, and to safeguard the villagers from any risk, you must be placed under guard."

"No, it is you who must follow me—and your colleagues with you."

Daktair flew into a rage. "Don't threaten me! Obey my orders, or I'll summon General Mehy's soldiers."

"I'm not threatening anyone. My only intention is to cure the sick man."

"You've just said publicly that you can't."

"Not by my medicine alone, true. But there are other ways."

The senior doctor glimpsed a way out. "Are we to understand that, once you had examined the patient, you would have entrusted him to specialists?"

"Not at all," replied the Wise Woman sweetly.

"You see?" raged Daktair. "She not only persists, she's mocking us, too!"

"In a case like this, the specialists would be as powerless as I am," Ubekhet went on calmly, "because the poison has already caused too much damage. All that remains is the last resort, whose outcome is unfortunately uncertain. That's why I'm asking you to follow me."

"It's pointless," said Daktair.

"It's essential," decreed Kenhir, rapping the ground with his walking stick. "Daktair, if you refuse to accept the Wise Woman's suggestion, I shall have you arraigned for failing to help a person in danger."

Daktair knew that the complaint would be successful, and that there was a danger of Ubekhet being found innocent. "Very well," he said resentfully, "let's go—but quickly."

"Carry the patient on a stretcher," ordered the Wise Woman, "and keep his lips and forehead moist."

It was harvesttime, the moment when the barley turned to gold, revealing the secret of nature's magic to those who had eyes to see. Because of the stifling heat, the procession made slow progress. The Wise Woman and the Scribe of the Tomb walked at the front, Paneb and Nakht the Strong carried the stretcher, while Daktair sweated like a pig and demanded drinking water constantly, for he was worn out by this tramp through the fields. Like Mehy, he loathed the countryside and did not so much as glance at the ears of barley, the earth's golden grains and the flesh of the risen Osiris.

▲

At the far end of a magnificent field a prayer shrine had been built, with a granite statue of a cobra crowned with a sun disk. Before it stood a small altar.

"Let us worship the goddess of the harvests," began Ubekhet. "May she protect the harvest and the granaries, and may our offerings appease her and persuade her to grant us her healing fire."

Bathed in sweat and gasping for breath, Daktair shrugged his shoulders. So this was the "last resort": a statue of a snake, the very embodiment of peasant superstitions!

Turquoise and Uabet the Pure approached the altar, bearing the offerings. These they handed one by one to Ubekhet, who presented them to the goddess.

"I offer you the first drop of water," began Ubekhet, "the first drop of beer, the first drop of wine, the first ear of wheat and the first piece of bread. Receive also this lettuce and this lotus flower, and grant us your magic."

Once the offerings had been laid on the altar, everyone fell to silent prayer. Everyone except Daktair, who could not bear the masquerade.

"Can you cure this sick man, yes or no?" he demanded.

The Wise Woman turned round. "What do you respect, Daktair?"

"New learning, not stupid old beliefs."

"You're right, and I share your opinion unreservedly."

Astrounded, he stared at her. "But you said . . ."

"I believe neither in this goddess nor in this statue, but I have learnt that the visible world is only an unworthy fragment of the invisible, in which creative powers are at work. And only one of those creative powers, embodied in this living stone, can cure the sick man."

Daktair burst out laughing. "For a moment, I thought you were at last giving up those stupid beliefs! Prison will soon set your ideas to rights."

Bearing the Revered Staff, which was made from precious wood decorated with gold leaf, Paneb approached the statue. Very gently, he touched its eyes with the tip of the staff.

Everyone took a hasty step back: for a split second, it seemed as if the eyes of the stone goddess kindled to flame.

"Take the statue out of the shrine and place it in full sunlight," the Wise Woman told Paneb.

Cautiously he did so. The stone was warm, as if life flowed through its veins.

"The sick man has been poisoned," declared the Wise Woman, "and ordinary remedies will not be enough to cure him. Neither I nor any doctor can prevent his death. Therefore I call to the goddess who gives birth to the golden ears of wheat and feeds mankind."

Slowly, she poured water onto the hieroglyphic inscriptions covering the column at the back of the statue; they were ancient incantations against snakes, scorpions, poisonous insects, and other visible and invisible creatures which sought to do harm. Now imbued with the inscriptions' magic, the water was collected in an ancient diorite cup, which was used only for this purpose.

"Drink," the Wise Woman urged the sick man, who was having difficulty breathing.

Paneb helped the man sit up, and he drank slowly before lying down again, his complexion grayish and his eyes half closed.

"Any more suggestions?" sneered Daktair.

"No, this is the final recourse," admitted Ubekhet.

"There's no point in our staying here any longer. We shall take the patient back to the palace, where we shall try to lessen his suffering. You have shown yourself to be incompetent, and will be suitably punished."

Paneb planted himself between Ubekhet and Daktair.

"Step aside," said Daktair angrily. "This attempt at intimidation is as unjustified as it is useless. If you continue, you'll also go to prison."

"Look!" exclaimed the most senior doctor. "Look, he's getting up."

His complexion rosy, as if new blood was flowing into his face, the sick man managed to get to his feet. He was still unsteady, and leant on Nakht the Strong's shoulder.

"My heart . . . it's beating properly. I felt as if I'd never be able to breathe properly again, but now I can!"

The heart doctor at once went to him and listened to his chest, and Ubekhet took the pulse on his stomach.

"The poison is being defeated," she concluded. "The healing water has won."

The eyes of all the doctors turned to Daktair, who stood transfixed and dumbfounded, nervously chewing his red beard.

Kenhir was radiant. "In view of the number and qualifications of the witnesses," he said, "I can now send a detailed report to His Majesty. I have the distinct feeling that the palace at Thebes will soon have a new head doctor—one worthy of the title."

▲

Daktair stamped about angrily. He had been kept waiting for more than an hour outside Mehy's office. As he had no appointment, the general's personal secretary had referred him first to two senior officers and a scribe of the granaries; and he was getting more and more impatient.

"General Mehy has consented to see you," the secretary informed him at last.

Daktair rushed furiously into the office, where Mehy was unrolling a papyrus on a large table.

"You must help me, Mehy!"

"In the first place, it's not for you to tell me what to do; and in the second place, lower your voice and calm yourself, or I'll have you thrown out."

"But I've just received the decree dismissing me from my post as head doctor."

"I know. If you'd read it more carefully, you'd have realized that I countersigned it after agreeing wholeheartedly with His Majesty's decision."

Stunned, Daktair collapsed onto a low chair, which groaned under his weight. "So you are abandoning me, are you?"

"Given your lamentable failure, I have no choice. I'm governor of this province, so how can I possibly support an incompetent official who—it would seem—deliberately fabricated a dispute with the Wise Woman of the Place of Truth? You should have succeeded, Daktair. Now you're a mere nothing."

"How could anyone believe that that ridiculous statue had the power to heal? I poisoned the man's food, as I said I would, and he should have died before the doctors' very eyes. It's incomprehensible!"

"You showed too much contempt for the old lore of the pharaohs, and it's taken its revenge. At least you're still head of the workshop. But if the new head doctor strips you of that post, too, I shan't object. There must be no sign of collusion between us."

Daktair sniveled. "You've no right to treat me like this—I can still be useful to you."

"Indeed, that may be so, but it will be for me to judge. Now leave. This conversation has lasted quite long enough."

From the look of utter defeat on Daktair's face as he left the office, it was obvious for all to see that Mehy had proved unbending and that he had, as usual, followed the path of justice.

18

News of the Wise Woman's triumph had reached the court at Pi-Ramses, which was buzzing with rumors about King Saptah's health and the fact that Queen Tausert must inevitably assume power. By dint of constant effort, the tjaty had succeeded in maintaining some semblance of consensus, but how long would that last?

When Bay entered the antechamber to his office, he found Setnakhte there, accompanied by a tall, middle-aged man whose gaze spoke of fathomless depths. The tjaty instantly suspected that serious problems awaited him.

Setnakhte went straight on the offensive. "I haven't requested an audience, but I wish to see you at once."

"I have countless matters awaiting my attention this morning, and I—"

"I shall wait as long as necessary."

Refusing to listen to Setnakhte, who was the leader of a rich and influential tribe, would have disastrous consequences for Tausert's future. Bay yielded. "Come in," he said, tugging at his little beard.

Setnakhte's companion did not move. The power of his personality was so great that Bay could not recall having ever encountered anything like it.

"My eldest son will wait for me in the antechamber," said Setnakhte, as they went into Bay's office. "We must speak alone."

Without waiting to be asked, he sat down on a chair made from precious wood, decorated with stylized lotus flowers. This little masterpiece, created by Didia the Carpenter, was so delightfully comfortable that he at once became less aggressive.

"Would you like a bowl of fresh milk with aromatic herbs?" asked Bay.

"Don't bother with niceties. I'm here to get accurate information and to give you some in return, because Egypt's in danger. No one sees King Saptah anymore because he remains shut away in the Temple of Amon, and it's even said that he's on his deathbed. Is that true?"

"No, it isn't."

"Then are you saying that he's in good health?"

How much of the truth could Bay conceal? Setnakhte was an intelligent man, and if he really wanted to know everything he'd find out in the end. So the tjaty decided not to lie.

"No, he's gravely ill. He is receiving the best of care, but he isn't expected to live much longer."

Setnakhte rested his hands on the arms of his chair. "You surprise me, Tjaty. I hadn't hoped for such frankness from you. In other words, the real pharaoh is Queen Tausert?"

"She has been since Saptah's coronation, for he has no taste for governing. He has spent happy years in the temple with the great sages of old and their writings; as for Egypt, it remains united and well governed."

"A clever strategy, Bay, but it has its limits. I don't deny that the country's prosperous, but you're closing your own eyes and Tausert's to the danger of invasion. For that reason, when Saptah dies I shall oppose her appointment as pharaoh. She wouldn't be able to defend the Two Lands, and we'd suffer another occupation—which, this time, might destroy our civilization."

"Have you gathered any reliable information?"

"You told the truth, Bay, so I shall do the same. Your minister for foreign affairs is an idiot and your intelligence-gathering service is made up of imbeciles who swallow anything the Canaanites, Syrians, and Libyans put their way. Do you think those peoples have become our allies and want to maintain friendly relations with us? You're wrong, Tjaty, very wrong. They just want what they've always wanted: to put our land to fire and the sword, and then seize our wealth. But even that isn't the worst thing. The princedoms beyond Canaan are in chaos, and the balance established by Ramses has been compromised. Savage, warlike tribes will attack Egypt, and your stupid diplomats won't have the faintest inkling of what's happening."

Bay reeled like a defeated, punch-drunk fighter. But he soon got his second wind. "Is your analysis based on specific facts?"

"You don't know me very well," said Setnakhte. "I'm a pragmatic man and I leave dreams and fantasies to others. My eldest son has carried out a long investigation, with the help of local informants who aren't stupid, gullible diplomats. Being cautious and skeptical, he gathered the information and sorted the wheat from the chaff before reaching these worrying conclusions. I am now passing them on to you because what I want is not power but the salvation of Egypt. Do you at last understand the seriousness of the situation?"

"Who knows about this, besides yourself and your son?"

"You, Tjaty. No one but you."

"You could destabilize the court, and even the government, if you made this information public."

"I tell you again, my only concern is to safeguard Egypt. And that's why I shall prevent Tausert from becoming pharaoh."

"If you do, you'll be making a bad mistake yourself."

"No woman, no matter how brave, has the necessary authority to defend the land and lead our armies to victory."

"I don't think we're at that point yet," said Bay. "Even if your predictions are accurate, you don't think war is imminent."

"Our enemies aren't yet ready to attack us, I agree."

"In that case, I shall submit the following proposal to the

queen: your son is to be appointed minister for foreign affairs, and you yourself shall be made our armies' commander in chief, in charge of all our troops and their weaponry."

"But I have absolutely no intention of working with Tausert."

"It is King Saptah who will sign the decrees appointing you, and you will have to answer to him and the queen for your actions. You know the situation better than I do and we must work together for the happiness of the Two Lands, so I shan't interfere with you in any way. And we shall meet in closed council each time the situation requires it."

Setnakhte looked at him narrowly. "Are you setting a trap for me?"

Bay raised his eyes a little, as if he could see the future. "It is strange, but I trust you, and I confess that I didn't until now. Ever since I attained high office, my one ambition has been to raise Queen Tausert to the throne of Egypt. You stand in my way now, but fortunately you're an honorable adversary: you don't seek personal gain, and you're motivated by deep convictions. If you're right, Egypt will owe you a great deal. Therefore I must choose you as my ally, be loyal to you and benefit from your skills. Moreover, by serving Queen Tausert faithfully you'll come to realize that she's worthy of becoming a new Horus. I've hidden nothing of my intentions from you, Setnakhte. Now you must decide."

"I must speak to my eldest son about your astonishing proposal, and take some time to consider."

"I shall discuss this with the queen, without waiting for your reply."

"And what if I refuse?"

"Egypt will suffer a great loss. You will pursue your course, and, as for me, I shall never betray Tausert. Inevitably we'll lock horns in a fight from which even the victor will emerge weakened."

"Thank you for your honesty, Tjaty."

"May the gods enable us to work together for the greatness of our people and our land, which we both love so much."

▲

Bay stole an hour from his overcrowded day and went to the great Temple of Amon, to talk with King Saptah. He feared he would be met by a young man bowed down by suffering, and did not know what words of comfort to speak; but the king's face wore an open smile, which contrasted starkly with the lines prematurely etched by sickness.

Bay bowed low. "I bring you good news, Majesty. The harvests were abundant, the Nile flood excellent, and the provincial governors have submitted encouraging reports on their regions' prosperity. Not one Egyptian child has an empty belly, and the gods may dwell among us in perfect serenity."

"Is my House of Eternity finished?"

"The paintings are being completed. All that remains is to lower the sarcophagi into place."

"I have spent many hours studying the symbolism of each corridor and each room, and I have read the *Invocation to Ra*, the *Book of the Stars' Creation* and the *Book of Doors* over and over again. Our wise men have seen the afterlife so clearly that our artists can draw the soul's path. What a marvel, Bay! Sometimes I can't wait to leave the earth and experience this journey, where the mortal body no longer imposes its limits upon us. My short existence will have been a solitary one, but I regret nothing, since I have had the good fortune to know the serenity of this temple and to prepare myself for another life."

"Majesty—"

"No, my friend, no useless words. I've learnt enough to have no illusions about my health. Pass on all my gratitude to Queen Tausert, who has so admirably exercised the highest responsibilities on my behalf, and who I am certain will be a great pharaoh."

"Majesty, I—"

"Forgive me, Bay, but talking tires me. To see you again has given me the greatest pleasure."

▲

The coughing spasm that racked Bay's chest as he climbed the palace steps alarmed him no more than the previous ones had. They subsided of their own accord, and he had no spare time to consult a doctor, who would only prescribe remedies Bay would forget to take. Tonight, after he'd seen the queen, he must put the finishing touches to the plan for creating new canals in the southern provinces and ensure that the distribution of wine was being done correctly.

Tausert was radiant. Surely, he thought, one look at her was enough to show anyone that her vocation was to reign.

"You don't look well, Bay."

"Just a touch of fatigue, Majesty. I must talk to you about a proposal I've put to Setnakhte and his eldest son."

"There's no need, Tjaty."

"You . . . you refuse to have any kind of understanding with them?"

"A confidential message has just reached me. They accept your proposal."

19

As if the Wise Woman's victory had unleashed benign forces, the Place of Truth enjoyed the benefits of the annual Nile flood in complete tranquility. Since the great building projects were well advanced, Kenhir had proved generous, granting the crews additional rest days. Some of the craftsmen stayed at home, others took advantage of the holiday to visit family members who lived a long way away. Some spent the time making beds, sarcophagi, or statues to be sold outside the village.

Sitting on a low dry-stone wall, Kenhir gazed at the sunlight bathing his tomb.

"The garden has grown well," commented Paneb.

"Not as well as Nefer the Silent's persea—that really is no ordinary tree."

"I think of the Master every day."

"He's always present among us," said the old scribe, "and he protects us. When we celebrate the cult of the ancestors, his spirit pours out its light upon us."

"But his murderer is still lurking in the shadows," Paneb reminded him, "and I think about him every day, too. I'll never be at peace so long as he goes unpunished."

"I feel the same way. I've been waiting and hoping to have a dream that will set us on his trail; but it hasn't come. Sometimes, I wonder if the guilty man was indeed that lay worker Libu, who was found dead. Since then, everything has been quiet."

"Sobek is more than skeptical."

"It's his job as well as his nature to be suspicious. But facts are facts: either the traitor must be dead, or else he's given up trying to harm us."

Paneb would have loved to believe that Kenhir was right, but . . .

Pai the Good Bread's wife came hurrying up to them. "The messenger's asking for you," she said.

Paneb helped Kenhir to his feet. On this beautiful October day, when the sun's rays were growing less harsh, the scribe showed his age.

"Let us hope this doesn't mean more bad news," he grumbled. "People say that King Saptah is slowly dying, and that when he dies there'll be a fierce struggle for power between Queen Tausert's supporters and Setnakhte's. This is all bad, very bad. Oh dear, how long it seems since the blessed years when Ramses the Great ruled over us. When he was king, we never had to fear the morrow. Let's make the most of this mild autumn weather, Paneb. The future is likely to be far less gentle."

The messenger, Uputy, was waiting for them at the main gate, his Staff of Thoth in his hand. He was renowned for his sure-footedness and his honesty. In obedience to the requirements of his position, he had never once opened a letter he carried, and his integrity was such that he was entrusted with many confidential missions.

Uputy took an enormous papyrus scroll out of his bag. "It's as heavy as a rock, this one."

"Where's it from?" asked Kenhir.

"The land registry in Thebes."

"Are you sure it's for us?"

"Absolutely. Sign here on this tablet, please, to confirm you've received it."

Kenhir placed his seal upon it, and Paneb carried the papyrus to the Scribe of the Tomb's office, where Niut was finishing her dusting.

"Don't you think there are enough rolls of papyrus in this place already?" she cried. "Soon, Kenhir will be taking over another room."

Paneb didn't reply. He broke the seal and unrolled the document. The two men read it quickly, then looked at each other in amazement.

"The land registry is actually daring to contest the extent of our lands!" exclaimed Kenhir indignantly.

▲

The Nile's floodwaters had receded. Everywhere, people were gathering dates and beginning to sow crops, except in the fields belonging to the Place of Truth or to those of its Servants who, like Kenhir and Paneb, had inherited them from their predecessors.

North Wind was carrying the materials Paneb would need to rectify the mistakes made by the scribes at the land registry. Forgetting his aches and pains, Kenhir had set off at a brisk pace, and his assistant, Imuni, was having difficulty keeping up, loaded down as he was with papyruses and writing materials.

As it did every year, the flood had wiped out the field boundaries and moved the marker stones. In an earthly projection of the celestial river, the Nile waters had fertilized the earth, and it had been reborn, as on the very first morning of creation. But some twisted individuals disregarded this wondrous re-creation, and thought of nothing but taking advantage of it to steal a piece of land from their neighbors. So officials from the land registry were responsible for reestablishing the boundaries fairly and punishing trickery.

Kenhir did not know the leader of the delegation from western Thebes, a bony thirty-year-old scribe with a jutting chin. The man had just been appointed by General Mehy, and had precise instructions.

"Are you the Scribe of the Tomb?" he asked.

Kenhir looked him up and down, and was not reassured by the expression in his eyes. "I am indeed."

"I am the new head of the land registry, and I have no intention of giving anyone preferential treatment, Place of Truth or not."

"You are to be congratulated on your impartiality."

"What's more, I won't let anyone think he's better than my specialists."

"Now there you're wrong. Anyone can make a mistake, yourself included."

"Be careful what you say," said the scribe. "I'm quite willing to charge you with slander if necessary."

"And I'm quite willing to charge you with incompetence! How dare you reduce our lands by a quarter, depriving the village of vital resources?"

"Because that is the result of our survey."

The specialists stood around their leader, nodding their agreement.

"Then we shall carry out a counterinvestigation," decided Kenhir.

"You're not qualified to do that."

"You're wrong again, dear colleague. Land registration is only an application of the art of building, and the Scribe of the Tomb has more than enough skill to measure the lands owned by the Place of Truth."

▲

Paneb drew a map on the ground, using the dimensions given on the papyrus scrolls Kenhir had unrolled. He quickly calculated the total surface area, which the head of the land registry could not dispute. Then he reached into the bags North Wind was carrying, took out the two pieces of a wooden measuring instrument, and assembled it, laying one across the other at right angles so that they formed a cross. The instrument, which was known as a *seba,* "the star," was placed on a post. At the ends of the arms of the cross, Paneb hung weights, forming plumb lines. Only two of them needed to be seen, superimposed on each other, to obtain or check an alignment.

Next, he took a knotted cord one hundred cubits long, which the donkey had carried without turning a hair. It was decorated at one end with a ram's head, and was an exact replica of the first surveyor's rope bequeathed to humans by Khnum and kept in his temple at Elephantine. It had been used to survey "the Head of Creation," the first province in Upper Egypt.

Taking account of previous years' measurements, which were given in detail in government scrolls, the giant proceeded to carry out a full survey of the village lands, watched in amazement by the land registry scribes. They all thought that he'd soon get weary and give up, but he continued with his task until it was done.

"You see, the truth has been reestablished," said Kenhir.

"I shall lodge a formal protest!" exclaimed the head of the land registry.

"Use the same instruments as Paneb, and you'll get the same results."

"I prefer to trust my own skills."

Kenhir gave the man an acerbic look. "At first, I thought this was simply one of those monumental imbecilities that are so normal in government. Now, though, I'm beginning to think you're guilty of malpractice."

"Rubbish," snapped the scribe.

"You hoped to win an easy victory, for you didn't know we have the means to thwart you."

"I have proof of what I'm saying!"

"Then let us see it."

The scribe signaled to one of his subordinates, who immediately brought him a little boundary stone covered in hieroglyphs.

"We found it at the foot of the acacia thicket you can see over there, and it marks out your lands exactly as we have calculated. As it was sunk deep into the earth and wedged in with stones, it was not dislodged by the flood. My scribes will bear witness to this."

"First, you should not have moved it; second, this is a forgery."

"No, it isn't. Look: it bears the name of the Place of Truth."

"Indeed, but it does not bear the mark of the craftsman who made it."

"He forgot to add it, that's all! In court, this proof will crush you."

"What if we submit it to the judgment of the celestial surveyor?" The Wise Woman's sweet voice made all the disputants spin round.

Although he had never seen her before, the scribe knew instantly who she was, and he had not the slightest wish to displease her. He asked, "Do you mean Thoth?"

"His ibis," explained Ubekhet. "Its step measures one cubit and its justice wipes away human quarrels. Will you accept its judgment, as we ourselves will?"

"Yes, of course, but we can't expect an ibis to come down from the sky and—"

"May the messenger of Thoth survey the lands of the Place of Truth," chanted Ubekhet.

A great white ibis swooped majestically down and landed so close to the scribe that he jumped backward in fright, bumped into one of his officials, and fell flat on his back in a muddy puddle.

Retracing the surveying work Paneb had done, the bird of Thoth paced out the land. It confirmed in every particular the boundaries Paneb had drawn.

20

"My dear Kenhir, I'm devastated," declared Mehy. "How could I have expected that the new head of the land registry would lose his head the moment he took office? His service record was impeccable, his career spotless. If you wish, I can show you the documents that convinced me."

"There's no need," replied the Scribe of the Tomb. "The most important thing is to ensure that this kind of thing doesn't happen again."

"Here's a duplicate of the land registry map, bearing the royal seal. You shall keep it in the village, and no one will ever again be able to challenge it. Incidentally, are you happy with the peasants working on your lands?"

"Yes, perfectly happy."

"I'm glad to hear it. The rogue who tried to harm you has been transferred to Canaan, where he will spend long years atoning for his mistake—with no hope of obtaining any other important post. Egypt is unforgiving to its incompetent officials—and quite right, too. And I can tell you, confidentially, that King Saptah holds the Place of Truth in such high esteem that he will permit no attack on its integrity."

Kenhir frowned worriedly. "There are more and more alarming rumors about his health."

"Yes, and I'm afraid they may be true. But Queen Tausert is an excellent ruler, and she has a firm grip on the helm of the ship of state. And I believe she, too, attaches the highest importance to your work." Mehy paused for a moment, then said, "May I ask a favor of you?"

Kenhir was instantly on his guard. "What is it?"

"I don't care for the furniture in my house on the west bank. I'd like to order several high-quality chairs, beds and jewelry boxes from the Brotherhood. The price is of no consequence."

"You're in luck, General. This is a quiet period, so the craftsmen have time to devote to this sort of work."

"I'm delighted to hear it."

As he accompanied the Scribe of the Tomb back to the main entrance of the building, Mehy managed to appear relaxed and pleased. But inside he was raging. That morning he'd received a message from the king, telling him Setnakhte had been appointed commander in chief of all Egypt's armies, and requiring him immediately to provide the commander with a detailed report on the Theban troops and the state of their weapons.

Such haste hinted at an attack on the country, either by the Libyans or else by the Syrians or one of the other northern peoples, and it delighted Mehy, for he could profit from chaos in Lower Egypt. On the other hand, Setnakhte's character worried him. He was rich, incorruptible, stubborn, and hardworking, and had been sufficiently influential to have his eldest son appointed minister for foreign affairs.

After meeting Setnakhte at Pi-Ramses, Mehy knew it would be difficult, or even impossible, to manipulate him. He could only hope that Queen Tausert, supported by the tjaty, would give him a hard fight and thus create major disturbances at the summit of the state—disturbances that Mehy would make the most of. More than ever, he needed the Stone of Light. But, despite searching and searching, that damned traitor still hadn't found its hiding place.

Mehy and Serketa had attacked the Wise Woman and Paneb, but their victims had won the day. However, not all the members of the crew could have the same strength of character. There must be a weak link in the chain, a weak link that could be broken, discrediting the Brotherhood.

It was therefore with a light heart that Mehy went home, to meet a priest from Karnak who spent part of the year as a temple steward. According to the report on him Mehy had obtained, the man was divorced and paid a substantial food pension to his wife, which had thrown him into debt. In exchange for the small service the unfortunate man was about to perform on his behalf, the general would become his benefactor.

▲

Casa the Rope was making an alabaster vase for the wife of a royal scribe. Fened, Unesh, Pai, and Didia were making luxury furniture for Mehy. Karo and Nakht were strengthening the low stone walls inside the village. Userhat was sculpting a *ka* statue for Kenhir's tomb. Ipuy, Renupe, Gau, and Ched were restoring craftsmen's tombs dating from the early years of the village; and Thuty the Learned was applying gold leaf to the chests destined for Saptah's House of Eternity.

Life was sweet, work joyful, the Place of Truth happy. People wanted to forget the pharaoh's interminable death throes and the period of instability that would follow his death. Only Paneb and Sobek were still on the alert. As they saw it, this peace was only temporary, for Nefer the Silent's murderer would not stop trying to harm the Brotherhood.

When Paneb entered the goldsmith's workshop, Thuty was thinking about his dead son, whose memory still gnawed at his heart.

"There's some work for you," Paneb said, "outside the village."

"I'm not interested."

"Not even if it's at Karnak?"

Before being initiated into the Place of Truth, Thuty had

worked in Amon's sacred city, where he had covered doors, statues, and boats with gold.

"Karnak?" he said. "That's different. What kind of work?"

"Something meticulous and delicate: gilding an internal door at the Temple of Ma'at."

"Karnak has excellent goldsmiths of its own."

"They're all busy with other work, and the temple steward's in a hurry. The court will soon be convening at this shrine and he wants the goddess of justice to be honored fittingly. Who can do that better than the goldsmith from the Place of Truth?"

"I'll need Kenhir's agreement."

"I've already asked him, and he agrees."

▲

Thuty could not have been welcomed more warmly by the temple steward, who ensured that he was comfortable and well fed. The goldsmith refused the tools he was offered, for he used only ones he had made himself. For him, gilding the door of a small temple like this one was child's play, but all the same he took his task extremely seriously.

In less than a week, the work was finished, and Thuty was already missing the village. True, Karnak was a magnificent place, where every stone was imbued with divine power, but he missed the spirit of the Brotherhood—even Kenhir's bad temper. He slipped his tools back into his bag, and waited for the temple steward's verdict on the work.

It was rapturous: "Magnificent, absolutely magnificent—and you have finished much sooner than I expected. It's easy to see why the Place of Truth chose you. Do you know that the post of head goldsmith at Karnak will soon be vacant? If you were to apply for it, no one would oppose you."

"Thank you, but I'm not interested."

"But what a fine end to your career it would be."

"I'm a craftsman. I don't care about careers."

"Forgive my curiosity, but what does the Place of Truth do to retain a goldsmith as talented as you?"

"It's simple: it is content to exist. And I thank it every day for accepting me into its heart."

"Before leaving, do me one service: check if the oldest gold plates are correctly fixed, and, if not, tell the workshop. I'll leave you now; I must take care of a delivery. May the gods protect you, Thuty."

▲

When Paneb entered Turquoise's house, just after the dawn rites, she was smoothing into her throat a balm made from honey, red natron, ass's milk, fenugreek seeds, and powdered alabaster. He gently cupped her naked breasts in his hands and kissed the nape of her neck.

Turquoise tried to contain her desire. "I wasn't expecting you."

"That's how you like me, isn't it?"

"What if I had urgent work to do?"

"What does this balm do?"

"It prevents wrinkles."

"You don't need it—you never get any older. Hathor has ordered the years to forget you."

"Anyone would think you were trying to seduce me," said Turquoise.

"Your intuition is remarkable. Let me continue this delicate work." He picked up the ointment pot, scooped up some balm with his little finger, and smeared it over his mistress's delightful navel.

Turquoise's defenses were swiftly breached. Naked, she lay down on her back, and Paneb continued to make her shiver with pleasure as he smoothed on the scented ointment that made her skin so supple and satin-smooth.

"The pot's empty," he lamented after a while.

"Then give me another sort of balm."

How could he resist an invitation given with such an enchanting smile? Paneb lay down on top of Turquoise, and their bodies were united in the unquenchable fire that marked each of their encounters.

▲

Turquoise had just got dressed and was putting on a pendant shaped like a mandragora fruit, when there was a timid knock at her door.

"Who's there?" she called.

"It's Renupe—Kenhir sent me. Open up quickly."

She opened the door a little way.

"Is Paneb still here?" asked Renupe.

"He was just about to leave."

"Tell him to go straight to Kenhir's house. Something serious is happening."

21

"I don't believe it for a moment!" roared Paneb. "Not Thuty—it can't be Thuty. We traveled together in the desert, and I know every corner of his soul. He is a righteous, thorough man. Since his son died, he's lived for nothing but his craft. This village is his motherland and his family."

"I agree," nodded Hay.

"And so do I," said the Wise Woman.

Kenhir was so angry that he rolled up a papyrus scroll too quickly, and creased it. "I agree, too, but Thuty has been formally accused of stealing two gold plates from the Temple of Ma'at at Karnak. Because he was there officially, in the name of the Place of Truth, the honesty of the whole Brotherhood is being questioned."

"Who accused him?" asked Paneb.

"The steward supervising the restoration work in the temple."

"I want to know everything about this fellow!"

"Sobek's already looking into it, but he has no authority to make inquiries in Karnak. I'm very much afraid that his investigation won't last long."

"What . . . what if Thuty really is the traitor and Nefer's murderer?" suggested Hay, embarrassed at putting forward such an appalling idea.

"Why ever should you think that?" asked Kenhir in astonishment.

"It could be a trick. By getting himself charged like this, he could damage the Place of Truth, probably fatally, in exchange for a lenient sentence."

"Such a thing would imply coconspirators at the highest levels of the Karnak priesthood. Can you imagine the size of the conspiracy?"

"I sincerely hope I'm wrong, Kenhir, but the traitor has shown how good he is at doing harm while hiding in the shadows."

"I must arrange a meeting with the high priest of Karnak," said Kenhir. "Together, he and I will decide what to do."

"Before we do anything else," cut in Paneb, "we must be sure Thuty's innocent."

"Who'll take charge of finding out?"

"As leader of the starboard crew, I will. And I swear to you that if he's guilty he'll talk."

▲

Paneb thought the goldsmith, a sensitive man, was going to burst into tears.

"Me, a thief? How could anyone be so vile as to drag me through the mud like this?"

"Did you know this temple steward?"

"No, it was the first time I'd seen him."

"He didn't seem shady to you?"

"Shady, no; condescending, yes. He even suggested I should apply to become head goldsmith at Karnak, and he seemed disappointed when I told him I wasn't interested."

"He accuses you of stealing two ancient gold plates."

"I checked them all, as he asked, and not a single one was missing when I left the temple."

"Were there any witnesses?"

Thuty looked like a beaten dog. "Unfortunately, no."

"I must search your house."

The goldsmith put a hand to his throat, as though suffocating. "You think I'm guilty?"

"Not at all, but we'll have to provide the court with hard evidence. I shall confirm that a thorough, verified search produced nothing."

Thuty huddled against a wall. "Go ahead, Paneb. Search everywhere."

▲

As he set his seal on Paneb's report, Kenhir sighed with relief. "Fortunately, you found nothing."

"Thuty collapsed—the Wise Woman's caring for him."

"Did you learn anything from him?"

"Only that he fell into a clever trap."

"And so did we! The Brotherhood is on the brink of the abyss, Paneb."

"Justice will recognize our innocence."

"We mustn't be too optimistic. Until I've met the high priest of Amon, I shall go on fearing the worst. I have written to tell the high priest that we are making our own inquiries, and I'm awaiting his reply. If he refuses to see me, our fate will be sealed."

"We can't let that happen," said Paneb vehemently. "I'll go and find that temple steward myself and make him confess."

"You will do nothing of the sort!" ordered Kenhir. "May Ma'at protect us."

Kenhir did not have to wait long for the high priest's reply, and it surprised him: this powerful man wished to meet the

Scribe of the Tomb at the guard post beside Ramses' Temple of a Million Years.

▲

The two men had opted for sober dress: an old-fashioned kilt and a plain linen tunic. The high priest of Amon and Kenhir shut themselves away in the senior guard's office, safe from indiscreet ears.

"It's a long time since I ventured on to the west bank," commented the high priest, "and I wish this short trip could have taken place in less dramatic circumstances. Are you in good health, Kenhir?"

"I get worse with each day that passes, but work enables me to forget it."

"I've heard that you have a young wife, who devotes all her attention to you."

"She's an excellent housekeeper—though a little too keen on cleaning my office. I regard her as a daughter, and she will inherit all my possessions. But you, High Priest, are resisting the years' decay much more successfully than I am."

"Only on the surface, my friend. If the king permits, I shall soon withdraw into one of the little houses by the sacred lake, and give up my post to a younger priest."

"Which king gives orders at Karnak, Saptah or Tausert?"

"Tausert decides, but Saptah still signs the decrees. I do not fear the queen. Since her stay here, and thanks to the Servants of the Place of Truth, she knows Thebes is not a potential enemy. My priests and I are well aware of what we owe you."

"And yet," said Kenhir, "one of the Servants of the Place of Truth stands accused of theft. What's more, the alleged theft took place in the Temple of Ma'at, our ruler and guide, and the whole Brotherhood might be pronounced guilty."

"That is so, I'm afraid."

"What kind of man is he, the steward who accused Thuty?"

"An administrator, and a close friend of the mayor. He works for two or three months a year at Karnak, oversees the upkeep of the buildings, and has always done his work satisfactorily. After Thuty left, he inspected the temple and discovered that two very fine gold plates, dating from the time of Thutmose III, were missing. He summoned the temple guards immediately, and drew up a charge. Only one person had been working there, only one person could have stolen the plates: the goldsmith from the Place of Truth."

"We searched his house thoroughly and found nothing."

"That isn't enough to clear him," replied the high priest.

"The Place of Truth's own court will try him."

"The theft took place at Karnak, and it's for the Karnak court to try him in the Temple of Ma'at, the very place where he committed his loathsome crime."

"The ramifications will probably be extremely damaging to us, especially if the death penalty is demanded."

"In such a serious case, it will be. However, there might perhaps be one solution . . ."

"Go on," said Kenhir.

"Let the investigators from Karnak enter the Place of Truth and search every single house in the village. If they don't find the gold plates, Thuty may be acquitted."

Kenhir froze. "That's impossible! That would violate one of our fundamental rules for the first time. Afterward, on any pretext whatsoever, any official could demand free access to the village. And I cannot endanger the entire village for the sake of one man."

"You are right, my friend; in your place, I'd do the same. But you're condemning Thuty and ruining the Brotherhood's reputation."

"Grant Commander Sobek permission to make inquiries about the steward, and let him question him."

"So long as the steward is resident in the temple, he is beyond the reach of a security officer—who in any case hasn't the skills to work in my domain. Besides, doing that would be bound to anger the jury before whom Thuty must appear. The

Place of Truth would be accused of using diversionary tactics to try and have one of its own people acquitted."

"A very clever trap indeed," murmured Kenhir.

"All you can do is charge Thuty and expel him from the village," said the high priest.

"But he's innocent! To abandon one of our men like that would be unforgivable cowardice."

"I'm glad to hear you talk like that, Kenhir."

"The steward has been bribed by a wicked man who wants to destroy us."

"Who on earth would be mad enough to attack the Place of Truth like that?" asked the high priest, in astonishment.

"I don't know—but we'll find out in the end."

"Yes, but that will be too late for Thuty."

"Since human beings can't act justly, why not turn to the gods?"

"You mean consult the oracle of Amenhotep I at Deir el-Bahri? But that won't save Thuty, because the theft was committed at Karnak."

"I haven't forgotten that. Do you remember that I am a specialist in dreams?"

"Ah, now I'm beginning to understand. You want to try to consult the oracle in a dream, to obtain the name of the real thief."

"Exactly."

"That's very dangerous," said the high priest with concern, "and there's no guarantee of a result."

"At my age, I've nothing left to fear."

"Because you're skilled in this area, the court won't allow you to try. Nor will it accept the Wise Woman, for her clairvoyant abilities are well known. If you insist on this course of action, find another candidate, someone who doesn't mind risking his life."

22

"In the name of your children, Paneb, I beg you not to take such a risk." Uabet put her delicately scented arms round her husband.

"I'm the leader of the starboard crew, and I must save Thuty from the trap he was lured into."

"You aren't responsible for what's happened. And if you die during this ordeal, the Brotherhood will be badly weakened."

"Unless we defend ourselves, its reputation will be destroyed—and then the village itself will die."

"I don't want to lose you, Paneb!"

The big man took his wife in his arms; she was as fragile and lovely as a blue lotus flower. "Uabet," he said gently, "you hold high rank among the priestesses of Hathor. Like me, you must put the Place of Truth before anything else."

"It's too dangerous."

"Why do you see me as defeated before I've even begun?"

▲

"No one's making you do this," said Nakht the Strong, "and if you change your mind no one will blame you."

"Well said," nodded Pai the Good Bread.

"Are you all agreed?" asked Paneb, staring hard at his crew, who had assembled outside his door.

"We are," confirmed Gau the Precise.

"I don't see Ched here."

"Oh, him," exclaimed Karo the Impatient. "He's always the same. He didn't say anything, but he must agree with us."

"All the same, I'd like to hear it from him."

"He's at the workshop."

A little while ago, Ched had been going blind. Ubekhet's treatment had saved his sight, but his strength was failing, and he had given most of his work to his erstwhile pupil, Paneb, who was now his superior. Ched was content to perfect certain details or bring colors back to life, with remarkable accuracy. He was particularly fond of looking after the old tombs, as if he preferred spending time with the Brotherhood's ancestors rather than with its living members.

When Paneb entered the workshop, Ched looked up and said, "Ah, it's you. They say you're leaving for Karnak?"

"You haven't told me what you think."

"What does it matter? When you make a decision, it is final."

"You don't think I should go, do you?"

"Let's see, what risks are you running? You might fall into an ambush laid by the priests of Amon, or go mad during the ordeal. But that isn't enough to make you deprive yourself of the experience, is it?"

"But supposing I succeed?"

"Now that is the true Paneb, pure and unblemished! When the road doesn't exist, you create one. Up to now, I grant, you've always chosen the right direction. But if you deprive the Place of Truth of one of the greatest painters it has known, I shall never forgive you."

▲

Paneb and the Wise Woman spent a long time meditating at one of the Brotherhood's prayer shrines; it was dedicated to Sekhmet, goddess of silence and queen of the Peak of the West. Meditation gave Paneb new strength, which he would sorely need when he confronted the darkness.

When they emerged from the shrine, the sun was beginning its descent toward the West.

"Soon," Ubekhet said, "it will be the moment of the *hotep*, the sunset's peace, which Nefer bore in his secret name. I have called upon him to enter your soul and help you."

"If you advise me not to take this risk, I'll obey you."

"I shall never recover from Nefer's death. If you were to die too, I'd have no son, and even the deep joy of the Brotherhood would no longer swell my heart. But I must not think only of myself. If Thuty is found guilty, guilt will also fall upon the Place of Truth, and you're the only one who can prevent that. When you enter the chamber of dreams, it's vital that there is no emptiness in your spirit. Think only of Thuty. Picture his face constantly, ask for the truth, and nothing else. Light and darkness will engage in a terrifying battle within you, but think only of the goldsmith. Tonight, I shall climb the Peak and call upon the goddess to nourish you with her fire."

They embraced, then Paneb headed for the main gate. All the villagers had gathered there in silence. Not one word was spoken as Paneb set off, alone, along the road.

▲

"What is your name?" asked the shaven-headed priest.

"Paneb, a Servant of the Place of Truth."

"Are you fully aware of the danger?"

"I'm not here to indulge in polite conversation."

"Your life hangs in the balance," said the priest.

"Not my life, the life of my Brotherhood."

"After purification, you will enter through this gate. Once on the other side, you must follow the trial through to its end."

The crew leader held out his hands, palms up, so that the ritualist could purify them with fresh water from the sacred lake. Then the priest washed his feet, and he put on white sandals. At the threshold of the temple, which bore the name "Ramses, who Heeds Prayers," stood a tall obelisk, a representation in stone of the dawn's first ray of light.

Paneb followed another priest into a room with pillars and a silver floor, representing the waters from which the first life had emerged. He halted at a small door, in front of which stood the high priest of Karnak.

"Kenhir has told me a lot about you," said the high priest. "You are regarded as a leader of men and a remarkable painter. Nefer the Silent, your spiritual father, would be proud of you. But would he not also say that a combination of talents such as yours is too rare and too precious to be risked in an ordeal like this?"

"I thought the time for talk was over."

"It is true what they say about your personality. Exceptionally, I should like to grant you a last chance to reconsider before you enter the chamber."

"I'm here to prove Thuty's innocence."

The high priest stepped aside. "May your body sleep if fatigue overcomes you, but not your spirit. Otherwise, you will be lost forever. May you attain God, and remember your visions."

Paneb found himself in a small room that had been freshly washed with water and natron. In the center stood a pedestal on which lay an acacia wood boat. In the boat burned a lamp with a single wick; like the lamps used by the craftsmen in tombs, it gave off no smoke.

The door closed behind him.

Paneb sat down on the ground and concentrated on the flame, all the time thinking of his brother Thuty, who had at last been soothed into a restorative sleep by the Wise Woman's remedies.

Suddenly the wick twisted and the flame danced as though trying to escape from Paneb's control. The painter approached it and, without fear of being burnt, cupped it in his hands, forming a reddish mirror in which he could make out the goldsmith's face.

"Tell me, Thuty, tell me everything."

Paneb felt as though his body was on fire, but he paid no heed, for a scene was taking shape in the circle of flame. He saw the goldsmith walking round the Temple of Ma'at, stopping at each gold plate fixed to the wall. One of them particularly attracted his attention.

"No, Thuty, no. You didn't do that!"

After checking that it was correctly fixed, the goldsmith walked away. Carrying his toolbag on his shoulder, he left the temple.

The flame licked Paneb's forehead but he did not even flinch, for another figure was appearing in the circle: the temple steward, whom Thuty had described in detail. After glancing behind him to check that no one was watching, the steward pried off a gold plate with the aid of a fine copper chisel. He did the same with a second plate, and then hurried away.

Paneb's eyes were misting over, and he longed for sleep. Resisting it took such intense effort that his body was drenched in sweat.

"Where are . . . the gold plates?" he asked, his voice cracking.

The jackal face of Anubis rose up in the middle of the flame. "Sleep, Paneb, sleep. Then you'll find the answer to all your questions."

"Help me, Thuty," gasped Paneb. "Fight with me, my brother!"

The goldsmith's features replaced those of the god, then came a series of confused images: the Nile, boats, a quay, women sitting down, baskets full of provisions.

"The market!" croaked Paneb.

He tried to stand up and push open the door, but he couldn't move. The flame went out, plunging the room into darkness. He fought to resist the deathly sleep in which his spirit was enmeshed.

Just as his eyes were closing, the door opened.

23

As instructed, as soon as his period of service at the temple was over, the steward set off for the market. The gold plates would be impossible to sell, but when he met his secret employer he'd exchange them for a silver ingot that would at last enable him to settle his debts and live a more comfortable life. True, he had had to steal, and the craftsman he had accused would be heavily punished in his place, but he regretted nothing. After all, every man had to fight his own battles.

The plates, hidden in thick papyrus wrappings, were in the leather bag he carried on his back. Now all he had to do was get through the main guard post.

"Is your work finished?" asked the head guard.

"I'll be back in a few months."

"A bad business, that theft."

"Fortunately, that sort of thing is very rare. Besides, the thief's been arrested."

"Open your bag."

His hands damp with sweat, the steward did so.

"What are you carrying?"

"The usual thing—a list of the repairs that have been done and the ones I must take care of next time I'm here. It's only a copy, of course; I gave the original to my superior this morning."

"Are you still working at the mayor's office?"

"For the moment, yes."

"Good. Well, I'll see you next time."

▲

Wearing the peasant costume that amused her so much, and carrying three baskets of figs, Serketa took up a position among the women who sold fruit and vegetables in the market. She had barely exchanged a few pleasantries with them when hordes of customers arrived, determined to haggle over prices. Several serving women who worked for her Theban friends were among them, but they merely glanced disdainfully at her, and Serketa even talked for a few moments with a rich landowner who was so miserly that she did her own shopping.

Following the other fruit sellers' example, Serketa was sometimes flexible over prices, sometimes stubborn, and she didn't sell too much, so as not to annoy her competitors.

Before long, she saw the steward appear, looking jumpy and ill at ease. He made his way through the crowd with difficulty, and headed for the fruit and vegetable sellers. As agreed, Serketa's figs had been laid out in three bright green baskets. He could not possibly choose the wrong woman to speak to.

Suddenly, all Serketa's senses were on the alert. Usually, two guard-baboons watched the market, ready to leap at pilferers' legs and bite them. Today there were four, and they were accompanied by several guards armed with sticks. Either the steward had talked or he had been followed. Whichever it was, Serketa was in danger of being caught red-handed.

He halted before the green baskets. "Do you sell watermelons?"

"Only nice ripe figs," she replied, according to the code on which they had agreed. "Taste this one."

The steward did so.

"Take a tray in return for your papyri," she whispered. "The guards are watching us."

"The guards? But—"

"Do it quickly."

Happy to be rid of his burden, the steward obeyed.

"The ingot is hidden at the bottom of the tray," muttered Serketa. "Buy some more fruit from the next seller and then carry on with your shopping. Above all, keep your nerve."

His throat tight and his hands trembling, the steward haggled over some grapes. As he turned his head to see if his accomplice was still there, his sight suddenly blurred. A jet of acid burned his throat, his heart pounded, and he couldn't breathe.

Seeing that her customer was unwell, the fruit seller got to her feet. "What's the matter?"

"I . . . She's . . ." His eyes rolling back in his head, the steward collapsed onto a pile of fresh onions.

"Help!" screamed the woman.

The guards came running up, but Sobek got there first. He pushed them aside. "This man is dead," he announced.

Panic began to grip the market, but the baboons bared their sharp teeth and calm was reestablished.

"Where has the woman from the next stall gone?" demanded Sobek.

"The fig seller? I don't know. I'd never seen her before, and she disappeared after talking to the man who's died."

"Did he buy anything from her?"

"The fruit that was in that overturned tray."

Sobek examined it. It contained only figs. "How did he pay her?"

"With lengths of papyrus, I think."

The commander examined the area where the murderess had been sitting. There, he found the papyri and, wrapped inside, the two fine gold plates that had been stolen from the Temple of Ma'at. For fear of the baboons, the false fruit seller had not dared take them with her.

▲

"How is he?" Kenhir asked Uabet the Pure.

"Judging by what happened last night," she replied with a mischievous smile, "he's in excellent health."

"Good, good. Can I see him?"

Uabet's pretty face fell. "You aren't bringing bad news, I hope?"

"On the contrary."

"In that case, come in."

Paneb was playing with Iuwen. He had made her a jointed doll, which he had painted to look like a priestess of Hathor, presenting a mirror as an offering. The little girl gently moved the doll's arm while her father watched closely.

"That's perfect, darling," he said. "And she can walk, too, you know."

Full of admiration and concentrating hard, Iuwen followed the doll's movements as if her life depended on it. "Will I be a priestess, too?"

"Would you like a beautiful mirror like that one?"

"It isn't just that."

"What else?"

"I want to know the secret of the mountain. And only a priestess of Hathor can ask the goddess. I asked Mummy, but she won't tell me."

"That's as it should be, Iuwen."

"So you won't tell me the secret, either?"

"I'm a craftsman, not a priestess."

The thought puzzled the little girl, but her face soon cleared. "All the same, you could take me to the Peak. You're strong, you're not afraid of any demon."

"You'll have to be patient for a while."

Kenhir gave a little cough. "Sorry to interrupt you, but I've just heard that the court at Karnak has found Thuty innocent. The high priest has invited him to finish decorating the little Temple of Ma'at, and will give him the value of the plates in ointments and clothing."

"How is he?" asked Paneb.

"Much better. The Wise Woman thinks he'll be back at work in a few days. Knowing he's been cleared of all blame has given him back the will to live. And how about you? How are you feeling?"

"I wouldn't wish to go through that again," confessed Paneb, taking his daughter in his arms. "When sleep took me, I thought the vision I'd had of the market would be worthless. Then there was a ray of light, and little by little I recovered the use of my limbs, all the time thinking about Thuty . . . Can it be that Brotherhood is stronger than death?"

To mask his emotion, Kenhir coughed again. "The temple steward was heavily in debt, and that's why he stole the plates, intending to exchange them at the market. Unfortunately, the guards were too much in evidence, and his accomplice, a fig seller, managed to escape, abandoning her booty."

"A fig seller?" Paneb was astonished.

"Yes, a peasant woman. No one knows anything about her."

"That doesn't make sense."

"According to Sobek, she was only a go-between, whose mission was to collect the plates—no doubt they were going to be melted down."

"In other words, there's a whole gang trying to destroy the

Place of Truth. And one of us, a man who claims to be our brother, is part of it."

Iuwen snuggled against her father. "Does that mean the darkness is going to eat the light?" she asked anxiously.

"It means that we shall fight to make sure the work goes on and that in the end the traitor is suffocated by his own treason."

24

A meeting of the Great Council had been convened on the authority of Queen Tausert. Setnakhte and his eldest son had arrived, and the only person they were waiting for was Tjaty Bay.

"He's never late," whispered the overseer of canals. "Her Majesty won't like it."

The queen exchanged a few words with her minister of finance, then addressed the assembly as a whole. "Does any of you know where the tjaty is?"

No one replied.

"The head steward shall go to Bay's rooms while we set to work. We shall begin with the report on the canals."

The steward left the council chamber and ran to Bay's office. It was empty. That left only his bedchamber, but the door was shut. The steward knocked. As no one answered, he dared to give it a push. The bolt was not drawn.

"My lord Tjaty, are you there?"

At the foot of his bed Bay was lying in a pool of blood.

▲

When the tjaty opened his eyes, he thought he had reached the paradise fields of the afterlife. He was surrounded by the mingled scent of lotus flowers and jasmine, and the wonderful face of Queen Tausert was bending over him.

"Bay," she said gently, "can you speak?"

"You mean . . . I'm not dead?"

"Several doctors are caring for you. What happened?"

"I remember. I had a coughing-spasm, more violent than before . . . and then blood, a lot of blood, and I fainted . . . But what am I thinking of? The Great Council—I've missed the Great Council!"

He tried to get up, but the queen laid a firm hand on his shoulder.

"Stay in bed, Tjaty, I command you."

He sank back on his pillows. "Very well, Majesty, very well. But did the discussions bear fruit?"

"Good decisions have been made."

"That's good. But there's still so much to do! Don't worry, Majesty, this is only a brief spell of tiredness. I'll be on my feet again tomorrow."

"You must rest a little."

"Is that another order, Majesty?"

"Of course."

"I'm sorry I wasn't at the Great Council. It won't happen again."

"We followed your recommendations, and the Treasury is satisfied."

"Majesty, I wanted to tell you . . ."

Bay's voice was barely audible. The queen took his hand.

"Majesty," he whispered, "take care of Egypt."

For a long time, Tausert remained there, standing very still.

A doctor approached. "Majesty, the tjaty is dead."

"No, doctor, he's resting at last."

▲

Walking with difficulty because of his club foot, King Saptah left the austere room he occupied at the Temple of Amon to go and meet the queen.

Tausert was struck by how much the young king had aged; and yet, in spite of the pain, his face radiated true serenity.

"You wish to see me, Majesty?" he asked.

"I have bad news."

"I should like to take a little stroll in the courtyard—I haven't seen the sun for several days. With my stick, I can still get about."

With admirable courage, the king managed to put aside the pain that had been gnawing away at him for several months, and stepped out into the fresh air.

"How splendid the sky is! It is up there that the souls of kings live . . . But you spoke of bad news?"

"Tjaty Bay has died."

Saptah crumpled as though he had been kicked in the stomach. "Bay, my friend and my benefactor. He wore himself out with work."

"His mummy will rest in the Valley of the Kings, close to your House of Eternity."

"What a magnificent journey Bay is about to undertake! I'm sure he'll welcome me into the Valley." The king sat down on a stone bench. "What a pitiful king I am! You talk to me of Egypt, and I think of nothing but myself."

"It will be impossible to replace Bay. He occupied a place apart, which he had created for himself through constant striving, and all the members of the government respected him. Now we are alone, you and I, facing them and the court."

"I shan't be able to help you, Tausert—you're even more alone than you think. All I can offer you is my unconditional support in the face of the vultures who will undoubtedly covet the throne. I shall sign the decrees you make, for I know that all that matters to you is to safeguard our land."

The queen bowed low before Pharaoh.

▲

Tausert entered an immense aviary housing many-colored birds given to the palace by travelers who had explored the Great South. The queen filled the little dishes with seeds herself, and poured fresh water into the drinking bowls. A hoopoe with a black and yellow crest landed on her shoulder and watched her, its head cocked to one side.

"Do you want your freedom?" she asked, showing it that the door was wide open.

The hoopoe flew off, hovered for a few moments, then returned to the back of the aviary.

"I can't escape, either," whispered the queen. As she turned away, she saw rugged Setnakhte striding toward her, even more determinedly than usual.

He bowed and said, "Will you grant me a private conversation, Majesty, or must I request an official audience?"

"I doubt that you have come here without a purpose, so let us talk now."

"The birds are noisy. Let us go and sit in the pavilion."

This wooden structure had the advantage of being both shady and isolated; no gardener would overhear their conversation. The queen and Setnakhte sat down on opposite sides of a low table, on which stood a basket of grapes.

"With Bay's death, Majesty, you have lost the only man who knew how to control the warring factions."

"No one is more aware of that than I am."

"To my mind, there is no one with the capacity to replace him."

"I agree."

"Are you planning to attend his funeral ceremonies?"

"They will take place in Thebes, and it is impossible for me to leave Pi-Ramses."

"I'm glad to hear you say that," said the general.

"Would you have tried to prevent me leaving?"

"Since you are remaining here, Majesty, the question doesn't arise. But I believe that, in the present situation, leaving would have been a serious mistake. Everyone knows King Saptah is dying, and he has entrusted you with the responsibility of reigning in his place. If the pharaoh had left the country, the task of governing would have fallen to you, and your position is therefore quite normal. You are not the first regent of the Two Lands, and today you embody the stability they need—so long as you do not leave the capital. So I and my eldest son will obey you unfailingly."

"I'm glad to hear you say that," said the queen with a faint smile.

"But I have to tell you once again that this obedience has limits. When Saptah dies, the regent must distance herself from the throne."

"And whom is she to abandon it to?"

"To an experienced man who will at last restore all-powerful pharaonic rule. We have suffered worryingly weak reigns in recent years, and no woman can put an end to this aimless drifting."

"Why do you believe you can?"

"Because that is my firm resolve."

"Even at the cost of a civil war, Setnakhte?"

"That would play into the hands of our enemies and condemn Egypt to death. When the moment comes, Majesty, withdraw and allow me to act."

▲

When the villagers learnt that the court of the Place of Truth had been convened, many of them were deeply worried. What new ordeal were they to face? It could not have anything to do with the Thuty affair, which had been conclusively resolved, and no one had heard of any recent disputes between craftsmen.

A whole host of rumors had spread. Some people said that Pai's wife was going to be punished for eating too many cakes, others that Karo's wife was going to be disciplined for swearing too much, but none of the tales seemed to have any foundation in truth.

"This must have something to do with the death of Tjaty Bay," concluded Unesh the Jackal. "The authorities have decided to reduce our deliveries of food and water."

Nakht the Strong disagreed. "No, I think the craftsmen at

Karnak are envious of us and want to stop us working outside the village."

"Whatever happens," said Fened the Nose firmly, "we won't let ourselves be manipulated."

To everyone's surprise, the court session did not last long; Kenhir refused to say anything, and the village remained in a state of suspense.

"Is it very serious?" Niut asked him when he got home.

"We've made a decision of the utmost importance for the Brotherhood's future," he replied, "and I hope we haven't made a mistake."

25

Acting as priest of the *ka,* Hay spoke the final words of resurrection over Tjaty Bay's sarcophagus, then he put out the lamps and climbed back up to the surface. The Servants of the Place of Truth were waiting there, among the fabrics, ointments, furniture, papyrus scrolls, and mummified foodstuffs they had brought to the tjaty's House of Eternity.

These were strange funeral ceremonies for the Valley of the Kings, for the dead man had not been a pharaoh, and the reigning pharaoh could not travel there and honor them with his presence. The wary Theban dignitaries had chosen to stay away, leaving to the craftsmen the task of taking care of Bay's mummy.

Paneb closed the door of the tomb, and set the seal of the Place of Truth on it. "Even Queen Tausert didn't come," he said.

"She can't leave the capital," said Hay. "Without the tjaty to support her, can you imagine the difficulties she's battling against?"

"If she really is capable of reigning, this is the time to prove it."

"According to what Kenhir's learnt, the queen's position is becoming more fragile by the day. Saptah is her last bulwark; when he dies, a military clique will take power."

"A clique that will regard our Brotherhood as utterly worthless."

"I fear that may be true," agreed Hay.

The craftsmen walked slowly away from the Valley of the Kings. As they crossed the pass, they took a last, wondering gaze at the Peak of the West and the sun-scorched hills in whose shade kings and queens rested, together with their faithful servants.

▲

Just as Paneb was about to enter the main gate of the village, Kenhir barred his way with his walking stick.

"I'm sorry, but you can't go back home."

"Why not?"

"Your deeds have made up our minds for us."

"Made up your minds? To do what?"

"The court of the Place of Truth has named you Master of the Brotherhood, and entrusts to you the task of carrying on Nefer the Silent's work."

Paneb was rooted to the spot, struck dumb with amazement.

"To fulfill this office and have access to the highest mysteries," Kenhir went on, "you must undergo a new initiation. Trust the hand that guides you."

Without further explanation, the Scribe of the Tomb turned his back on Paneb.

"Follow me," ordered Hay, and he set off along the path that led past Ramses' Temple of a Million Years.

Paneb thought the ceremony would take place inside the temple, but Hay walked on until he reached the landing stage.

"Are we going to the eastern bank?" asked Paneb.

"Yes, but not on the usual ferry."

The two men walked along the bank to an isolated spot where a boat was waiting for them. At the tiller was a strange sailor with a shaven head and two eyes painted on the back of his neck, as if he had the power to see behind him.

"Have you the means to pay?" he asked.

"The fare is the gods' Ennead, which contains and reveals unity," replied Hay, showing his ten fingers.

The crossing took place in silence until they reached the landing stage at Karnak, which was empty of all human presence. The sacred city was steeped in silence.

"Here, the eye of the master of the universe is opened," declared Hay when they had stepped ashore, "and this shrine is the place where his heart speaks. Here, that which was scattered is made whole again."

After skirting the curtain wall, he led Paneb to the Temple of the East.

The big man said quietly, "Must I go through the chamber of dreams again?"

"Would you flinch before the ordeal, if you had to?"

Paneb gazed straight ahead.

"Look at the primordial mound," Hay advised him, "the island that was born from the very first ocean. It contains the radiant energy that enables the stone to live and the builders' hands to build. The sun rises on it every morning; it enlightens those who wander in darkness, and safeguards the path they take."

Paneb stepped forward, and the temple door opened.

"Your bonds have been removed," chanted a priest in a solemn voice. "The gates of the heavens open for you; everything is given to you; everything belongs to you. You enter as a falcon, but you will leave as a phoenix. May the star of morning open the way to you and enable you to gaze upon the master of life."

Paneb followed a ritualist, who measured his steps by striking the ground with a long staff of gilded wood. He walked past the giant statues of Ramses and knelt to worship the obelisk, whose gold pyramid reflected the light of the sun.

The priest continued, "Now you have arrived at the place where Ra's breath took form, rich in miracles. Feed upon its radiance and enter the divine workshop."

The painter was shown not into the chamber of dreams but into a small room occupied by two priests, one wearing the mask of an ibis and the other that of a falcon. They purified him before taking him to the shrine of Thutmose III, "He whose Monuments Glitter with Light."[2]

Here, the high priests of Karnak were initiated, and the Masters of the Place of Truth received the illumination necessary for their spirits and their hands to be united forever.

"To give the work direction," intoned the falcon-mask priest, "you must enter the Light and see as it sees. What do you ask, on this day when the sun shines in the dead of night?"

"I come to you, ruler of the sacred space, for I have practiced the rule of Ma'at. Permit me to join those who follow you and to know your radiance, in heaven as upon earth."

"To become a being of Light, you must transform the mortal into the eternal, assemble the materials to form a new, unchanging body, be the craftsman who gives life. Your hand will know God's designs and your mouth will speak the words of transfiguration. Then you shall move like a star in the belly of your mother, the sky, you shall shine like gold and you shall accomplish the Work. Remember that the Light of Ma'at grants fruitfulness to those who practice her ways."

Paneb went on into a vast hall whose pillars were decorated with wonderful paintings showing the pharaoh communing with the gods. Brightness shone forth from the warm hues, overwhelming him.

"Light is in heaven, power upon earth," chanted the High Priest of Amon, presenting Paneb with a gold statue of Amon, one cubit tall. "Paneb the Ardent, if you are able, complete the work begun by your predecessor, Nefer the Silent."

He went out, leaving Paneb alone in the presence of the god.

Paneb had no tools with him, and he found the sculpture so perfect that he could not change any aspect of it. Down to the smallest detail, Nefer had attained such beauty that it swelled his heart. Then he bowed before the fragile statuette and worshipped the power it bore within it.

The paintings of the pharaoh seemed to come to life on the pillars, the offerings seemed to grow in number, and concentrate themselves into a single ray of light that entered the statuette's head. And the head came away, revealing a stone similar to the Stone of Light used by the Place of Truth to empower its works.

Paneb saw that the elements making up a material could be taken apart and put together in another way, and that the craftsmen could carry out these transmutations as long as they knew how to use the Stone.

All at once, a ray of light shone forth, so intense that it lit up the whole temple. Reason ought to have told the painter to close his eyes and cover his face, but he opened up his entire being to this energy, which came from the heart of the universe.

He heard the voice of the high priest say, "Carry this and you shall hold Light in your hands."

He lifted the stone, which was at once heavy and light.

"The initiate is a rough stone," the high priest went on. "When he enters the temple, he becomes refined like the mineral born in the belly of the mountain, and he rises up from the depths to be born to the day and become one with the Stone of Light. You have seen the secret, Paneb the Ardent, and you must now build it and pass it on. Here, in this temple, your predecessors built the land of Light in which the rites take place. In the Place of Truth, the radiant souls of the ancestors maintain the power of the primordial Stone. And you, Master, must preserve the unity of the Brotherhood."

An atmosphere of profound peace filled the shrine, like the peace of a sunset at the end of a long day's work. But Paneb sensed that, for him, the time had not yet come to enjoy this happiness.

When he left the temple, he saw a huge blue bird, a phoenix from the East, flying toward the Place of Truth.

26

The announcement of Paneb's appointment as Master of the Place of Truth came on the twenty-ninth day of the third month of the season of sowing. In fact, it coincided precisely with the great festival in honor of King Amenhotep I, founder and Master of the village. The villagers carried the statue of their protector in procession, before sitting down to an immense banquet of roast quail, pigeon stew, kidneys, sides of beef, several sorts of fish, cheeses, berries, stewed figs, and cakes made with honey and date wine.

The craftsmen had prepared the meat, the women the other dishes; and the serpentine cooking pots and precious dinnerware given by pharaohs were brought out specially. There were alabaster cups and plates, and gold goblets that were filled with the fine wines Kenhir had brought from his cellar.

When Userhat the Lion raised the ram-headed staff, the symbol of Amon, everyone fell silent.

"He who is deaf to the voice of Ma'at has no brother, and there is no feast day for the greedy man," the Scribe of the Tomb reminded them. "We are fortunate to be living through a period of harmony and to have Paneb the Ardent at our head, to carry on the Great Work and defend us against our enemies. Together, let us make this day joyful."

Together: that was the all-important word. That was why Ebony, Bad Girl, Aapehti's pet green monkey, and Charmer all had a right to enjoy the same food as the humans. As a very special favor, North Wind was given permission to enter the village, too, and join in the celebrations.

The donkey's large ears twitched in enjoyment of the concert given by three priestesses of Hathor. One played a double pipe, made from two long, thin reed-stems, the second a single pipe, and the third a curved harp carved from the trunk of an acacia tree. The harpist was none other than Turquoise, whose beauty and jewels naturally attracted a few pointed remarks from those women to whom nature had been less generous; but the musician paid heed only to her instrument and, with her eyes closed, let her fingers run over the seven strings.

"You don't look very happy," Renupe remarked to Paneb, easing his waistband, which was threatening to burst.

"Responsibilities only make people happy when they don't understand them," observed Unesh.

"That's true enough," agreed Gau the Precise, whose long nose was starting to turn red.

"We'll see about that tomorrow," said Didia the Generous. "For now, let's do justice to the banquet and these jars of fine old wine."

Casa the Rope would gladly have agreed with the carpenter, but he was past the point of being able to see what was going on around him, and could no longer speak.

Kenhir was obliged to stay reasonably sober because of Niut's angry looks, but he noticed that the priestesses of Hathor were drinking no water at all. No doubt the Wise Woman would have many sore heads and upset stomachs to treat.

Throughout the evening, Paneb seemed distracted, as though the celebrations had nothing to do with him.

"You're thinking about Nefer, aren't you?" Ubekhet asked him.

"He should have presided over this banquet, not me. I saw his masterwork, at Karnak, and I can't add anything to it."

"When he was in the situation you're in now, he said exactly the same thing. And all he dreamt of was withdrawing into his workshop to be alone with his tools and his materials."

"In other words, it's impossible to give up a mission the Place of Truth has given you."

"That's indeed what Nefer came to understand," said Ubekhet. "But surely everyone is free to choose his own destiny?"

"I always had one burning desire: to belong to this Brotherhood, to paint the fire of life, to attain eternal Light. But I never wanted to be a leader."

"Neither did Nefer. On our road, it is only when we don't seek power that it is given to us. And then we feel how heavy a burden it is."

Rarely had a celebration been so joyful. Since the village had a Master once more, worries were melting away. When the last wine jar was empty, torches were handed out to the revelers. They lit up the Place of Truth, which sparkled for a long time in the starry night.

▲

Uabet the Pure had made up her face very elegantly. Putting on her most beautiful dress, which was a soft green in color, she was ready at last.

Iuwen was growing impatient. "Are you coming, Mummy?"

Uabet took one last look round the house, to make sure absolutely nothing had been forgotten. Already, the craftsmen were carrying the furniture to the Master's new home, which was almost as big as the Scribe of the Tomb's house. Uabet had to show them where to put each piece of furniture, and give the servants their instructions. Young men and girls from the village had fallen over themselves in the hope of working for Paneb's wife. Uabet had engaged five of them but had insisted that they meet her own high standards, starting with rigorous cleanliness.

"Where is Paneb?" she asked Nakht the Strong, who was carrying a wooden chest filled with linen.

"At the temple, supervising the handing-in of the tools."

"Just you be careful! That's my best linen chest."

Uabet was annoyed and delighted, all at once. From their first meeting, she had sensed that Paneb had the makings of a leader, and she congratulated herself on his success, which was due to his courage and talent. Her love for him was mixed with profound admiration, and her only concern was to be a worthy wife to him.

"Where shall I put the sewing baskets?" asked Karo.

"Follow me."

Iuwen had already taken possession of her bedroom, where she was playing with her doll. As for Aapehti, he preferred to practice wrestling with his friends. Fearing he might break the fragile objects, his mother had raised no objections to this new show of laziness.

Uabet had rejoiced at Turquoise's behavior. Not once during the banquet had her spiritual sister spoken to Paneb, leaving his legitimate wife to take the center stage. Uabet had feared that her husband's appointment might cause the beautiful redhead to make unseemly demands, but she had known what was right.

"What a beautiful house," exclaimed Pai the Good Bread. "How happy you must be, Uabet. You were right: Paneb really isn't like any other man."

▲

"Here is the Master's cubit," said the Wise Woman, handing Paneb a golden tool on which divisions were marked in hand spans and shorter lengths. "It is the royal cubit, made sacred by four gods, Horus to the east, Osiris to the west, Ptah to the north, and Amon to the south. You shall invoke these angles of creation and embody them in all your work."

Then she handed him the cubit he would use at work. It was made from ebony and upon it was engraved an invocation to Osiris and Anubis. "This will enable you to bring the correct proportions to life, but the measurement you use in your constructions will be your own arm. In that way, the eternal cubit and its embodiment shall be united."

Next, the Wise Woman gave the Master the three other main tools of his office. These were the set square, one of whose names was "the star," and which corresponded to a triangle with sides in the ratio 3:4:5; the level; and the plumb line. The last two were marked with the hieroglyph representing the heart.

"May Ptah, master of builders, make these tools effective. With their aid, you will bring together the scattered parts of the eye and make it whole again. You will see what must be seen, what is clear and what is hidden, in the visible world as in the invisible. In order to do so, your first duty will be to prepare your own House of Eternity, the place where you will live outside time."

The Wise Woman approached Paneb and placed the gold apron about his waist: it was the same apron Nefer the Silent had worn.

"Do what is right and just, Paneb; be clear and calm; may your character be firm and capable of bearing misfortune as well as happiness; may your heart be vigilant and your tongue keen-edged."

Paneb felt as though dozens of enormous stones were falling onto his shoulders, but he did not give way beneath the heavy load, though he was a peasant's son who had only wanted to become an artist so that he could slake his burning passion.

The Wise Woman guided the Master into the shrine of the main temple of the Place of Truth. There, like his spiritual father before him, he walked the two paths, that of Ma'at, the eternal ruler of the universe, and that of Hathor, creative love, and discovered that they were one and the same.

27

The Nubian serving girl smoothed a little too much of the slimming ointment onto Serketa's thighs.

"Little idiot!" Serketa yelled, slapping her. "You'll burn my skin!"

The young black girl, whose beauty made her mistress's friends jealous, held back her tears. Although she was far from her home village, poorly paid, and brutally treated, this was her first job in a luxurious home, and even her horrible mistress was not going to make her leave it.

"I'm sorry, madam."

Serketa shrugged. "Bring me my cosmetic sticks."

Terrified of gray hairs and wrinkles, Serketa was using more and more beauty aids: green and black eye makeup, red ocher for her lips, gentle powders and creams for her face, and regenerative tints and oils for her hair. Consequently her bathroom was overflowing with jars, each more expensive than the last, and the crowning glory was a perfume vase made from perfectly transparent glass.

"My breakfast," she demanded.

The servant-girl brought soured cream, and butter mixed with fenugreek and caraway; spread on hot bread, it contributed to Serketa's swelling curves, but she could not resist it.

Mehy burst into his wife's room, dressed in a splendid pleated robe. "Get out," he ordered the Nubian girl, who fled.

"Ready so soon, darling?" asked Serketa in surprise.

"I've called a meeting of my senior officers to put the final touches to the report for Setnakhte."

"That won't cause you any problems, I hope?"

"No, it's routine. The important thing is that confrontation between Setnakhte and Tausert is now inevitable."

"Who do you think will win?"

"Let's hope they destroy each other."

Serketa threw her arms round her husband's neck. "If only you knew how excited I was, at the market! Those stupid guards were so close to me—can you imagine?"

"You take too many risks, my sweet."

"No I don't, my tender lion! They'll never catch me. I can sense danger more keenly than a wild animal can."

"All the same, the guards now know a woman's involved."

Serketa sneered. "They know nothing—except perhaps that there's a well-organized conspiracy."

"Have you heard anything from the traitor?"

"Paneb has been appointed Master, so he is bound to use the Stone sooner or later, and our man is watching him constantly. He also has an idea for causing trouble in the village and disrupting the start of Paneb's reign."

"So have I. We mustn't let Paneb have a moment's peace. He's much less levelheaded than Nefer, and in the end he'll explode like a stone smashed by a sledgehammer."

▲

For the first time, Paneb was presiding over the village court, which had convened to establish working conditions and answer certain craftsmen's concerns.

Karo was quick to attack. "There's a rumor that you want to increase the work rate."

"That isn't true," replied Paneb. "The crews will work on the site for eight days at a time, from eight until noon and from two till six; then they'll have two rest days, and, of course, festivals and special holidays. That is the village tradition and I have no intention of changing it. I shall try to deal with any emergencies by using Hay and a small number of volunteers, who will be generously paid for their extra hours."

"While we're on the subject," cut in Unesh, "let's talk about pay. People are saying you intend to cut it."

"That isn't true, either. As always, you'll always be paid on the twenty-eighth day of each month: five sacks of spelt and two of barley for the Scribe of the Tomb, the leader of the port crew, and myself; four of spelt and one of barley per craftsman as the minimum."

"A whole one of barley instead of half? You're giving us a pay raise?"

"Kenhir has obtained the government's agreement."

"That doesn't mean the other rations will be cut, does it?" asked Renupe anxiously.

"Not at all. Every day there will be bread, fresh vegetables, milk, beer, and fresh or dried fish for everyone."

"And salt, soap, oils, and ointments every ten days?"

"Of course."

"Then nothing's changed!" exclaimed Userhat.

Paneb smiled. "Why change something that suits us?"

"To be frank," confessed Nakht in some embarrassment, "some people had laid bets that you were going to abolish the old customs."

"I believe that unthinking routine is dangerous, to the hand and to the mind; but our ancestors have bequeathed us a number of useful customs and those are among the treasures I intend to preserve, with your support."

These calm words surprised the craftsmen.

"I've won my bet," announced Ched drily. "No one thought Paneb would really be Nefer's successor. Since a Master always keeps his word, you can all sleep peacefully."

▲

Setnakhte was reading the last report from his eldest son; he was traveling widely in Syria and Canaan to establish a network of informants, who could alert the capital at the first signs of any disturbance.

"Queen Tausert wishes to speak with you," his steward informed him.

"The queen is here? In my house?"

The steward nodded. In amazement, Setnakhte left his office and hurried to meet Tausert, who was seated comfortably in a cushioned chair.

"Majesty, I never thought you'd—"

"Did you not promise me obedience?"

"Yes, in the current circumstances and for as long as—"

"Do you often break your word?"

Setnakhte was insulted. "Never, Majesty! And I can find dozens of witnesses to confirm that."

"In that case, why have you not sent me the latest report on Syria and Canaan?"

"It was my eldest son who produced it, and—"

"He is first and foremost minister for foreign affairs. The pharaoh and myself have a right to know of his work, and, if necessary, to keep it secret—even from you."

A stickler for legalities, Setnakhte had to admit that the queen was right, but nevertheless he protested, "King Saptah wouldn't understand the importance of a report like that."

"Don't deceive yourself. Each morning I go to his bedside and give him the main points arising from information received. In return, he gives me the enlightened opinion of a man who is detached from the world. I keep my promises, Setnakhte."

The old courtier was annoyed, but bowed. "I'll give you the minister's report immediately, Majesty."

"Since you have read it," said the queen with a faint smile, "summarize its contents for me."

Aware that this was a sign of trust, Setnakhte hid nothing. "Syria and Canaan are calm, but here and there many small groups are forming to protest against the Egyptian protectorate, even though it ensures the region's prosperity. These are only the usual minor disturbances, which the local troops can repress. On the other hand, the situation in the hinterland is worrying; kingdoms are crumbling, warlike dynasties are seizing power, and no one can tell what will emerge from this melting pot. Nothing good for Egypt, that's certain. This is still the country everyone wants to conquer."

"What do you recommend we do?"

"We should keep a constant watch on the northeastern invasion corridor, maintain heavily armed and well-paid garrisons, strengthen the forts that are our first line of defense, build new warships, and order the arsenals at Pi-Ramses to produce more weapons."

"And what about the Libyan threat?"

"We should take it very seriously. The tribes are still divided, but all it takes is one warlord who is more fanatical than the rest, and they'll launch an attack and try to conquer the Delta, especially if the attack comes from the east."

"We must make sure we can gather detailed information," said the queen. "Have you enough agents in place?"

"I'm afraid not, and infiltration is very dangerous. Many of my people have already lost their lives in the attempt. According to the information we do have, the Libyan tribes will soon be fully armed."

"Have you established the precise condition of our armies?"

"The generals have responded quickly and in full detail. I think we'll have the means to defend ourselves. But you know my position: it would be better to launch a preemptive attack."

"I disagree," said Tausert. "Now, what about the Theban army?"

"General Mehy has a large force of well-trained troops. Thanks to him, Upper Egypt and the Great South are under control."

"When will the minister for foreign affairs be returning to Pi-Ramses?"

"Not for several days, Majesty, because he wants to check everything himself."

"From now on, he is to address his reports directly to Pharaoh."

Setnakhte bowed again.

28

Sobek was consulting the Wise Woman for the first time in his life. Although he'd never been ill, he had made up his mind to ask her advice, for he had been lying awake night after night.

"You're in excellent health," said Ubekhet when she had finished her examination.

"But I can't sleep," he said.

"Nevertheless, given the quality of your blood, you are managing to rest with your eyes open. No medicine will drive away the thoughts that torment you."

"I'm in charge of the village's safety, and yet a murderer can still prowl its streets with impunity. I'm certain that the same man killed both one of my guards and Nefer the Silent, and that he's a member of the starboard crew."

"Why are you so sure?"

"Instinct, only instinct—and I'm going mad for lack of any serious leads."

"Don't give up, Sobek."

The commander looked at her sharply. "Does that mean you suspect someone?"

"I simply know that you're right and that the traitor has shrouded himself in so much darkness that no thought, however strong, can now break through it. But this situation won't last forever."

"He hasn't put a foot wrong, all these years. Why would he lower his guard now?"

"Evil has its own vanity," said Ubekhet, "and the man you're hunting will eventually fall prey to it."

"We haven't even been able to identify the peasant woman! We've questioned dozens of women, but we haven't one single clue—not so much as a rumor among the peasants—to set us on the right track. Anyone would think the fig seller didn't exist."

"I don't think she does."

Sobek tensed. "Do you mean she's an evil spirit?"

"No, but she probably isn't a peasant."

"A disguise? Is that what you're thinking of?"

"What better way of passing unnoticed? If she were a real fig seller, living in a village nearby, you'd certainly have found some trace of her."

"A disguise, yes . . . But I can't set men to watch every single woman in the province in order to uncover our suspect. And who can she be? A woman from the city? A foreigner?" Despite the difficulties, Sobek was yet pleased to have found a thread to cling to, however tenuously. The sounds of a fierce argument disturbed his train of thought. He sighed. "It sounds as if there's trouble with the food deliveries. I'd better go and settle it."

"The consultation is over," said Ubekhet. "If you want a decoction of calming plants, I'll make it for you; but will you drink it?"

"Thank you for everything—I'm feeling much better. Now I must go and re-establish order."

Sobek discovered the beginnings of a scuffle between the village women and the fishermen, whose leader was a hairy, ill-tempered man called Nia. Despite his size and strength, he was cowering in front of Niut, who was brandishing a broom handle and clearly intended to thrash him with it.

The tall Nubian stepped between them. "What's going on here?"

"Nia's nothing but a bandit," exclaimed Niut.

"I've delivered my fish, as usual."

"Yes," she said angrily, "let's talk about your fish. There's no mullet, and no carp. And just look at the perch you've dared to bring us!" She reached into a willow basket and snatched up a dull-eyed fish with sagging gills and a suspect smell. "You call this rubbish fresh fish? Go on, admit it: you're trying to poison us!"

"I've delivered what I was told to deliver—besides, you've got plenty of dried fish."

Niut opened another basket and kicked it onto its side so that its contents spilt onto the ground. "Badly prepared and inedible! Are you trying to make fools of us?"

"Look," protested Nia, "I'm just a lay worker, and I've got my orders."

"Orders from whom?" demanded Paneb, shouldering his way through the crowd.

Nia hid behind his men. "Don't touch me," he begged fearfully; once before, he had felt the force of Paneb's anger.

"Answer my question, and all will be well."

"Orders from the government."

"I'm the one who gives the orders here," said Paneb. "Take this rubbish away and bring us best-quality fresh and dried fish this very day. And don't dawdle, or I'll come and find you."

Laden with their baskets, the fishermen left the lay workers' camp. But before Paneb could go back inside the village, Pai the Good Bread's wife came rushing out through the gate.

"The grain sacks contain less than they should," she said furiously.

"Are you sure?" asked Paneb.

"I've got eyes, believe me! You can check."

The Master entrusted the task to Gau the Precise, who used the village's official measure.

"A tenth of the usual amount is missing," Gau announced. "The people who filled the sacks used a different measure."

"I'm going straight to the government offices," declared Paneb. "And Nakht the Strong is coming with me."

▲

Although he was extremely fit and strong, Nakht had great difficulty keeping up. Paneb was in a dreadful mood, and seemed even more gigantic than he had before his appointment.

"I'm sorry for you, Paneb," panted Nakht. "With all these problems, you haven't had a very pleasant start as Master."

"Problems are part of the job."

"But there are an awful lot of them. It's almost as if someone's trying to harm and dishearten you."

"Have you got someone in mind?"

"No one in particular. When you became a crew leader, that ended the rivalry between us. And I'm sure the court was right to appoint you Master."

"Didn't you think you deserved to be Master yourself?"

"Me? Certainly not! I love the Brotherhood and my work, I am happy in the village, and I know my limits. Leading isn't my strong point. It's not just that I don't envy you, I actually feel sorry for you. From now on every problem, big or small, is yours to sort out."

As usual, the soldiers guarding the central government buildings were alert.

"The Master of the Place of Truth wishes to see General Mehy," said Paneb calmly. "It's very urgent."

An officer ran to the stables, where Mehy was examining two horses to see if they would be suitable for his battle chariot.

"These aren't good enough," he concluded. "Groom, give them to an inexperienced charioteer and find me some good, strong animals."

He strolled unhurriedly toward the two craftsmen. "I wasn't informed you were coming."

"And I wasn't informed that the village was going to be sent rotten fish and underweight sacks of grain," retorted Paneb.

Mehy looked surprised. "Are you sure, Master? That's what I must call you, isn't it?"

"Absolutely sure. Since this is a serious mistake by your government, I demand immediate compensation."

"Will you follow me to my office?"

Once there, Mehy consulted some wooden tablets. "Let's see . . . According to the stewards' latest report, Nia has indeed delivered the fish, and the sacks of grain have arrived on time from the bakery at Ramses' temple."

"Rotten fish and a short weight of grain," Paneb reminded

him. "It would seem that the measurement was changed illegally."

The general smiled condescendingly. "Tell me, Paneb, are you really in charge of the Place of Truth?"

"Why do you ask?"

"My government is in no way responsible for your difficulties, and in any case you seem unaware of what's happening in your own village."

Paneb felt his anger rising. "Just what do you mean by that?"

"My department received a written order, bearing the seal of the Place of Truth. It instructed Nia to deliver his stock exactly as you received it, and the official in charge of the grain stores at Ramses' temple to change the measurement and content of the sacks. Naturally, the order was obeyed."

"Let me see the order."

"Gladly."

The wooden tablet was genuine. Next to the seal of the Place of Truth, there was another: that of the craftsman who had given the order on the Master's behalf.

29

The Master, the Scribe of the Tomb and the Wise Woman examined the tablet together.

Kenhir was devastated. "So he was the one . . . He was the traitor and the murderer!"

"Let's not jump to conclusions," advised Paneb.

"But this is his personal seal, here, on this tablet."

"For the time being, we can accuse him only of abusing his authority."

"Don't you see? He tried to discredit you, so that he could

take your place and then profit from his crimes. The court must be convened at once."

"First we should question the suspect," suggested the Wise Woman.

"Surely this is proof enough," said Kenhir.

"I'll go and find him," said Paneb.

Ubekhet was serene, Kenhir impatient.

When Paneb came back with the craftsman suspected of these terrible crimes, Kenhir rose to his feet and fixed the man with a steely gaze.

"Well, Userhat the Lion, what have you to say in your defense?"

The sculptor looked utterly bewildered. "My defense? But what am I accused of?"

"Your seal's the head of a lion, isn't it?" With ice-cold anger, Kenhir showed Userhat the wooden tablet.

"Yes, that's my seal." Userhat read the document quickly. "I never wrote that! Where did this come from?"

"As if you didn't know!"

"Of course I don't know," said the sculptor angrily. "And I won't let anyone doubt my word."

"General Mehy gave it to me," said Paneb.

"I don't have anything to do with the government offices. That's a job for the Scribe of the Tomb and the crew leaders."

"Mehy received this tablet from our official messenger, Uputy."

Userhat's agitation lasted only a moment. "Someone has copied my seal."

"Can you prove that?" demanded Kenhir.

"First of all, there's my word as a Servant of the Place of Truth. If need be, I'll swear before Ma'at and the court that I didn't write this tablet. Also, when I print my personal seal, it's always on stone, never on wood. The sculptors will tell you that's true. Do you need any more proof?"

Kenhir frowned.

"No, that's enough," said Paneb.

"Someone's tried to discredit us both," said Userhat.

When the sculptor, his head held high, had gone, Kenhir made it clear he still wasn't happy. "We must tell Sobek about this incident, so that he can keep a close watch on Userhat."

Deep in thought, the Master agreed.

▲

That morning, Kenhir had woken before Niut, who was going to cleanse and purify the entire house, including his office. Resigned to this, he had decided to leave home without washing his hair, and go and gaze at his tomb as the sun rose over it.

The tomb had been cut out of rather poor rock, at the far end of the terraced burial ground. Although its shrine was very plain, it had an alcove in which the Scribe of the Tomb was shown as eternally young, standing before Osiris, Hathor, and Isis. This wonderful privilege had made him forget that his *Key of Dreams* was still not finished.

A small, pointed pyramid crowned his House of Eternity, in the tradition reserved for important members of the Brotherhood. As he gazed up at it, the old scribe mused that his greatest work was the Journal of the Tomb, in which he had related every event in the life of the Place of Truth.

The rays of the rising sun brought each little pyramid to life in turn, and gave rebirth to stelae depicting the dead on their knees, worshipping the sun disk. Soon, Kenhir would go to join the ancestors, and he hoped he would not be judged too severely by the living.

"Up already, Kenhir?" The Master's booming voice made the old man start.

"When you're old, you don't sleep so much. And I want to savor every morning I have left in this village where I have known so much happiness."

"Would you like me to decorate your House of Eternity?"

"Everything has been ready for me for a long time. It's better that you concentrate on your own. A Master's tomb must do honor to his rank."

"Very well. But I must send a crew to the Valley of the Kings to tidy the entrances to the royal tombs."

"A good idea. I'm too tired to go there myself, though, so Imuni will go in my place."

The Master smiled. "A spot of exercise will do that little scribe the world of good. He spends so much time shut away with his papyrus scrolls that he's in danger of mummifying before his time."

▲

Assistant Scribe Imuni was a confirmed bachelor, who feared women more than a plague sent by the lion-goddess Sekhmet. He looked after his modest house himself. It stood in the western part of the village, next to the house belonging to the leader of the port crew. Given his position, Imuni was entitled to several hours' housework per week, at a favorable rate, but the little rat-faced scribe preferred to keep the whole of his salary for himself.

For several months, Imuni had been suffering from stomach pains, whose cause he knew only too well: Kenhir seemed immortal and Paneb had become Master of the Brotherhood. The situation could not be worse, and he was not going to become Scribe of the Tomb or get rid of Paneb by washing his writing brushes fifteen times a day and scraping his palette until he wore it out.

Why didn't old Kenhir name his assistant as his successor, and then retire? Imuni carried out his duties meticulously, kept flawless accounts, and never let even the smallest irregularity pass. Thanks to him, no one could find fault with the management of the Brotherhood. And as he knew how to observe people without being noticed, he had learnt a great deal about the craftsmen's techniques; one day, he would be capable of being not only Scribe of the Tomb but also leader of the two crews. But he still had to find a legal way to get rid of Paneb, who would always oppose his rightful ambitions.

Someone banged hard on his door, and Imuni dropped his brush.

"Move yourself," ordered Nakht.

"Move myself? Where to?"

"We're going to tidy up the Valley of the Kings."

"But it's the Scribe of the Tomb who—"

"Kenhir's tired, so you're taking his place. Come on, we're ready and we don't like being kept waiting."

Hurriedly, Imuni got together all the materials he would need and ran after the group leaving for the Valley.

▲

Pai the Good Bread was in a state of great anxiety. "It's not my heart? You're sure of that?"

"Absolutely," replied the Wise Woman. "Its voice is clear, and the energy it gives out is circulating properly around your body's channels."

"But it was racing!"

"I realize it's alarming, but the cause isn't serious. It's just an attack of nerves."

"And will it happen again?"

"That depends on you, Pai. I imagine you flew into a rage about something, and the effects have barely worn off."

The artist hung his head. "There's some truth in that."

"What made you lose your temper so badly?"

"It was my wife. She keeps complaining about how difficult life is in the village, especially about the fact that Sobek and his men are keeping watch on us."

"Does she want to leave?"

"Well, sort of. I brought matters to a head, voices were raised, and I punched our linen chest."

"If your wife really wants to leave, she's perfectly free to do so," Ubekhet reminded him, "and your anger won't keep her here."

"I know that," conceded Pai, "but the reason for the quarrel wasn't really a serious one—in fact, she was telling me off for drinking too much with the other painters and not attending to the repairs that need doing in our house. I've been promising her a new kitchen for more than a year, but there are so many festivals to celebrate and banquets to organize."

The Wise Woman smiled. "When a craftsman starts a family, shouldn't he ensure that it's a harmonious one?"

"If I do what's needed, will my heart work properly?"

"Of course it will."

▲

Despite the physical effort, Imuni was proud to be taking Kenhir's place and overseeing the craftsmen's work. Leveling the entrances to the royal tombs and taking away the stone debris that littered the Valley of the Kings was no mean task; but the crew, made up of Casa, Fened, Karo, Nakht, and Didia, set about it with a will. The rest of the starboard crew were engaged in building Paneb's tomb, and the five men were in a hurry to finish in the Great Meadow so that they could join them.

"That runt gets on my nerves," confided Casa to Fened. "If somebody dropped a block of stone on his foot, he'd leave us alone."

"Don't pay any attention to him."

"When I go to make water, he notes it down on his tablet! Kenhir's no joke, but at least he knows the limits and doesn't overstep them."

"Imuni's harmless," said Karo. "As long as he doesn't try to interfere with our way of working, of course."

"He hates our new Master," observed Didia.

"Do you think he might try to do him harm?" asked Nakht.

The carpenter nodded.

"Let's not get carried away," advised Fened. "That runt with his stupid little mustache would never dare attack Paneb. All Imuni wants is the job of Scribe of the Tomb. And I'll wager Kenhir will lead him a merry dance to make sure he doesn't get it."

"You're ascribing some pretty bad intentions to Kenhir," remarked Casa, running a hand through his black hair.

Imuni came over to the group. "When will you be finished?" he asked in an unctuous voice.

"Sooner than expected if you lend us a hand," replied Didia.

"That's not my job," protested the scribe.

"We'll finish when we finish," said Nakht firmly.

"It isn't very hot now—you could work faster."

Nakht the Strong's massive bulk loomed over the scribe. "You oversee but you don't give advice. Are we agreed?"

Imuni took a step back. The craftsmen turned their backs on him and continued to fill their baskets with limestone debris. They used it to strengthen the protective walls that prevented mud slides from damaging the doors to the royal tombs.

They finished with the entrance to the tomb of King Meneptah, where Fened discovered several fine blocks of limestone that could be trimmed and used again.

"How about giving the Master a surprise?" he suggested to his companions.

They all agreed.

"They'll be heavy to transport, though," remarked Casa.

"We're not weaklings," cut in Nakht.

When they left the Valley, carrying their burden, no one noticed Imuni's sly smile.

30

Paneb and Uabet were listening to little Iuwen telling them about a beautiful dream, in which she had turned into an ibis and soared above the mountain.

Her story was interrupted by Karo, who burst into the

house. "You must come at once," he told Paneb. "The leader of the lay workers says one of your bullocks is sick and the quails are about to attack your field. If you don't do something, your harvest will be ruined."

As the harvest was an important food supplement for some of the village families, Paneb took the matter seriously and went immediately to see Kenhir. Because of a severe pain in his elbow, the Scribe of the Tomb had been forced to dictate the Journal of the Tomb to Imuni.

Paneb explained the situation and said, "I must leave the village with at least two men from the starboard crew."

The old scribe frowned. "You know it's forbidden to use craftsmen from the Place of Truth for that sort of work."

"It isn't work. They're simply lending a hand so that we can put nets in place to protect the wheat and catch as many quails as possible. The birds will of course be roasted and eaten."

Kenhir muttered a few vague words of approval and the Master was content. But they had not seen the satisfied leer on Imuni's face.

▲

Paneb arrived at the field, accompanied by Nakht and Didia.

"What could we do?" complained one of the five peasants who worked for Paneb. "We told you straightaway—that's as much as you can expect of us."

Paneb didn't reply. Instead he examined his bullock, which was having difficulty breathing.

"Take it to the lay workers' camp," he told Nakht, "and ask the Wise Woman to treat it. Then hurry back here."

Lookouts had warned the Theban authorities about the first flocks of quail, which were so numerous that they blocked out the sun as they swooped down onto the fields. So Paneb, Didia, and the peasants spread out a fine-meshed net between sticks sunk deep into the ground. To avoid hurting their feet, they put on rough papyrus sandals.

"There they are!" shouted one of the peasants.

A cloud of birds approached, with a deafening whirr of wings. The hunters shook scraps of material, which unsettled the quails and made many of them fall into the net, where their feet became entangled in the mesh.

"What a feast we shall have!" declared Didia in delight.

Just then Nakht reappeared. "The Wise Woman can cure your bullock," he told Paneb.

▲

The hot wind caressed Turquoise's naked body as she lay stretched out on the terrace of her house in the morning sunshine. Although Paneb had climbed the staircase as silently as a cat, she knew he was there.

"Come here," she said.

"I thought I'd find you at the goddess of silence's temple, preparing for the festival with the other priestesses of Hathor."

"But you came here."

"You were waiting for me, weren't you?"

Turquoise confined herself to a smile. And, as ever, an irresistible desire flared up within Paneb, drawing him toward this magnificent woman. The years had no hold on her; in fact, time only made her lovelier, adding a sweet and tender charm to the wild beauty of her youth.

Paneb lay down on top of her, but she pushed him away, and said, "Paneb the Ardent, you have become Master of this Brotherhood. What stamp will you make upon it, and what destiny do you offer it?"

For a long time, the lovers gazed into each other's eyes. Paneb was no longer looking at a loving woman; he saw a creature of the world beyond, who was beautiful enough to die for but who would not give him back his freedom until he had answered her.

"The Brotherhood doesn't belong to me," he said. "I chose it, it chose me, and only the total love that unites us can enable me to lead it. Its destiny is written for all eternity. But I shall place my stamp upon it, it is true, for I want to create a Place of

Truth whose heartbeat embodies the words of the gods with wisdom, strength, and harmony. I shall fail, of course, but I shall never stop trying. And when I die, another Master will try in my place."

Gently, Turquoise took his hands. "From my terrace, I can see your tomb, that magical dwelling where your strength will outlive you. Since your new power hasn't corrupted your spirit, you may make love to me."

▲

The starboard crew had worked hard, and the construction of Paneb's tomb had progressed surprisingly swiftly. Userhat urged his brothers to give of their best, for there was much to be done. The well must be dug, the vaulted funerary chamber must be carved out of the rock, and the entranceway must be built, along with those rooms which the living were permitted to enter. Then there was the lake, representing the primordial water from which all life originated and to which it returned, and the garden, where the dead man's soul would rest at sunset.

When the Master went to inspect the site, at the end of a gentle autumn day, he found it deserted and silent.

At the entrance were four sturdy columns; then a vast terrace leading to the shrine which was topped by a sharply pointed pyramid. To the left of the door was an altar; to the right, a lake of purification. A corridor led to a large chamber decorated with carved panels showing the craftsmen at work and Paneb's *ka* meeting the gods.

Through a narrow slit in the back wall, the Master gazed at his statue; its eyes were slightly raised toward the heavens, where they could perceive other universes. He felt himself changing, becoming a different being, as Nefer had done before him. Now that Nefer's radiant presence dwelt in him, opening the way to him, he had received his inheritance in full.

All the members of the starboard crew were seated in the

furthermost shrine, which was decorated with wonderful paintings, including some featuring Isis the magician, Osiris the Risen One, and Ptah, the patron god of builders.

Ched was first to get to his feet, but his companions soon followed. Together, they formed a circle round the Master, whose gaze lingered on the rosettes, diamonds, and spirals that decorated the upper part of the walls and the ceiling, depicting the stages on the path of initiation in geometrical shapes.

"May you breathe the breath of life forever," declared Userhat in the name of the sculptors.

"The artists offer you the lotus, from which the sun springs forth each morning," said Unesh.

"Sail eternally in the Brotherhood's ship," exhorted Nakht, the stonecutters' spokesman.

The sail symbolizing the breath of life, the lotus, the ship . . . they were all here, painted on the walls of this House of Eternity, in which Paneb the Ardent's essential nature was set forth.

Standing at the center of the circle, he felt the light radiating out from his brothers, a light more intense than a summer sun. But how could the Master forget that among the hands reaching out to transmit their energy to him were the hands of a traitor?

▲

The traitor was convinced that, sooner or later, the Stone of Light would be hidden in Paneb's tomb. But the construction work was coming to an end and still the treasure he so coveted had not appeared.

Didia presented Paneb with a superb acacia wood sarcophagus, designed to receive his body of light. "With a boat as fine as this," he said, "you'll cross eternity without the slightest problem."

"There's no hurry," commented Pai. "Kenhir has gone into his cellar and taken out two jars of red wine dating from the first year of Seti II's reign. They're waiting impatiently to be drunk." Everyone agreed with his wise decision, and he was the first to sample the nectar. "Full-bodied and joyful," he declared, his cheeks already turning red. "It's certainly worthy of the occasion."

"Seti should be honored," added Thuty, "for here's some fabric with golden palm leaves which I'd meant to include in his burial goods, but couldn't finish in time. It shall veil the head of Paneb's sarcophagus."

The craftsmen pledged their leader's good health, and each raised his cup with gusto.

"The decoration of your tomb will be my last work," Ched confided to Paneb.

"Why do you say that? Surely you'll be able to work for years yet."

"No, I shan't, because I am being attacked by an enemy you don't know: exhaustion. From now on, I shall devote myself to making sketches for your future projects, and our team of artists will serve you faithfully. We all know that King Saptah is dying and that a grave crisis is in the offing; you are the only one who can cope with it."

"It's not like you to pay such compliments."

"Age is making me soft."

Karo, who was completely drunk, lurched over and tapped Paneb on the shoulder. Ched threw him a black look and advised him, "Do whatever stupid things you like, but never fail to show your Master the proper respect."

Karo staggered away.

Imuni was delighted with what he had just witnessed. His collection of evidence was growing so huge that he was more convinced than ever that he would soon triumph and bring about Paneb's downfall.

31

Setnakhte had been working tirelessly and methodically. In the greatest secrecy, he had met each of Tausert's ministers in turn, in an attempt to persuade them all that the queen was incapable of ruling the country or commanding the army in a crisis. Some had agreed unreservedly, others had been undecided, and two were openly hostile. However, this had not discouraged Setnakhte, and he had eventually coaxed the waverers over to his camp while persuading his opponents to remain neutral.

He had got the result he wanted. At the next full meeting of the Great Council, he would declare openly that he had no confidence in the queen, and he would have the support of the great majority of the councillors. That would be the first step toward gently removing her from power.

Setnakhte felt no animosity toward Tausert; on the contrary, he admired her more each day for her intelligence and her real talent for handling matters of state. But he still believed she lacked the necessary authority to defend Egypt against the invasions that his eldest son believed were inevitable. As the only eminent person aware of the terrible danger facing the country, Setnakhte owed it to himself to act accordingly.

His personal scribe announced the visitor he had been hoping for: the treasurer of the great Temple of Amon. It took a long time to persuade the treasurer to tell him all he needed to know about King Saptah's health.

To everyone's astonishment, the young king was resisting death with an energy that, though it ebbed away at sunset, was reborn each sunrise, after he had woken the Divine presence in the shrine. Although he took to his bed for the remainder of the day, and ate little, he continued to read the works of the sages of the Old Empire, and never failed to study the summarized report sent to him from the royal palace. And he was always happy to see the queen, in whom he had complete trust and confidence.

The treasurer bowed before Setnakhte. "There is one important piece of news, my lord: King Saptah did not leave his bedchamber this morning. The High Priest of Amon celebrated the ritual in his place, and the king's doctor thinks His Majesty is on the brink of death."

"Is this supposition or a certainty?"

"The king's absence leaves no room for doubt regarding the grave state of his health."

Setnakhte dismissed the treasurer. There was less than an hour until the Great Council met. What he had just learnt would strengthen his position still further.

▲

The ministers were astonished to be directed, one by one, to the great audience chamber of the royal palace under the watchful eyes of Pharaoh's personal bodyguard.

"Why aren't we meeting in the council chamber?" asked Setnakhte, who was not at all happy.

"It is the queen-regent's orders," replied an officer.

Setnakhte hesitated on the threshold. What if Tausert had decided to have all her opponents killed? No, that was impossible. Only tyrants behaved like that, and, like her subjects, the queen bowed to the law of Ma'at. She would never resort to violence and crime to secure power.

When his turn came, Setnakhte entered the vast hall, which was lit by high, narrow windows. Several ministers turned their eyes toward him, and were reassured by his calm demeanor.

Everyone remained standing until the queen entered, dressed in a long turquoise dress. Her noble features were complemented perfectly by a fine gold diadem and earrings.

By the time Tausert sat down on a plain throne of gilded

wood, she had already won back the hearts of several dignitaries who had thought of deserting her for Setnakhte.

"I have brought you together in these solemn surroundings to take stock of the tasks I have entrusted to you. If you fail, others will be appointed in your place. Serving Egypt is exhilarating; anyone who does not realize that deserves no leniency."

"We all realize that, Majesty," declared Setnakhte, "and you will find no man here who is lazy or irresponsible. Before examining the condition of the country, may we know that of the rightful pharaoh?"

"During the last hour of the night, King Saptah fell victim to a sickness that almost killed him. That is why he was not able to celebrate the morning ritual. He has just regained consciousness, and his soul remains joined to his body. I spoke to him about this audience, and he is waiting to hear the results of it. Let us begin by hearing the agriculture minister's report."

The minister unrolled a papyrus scroll and, province by province, detailed the quantities of cereal crops harvested, comparing them with the previous year's figures.

Tausert's comments were precise and trenchant. She emphasized the report's weak points, demanded that several figures be checked, and suggested improvements to the management of certain provinces. She showed equal skill in the other sectors of government. Eventually, all that remained was foreign affairs.

"Since the minister for foreign affairs is absent, Setnakhte will outline the dangers that threaten us."

He got to his feet. "According to the latest information from the hinterland beyond Syria and Canaan—Her Majesty has of course already been informed of this—we must expect profound upheavals that will affect our alliances and present us with new and powerful enemies. More than ever, Egypt has the look of a prosperous country ripe for conquest, and the invaders will undoubtedly attack via the Syria-Canaan corridor. Those who call me a pessimist are badly mistaken; I am only describing reality, and the threat is far from illusory."

"Your words have been heard," said Tausert, "and our defenses are continually being strengthened."

"Every one of your subjects will be grateful to you for that, Majesty, but should we not go further and—following the example of glorious pharaohs of the past—launch a preemptive attack?"

"Against whom, and on what scale? The situation is much too fluid to throw ourselves into an adventure whose outcome is so uncertain. Thanks to you and your son, our network of spies has been reconstructed and is providing us with the information we need. According to the current intelligence, we should indeed favor a defensive stance."

Setnakhte was hoping that several ministers would fly to his aid, but Tausert's authority and arguments had won everyone over.

Defeated, he could do nothing but bow to the general will.

As his colleagues were leaving the audience chamber, Setnakhte approached the queen.

"I offer my congratulations, Majesty. Like the others, I was dazzled. No one can doubt your ability to govern the Two Lands."

"Then why did you try to set my ministers against me?"

So the waverers had spoken! Setnakhte felt the ground quake beneath his feet, but he nevertheless had the courage to be direct. "For the same reason as before, Majesty: there will inevitably be war with peoples determined to conquer Egypt, and you cannot lead our armies. What is more, you reject the only possible policy."

"The fact that our opinions diverge and you express your own openly does me no harm. But you owe me obedience; and plotting against me weakens Egypt. Never forget that, Setnakhte."

More impressed by the queen than he was willing to admit, he realized that the warning she had just given him would be the last one. He bowed low to her and withdrew.

Though she was exhausted after the fierce struggle from which she had just emerged victorious, Tausert had no chance to rest, for her personal scribe intercepted her before she had reached her private apartments.

"Majesty," he said anxiously, "there's bad news."

"King Saptah?"

"No, no, Majesty. But there's a message from Thebes."

"Have there been disturbances in the province?"

"No, Majesty, do not worry on that score. But a serious scandal is looming on the horizon. The governor of Thebes has received compromising evidence concerning the Master of the Place of Truth, Paneb the Ardent."

"Compromising? In what way?"

"He is accused of all sorts of barbaric acts. Since the accusations partly concern the Valley of the Kings, if there is evidence to support them Paneb will have to be arrested and tried. And if he's found guilty his sentence will undoubtedly be severe. There is a fear that the Brotherhood might rebel and stop working. That would have ramifications beyond the Theban region and sow turmoil all over the country. The importance of the Place of Truth—"

"I am well aware of its importance," the queen reminded him irritably. "Who is the author of this report accusing Paneb?"

"It is anonymous, Majesty."

"In that case, we shall pay it no heed."

"That would indeed be desirable, Majesty, but it passed through several hands before reaching the tjaty of the South, and I fear that confidentiality can no longer be assured. If we don't act, rumors will circulate, the judiciary will be accused of idleness, and your reputation will suffer."

King Saptah was dying, Setnakhte was preparing to seize

the throne, the Place of Truth was on the edge of the abyss. . . . The dangers were becoming so pressing that for a moment Tausert longed to rid herself of her burden. But no one would ever accuse her of desertion.

"Is this tjaty loyal to me?"

"He is an unassuming man, who spent his entire career running the granaries before being appointed to this post on General Mehy's recommendation and with Tjaty Bay's approval."

"Tell him to make quick, discreet inquiries into Paneb the Ardent and send the results to me without delay."

▲

"Your liver isn't working properly," said the Wise Woman.

"Are you sure?" Renupe was astonished. "But I'm so moderate in what I eat."

"Then your diet isn't the cause of your troubles. I don't think my medicine will work."

Every ounce of cheerfulness drained from the craftsman's face. "Must I go and consult a specialist, on the east bank?"

"The only doctor who can cure you is yourself."

"I don't understand."

"Don't you know that the liver is the seat of Ma'at? What you're suffering from is not a physical affliction but a lack of truth. Are you being eaten away by a lie, Renupe?"

He froze. "No, of course not—well, not completely. But it's so difficult to say."

"Have you hidden something important?" asked Ubekhet gently.

"A memory, a simple memory which has been obsessing me for several weeks. It's so terrible. If I say anything, I'll be denouncing a colleague and behaving like an informer."

The Wise Woman was unruffled. "Let your heart tell you what to do."

Renupe took a deep breath. "A long time before Nefer was appointed Master, we were discussing everyone's abilities to lead the Brotherhood. Everyone was in favor of Nefer except

Unesh the Jackal, who was undecided, and Gau the Precise, who confided in me. Gau and Ched the Savior both thought they were worthy to lead us. You can see what that means. Gau must have become embittered, and I daren't imagine what revenge he wanted."

▲

In the pillared hall of the temple, the atmosphere was one of profound peace. Gau the Precise stood calmly before the Wise Woman and the Master.

"Why have you summoned me here?" he asked.

"Because here Ma'at reigns," replied the Wise Woman, "and here no lie can be spoken, under pain of seeing its author's soul condemned to the second death. Did you wish to hold the office of Master, Gau, in place of Nefer?"

After a long silence, he said, "It's true, I did want to. At that time, I felt that only Ched the Savior was fit to run the Brotherhood, but he refused the office. I believed Nefer did not have the necessary experience. I was wrong, very wrong."

"Did you hate Nefer so much that—"

"I never hated Nefer. I underestimated him, envied him, then admired him—most of us did, in fact. But I've never hidden my opinions, and if they harm me that's just too bad: I prefer to live up to my nickname of 'Precise.' "

"Here is a gold necklace intended for the statue of Ma'at," said the Wise Woman. "Are your hands pure enough to lay it before her statue?"

Gau did not hesitate for a moment. "Look at my hands!" he demanded, his voice full of indignation. "These are the hands of a Servant of the Place of Truth and they will accept any and every task you entrust them with." And he laid the necklace before Ma'at.

Although relieved, Ubekhet and Paneb were still not altogether reassured. Why had Renupe's memory been so slow to return?

32

Sobek looked on gloomily as the lay workers carried out their work, all the time scratching the scar beneath his left eye. For the first time in many years, he had risen late and had hardly listened to the reports by his men—fortunately, nothing untoward had happened during the night.

Nothing untoward. Just a series of murders, carried out by people who remained unpunished.

He went back to his office in the Fifth Fort, and concentrated resolutely on his work; when the Master came in, he did not even look up.

"Are you ill?" asked Paneb.

"I'm wondering if I'm still any use for anything," confessed Sobek. "I can't catch criminals—just look at my disastrous record. You'd better replace me, or else I'd better resign."

"Let's get out of this hole and go for a walk in the hills. You need some fresh air and sunshine."

Reluctantly, the Nubian agreed.

Although Sobek was almost as tall and broad as Paneb, he seemed to have aged and had a defeated look. However, by making him climb briskly, Paneb managed to restore some of his energy.

"I love this place," murmured Sobek. "As the sun burns the desert, it gives us another life, so different from life in the Valley. Here there is neither cheating nor pretense. We have to confront reality in all its savagery, and must fear neither snakes nor scorpions. And yet a shadow has masked the light and I cannot drive it away."

"Have you been watching Userhat?"

"Of course I have—and all the others. And I have discovered not a thing." Sobek sat down on a burning-hot stone. "I've begun to wonder if some demon isn't amusing itself by assuming different human forms to strike its victims, so as to mislead us more effectively. Let the Wise Woman use her magic, and find another officer to deal with the matter. I've failed."

Paneb scooped up a little sand and let it trickle between his fingers. "Your task is to ensure the safety of the village and its inhabitants. I consider that you have carried it out well."

"What? With this murderous shadow sneering at us?"

"The Brotherhood has nurtured a serpent in its breast. We must get rid of it ourselves, with your help."

"You're wrong to leave me in my post," said Sobek.

"It won't be my first mistake or my last. Lift your men's hearts again, my friend, and convince yourself that we haven't yet lost the battle."

▲

When Paneb took his place in the Master's chair where Nefer the Silent had sat, he closed his eyes and called upon his spiritual father to help him lead the Brotherhood.

The starboard crew had gathered at the Brotherhood's meeting place, together with Hay, whose own crew was restoring the tombs in the Valley of the Queens. After the purification ritual, Paneb made a heartfelt appeal to the ancestors, and everyone sensed that the office of Master had begun to take possession of him.

The Servants of the Place of Truth were seated in stalls on stone benches. They were worried; one look at Paneb's preoccupied expression told them that the news was not good.

"At the moment," said the Master, "we aren't working on any projects in the Valley of the Kings. Given his frail health, King Saptah's death may come at any moment. But the months are passing and, in reality, the Scribe of the Tomb has no definite information. For that reason, I've decided to accept several outside orders, in order to preserve the Brotherhood's reputation and prove its expertise in a wide range of areas."

"You're not going to increase the work rate, are you?" asked Karo.

"Our rule will be respected, and you will receive additional bonuses if you answer my call."

"Who'll pay them?" asked Unesh doubtfully.

"The customers, and the bonuses will be paid in full to those who complete their work within the time allowed."

"Is it really necessary to give so much importance to the outside world?" protested Gau. "Several shrines in the village could do with restoration, and so could some of the tombs."

"I'm planning to allocate those tasks to the port crew, with the agreement of its leader."

Hay nodded in confirmation.

"If I understand you correctly," said Ched drily, "you're putting us to the test."

"What test?" asked Pai.

"The Master fears we may lapse into vanity and routine," explained Ched.

"That's enough talk," cut in Casa. "What are these wonderful outside orders?"

"A series of traps," replied Paneb.

The announcement was followed by a heavy silence.

"Are you joking?" asked Unesh.

"It seems that there's upheaval in the central government—of what kind and how serious, we don't know. If the government falls, the very existence of the Place of Truth will be threatened. My first duty is to preserve it, even in a time of violent change. The arrival of these orders is no coincidence. The outside world wants to know if we're good for anything besides building Houses of Eternity, so people are setting us challenges—which we're going to meet."

"But what if we can't?" fretted Gau.

"We have no reason to doubt that we can," said Userhat. "Besides, we possess the Stone of Light. Each time a vital question has been put to it, it has answered by lighting our way."

"In other words," concluded Thuty, "we'll all have to volunteer, because the only way we can succeed is as a team."

No one contradicted him.

So," said Fened, "what have we got to make?"

"First of all, a large number of thanksgiving plaques for temples in the Theban region," replied the Master. "We must work with small fragments of very fine limestone and sculpt them into small plaques, which will be laid in shrines or inserted into the walls of temples. All that remains for us to do is to choose the theme for the engraving."

"There's one obvious one," ventured Ipuy. "Ptah, patron of builders, protected by the wings of Ma'at. She alone can give the breath of life to the great master builder who recreates a harmonious universe each day."

"Couldn't we find something simpler?" objected Renupe.

"The idea seems an excellent one to me," decided Paneb. "It conveys the ideal of the Place of Truth without betraying it."

"Of course," grunted Karo, "that isn't all we'll have to do."

"Of course," nodded the Master with a broad smile. "We must also supply Karnak with statues and stelae, not forgetting copies of the *Book of Going Forth by Day,* with as many drawings as possible, designed to illustrate the soul's transformations."

"Which chapters are we to copy?" asked Gau.

"It's up to us to choose. But there are one or two rather more difficult things than that."

All eyes focused on the Master.

"The government has ordered porcelain vases in a perfect shade of blue to decorate the royal apartments."

Casa let out a disapproving whistle. "Can we make them?"

"I think so," replied Thuty, "but we'll have to consult the records of our master potters."

"My initiator was one," recalled Hay, "and I have forgotten nothing of what he taught me, but I'll need help if the order's a large one."

"It is," said Paneb. "First thing tomorrow, we shall open a workshop specifically for making these vases."

"Have we got enough sand with a high quartz content?" asked Hay.

"I'm sure we haven't," said Thuty, "but I know where to find some."

"There's just one more thing," Paneb went on.

"But what you've set us already is crippling," protested Casa.

"The tjaty of the South himself has sent us an urgent order."

Fened was amazed. "That old relic? All he cares about is getting through the day's business while he waits to be replaced. And he's never even set foot in the village."

"The tjaty needs two large wooden sarcophagi."

"Can't the carpenters at Karnak supply them?" asked Didia.

"He's ordered them from us. You're the carpenter; you shall make them."

"In that case, it might be better if we stop talking, have a good drink, and set to work."

Didia's suggestion met with unanimous approval. At the Master's invitation, the craftsmen joined hands to feel the energy flowing through the crew.

When the door of the meeting place closed once more, Paneb was left alone. He looked up at the starry sky. "Don't leave me, Nefer; and let your silence become words. I'm listening to your voice, I'm living with your life, my hand continues what your hand began, and through me you shall live on."

33

Kenhir had consulted the records left by the master potters of the time of Thutmose III, who had produced countless masterpieces. But following their instructions had proved disappointing.

When the first vases came out of the new workshop they

looked superb, a glittering blue. But when set beside the ancient vase Paneb took out of the strong room for comparison, they looked thoroughly second-rate.

"Did you use sand with a high quartz content, and did you crush it finely?" Paneb asked.

"Not once but twice," replied Hay, "and I added soda and vegetable ashes as a melting agent, as I was taught. The ingredients were well mixed into a solid, porous mass, I heated it to the correct temperature and applied the glaze. But beside the reference model, the color seems dull."

"We must have left out a vital ingredient. I'll go and ask the Wise Woman."

Ubekhet watched while a vase was made. Her verdict was definite. "Something vital is indeed missing. Leave me alone with the Master."

When the craftsmen had left, and the door of the workshop was securely bolted, Paneb opened a large sack filled with sand—or, rather, half filled: underneath the sand was the Stone of Light.

"Are you sure no one saw you take it from its hiding place?" asked Ubekhet.

"I went to fetch it in the middle of the night, with Ebony and Bad Girl. No one could have followed me without being spotted."

"Any good potter could make the blue we've produced. Our ancestors' blue was of an altogether different nature, which must derive from the Stone of Light. At each stage of the process, the materials should be exposed to the Stone's radiance."

Carefully, Paneb compacted the sand, added the ashes and soda, formed the mixture into a simple shape and covered it with a layer of colored paste, which was duller than that used by Hay. Then he heated the furnace. As the temperature rose, the light shining out of the Stone became more intense. Marveling, Ubekhet and Paneb watched as an extraordinarily pure blue coated the whole of the vase like some precious garment.

Its work done, the Stone's light grew dimmer and it seemed almost inert.

In a wide-mouthed cup set next to the vase, some pigments had been deposited.

"Cobalt blue," said the Wise Woman. "The scrolls spoke of it, but I didn't believe it could be found. That's the ingredient that produces this matchless color.[3]

▲

The traitor was in no doubt: if the Wise Woman and the Master had locked themselves away in the workshop, it was so that they could use the Stone of Light without being seen or heard. And since the Stone had been taken into the workshop, it would have to be taken out again, inevitably by Paneb. It was up to the traitor to be there at the right moment, and to follow Paneb to the Stone's hiding place.

With the other members of the starboard crew, the traitor saw the Wise Woman emerge from the workshop bearing a wide-mouthed blue vase. For several moments, everyone was speechless. The blue was so intense and yet so soft, lit up by a supernatural radiance.

"You've done it!" exclaimed Thuty in wonder.

"We have enough pigment to make many vases and several amulets," said Paneb. "This collection will be worthy of our ancestors."

"Such success deserves a banquet," declared Pai. "I shall give you meat grilled on skewers, and fillets of perch."

"Get everything ready," said Paneb. "I'll tidy up and put out the furnaces."

The traitor had to help his comrades, but they had the good idea of setting out tables and seats not far from the workshop, and he never took his eyes off its door.

▲

As soon as the meal was over, Paneb shut himself away in the workshop again.

Instead of going home like his brothers, the traitor hid on

the terrace of an empty house and continued to keep watch. The wait seemed never ending, but it augured well. If Paneb was letting darkness close in like this, it was so that he could be sure the whole village was asleep when he returned the Stone to its hiding place.

Just as a cloud drifted across the moon's slender crescent, the door of the workshop opened and Paneb came out, carrying a sack on his shoulder. He glanced around.

A sack of sand. So that was the trick the Master had used! Without the Stone, he would never have been able to obtain the same blue as the ancestors, for it was the Stone that illuminated all matter, bringing it to perfection.

When he murdered Nefer the Silent, the traitor had also killed all emotion within himself. Icy blood flowed in his veins, giving him supreme self-control. So he descended the stairs unhurriedly and followed Paneb at a distance, hiding first in a corner by a house, then behind a water jar.

Because of the weight he was carrying, Paneb walked slowly toward the temple.

The temple: the ideal hiding place. During the day, rites were celebrated there, perfumes were burnt, ritual objects were washed. At night, the Divine power rested there behind the sealed door of the innermost shrine. None of the villagers would ever imagine a craftsman daring to break the door seal and violate the sacred place.

Paneb walked through the gateway, crossed the courtyard, and entered the building.

The traitor crouched behind a stele, waiting for him to come out again. The Master must have fashioned movable stones, which had only to be pivoted to reveal a space where the Stone was hidden. One unexpected detail put him on the alert: neither Bad Girl nor Ebony was on patrol here. If Paneb had left the goose and the dog at home, he must be setting a trap.

So, when Paneb at last left the temple without his burden, the traitor slunk back home along the walls of the houses.

Scarcely had he closed his door when he heard Bad Girl cackling and Ebony barking.

Paneb would be disappointed that his quarry had escaped him yet again. But the traitor was jubilant: the Stone of Light was indeed hidden in the Temple of Ma'at and Hathor.

▲

Because of his painful elbow, Kenhir had agreed to let Niut massage his scalp, though he hated having to be so dependent. Thanks to Ubekhet's treatment, the old scribe could at least write the Journal of the Tomb without the help of Imuni, who had recently been lavishing rather too much flattery on his superior, as though he were hoping for a reward.

Imuni understood nothing of the spirit of the Brotherhood, and he was behaving like any little scribe who wanted to make a career for himself; he had no understanding of the adventure to which he was linked.

Kenhir knew Imuni's sole ambition: to become Scribe of the Tomb and impose his authority on the two crews. The little weasel did not lack skill, and he must not be underestimated.

"I'm going to the temple," Kenhir told Niut.

"That isn't a good idea. You ought to rest."

"I'm feeling better this morning."

"I'm starting lunch. Don't be late."

Given the quality of Niut's grilled pigeon with spices, there was no danger of that. Rightly considered the best cook in the village, she was constantly inventing new recipes which whetted Kenhir's considerable appetite.

The old scribe set off down the main street, grumbling a response to the villagers' cheery greetings.

The Master was installing a new doorstep.

"Did the traitor fall into the trap?" asked Kenhir.

"Unfortunately not."

"It's incredible. You'd swear someone was telling him our plans."

"Let's hope it's simply that he has a strong instinct for danger. He must have suspected something when he saw that Ebony and Bad Girl weren't there."

"How are we ever going to catch this devil?"

"I'm sure our tactics are the right ones."

"But he's still free and unpunished," Kenhir pointed out.

"How can a man be free when he's the slave of his own greed? The Stone of Light obsesses him—he thinks of nothing but stealing it. Let's go on following our plan."

"I wish the monster could be caught and locked up this very night."

Paneb grinned. "Wasn't it you, Kenhir, who taught me how to be patient?"

34

After squaring off two well-dried sycamore trunks with an ax, Didia the Generous sawed them into planks with a true craftsman's meticulous accuracy. He planed them down with a long-handled adze, then used a bow-drill to make the holes for the pegs.

When Paneb entered the carpenter's workshop, the tjaty's two sarcophagi already looked impressive.

"Any problems?" asked the Master.

"No, none. If you agree, I shall make a slightly curved sliding lid. Everything will be put together with wooden pegs, and I shall use cedar wood wedges to ensure that the lid is properly joined to the interior."

Paneb checked that the side planks were perfectly adjusted to the corner props and that the tenons, which were in the form of half-dovetails and fixed with tongues, were of excellent quality. Certain joints, which determined the way the base frame fitted to the lid, were concealed.

"Shall I fashion an Osiran face from acacia wood?"

"A good idea," agreed Paneb. "On the lid, I shall paint the tjaty as Osiris, with Isis and Nephthys on either side; at the foot, I shall paint Anubis lying in the embalming shrine."

"He's a lucky devil, our tjaty. Considering what a colorless, bureaucratic life he leads, I'm not sure he deserves a gift like this."

"Don't worry. He'll pay the full price for it."

"A fine sarcophagus can be traded for a shirt, a sack of spelt, a wooden door, four mats, a bed, and three pots of fat. So you can imagine how much these two are worth."

"We'll get much more than that for them, especially as you're at the height of your talents."

"Don't say that," said Didia hastily. "It brings bad luck!"

"Forgive me, but these two sarcophagi are real works of art."

"There's always a detail that can be improved—you know that as well as I do. That's what gives our craft its nobility, the mystery that unites the hand and the spirit in an act of love. It's your first duty, as Master, to see that this mystery is accomplished, and fortunately you understand that."

Paneb paused for a moment, then asked, "Have you any suspicions as to who the traitor is?"

"I can't even accept the fact that he exists," confessed Didia.

▲

Imuni handed Kenhir a papyrus. "An urgent message from the tjaty's office."

Kenhir broke the seal and read the scroll. "He summons the Master to a meeting tomorrow morning. Who does he think he is, this useless old fool?"

"As an instrument of Pharaoh's will, he's quite within his rights," said Imuni in his unctuous voice.

"True," agreed Kenhir, "but I could oppose him and ask the king to intervene."

"Yes, but in the time it would take for messages to go to and from His Majesty at Pi-Ramses, the tjaty could use force to make the Master appear before him."

"If he did, I'd order Sobek to drive the tjaty's men back."

"It would be better to avoid such a disastrous confrontation," purred Imuni.

"Go and find Paneb."

▲

When he heard the news, the Master was unruffled. "I expect the tjaty's impatient to see his sarcophagi," he said. "I'll explain that they aren't finished yet, and that haste might harm their quality. To pacify him, I'll take him one of the vases intended for the royal palace."

"I very much want to come with you," said Kenhir.

"Don't tire yourself out needlessly."

"Listen to what that snake says to you, Paneb—and don't lose your temper! Above all, don't say a word more than you have to. If he tries to wear you down with administrative problems, simply tell him they're for me to resolve."

"Don't worry. I shall be as good as gold."

▲

Mehy galloped his horse home from the government buildings in record time. The gatekeeper barely had time to throw himself into a clump of tamarisks to avoid being trampled, and a frightened servingwoman dropped two jugs of milk, which fell to the ground and smashed.

Paying no heed to these domestic dramas, Mehy jumped down from his horse and rushed into Serketa's bathing room, where she was having her body hair plucked out.

"I have good news," he announced with a beaming smile.

"My sufferings are almost over, sweet darling. Have some cool wine. I shall be with you directly."

Aware of what his master would want, the steward brought a fine oasis wine and some fillets of perch in hot pepper sauce. Mehy had just finished devouring this snack and emptying his first wine jar when his wife appeared, scantily clad in a wrap that hid nothing of her opulent curves.

"Am I not your delicious little girl?"

"Come here." After kneading Serketa's buttocks with his usual roughness, Mehy dragged her down on to his lap. "We shall soon be rid of Paneb the Ardent," he said.

"Have you decided to kill him?"

"The tjaty of Thebes I appointed will do that for me—and in the most legal way imaginable. The old fool has just received evidence supporting grave accusations against the Master."

"Is this the traitor's work?"

"If so, he's done it well. The accusations have been formulated as though by a scribe, and the facts are precise and detailed. Paneb has no chance of emerging from the tjaty's office a free man."

"Have you actually seen the evidence?"

"Of course—that old fool of a tjaty wouldn't dare not show it to me. For once, he's going to be useful. And I didn't even have to prompt him, because it's a very simple case. All he has to do is apply the law, and the Place of Truth will be decapitated. After Nefer the Silent, Paneb the Ardent . . . Kenhir's too old to resist the whirlwind that will destroy the Place of Truth. Either the traitor will succeed in becoming Master, or I shall dissolve the Brotherhood. Either way, the Stone of Light will belong to us. And with it, we shall possess absolute power."

Serketa seemed less than enthusiastic. "Paneb must have prepared his defense."

"He knows nothing! He probably thinks the tjaty wants him to talk about his sarcophagi."

"Paneb will guess it's a trap, and he won't go."

"In that case, the tjaty will use force. And force means my army."

"The Brotherhood will defend itself."

"It won't be able to."

Serketa slid off her husband's lap and paced the room nervously. "A direct confrontation would be damaging to you. You'd be accused of using violence, and your reputation as a cautious, careful administrator would be in tatters. We mustn't let that happen."

"We aren't at that stage yet, my little dove. Paneb has no reason to be suspicious. He'll go to see the tjaty—and be thrown into prison."

▲

The old tjaty of the South was under the thumb of Mehy, to whom he owed his appointment, and he had adopted the same attitude as the mayor of Thebes. He never used his initiative, he obeyed the general's instructions to the letter, and he confined himself to sorting out current business, referring matters to the general at the slightest sign of difficulty. By following this line, the official ensured himself a quiet life and could relax as much as he liked in his comfortable official residence, on the banks of the Nile.

In a city as safe as Thebes, where crime was almost nonexistent, Mehy had gained himself a reputation as an honest general, capable of imposing order in any circumstances, to the citizens' great satisfaction. Consequently, it was a long time since the tjaty had convened the highest court, where murderers and other serious criminals were tried.

When he received the anonymous accusations against the Master of the Place of Truth, the old tjaty had been horror stricken. Of course, his first reflex had been to show it to Mehy, who had advised him to apply the law, after first alerting the central government by official messenger.

The old man hoped the Master wouldn't answer his summons, because he'd heard that Paneb was a wild, hot-tempered man. If Paneb proved recalcitrant, Mehy would have to intervene by force, and he, the tjaty, would be absolved of any responsibility.

"Any petitioners this morning?" he asked his secretary, a thin, pale scribe.

"No one important. Your assistants are dealing with them."

"Nothing urgent to be dealt with?"

"Thebes is perfectly calm. Thanks to the guard-baboons, there haven't even been any petty thefts from the markets."

A servant entered and said, "Paneb the Ardent, Master of the Place of Truth, wishes to see the tjaty."

35

The old man swallowed hard at the thought of meeting this violent, vengeful man, who was said to have beaten nine opponents, single-handed.

"Is everything ready?" he asked.

"Don't worry," his secretary promised him, "you'll be quite safe."

"Good, good. Bring him in, then."

When the big man appeared, the tjaty suddenly felt older and weaker. He shrank into his chair and was careful to avoid looking into Paneb's eyes, which were as intense as a flame.

"Your sarcophagi aren't quite finished," Paneb told him, "but I can assure you that they'll be exceptionally beautiful. The other orders are nearly ready, too, and here's a sample of our work." Holding the blue vase as if it were a sacred offering, he took a step toward the tjaty.

"Get back!"

Paneb halted in surprise.

"You're under arrest," quavered the tjaty, and as he spoke a dozen guards poured into the office and surrounded Paneb, pointing their spears at him.

"What on earth is this nonsense?" demanded Paneb.

"You're a dangerous criminal, and I have overwhelming evidence to prove it. At the slightest sign of resistance, you'll be killed."

The soldiers threatening Paneb were no weaklings, and they had had the benefit of surprise. One put wooden manacles on his wrists, while another shackled his ankles. And all the time, spear points were pressing into his neck, chest and back. In a few moments he was securely restrained, with no freedom of movement at all.

"May I at least know what I am accused of?" he asked.

"You'll know soon enough. Men, take this criminal to prison."

▲

Mehy grabbed his bow, drew the bowstring back so fiercely that it almost snapped, and took aim at a peregrine falcon that had been unwise enough to fly over his house, tracing broad circles in the sky. No hunter ever attacked this bird of prey, for it was the incarnation of Horus, the protector of royalty, but the general had only contempt for such superstitions.

A small cry disturbed Mehy's concentration, and he let fly his arrow a moment too soon. The bird's sharp eyes saw the danger, and it escaped at the last moment by beating its powerful wings and soaring up toward the sun.

Whirling round, he saw Serketa's pretty Nubian serving girl; she was on her knees, tears in her eyes.

"Forgive me, my lord," she pleaded, "but I was afraid for the bird."

Mehy slapped her so hard that she was flung down onto the sandy path. "Little idiot, you made me miss my shot! Get out of my sight and never cross me again, or else . . ."

A hand to her bruised face, the girl got to her feet and fled. Mehy would have liked to rape her, but he was wary of Serketa. If he deceived her, she would find out one way or another and would take her revenge. Now, when he was on the eve of a great victory, was certainly not the moment to do something so stupid. When Serketa had got so fat that she lost her looks and was no longer any use to him, it would be time to review matters.

Smiling at the thought, he went into the house and summoned his head steward. "Still nothing?" he asked.

"The usual messages, my lord, but nothing from the tjaty's office yet."

Mehy heard a horse approaching at full gallop, and ran to the front door. It was indeed an envoy from the tjaty, bearing an urgent message.

The opening words delighted him: Paneb had been arrested and imprisoned. But what came next disturbed him: an important visitor had just arrived, unannounced, in Thebes. And Mehy did not know what that meant.

▲

Evening was falling, and Paneb had still not returned.

"Aren't you hungry?" Niut asked Kenhir, who had not touched his delicious supper of gray mullet grilled with lentils.

"Something's gone wrong."

"I expect the tjaty has invited the Master to dinner."

"If so, Paneb would have sent us a message."

Despite her comforting words, Niut was as worried as Kenhir, and she did not try to hold him back when he got to his feet and picked up his walking stick.

Before he went out, she put a cloak round his shoulders. "There's a cool wind. Don't catch a cold."

Kenhir went to the Fifth Fort. "Is Sobek here?" he asked the Nubian guard on duty.

"No. He took the official chariot and went to the landing stage."

So Sobek was worried, too, worried enough to go off in search of information.

"Give me a stool," said Kenhir. "I'll wait."

"I've nothing very comfortable."

"That doesn't matter."

So it had indeed been a trap. But who had set the trap? Not that old imbecile of a tjaty—he would never dare pick a quarrel with the Master of the Place of Truth. The order must have come from the real lord of Thebes, General Mehy. But part of his role as governor of the west bank was to ensure that the Brotherhood was protected. Besides, he had no reason to wish it harm. Above Mehy, there was only the supreme Master of the Brotherhood, Pharaoh. Clearly, the unfortunate Saptah could not have set the trap, so Queen Tausert must have been responsible.

Kenhir shivered. If he was right, the queen regent had—for reasons unknown—signed the Brotherhood's death warrant. First, enfeeble it by having the Master arrested, then—

"Here comes Sobek," said the guard.

The big Nubian brought his chariot to an abrupt halt, but he did not forget to stroke his horse before coming to meet the Scribe of the Tomb.

"Paneb has been imprisoned at the palace," he revealed.

"Why?" asked Kenhir, appalled.

"I don't know any details, but several serious accusations have been made against him."

"By whom?

"I don't know that, either. Apparently, the tjaty received a detailed report which left no room for doubt about Paneb's guilt."

"The traitor—it must be. I'm going to request an audience with the tjaty."

▲

Kenhir's old bones did not appreciate the bumps in the road, but he ignored his aches and pains and thought only of the Master. He must convince the tjaty that this was a cunning deception and that Paneb should be freed immediately.

Sobek woke a ferryman, who grudgingly agreed to cross the Nile even though night had fallen. The Nubian's imperious tone and daunting size dissuaded him from arguing too vociferously.

The tjaty's apartments were next to the royal palace at Karnak, and it took all the strength of Kenhir's convictions to persuade the commander of the guards to rouse him.

Taken by surprise, the tjaty agreed to receive Kenhir in the antechamber where his visitors usually waited. Fearing that this ill-tempered scribe would provoke a scandal, he felt it wise not to put off the inevitable confrontation.

"Is our Master being held prisoner here?" demanded Kenhir.

"Indeed he is."

"Why? What is he accused of?"

"I don't have to tell you that."

"Of course you do! As Scribe of the Tomb, I have access to all official documents concerning the Brotherhood."

"This is an exceptional case—"

"To say the least!"

The tjaty was unnerved by Kenhir's anger, but he knew he could not back down. "In an exceptional case, exceptional procedures are fitting," he said, his voice trembling.

"You are the tjaty, and for that precise reason you must respect the law of Ma'at."

"Listen, Kenhir—"

"Send me the document outlining the charges, and free the Master of the Place of Truth immediately."

"I can't."

"Then I shall write at once to His Majesty, tell him what you have done, and demand your dismissal."

"That is your right, Kenhir."

"You'd do better to meet my demands."

"I told you, I can't."

Kenhir drew himself up. "Very well. Since you want war, you shall have it."

▲

Paneb could have broken down the door of his cell, attacked the guards, and tried to escape from the palace. But that would have been acting illegally, and his office forbade him to do so. Moreover, he wanted to know why he had been arrested, and who was trying to destroy the Brotherhood through the accusations leveled against him.

So he lay down on his rough bed to spend a peaceful night and prepare himself to appear before the court. There, he would have ample opportunity to explain himself, and in the meantime Kenhir was sure to battle fiercely to have him set free. Egypt was a country where the law of Ma'at was respected, beginning with the tjaty, who stood as guarantor for it.

His awakening was brutal: two spear points jabbed him in the side.

"Follow us," ordered a guard.

Paneb was led to a small room with two pillars. It did not look like a courtroom. The tjaty was seated on a low chair, a papyrus spread across his knees.

Avoiding the prisoner's eyes, he said, "Paneb the Ardent, the time has come to answer for your crimes."

36

"Is this a private conversation, or an official audience?" asked the Master.

"I'm obeying my instructions as I understand them," replied the tjaty, "and I command you to answer the accusations brought against you."

"Who is my accuser?"

"You don't need to know that."

"The law obliges you to tell me his name. If you refuse, the case will be declared null and void."

The tjaty looked embarrassed. "As a matter of fact, we're dealing with an . . . anonymous document."

"Then it has no legal value."

"The accusations are so serious that I shall let that detail pass."

"That is unacceptable. Either you give me the name or I leave this room."

"The document really is anonymous, and I have no means of identifying its author. Will you nevertheless consent to know what you are accused of?"

"As I have a clear conscience, why not?"

The tjaty cleared his throat. "I'll begin with the least serious crime, though even that one is unforgivable: you had a craftsman from the Brotherhood look after your bullock, and made two Servants of the Place of Truth work in your field, which is strictly forbidden."

"That's nonsense. Two craftsmen did indeed help me, but of their own free will and without any compulsion. All you have to do to learn the truth is ask them, and the five peasants who work perfectly legally for me will confirm what I say."

"That may be. But there's a more delicate matter. You're accused of having seduced several married women and caused trouble in the village families."

Paneb burst out laughing. "Have any women complained? Who are they?"

"The document does not go into that much detail. Do you deny the facts?"

"My wife will bear witness for me, and she'll explain that my behavior doesn't compromise the harmony of the village in any way."

"Very well. Let us move on to the next charge: you have a pickax which only you use, something contrary to the rules."

"The Scribe of the Tomb will tell you that this pickax is my personal property—as everyone in the village knows—and that it's marked with a seal so individual that it couldn't possibly be confused with another one. So my pickax doesn't have to be handed in to the Brotherhood's store after use."

"The government should have been notified of this exception."

"It's all set down in the Journal of the Tomb, which Kenhir will make available to you."

"I see. But you did steal a bed from a village tomb."

"If I had," retorted Paneb, "I'd have been tried and sentenced by the Brotherhood's court. No theft has ever been committed in our ancestors' Houses of Eternity, for they watch over us and we worship them every day. A bed was officially given to me with the agreement of the Scribe of the Tomb, and the gift was noted down in the Journal."

"Let us come to the most serious accusations, which are punishable by death."

Paneb's eyes almost popped out of his head. "Are you serious?"

"The charges certainly are: the first is that you violated tombs in the Valley of the Kings."

At this, Paneb lost his temper. "Have you gone quite mad?"

"Kindly respect my office," pleaded the tjaty, whose throat felt horribly tight. "It's my job to establish the truth, and—"

"Then tell me what you're talking about."

Still not daring to look the giant in the eyes, the old man buried his nose in the papyrus. "You stole a piece of precious fabric from the tomb of King Seti II, and to celebrate this exploit you got drunk, standing on his sarcophagus."

"There's some truth in that."

The tjaty raised his head a fraction. "You . . . you admit it?"

"I admit that I got drunk. As to the rest, the informer has given you a tissue of crude lies. The fabric in question was not in Seti's tomb, and the sarcophagus beside which I and my companions enjoyed some excellent wine wasn't his, either. On those points, I can supply witnesses who'll disprove these allegations—which are as grotesque as they are libelous."

"You have witnesses? Really?"

"They will give testimony under oath, before the village court presided over by the Scribe of the Tomb, and then before you, if you demand it. And you'll be shown both the piece of fabric and the sarcophagus."

"Very well. But there remains one exceptionally grave charge."

"I'm listening."

As Paneb had calmed down, the tjaty felt more confident. "Stone blocks belonging to King Meneptah's tomb were moved from the Valley of the Kings to the village, and were used to construct four pillars in your own House of Eternity."

"That's right," agreed Paneb.

"So you, the Master of the Place of Truth, robbed a king's tomb which you had excavated and decorated,"

"That's wrong."

"But . . . you've just admitted your crime!"

"There was no crime. The stone blocks in question were salvaged materials. I asked a small crew to tidy up the Valley of the Kings by getting rid of the debris that had accumulated where we were working. They brought back some stones to use in constructing my tomb, as my companions had decided to give me this magnificent gift."

"And are they also prepared to testify?"

"Of course."

The old tjaty rolled up the papyrus. "You have reduced the accusations to nothing, Master."

"Is that everything?"

"Don't you think those charges were enough?"

"If I understand you correctly, you're withdrawing them all. Is that right?"

"Your explanations have convinced me. But a judge in the highest court might perhaps take a different view."

Queen Tausert appeared in the doorway. The tjaty and the Master rose instantly to their feet and bowed to her.

"I heard everything," she said, "and I have reached the same conclusion as the tjaty. The Master shed clear light upon the matter and has demolished the anonymous evidence, which is the work of some vile slanderer."

Still bowing low, the tjaty withdrew.

▲

Paneb gazed at the queen, whose beauty was almost the equal of Turquoise's: the same proud nobility, the same finely sculpted features, the same clear gaze. But the queen's eyes held more loneliness and controlled suffering.

Tausert was surprised by Paneb's strength and by the energy that radiated from him. For a moment, she mused that he would make a pharaoh comparable to the greatest who had ever ruled, and that a man like him would be capable of ruling Egypt.

"Had you been found guilty, it would have caused a crisis so profound that my regency would have been undermined," she said.

"I am innocent, Majesty, and both your reputation and that of the Place of Truth remain intact."

"I preferred to make sure of that myself, for the most alarming rumors about you were circulating, and I was not certain that the tjaty of the South would be impartial. He shall be replaced first thing tomorrow, by someone who can distinguish truth from lies, and I hope nothing like this will ever happen again."

"Forgive my impudence, Majesty, but why not hear the witnesses, who would dispel any lingering doubts?"

A dazzling smile lit up the queen's face. "Because I trust you, Paneb. Don't you know how to trust people?"

"When one leads a Brotherhood or a country, perhaps one cannot afford to do so."

"That is indeed what several great pharaohs advised. But I am only a regent, and it is my weakness to believe you. In exercising power I have learnt to read people's characters, and I don't believe you are capable of telling a lie."

Paneb was so moved that he could not reply.

"Someone tried to destroy you," Tausert went on, "and it's vital that you find out who."

"I already have, Majesty. And I beg you to do me the favor of judging him according to the laws of our Brotherhood."

"I must remind you that only the tjaty's court can impose the supreme punishment."

"You need not fear: the criminal will emerge from our Brotherhood alive—if one can call the fate that awaits him a life."

"Act according to the rule of Ma'at," warned the queen.

Paneb bowed. "Will you grant us the honor of a visit, Majesty?"

"I cannot. I must leave to return to Pi-Ramses immediately. King Saptah's health is in irreversible decline. Ensure that everything is ready for his funeral ceremonies."

"You have my word, Majesty."

37

In his capacity as Master, Paneb presided over the village court, which had convened before the gateway of the Temple of Ma'at and Hathor.

The jury was made up of the Wise Woman, the Scribe of the Tomb, the leader of the port crew, Ched the Savior, and two priestesses of Hathor. All the villagers were present, for this promised to be a most unusual session.

Paneb had made no official announcement since his return, and everyone was still wondering why he had been arrested. So absolute silence fell when he rose to speak.

He said, "False accusations were made against me by a member of this village, who did not even have the courage to sign the document he sent to the tjaty. I was imprisoned like a criminal, but thanks to Queen Tausert I had a chance to defend myself, and I proved my innocence. All that remains is to identify the informer, a man who resorted to crime in an attempt to gain power over the village, a man who has always hated me and who is sustained only by ambition."

Horrified murmurs ran round the assembled throng.

"This vermin must give himself up at once," demanded Nakht.

A path to the court was cleared, but no one stepped forward.

Fened asked, "Master, do you really know who it is?"

"His own accusations gave him away. Only one person could have framed them and distorted reality with so much mean-spiritedness and hatred."

The craftsmen exchanged looks, but no one could believe that one of his companions could have acted so basely.

Paneb turned to Imuni, who was hiding behind Didia. "At least have the courage to confess," he urged him.

The little rat-faced scribe with the shifty eyes tried to back away, but Karo and Casa blocked his way.

"I don't understand," stammered Imuni, in the syrupy voice that had always exasperated Kenhir. "I've always done my work well, and I—"

"Come here," ordered the Master.

Obediently, Imuni went to stand before Paneb, the Wise Woman, and the Scribe of the Tomb.

At first he put on a show of humility. "Perhaps I made a few mistakes, but I didn't mean to do any harm. An unfortunate combination of circumstances threw suspicion onto Paneb and he was accused of crimes he hadn't committed."

"Was it indeed you who sent a collection of evidence to the tjaty?"

"There were certain things I felt I had to tell—"

"Without going through me?" thundered Kenhir.

"I . . . I didn't want to bother you."

"Do you take me for a fool, Imuni? You have betrayed my trust, slandered the Master, and become the enemy of the entire village."

The little scribe drew himself up and went on to the attack. "You've never recognized my talents or my rights!" he bawled. "I should have been made Scribe of the Tomb long ago—I'm the best qualified of all of you! Why won't you admit it?"

Paneb looked Imuni straight in the eye. "Was it you who murdered Nefer the Silent?"

"No, no, of course not! I swear I'm innocent!"

Paneb sensed that Imuni was too afraid of him to lie.

"Let's give the little runt a good thrashing!" cried Karo.

"Calm down," ordered Paneb. "Nothing must be done that diminishes the dignity of this court."

Kenhir was devastated. He had never liked his assistant, but had never even begun to guess how badly envy and hatred had eaten away at him.

"Imuni's treason has been proved," said Hay, and the other members of the Brotherhood agreed emphatically.

"Then he must be punished as our rule requires," pronounced Paneb. "He must be expelled from the village forever."

The jurors agreed.

Imuni went white. "You . . . you have no right!"

"You may no longer pass through the gate of the Place of Truth," Paneb continued. "You may not even enter the lay workers' village. A complaint will be made to the tjaty about you, charging you with abuse of a magistrate and slanderous defamation. Farewell, Imuni."

Casa and Karo seized the little scribe by the collar of his tunic and dragged him along the main street, followed by all the other craftsmen.

Imuni was afraid he would be beaten, but the two stonecutters were content to take him to the great gate, which Renupe opened.

The port and starboard crews arranged themselves into lines on either side of the gate.

"Get out, runt!" ordered Userhat.

Imuni hesitated. "You don't know what you're losing! I'd have—"

Fened picked up a pebble and shied it at the little scribe's backside. Imuni squealed with pain.

"Be off with you, or we'll stone you!"

Imuni took to his heels and fled from the Place of Truth, pursued by the craftsmen's jeers.

▲

The banquet given by Mehy and Serketa was sure to rank among the most successful events of the year. The governor was using this opportunity to honor the new tjaty of the South whom Queen Tausert had appointed, an obscure priest from Karnak.

Mehy had conversed briefly with Tausert before she embarked for Pi-Ramses, and warmly commended her for replacing the old tjaty, a move that he had in fact been going to suggest himself. He also congratulated himself on the swift rehabilitation of Paneb the Ardent, who was a remarkable Master, even if his manner was sometimes abrupt. And Mehy had of course assured the queen of his total loyalty. Confidential conversations with officials from all over the province had reassured him that his own reputation and influence remained intact.

At the banquet, Mehy did not much enjoy the gyrations of the naked dancing girls in their diaphanous pink veils. He did not even get drunk, despite the wonderful vintage wines, and he withdrew to his own rooms well before the end of the festivities.

As she smiled endlessly at her guests and shared their confidences, Serketa hammered home the message that must be got across to them: she and Mehy were a happy, generous couple, fate had granted them everything they wished for, and their only ambition was to serve their country. The prosperity of Thebes was surely ample proof of her husband's abilities as an administrator, and he was the very model of an honest, upstanding man.

Once the last guests had left, Serketa went to Mehy's bedchamber and sank into a chair. She had her Nubian servant fetched, and ordered her to massage her feet.

"We still have one guest to consult," said Mehy.

"Oh no! I've met enough idiots for this evening, my sweet darling."

"This one should interest you more than the others."

"You intrigue me. Who is it?"

The general ushered in a little scribe with a weasel face and shifty eyes. "Allow me to present Imuni, the Scribe of the Tomb's former assistant."

Serketa put on a sympathetic expression. "You've been the victim of a terrible injustice, haven't you?"

"Yes, I have, and I don't know how to defend myself."

"Why don't you tell us all about it?" suggested Mehy. "As protector of the Place of Truth, I owe it to myself to collect as much information as possible, to avoid making mistakes."

Imuni did not need to be asked again; Mehy and Serketa listened attentively to his story.

"So you feel cheated," said Mehy when the scribe had finished, "because you feel you're the one who should be leading the Brotherhood."

"That's it exactly, General."

"Your situation is delicate, very delicate. Paneb has been found innocent, your accusations have been judged unfounded, and the new tjaty is not willing to reconsider the case. However . . ."

The little scribe's eyes glittered with greed.

"However, I am a man who sets great store by justice, and your sincerity moves me. For the moment, your career has been shattered, and I cannot oppose the Brotherhood's court. But if you tell me everything you know about the Place of Truth, I shall understand this painful affair better and may be able to help you."

Imuni smoothed his mustache with his index finger. "Information like that is so confidential that it's very valuable."

"Everything has its price, that's true; but you can't sell to anyone but me. For if you became too talkative, the tjaty would have you arrested for high treason. Which means, of course, that this conversation must remain secret. In exchange for your friendship, I shall set you up in a house in Middle Egypt, where you shall work while you await better things."

Imuni talked for a long time, delighted to have found such a powerful ally; one, moreover, who was offering him the future he had dreamt of: ousting Paneb and becoming Master of the Brotherhood. All he needed was patience, and the scribe had no lack of that.

Serketa learnt nothing new about the village and its running, but she was delighted by the little scribe's rancor. He would be an amusing toy in her husband's hands. And she rejoiced above all in the Brotherhood's naïveté, for they were convinced that Imuni's expulsion had at last rid them of the traitor.

But of course the traitor was someone else.

38

Niut the Lively laid the damp fabric between two grooved wooden planks. Pressing it like that would produce fine pleats, and the Scribe of the Tomb would have a ceremonial shirt worthy of the name.

Although deeply shaken by the revelations about Imuni, Kenhir had managed to sleep, with the aid of drugs prescribed by Ubekhet, and his appetite was good.

And yet, when he returned from his private meeting with the Wise Woman and the two crew leaders, his face was solemn.

"Is there another problem?" asked Niut.

"No, not exactly. Tell me, though, what did you think of Imuni?"

"I've already told you—several times. When a man looks like a rat, he behaves like one; when he has an oily voice, he flatters people; and when he flatters people, he tells lies. But you never listen to a word I say."

"I did listen," said Kenhir, "but I simply couldn't believe he was so bad."

"And you still don't believe it, because you can't imagine the kind of monster who comes from a combination of mean-spiritedness and ambition."

"The council has decided to appoint a new assistant scribe."

"I'm glad to hear it. At your age, you need help."

"I put forward a candidate, and my suggestion was accepted unanimously."

"I'm glad to hear that, too. For his official appointment, you shall have a beautifully pleated shirt to wear."

"The new assistant hasn't yet accepted the appointment."

"Why not? Who is he?"

"You, Niut. You are more than an exceptional housekeeper and cook, for you can also read and write. Everyone knows how thorough and hardworking you are, and the council believes, as I do, that there is no better candidate for the post."

Niut examined the shirt. "I can do better pleats than these, but I'd need finer fabric. Very well, let's get to work. Do you want to dictate today's entry for the Journal of the Tomb?"

▲

The pretty, fifteen-year-old daughter of a sculptor from the port crew came to the door of Paneb and Uabet's house. She was crying bitterly.

"What's the matter?" Uabet asked, stroking the girl's shining brown hair.

"I wanted . . . I wanted to tell you, but I daren't now . . . And, and . . ."

"Come inside."

Uabet's home was enchanting, decorated with shimmering paintings by Paneb, who took pleasure in bringing them back to life as soon as a color faded. Geometrical shapes, vines, lotus leaves, birds frolicking in the papyrus forests: all combined to create a miniature palace, whose mistress tended it with love and pride.

Uabet invited the girl to sit down on the orange cushions she had embroidered herself.

"You wanted to speak to me?"

"Yes—no. Let me leave, I beg you."

"Calm yourself, little one, I am ready to listen, whatever you have to tell me."

The girl looked up, her eyes still full with tears. "Really?"

"Really."

"Could I have a drink of water?"

The girl drank greedily, as though she had just crossed a desert. "You'll be so angry with me."

"I promise I won't."

The girl hugged her knees. "The other girls and I, we were flirting with the boys last night, after the sun went down. We danced bare-breasted as we always do, but we didn't stop there. We'd drunk some rather strong beer and it was very hot, so we took off our kilts, too, to make it easier to do acrobatics."

"And the boys took theirs off, too, I suppose?"

"At the end of the dance, yes. But all we did was look at each other, and laugh, and then everyone went home. But I . . . I couldn't."

"Why not?"

"Because of Aapehti." The girl broke down and sobbed.

"Did he rape you?"

"Yes and no. When he came up to me, he was still naked and so was I. At first, I thought he just wanted to caress me, and the thing is, he's so handsome and so strong . . . I should have screamed, fought him off, called for help."

"But you didn't?"

"No," confessed the girl shamefacedly.

"So you made love, and now you're no longer a virgin."

The girl nodded nervously.

"Are you in love with Aapehti?"

"I don't know. I think so. But I daren't say anything to my parents."

"Have you seen him since last night?"

"No. Oh no!"

▲

Aapehti's fist made contact with the chin of his opponent, who fell flat on his back.

"I win!" exclaimed the young man, who had never yet been beaten in unarmed combat.

"You're nineteen now, and yet to you life is nothing but a sparring match," said Paneb, his voice cutting.

Abashed, Aapehti dared not look his father in the face.

"You've become a good plasterer. It's time to move into your own house and marry the woman you seduced and whom you love."

"But I don't love any woman!"

"Oh yes you do, remember? A pretty brown-haired girl to whom you proved you're a man."

"We were just having a bit of fun, that's all."

"It wasn't 'a bit of fun' for her, and it isn't for you anymore. Either you restore the little house the Scribe of the Tomb is giving you, and live there with your wife, or else you leave the village."

▲

Ubekhet was feeling very alone, as she did every evening when she had finished seeing patients. She rose before dawn, for the morning rites, then busied herself with her healing work, all the time thinking of the village's well-being. She was happy that she had stabilized Ched's sight, and there were no serious illnesses that would require sending the patient to Thebes.

Once the last patient had left, she felt the full weight of Nefer's loss again, and she knew only too well that the emptiness could never again be filled. Despite her great love for the

Brotherhood, the ordeal of separation from her husband was so cruel that she longed to join him soon.

As night fell, Ubekhet felt an immense weariness. She was not hungry, and she knew that sleep itself would bring her no comfort. So she decided to climb to the summit of the Peak of the West, in the hope that the goddess of silence would accept her into her breast and allow her through the gates of the world beyond.

When she opened her door, sitting on the doorstep she found seven-year-old Iuwen, tightly clasping three little linen bags containing grape seeds, dates, and barley.

"What are you doing here?" asked Ubekhet.

"I've prepared my own offerings to the goddess of the Peak of the West. You promised you'd take me, remember? I'm ready."

A golden light burned in the child's eyes. At that moment, Ubekhet knew that destiny had chosen the future Wise Woman of the Place of Truth, and that from now on she must devote a good part of her time to training her.

"Give me a few moments," she said.

When she reappeared, she was dressed in a pink and white robe of pleated linen, and wore a broad gold necklace and bracelets. Her wig was surmounted by a lotus and held firmly in place by a gold circlet.

"How beautiful you look!" said Iuwen.

"That's to honor the goddess. I'm sure she'll approve of your offerings."

The Wise Woman and the child began a slow climb, in the last rays of the setting sun. Iuwen held Ubekhet's hand very tightly, but never took her eyes off the summit.

"Worship the goddess of silence, who dwells at the summit of the mountain," the Wise Woman urged her. "Sometimes her appearance is frightening, but in her dwells the fire of creation. When I have returned to the West, may she become your guide and your eyes."

When they reached the summit, the female royal cobra emerged from its lair. Iuwen held Ubekhet's hand even more tightly.

"Stand behind me and do everything I do," said the Wise Woman.

The ritual dance of the snake and the Wise Woman was celebrated in perfect harmony. Pacified by the gifts, the cobra returned to the kingdom of silence.

Ubekhet and Iuwen sat down side by side, to savor the coolness of dusk.

"We shall travel through the night hours together," said Ubekhet. "One day, you shall touch the great serpent, the incarnation of the goddess, and she will transmit her energy to you."

The little girl stayed awake all night; not for one moment did she feel sleepy. Just before sunrise, Ubekhet gathered the dew that flowed from the highest stone on the Peak, the regenerative water that came from the stars, and gave it to Iuwen to drink.

Then they set off back toward the village.

▲

Paneb was standing outside the village, where the path began. The little girl ran to her father, and fell asleep the instant he took her up in his arms. The Wise Woman's eyes met the Master's; neither of them needed to say a word.

And for the first time, Ubekhet saw the big man weep.

39

All the orders for the outside world had been finished and delivered, to the complete satisfaction of the temple at Karnak and even of the former tjaty, who had paid dearly for his two sarcophagi.

After the success of their tremendous efforts, the villagers were enjoying a respite. The late May heat was unbearable, and everyone was living life in slow motion.

▲

Ubekhet spent long hours at the foot of the persea tree that had been planted on Nefer's tomb. The tree grew almost as she looked at it, and exuded the calming presence of the man she continued to love as fervently as ever.

The craftsmen were happily playing dice with five stones of different shapes, symbolizing fire, water, air, earth, and the universal essence. Nakht was just about to take his turn when Paneb's enormous cat stepped right in front of him, all the hairs on its back bristling and its claws extended.

"What's the matter, Charmer?" he asked.

The animal answered with a yowl.

"He's warning us of danger," said Fened.

The craftsmen laid down their dice and followed the cat, which stalked along, its tail fluffed out and its whiskers quivering. It led them to the great gate, which it began to claw at wildly.

"That animal's gone mad," said Pai. "I'm going to find Paneb. Whatever you do, don't go near it: it could scratch you badly."

Suddenly, someone banged hard on the gate.

"It's the gatekeeper," said Pai.

"The cat's not as mad as you think," said Casa drily. "Go and tell the Master."

In a few moments, all the villagers were crowding round the great gate.

"Let me through," ordered Paneb.

When the gate swung open, they saw Uputy, the messenger, standing beside the gatekeeper.

"I have two messages for you, Master," he said, "one verbal and one written. Here is the first. It is my duty to inform you that the soul of King Saptah has taken flight for the celestial paradise, to unite with the Light from which it came. And here"—he handed Paneb a papyrus bearing the regent's seal—"is the written message."

What Paneb read angered him so much that he immediately summoned the Wise Woman, the Scribe of the Tomb, and the leader of the port crew to a meeting.

"To honor Saptah's memory," he told them, "the queen orders us to enlarge his tomb."

"I suppose we could lengthen it," suggested Hay.

"I consider our work finished. The tomb's size and proportions respect the laws of harmony, as does its decoration."

"But this is an order from the queen regent," said Kenhir. "You can't just ignore it."

"Saptah is dead, his mummification will last seventy days, and then he'll be buried in his House of Eternity. How could we possibly excavate, sculpt, and paint properly in such a short time?"

"All the Servants of the Place of Truth can work well when they work fast—including yourself," disagreed Hay.

"It isn't the Brotherhood's abilities that worry you, is it?" said the Wise Woman. "Why is it that you're so strongly against this decision?"

"Because we'd run headlong into trouble. Touching that tomb would be a disaster."

"You can take all the necessary precautions," said Kenhir.

"Shouldn't you write to the queen," asked Paneb, "to tell her we disagree with her decision?"

"No," said Kenhir, "I don't think that would be a very good idea. At Pi-Ramses, the war of succession must already have begun, and I don't think Tausert would care to be thwarted by the Place of Truth's disobedience. What I know of her leads me to think she won't change her mind."

"Write to her anyway," persisted Paneb, "and tell her we have serious reservations about enlarging Saptah's tomb."

Kenhir was getting worried. "Will you at least agree to reopen the site?"

"Have I any choice?"

▲

Immediately after the king's death was officially announced, the queen regent convened the Great Council. She informed its members that the embalming ritual was beginning, and that she had ordered the Place of Truth to embellish Saptah's last dwelling.

Setnakhte was astonished by the decision, which was bound to delay the funeral ceremonies; but the queen made her position clear, claiming that the king, who had respected the law of Ma'at throughout his too-brief life, well deserved this final act of homage.

Setnakhte was still angry when he arrived home.

"Your eldest son is here," his steward informed him.

The minister for foreign affairs looked worried. "Rumors are flying on all sides, Father. Has King Saptah really returned to the celestial paradise?"

"He has indeed. What news have you brought me?"

"Nothing good—but nothing disastrous, either. Our diplomats are doing their best, but I'm afraid I have little faith in their success. Egypt looks more and more like a luxuriant land ripe for conquest."

"The queen refuses to admit it."

"Who's going to succeed Saptah?"

"It's possible that Tausert might, but that would be a disaster for Egypt."

"Do you mean you're going to fight her?"

Setnakhte was slow to answer. "It's such a serious decision that I am still reluctant to make it. Civil war fills me with horror, for it brings nothing but misery and desolation. But how can it be avoided, if the queen persists in her blindness? It is not my own future that concerns me, it is Egypt's. I'm the only person who can unite Tausert's opponents and prevent our armies from crumbling away."

"The queen regent holds her office by right, Father," said his son quietly.

"Until Saptah is buried, that's true. But when the door of his tomb closes, a new pharaoh must be appointed."

The two men stared at each other for a long time.

"Will you be with me or against me, my son?"

"With you, Father."

▲

Greatly affected by the young king's death, Tausert had attended the beginning of the mummification rites, which were carried out by specialists from the Temple of Amon. In the presence of the priest who wore the mask of Anubis, she stated that the king had behaved justly, had committed no grave errors, and that he deserved to be recognized as a just man by the court of Osiris.

During the meeting of the Great Council, the queen had the weight of critical looks upon her, as if she were responsible for Saptah's death. So she restricted herself to a brief declaration, postponing the reading of the reports until later.

At her request, almost everyone then left the council chamber; the queen was left alone with the scribe who was acting as tjaty until a new tjaty could be appointed.

"What do you think of my decision to embellish Saptah's tomb?" asked Tausert.

"What everyone thinks, Majesty: you wish to pay a last act of homage to a king whom you hold in great esteem."

"Now tell me the truth."

"Well . . . some people do consider the honor excessive, bearing in mind his rather retiring reign, and they think you're trying to gain time by extending the mourning period."

"And they're quite right," confirmed Tausert.

"Your minister for foreign affairs has just returned to Pi-Ramses, Majesty. He went straight to see his father, who is receiving a constant stream of influential people."

"Setnakhte doesn't bother to hide his intentions anymore. Has he summoned you, too?"

The scribe was embarrassed, but dared not lie. "He has invited me to dinner, Majesty."

"Refuse the invitation."

"Majesty," he said awkwardly, "it would be unwise to create more tension. Also, the meeting may have a diplomatic aspect that could be useful to you. I shall try to persuade Setnakhte not to do anything unwise."

"What do you advise me to do?"

"To think only of Egypt and her happiness, Majesty."

Turning away from him, Tausert went into the palace garden, which was filled with birdsong. Even here, in the North, the day promised to be unbearably hot.

How alone she felt! If Bay had been at her side, he would have devised a way to prevent Setnakhte from harming her. And Paneb would not have restricted himself to hollow clichés and bland advice. But Bay was dead, and the Master of the Place of Truth was carrying out his sacred office, far from Pi-Ramses. Tausert could rely on no one but herself as she made her all-important decision: to give up the throne and leave the field free for Setnakhte, or to confront her adversary in a merciless battle.

40

Rumors were rife at the main barracks in Thebes: civil war, a seizure of power by the military, the violent death of Tausert, a Libyan attack. The fact that the troops had been placed on alert confirmed that something serious had happened, and that the stability of the Two Lands was threatened.

Every soldier was waiting impatiently for General Mehy to arrive. Around midmorning, he entered the great courtyard in a chariot drawn by two horses. After the officers had called the ranks to attention, he addressed the regiments.

"Soldiers, King Saptah has returned to the sun, and Queen Tausert will continue to exercise regency until the end of his funeral ceremonies. The northern garrisons and those on the frontiers have been placed on a war footing, to discourage any attempt at invasion during the period of mourning.

"And you need have no worries about your pay. I have just met the high priest of Amon and he assures me that, if the government at Pi-Ramses should fail to pay you, the temple at Karnak would see that you received everything due to you. You know that you have the newest and most effective weapons in the world. Thanks to this, and to your skill and courage, Thebes is well protected and has nothing to fear from the future: it will remain prosperous, whatever happens. And I am delighted to announce that, with my own money, I shall be paying you an added bonus, to reward you for all the intensive training you've undergone."

The good news was greeted with cheers. This lie did not cost Mehy very dearly for, by cleverly juggling his accounting figures, he had transferred a few assets from the town to the barracks without touching his own possessions.

Once the playacting was at an end, the general called a meeting of his general staff. They were all career soldiers whom he had bought and made wealthy; and they all obeyed him without question, particularly since they had to keep a close eye on their colleagues. Each man was quite willing to denounce another in order to retain Mehy's trust, and each knew that the smallest lapse would be fatal.

"This meeting will not be mentioned in any report," the general began. "Only one thing is certain: civil war is inevitable, and sooner or later the Theban troops will be asked to take sides."

"Is there any reliable information about what's happening?" asked a senior officer.

"We are going to hear from one of our agents, who has just come from the capital."

The man was utterly exhausted, but Mehy had given him no time to rest.

"Tell me, my man, who rules in Pi-Ramses?" he asked.

"The situation is very complex, General. The regent is still exercising power, and Setnakhte has not yet made a move against her. But his eldest son has resigned as minister for foreign affairs, in order to work with his father, who heads a powerful tribe. Setnakhte has never hidden the fact that he will not allow Tausert to become pharaoh."

"So the queen is isolated and will very soon be forced to withdraw."

"That's by no means certain. Tausert is considered an excellent administrator—much better than Setnakhte—and a number of senior officials would like to see her take supreme power. Setnakhte hasn't swayed them, and they have no intention of abandoning the queen, because they want to avoid a forcible seizure of power that might be followed by many others. And their position seems to be getting stronger."

"What about the army?" asked Mehy.

"It is very divided, General. Some officers share Setnakhte's wish to launch an offensive in Syria and Canaan and in the hinterland, so that our enemies give up all thought of attacking. Others favor Tausert's strategy of strengthening our lines of defense."

"In other words, the outcome of the battle between Tausert and Setnakhte is still uncertain."

"Assuming there is a battle . . ."

"What do you mean?

"Setnakhte is unwilling to start a civil war, and Tausert believes she is too weak to win one. They are watching each other like wild beasts defending their territory, neither of them knowing who will attack first."

"Who do you think would win?"

"At this moment, General, I cannot say."

Mehy thought for a moment, then asked, "What do people think of me, in Pi-Ramses?"

"You are seen as a powerful, honest man with a proper respect for the law of Egypt. Everyone knows how good the Theban troops are and admires the way you run the province. The new pharaoh, whoever that turns out to be, will need your support."

A wave of satisfaction washed over the general, but public recognition of his admirable qualities would not be enough. In such troubled times, he must be seen as the country's last and best hope.

"Go straight back to Pi-Ramses," he ordered his agent, "and set up a fast, confidential message system that will provide me with daily information on events as they unfold."

▲

As they made love Serketa feigned pleasure, though she was crushed beneath the weight of her husband, who had been getting visibly fatter in recent months.

Mehy was a dreadful lover, but she humored him because she knew he could sweep away the last few obstacles separating him from absolute power. Once that was done, and their position was secure, she would find consolation among better lovers—taking care that Mehy did not find out, for he set great store by his virility.

Sated, Mehy rolled on to his back. "I'm worried, my sweet love."

Serketa stroked the chubby feet he was so proud of. "Can't you put these uncertain times to good use?"

"I thought so before my informant arrived. But now I can't make up my mind whom to support."

"Setnakhte, of course."

"That might not be wise."

"Why not?"

"Because Tausert and Setnakhte are both predators, each as formidable as the other. I thought that when Saptah died the queen would no longer have the strength to fight, but I was wrong: she is demanding that his tomb be enlarged. In other words, she's planning to extend the official mourning period in order to gain the time she needs to consolidate her alliances with influential civilian and military officials, and then she'll try to strike Setnakhte down. If we side with him and she wins, she'll make us pay dearly for it. At best, I'd be sent into retirement; at worst, she'd have me sentenced for high treason. But there is no proof that she'll defeat Setnakhte. For years, he's been preparing for a decisive move to seize the throne, and I'm sure he won't give up at the last moment. Like the queen, he can't manage without Thebes and my support. So, my love, which side am I to choose?"

"At the moment, neither," replied Serketa. "We know Tausert and Setnakhte no longer have any direct contact at all, so assure each of them of your absolute loyalty. According to our information, whoever wins will emerge considerably weakened. And then we shall strike."

"You mean . . . ?"

"Yes, you must leave for the North with the main body of the Theban troops, and have yourself crowned pharaoh. Everyone will see you as a peacemaker, and no one will challenge your authority."

Mehy felt suddenly dizzy. "You really think . . . ?"

"The time is near, my tender love. Tausert's only a woman, and Setnakhte's an old man. Circumstances have never favored us so much."

The general leapt out of bed and slammed his fist into the pillow. "But there's still one thing standing in my way. The Place of Truth! It's because of that damned village that Tausert was able to extend the mourning period. If she hadn't done that, Setnakhte would easily have ousted her. Have you had any news from our ally in the village?"

"In his last letter he said he's now certain that the Stone of Light is hidden in the Brotherhood's main temple."

"Why doesn't he take it? What's he waiting for?"

"The temple's the most closely watched place in the village, after the strong room. There must be movable blocks of stone in the walls of the shrine."

"A sort of crypt?"

"Either underground or in a wall."

Mehy poured himself a cup of wine. "This time we really are getting close, I can feel it! Has our man got a plan?"

"He must be careful. Paneb made another attempt to lure him into an ambush, and only suspicion enabled him to escape."

"If we had the Stone, Tausert and Setnakhte would be nothing but puppets."

Serketa embraced her husband. "Be patient just a little longer, my tender lion. So far we haven't made a single mistake, and your reputation continues to grow."

He seized her by the hair. "Do you want power, too?"

"Only through you, my sweet love."

Mehy knew she was more dangerous and untrustworthy than a scorpion, but the future master of the country needed a woman like that.

— 41 —

How was he going to get into the Temple of Ma'at and Hathor without anyone seeing him, and have enough time there to find where the Stone of Light was hidden? The question obsessed the traitor, but he could find no answer to it. It kept him awake at night, and was making him lose his appetite.

Noting this, his wife had tried several times to persuade him to abandon his appallingly dangerous plan. This evening, she tried once again: "Even if you know where the Master has hidden the Stone, you'll never get at it. Why keep trying?"

"Because we have no future in this village, whereas a substantial fortune awaits us on the outside if we just keep our side of the bargain."

"If you're caught, the court will punish you severely."

"Stop being afraid, and concentrate on the fact that we're at last within reach of our goal. Instead of going with the others to the Valley of the Kings, I'm going to pretend to be ill. No, that's a bad idea—Ubekhet would be able to tell. Give me something harmful to eat. I must be genuinely ill."

"But the temple won't be left unguarded, will it? In any case, if you're the only craftsman from the starboard crew in the village and anything at all happens, you'll be the obvious suspect."

"You're right. I must think of something better."

Not at all reassured, she served him overcooked beans. "I've just heard something odd," she said, "but I don't know if it'll be any use to you."

"Tell me anyway."

"The wife of the port crew's goldsmith told me—in the strictest confidence—that the Master had ordered a golden goose from him."

"A goose? Are you sure you understood her properly?"

"Of course I am. When a sculptor was restoring the tomb of one of Ramses' daughters in the Valley of the Queens, he noticed that her funerary goods contained a damaged model of a goose. So Paneb has decided to have another one made."

"A golden goose," mused the traitor, "a guard goose, fat enough to hide the Stone of Light . . . not here, in the village, but in the Valley of the Queens. Can you find out any more about the tomb?"

"That woman's as talkative as she's self-important—it'll be easy."

▲

The court was buzzing with rumors, all on the same theme: Queen Tausert had admitted that she could not withstand the combined might of Setnakhte and his son. For several days in succession, she had spent long hours in conversation with the highest civilian and military authorities, and she had listened a great deal. So when a special meeting of the Great Council was convened, and Setnakhte was invited, he was in no doubt about the outcome of his conflict with her.

"Tausert has added clear-sightedness to her intelligence," he observed to his son. "Are you coming with me?"

"Since my resignation, I hold no government office. It would be pointless to provoke the queen."

"You've become a diplomat," said Setnakhte drily. "Tell my bearers to bring my litter."

The old man was so afflicted with rheumatism that he could barely walk, and he had no illusions about how long his reign would last. It would consist of waging a vigorous military campaign in Syria and Canaan before his son succeeded him.

When Setnakhte arrived at the palace, he was greeted with more marked courtesy than usual. He smiled to himself. The courtiers had recognized him as the new master of Egypt, and were congratulating themselves on this peaceful transfer of power.

When the queen appeared, dressed in a golden robe and wearing the Red Crown, Setnakhte could not suppress his admiration. Many, many men must have fallen in love with her, yet all had failed to break her oath of fidelity to her dead husband.

Tausert sat down on the throne.

"It is twenty days since King Saptah's mummification began," she announced. "Although we are in a period of deep mourning, we must continue to govern. That is what has led me to make a decision vital for the country's future."

She could have waited until the end of the mummification period to step down, thought Setnakhte, but perhaps it's better this way. Once the name of the future pharaoh is known, tensions will ease and Egypt will be the stronger for it.

"I have chosen a new tjaty," said the queen.

If lightning had struck the throne room, it could not have had more effect than those few words. By appointing a new tjaty, the regent was clearly stating her claim to become pharaoh.

Setnakhte understood: she was going to appoint him tjaty, in order to tie his hands more effectively. But in doing so, she was making a grave mistake. He would refuse emphatically, proving to the regent that he had nothing to fear from her.

"Tjaty Hori," commanded the queen, "come forward and swear the oath by the name of Pharaoh and according to the rule of Ma'at."

Hori, one of the priests from the Temple of Amon who had introduced the young Saptah to the sacred texts, was brought into the throne room. Tausert raised a golden feather, the symbol of Ma'at, and the new tjaty swore that he would faithfully fulfill his office, which the sages had said was "as bitter as bile."

Two priests dressed him in a heavy robe and a necklace decorated with two pendants, one heart-shaped, the other depicting Ma'at.

▲

Setnakhte's anger was worthy of the god whose name he bore. A positive thunderstorm had erupted in his Theban home.

"If she wants war," he bellowed, "she shall have it! Does she think for one moment that I'll bow the knee to her like this?

I'm not taking orders from her puppet tjaty!" Puce with rage, he at last ran out of breath.

Before he could start again, his eldest son said quietly, "I advise you to be careful, Father."

This warning stunned Setnakhte. "Surely you don't intend to switch to Tausert's side?"

"Of course not. It's simply that I've received some information about Tjaty Hori. On one hand, he should please you: he's honest, hardworking, free of personal ambition, thorough, and not easy to influence. On the other hand, his appointment means that the queen has made a judicious choice and that her new first minister will be neither a man of straw nor a puppet. He's already moved into Bay's office and started studying the decrees the queen plans to issue."

Setnakhte frowned. "This is simply a crude tactic to try to impress us."

"I don't think so, Father. Tausert wants to become pharaoh and she's giving herself the means to succeed."

"The means? An inexperienced little tjaty?"

"A new man, free from the taint of scandal or privileged relations with any tribe."

Setnakhte considered what his son had said. "But Hori has fewer than fifty days left in which to establish himself. No matter how talented he is, he won't manage it."

"You know perfectly well that Tausert will get round that obstacle by claiming that the new tomb isn't ready and that the date of the funeral rites must depend upon its completion."

"Then the Place of Truth must work faster."

"We have no hold over it, Father."

"Then who has?"

"Tausert herself, as regent and Pharaoh's substitute."

"Has the state no representative in the Brotherhood?"

"Yes, the Scribe of the Tomb."

"And what sort of man is he?"

"An old man called Kenhir, who has lived in the village for

many years and will not allow the government to interfere with its prerogatives in any way."

"You are remarkably well informed, my son."

"The Place of Truth has interested me for a long time. Without it, our kings would have had only an earthly existence; thanks to the Houses of Eternity created by the craftsmen, they continue to shine beyond death. In trying to use the Brotherhood for her own ends, Tausert is making a skillful move that we can't counter."

Setnakhte thought for a moment. "The most powerful man in Thebes is General Mehy. What will his attitude be, do you think?"

"He has always obeyed the rightful power."

"So he'll be loyal to Tausert."

"It seems likely."

Setnakhte felt very tired. "Everything I've built suddenly seems so fragile. I've never underestimated the queen, but she's even more formidable than I thought. She never reacts in the way one would expect."

"Precisely, because she is a true queen."

"So you admire her, too, do you?"

"She's a truly exceptional woman. How could anyone not feel profound respect for her?"

"Then we're beaten."

"Certainly not."

"What hope is there?"

"Let us stick to the line we have always followed. We don't wish to destroy Queen Tausert; we wish to save Egypt from very real danger. That wish must live in our hearts all the time; if we're right, it will give us victory."

Setnakhte felt the years weigh less heavily upon him; his son's words had given him new energy. "Tausert is wrong," he said, "and she's putting Egypt at risk. She must step aside."

42

Aapehti showed his father the little house that had formerly belonged to Imuni; the Scribe of the Tomb had granted it to the lad, who had refurbished it a little. "Are you satisfied?" he asked.

"You've done only the bare minimum," observed Paneb.

"Considering how little time I had, it's not too bad."

"You'll have to replaster the upper part of the walls, repair the front door, and renovate the kitchen. You must make your wife happy, and you can start by giving her a beautiful house."

The pretty, brown-haired girl sang to herself as she sorted the linen.

"I didn't want to get married," said Aahpeti sulkily.

"Too bad. It's done now, and you must become a responsible husband."

"Well I don't want to stay a plasterer all my life."

"Indeed? So what do you want?"

"You're the Master, I'm your son. Appoint me assistant crew leader."

Paneb raised his eyebrows. "Is that all!"

"I can supervise workmen just as well as you can."

"They are workmen, that's true, but first and foremost they are craftsmen and, even more importantly, they are Servants of the Place of Truth, whose call they have heard. So they don't like being told what to do by all and sundry."

"I'm not all and sundry!"

"Do you know how to draw a plan, build, draw, and paint?"

"Each unto his own. I was born to be a leader."

"To be a leader here," said Paneb, "you must have obeyed a great deal and understood the meaning of the work. You are still a long way from that."

"Everyone here's afraid of me. Isn't that enough?"

"It would be better if everyone loved and respected you.

Well, you can begin by restoring this house to perfect condition. After that, we'll see."

As the Master walked away, Aapehti contemptuously surveyed his modest home. Its furnishings consisted of two mats, three storage chests, a container for storing wheat, and some oil jars. His wife was washing the cooking pot and bowls before preparing the meal.

This second-rate existence was not what he wanted! He was already tiring of the brown-haired girl. He had his eye on the daughter of a stonecutter in the port crew; he was planning to take her on as a cleaning woman. Then there were the two married women who never failed to stick out their magnificent breasts to attract his attention whenever they went to fetch water.

Aapehti decided to enjoy himself and take advantage of life. And he wasn't about to take lessons in morality from his father, whose liaison with Turquoise was notorious!

"What do you want to eat, darling?" asked his wife.

"Eat on your own. I'm going out for a walk."

▲

Paneb hacked at the temporary seal on the door of King Saptah's tomb. During the craftsmen's journey from the village to the Valley of the Kings, he had not said a word. And, as Ched the Savior had refrained from making sarcastic remarks, the atmosphere was positively ominous.

The Master glanced up at the cliff tops, where Sobek's guards were posted.

"What's bothering you?" asked Unesh.

"Nothing specific."

"I had a nightmare last night, but I didn't tell Kenhir about it—if I had, he'd have interpreted it for hours. Like you, I'm uneasy."

The fragile, dried-mud seal resisted.

"Perhaps we should give up," suggested Karo, who was looking for signs of the presence of the evil eye.

"It's giving way at last," said Nakht.

"The Master must enter first," Pai reminded him, "but first of all we must have light."

A dozen torches were lit.

Inside, nothing seemed to have disturbed the peace of the tomb. The sculptures shone, the paintings lived, the hieroglyphs spoke.

"King Saptah shouldn't be unhappy with his eternity," commented Ched. "He'll certainly find it more joyful than his earthly life. Are we going farther in?"

Paneb led the way down the sloping passageway, lingering over each detail, as if afraid that the work might have deteriorated; but all the symbolic decoration was intact.

"It's impossible to enlarge it," said Ched. "We'd have to destroy all our work, push back the walls, and begin all over again. There's never been such an upheaval in the Valley."

"Then all we can do is excavate so as to lengthen the tomb," said Fened.

"The harmony would be destroyed, because the proportions would be wrong," objected Gau.

"We are all well aware of that," said Karo, "but we can't argue with a command from Pharaoh."

"This command's only from the queen regent," Casa reminded him.

"But she is acting as queen of Egypt, and as far as we're concerned her word has the force of law," said Thuty.

Fened examined the back wall of the tomb for more than an hour.

"What do you think?" asked the Master, when Fened had finished.

"We were right to stop here. Excavating any farther would be a big mistake. Either the rock holds some unpleasant surprises for us, or there is an abandoned funerary well back there, and we'd fall into it. In my opinion, it's impossible for us to obey the queen's command."

▲

The Master passed the news on to the Scribe of the Tomb and his new assistant.

Kenhir was furious. "I can't write to the regent and tell her you refuse to enlarge Saptah's tomb."

"We aren't refusing," said Paneb. "It's a question of insurmountable difficulties."

"Tausert will never permit a Master of the Place of Truth to speak in those terms. Difficulties are made to be overcome, are they not?"

"Usually, yes, but in some cases we have to yield to our raw material."

"That isn't like you, Paneb," said Kenhir acidly.

"Fened is absolutely adamant—and he's never been wrong."

"His position suits you very well," grumbled the old scribe, "seeing as you don't want to alter the tomb's proportions."

"Whether it suits me or not, it's a fact. If we pierce the back wall, we'll do great harm to King Saptah's House of Eternity. Surely the queen doesn't want that?"

Kenhir looked harassed. "I'm worried we may have got bogged down in the morass of politics. The queen needs time to strengthen her alliances and foil Setnakhte, so she's demanding extra work that will lengthen the mourning period."

"In other words, she's using us," said Paneb.

"And why not?" cut in Niut. "Her cause is a just one, so we should support her. Every woman who's reigned over Egypt has been an excellent ruler. Why should we side with an ambitious old courtier who ought to be obeying her? That man Setnakhte is a woman-hater, and that's all there is to it."

Kenhir felt his assistant's analysis was a little hasty, but he decided not to argue about it.

"I must speak to the queen," said the Master.

"That's just wishful thinking," retorted Kenhir. "With things as they are, she can't leave Pi-Ramses, where the situation probably changes from one hour to the next."

"In that case I shall go to her—I'll leave at once. I shall see Tausert and explain the facts to her."

▲

The Theban army, veteran and newly recruited regiments alike, was undergoing rigorous training. Most of the experienced soldiers were delighted to emerge from their usual state of inactivity, and the young recruits were trying out their new weapons, by which they were amazed and impressed.

Mehy galvanized even the slowest men, and he had no hesitation in wielding the bow or sword himself, to prove that he, too, was a warrior. He paid particular attention to the charioteers, the best in the land, and every day he was more delighted with his troops.

The news from the capital was that destiny had not yet chosen the victor. The appointment of Hori as tjaty had been a master stroke, and many courtiers and most senior officers were still wavering between Tausert and Setnakhte.

"General," his assistant informed him, "an officer from the river guards wishes to speak with you."

"Send him in."

The man was aged around forty, tanned and self-confident. He saluted and said, "General, you ordered us to inform you of any unusual activity on the river, and something unusual has happened. The Scribe of the Tomb has hired a fast boat."

"Where is it heading?"

"To Pi-Ramses."

"And is he on board?"

"No, the passenger's a giant of a man, at least four hand spans taller than I am."

So the Master was heading for the capital . . . but why? Could Tausert have summoned him, to appoint him to a senior position in her government? Mehy would have to take immediate action.

43

At long last, the wife of an artist from the port crew yielded to Aapehti's blandishments. It was a hot day, and she was sweeping her front step, bare-breasted and with her hair hanging loose, as he passed her house in the deserted alleyway. Filled with desire, their eyes met. She took off the reed kilt that she wore when doing the housework, and he took her in his arms.

Aapehti was still thinking about his mistress when he arrived home.

His young wife smiled at him. "I've made you a good lunch."

"Eat it yourself."

"I promise you it's delicious, darling. Won't you at least try some?"

"I've got to go out."

"Where?"

"To the boatmen's festival at Thebes. I'm taking part in the boat-pole match, and I'm going to win."

"May I come with you?"

"Certainly not. A housewife's job is to look after her house."

"Aapehti, I—"

He slapped her. "Stop pestering me. I hate women who never stop talking."

▲

Standing in the bow of a boat, a long, heavy pole in his hands, Aapehti was facing his fourth opponent. His aggression was frightening: he'd seriously wounded the three previous ones. Another two victories, and he'd be the hero of the festival—and this feeble specimen wasn't going to stop him.

As the twenty-eight oarsmen rowed the two boats toward each other, Aapehti let out an enraged roar and aimed a blow at his enemy's head.

Swift as lightning, the man dodged out of the way.

Aapehti's pole brushed his temple, but with his own he hit the young man in the belly and threw him off balance. To the immense satisfaction of the watching crowd, Aapehti fell into the water.

Despite the pain, he swam to the riverbank, where two young women helped him to his feet.

"I am a nurse," said the prettier one. "Let me see your wound."

"With pleasure."

"Where are you from?" she asked.

"My name's Aapehti and I'm the assistant to a crew leader at the Place of Truth."

"The craftsmen's secret village?"

"None other."

"So you know all the mysteries?"

"All of them."

"Are the other craftsmen as strong as you?" she cooed.

"I'm their champion. No one's ever beaten me."

"Except that skinny little boatman."

"He used cunning, the coward's weapon! If I ever meet him again, I'll smash him into a thousand pieces."

"Let's take a look at the damage."

As she was bending over him, Aapehti caught one of her breasts in his right hand. And he did the same to her friend with his left.

"That's enough of that, my boy," said the first woman firmly. "We're both married."

"In that case . . ."

Aapehti let himself be led to a temporary shelter erected on the bank. He lay down on a mat, gazing up at the sky. "I'm in a lot of pain. Is it serious?"

"It was a fierce blow, and you have a magnificent bruise. I'll apply some soothing herbs, but you should see a doctor."

"I'll think about it. But wouldn't a good massage be enough?"

"My friend will help me."

The two women busied themselves with one shoulder each. Offering no further resistance to what he considered caresses, Aapehti pulled them both toward him.

"That's enough!" protested the nurse again.

"You want me, and I want you—let's not make life complicated."

Furious, the friend tried to resist. He pushed her aside with the back of his hand. "Wait your turn, my little one. I'll deal with you afterward."

Aapehti tore the nurse's dress and revealed two round breasts, rather small but very appetizing.

"Let go of me, you brute! I don't want this!"

"Oh yes you do."

As he straddled his victim, her friend shouted for help. Aapehti ought to have shut her up, but he was too captivated by the delectable body of his victim, who was struggling in vain.

Just as he was about to rape her, several boatmen entered the hut and hurled themselves on him.

▲

Throughout the voyage, Paneb was silent, thinking of the journey he had made with Nefer when the Master showed him the three pyramids on the Giza plateau. Today, alone at the head of the Brotherhood, he was journeying to confront the queen regent in a world whose laws he did not know.

Thanks to a strong current and the skill of the sailors, who had agreed to sail at night, the distance was covered in less than six days, a record time.

At the landing stage in Pi-Ramses, he was stopped by some soldiers.

"I am Paneb the Ardent, Master of the Place of Truth."

The soldiers' commander looked at him in surprise. "No one told us you were coming," he said.

"I wish to see Queen Tausert as a matter of urgency."

"I shall go and inform her you are here. In the meantime, you are to stay aboard your boat."

Paneb could see nothing of the capital except the great canal lined with lush gardens and the port where warships were moored. The atmosphere was feverish, with soldiers patrolling the quays and the adjacent alleyways. He began to wonder if his journey might not end in crushing failure. Tausert was clearly engaged in a fierce battle for her own survival. Would she have time to receive him and listen to what he had to say?

Worriedly, he ate alone in his cabin, but the dried meat seemed flavorless and the red wine acid. So he went back up on to the deck, which the sailors were swabbing down with water. At the foot of the gangplank, the captain was talking with a colleague.

When he came back on board, Paneb asked, "Do you know what's happening in the city?"

"Everything's calm, but there are soldiers everywhere."

"Is Queen Tausert still regent?"

"Her authority still holds, and she's just celebrated a ritual to pacify Sekhmet, as if she wanted to prove her ability to dispel unrest."

"But has Setnakhte given up?"

"No, and he still has a lot of determined supporters. If you want my advice, it would be best to be like me and stay on the sidelines. I'm going to have a nap."

By refusing to enlarge Saptah's tomb, the Master of the Place of Truth was perhaps changing the destiny of Egypt. But his craft had its demands, and he must be the first to defend them.

The sun was beginning to set. As he lay down on his traveling mat, Paneb thought again of Nefer. In this situation, he would not have yielded a hand span of ground. Neither threats nor false promises would have made him deviate from the way of Ma'at. He, Nefer's spiritual son, swore that he would follow his father's example.

Just as he was dozing off, there came a knock at the door of his cabin.

"Soldiers are asking for you," said the captain's deep voice.

Paneb opened the door. "Who sent them?"

"The regent."

Although he was more sturdily built than Imuni, the officer who took charge of the Master had the same weasel face. "Hurry up," he demanded hoarsely. "The regent is impatient to see you."

The officer led the way while a soldier walked on either side of Paneb, and two others followed him.

"Anyone would think I was a prisoner," remarked Paneb.

"It's just a security measure."

"Will it take long to get to the palace?"

"Not too long, if we walk quickly."

Although he knew nothing of the layout of the capital, Paneb was intrigued by their route, which took them from alleyway to alleyway and into a suburb where, as they went, they saw fewer and fewer people.

When he saw half-built houses, he halted. "My foot's hurting—must be a sliver of stone."

The giant sat down and pretended to examine his right foot, but he leapt back up suddenly and, before they could react, grabbed the two rear guard soldiers by the hair and slammed their heads together. They dropped their clubs and collapsed, unconscious.

The officer tried to club Paneb on the back of the neck, but the Master rushed at him and kicked him in the belly, before leaping to one side to avoid a joint attack from the two remaining soldiers; their clubs met empty air. The giant knocked out the first of them with a blow from the side of his hand, then broke the second man's ribs with his elbow.

"Who sent you?" demanded Paneb as the false officer writhed in pain.

"We're . . . mercenaries," and he shut his mouth hard. It seemed the scoundrel was not going to reveal who was behind this attack.

Paneb turned to the other man and threatened to kick

him in his broken ribs. "Which way is the palace?" he said coldly.

"Second alleyway on the left . . . then head north."

Ignoring the defeated men's moans of pain, the big man strode away.

44

As soon as he saw Paneb approaching, the man guarding the first gate in the palace wall knew he was in for trouble. So he aimed his pike at this alarming visitor's belly and called other soldiers to his aid.

"My name is Paneb the Ardent, and I am Master of the Brotherhood of the Place of Truth. I wish to see Queen Tausert as a matter of urgency."

If he had not mentioned the mysterious Brotherhood, which even the most ignorant soldier had heard about, the guards would have given him short shrift.

An officer arrived, and again Paneb gave his name and his title.

The officer eyed him up and down. "Are you really who you claim to be?"

"Upon the name of Pharaoh, I swear it."

"I'll tell one of Her Majesty's scribes."

"You must tell the queen herself—at once."

"That's impossible. You must wait for an official audience and—"

"Believe me, I haven't time to wait."

The officer saw a strange, almost inhuman light in Paneb's eyes, and said, "Wait here. I'll try."

The soldiers were relieved. They too had sensed that the

big man would try to force his way through, and that his fists would be devastatingly effective.

Paneb sat down calmly on the ground. Slowly, one by one, the soldiers' pikes returned to the vertical. A long hour passed, but he showed no sign of impatience. Then a scribe appeared, accompanied by four guards armed with short swords.

The Master got to his feet.

"Please follow me," said the scribe. "Her Majesty has agreed to see you."

The flabbergasted soldiers realized that the magical power of the Place of Truth was no mere legend.

▲

As he climbed a great carved staircase, then walked down a long corridor, Paneb imagined how Nefer would have handled this meeting with a queen: by going straight to the heart of the matter and not mincing his words. But Nefer had possessed great calm, and that was not exactly Paneb's strongest point.

The high ceiling of the audience chamber was supported by two porphyry pillars, and the walls were decorated with palm fronds and spirals in soft blue.

The queen was sitting on an ebony chair whose feet were shaped like a lion's paws. She wore an austere brown tunic, and her hair was twisted into a simple bun, held in place by gold pins, throwing the perfect oval of her face into relief. She was lightly made up, accentuating the delicate features that made her the most beautiful woman in Egypt.

Instantly under her spell, Paneb bowed low.

"Tell me, Master," said the queen, "why have you undertaken this long journey without officially requesting an audience?"

"Because the order you gave me runs against the realities of the rock."

"What do you mean?"

"King Saptah's House of Eternity is ready to receive his body of light. As is the rule, it will look unfinished, but we cannot widen or lengthen it because the rock is unsound. If we tried, we'd almost certainly cause a disaster."

The queen stood up and leant gracefully against a pillar. "I am grateful to you. But do you understand the full weight of an order from the head of state?"

"I well know that Pharaoh is the supreme Master of the Brotherhood, and that I owe him obedience."

"Then perhaps you consider a queen regent's orders unimportant?"

"Indeed not, Majesty. That's precisely why I wanted to plead my cause in person. And I should tell you that the moment I arrived in Pi-Ramses someone tried to kill me."

Tausert was horrified. "Who dared do such a thing?"

"I was attacked by some mercenaries. I beat them, but they wouldn't say who hired them."

"Setnakhte—it must be. While you are here, you shall stay in the palace, and two soldiers will guard your room. You must understand that I need time, Paneb, and that the only way to gain it is to extend the seventy days of mummification and mourning for Saptah. And the only way of doing that is to resume work on his tomb. If you refuse, you will condemn me to death."

"Majesty . . ."

"Seventy days are not enough. I need longer."

"To destroy the finished work would be an unforgivable sin."

"I am not asking you to destroy it," said the queen, "or to build another tomb. That would take too long, and I must remain within limits my opponents will accept."

"And what are those limits, Majesty?"

"Another hundred days. If you take all the necessary precautions, surely you can do it?"

"We'd be certain to break through into a funerary well and cause serious damage to the tomb. Worse than that, such work would destroy its harmony. King Saptah's body of light would not lie in the magic crucible designed for it, and its survival could not be guaranteed."

The queen closed her eyes for a few seconds. "You could have put forward no better argument, Master. I felt deep affection for the late pharaoh and I shall do nothing that might harm him. The order is therefore canceled. Tjaty Hori will write to you to confirm my decision." She looked up at him. "The Place of Truth always wins its battles, doesn't it? It should give me a little of its strength."

"I was going to suggest precisely that, Majesty."

Tausert's look sharpened.

"We can't alter the structure and decoration of the tomb, but we certainly could gain time over his burial goods. Order beds, thrones, vases, and other precious things from us, things we couldn't make in the forty days between now and the end of the mummification. Without lying to you, and without betraying the spirit of the Brotherhood, I can tell you that we'll definitely need extra time—at least three months, in fact."

"It's a tempting idea, Paneb. But Setnakhte knows that Saptah's burial goods are already made and he knows how skillful the members of the Brotherhood are. Making a few extra pieces wouldn't take you so long."

The objection was a valid one, and Paneb could not answer it.

The queen returned to her throne and sat down again, her face serious. "Thanks to the Stone of Light, you create gold, do you not?"

The Master took some time to reply. "In certain circumstances," he said carefully.

"Then this is what I shall tell the court: the final work shall be done on Saptah's tomb, and several exceptional items will be created, notably gold scepters, crowns, and a large gold prayer shrine. The necessary gold will be taken from the Treasury and delivered to the village as soon as possible by special boat."

"In that case," said Paneb, puzzled, "there's no point making it by magic."

"There certainly is. I shall order so much gold that

Setnakhte will be provoked into reacting. He will protest loud and long that the Treasury will soon have to finance a war and that it must not give up its wealth like this. After much debate I shall agree, but I shall hold to my demands concerning Saptah's funerary goods. We shall then be in an impasse."

Paneb smiled slowly. "And you'll have to reveal that the Brotherhood can supply the extra gold but that it will take more time."

"There is one difficulty, though. Setnakhte will realize that the Place of Truth can create gold. Will its Master permit the regent to reveal that secret?"

"If the regent becomes pharaoh and continues to protect the village, why not?"

"But even if I do this, I am not certain to win," warned Tausert.

"Thank you for your honesty, Majesty."

"What is your decision, Master?"

"Since you are asking me to add to the deceased pharaoh's funerary goods, I have no reason to refuse."

Tausert turned her face away to hide her emotion. Once again, she saw Paneb as a statesman of great stature; but was he not one already, in the office he held?

"Majesty," Paneb asked awkwardly, "what will happen to you if you fail?"

"I do not know and I do not care. All I want is to save the country from a preemptive war, which would be a disaster. That is the only reason why I am fighting to hold on to power."

Paneb knew she was sincere. At that moment, she needed comfort so badly that she seemed fragile. If he had taken her in his arms, she would undoubtedly not have resisted him. But she was queen of Egypt and regent of the Two Lands, and he was the Master of the Place of Truth. What they had to build together was more important than a passion that had no tomorrow, since he would never leave the village or the Brotherhood.

45

After waiting impatiently for several days because of damage to his boat, which the boatyard took a ridiculously long time to repair, Paneb was at last ready to set off back to Thebes.

As he was leaving the palace, an officer of the guard hailed him. "Tjaty Hori wants to see you."

"The tjaty? But my boat is waiting, and—"

"Follow me."

There was urgency in the officer's voice. No doubt Queen Tausert had told Hori to give the Master more details about the plan.

The new tjaty had been at work since dawn. He was a stern, cold man, not given to pleasantries. As soon as he had—much to his dismay—been appointed, he had studied all the scrolls the queen had entrusted to him. Then he had had private meetings with each minister in turn, Setnakhte included, to gain an understanding of all their different areas of activity.

When Paneb was shown into his office, he looked up from his work and asked, "You are the Master of the Place of Truth, Paneb the Ardent?"

"I am."

"Do you consider yourself responsible for the craftsmen you command?"

The question took Paneb aback. "How dare you doubt it?"

"How can one fail to doubt a leader who appoints a criminal to an important post?"

"A criminal?" said Paneb, astounded. "Who on earth are you talking about?"

"The authorities in Thebes have sent me information about serious crimes committed by one of your craftsmen during the boatmen's festival. He unlawfully detained two women and tried to rape them. He admits that he is married and has been deceiving his young wife with his colleagues' wives. I sincerely hope the matter will be dealt with decisively, particularly since the guilty party is one of your right-hand men."

Paneb was appalled. "Tell me his name," he demanded.

"He is an assistant crew leader, and his name is Aapehti."

The Master felt as if the entire royal palace was falling about his ears. "Aapehti is my son," he revealed. "He is not an assistant crew leader, he's a humble plasterer."

The tjaty's face betrayed not a trace of emotion. "The case is too serious to be hushed up, particularly since your son was arrested outside the lands belonging to the Place of Truth. It is clear, however, that the village cannot be held responsible."

"Can he not be tried in our own court?"

"You have the right to ask that, certainly; but I would warn you against doing so. By trying to find extenuating circumstances, you would only slow down the case, and the matter would still be referred back to my court. And do not, I warn you, expect me to be lenient."

"Never mind the fact that he's my son. Aapehti is a craftsman plasterer, and he must be judged by those who trained him."

Hori stood up. "You are wrong to defy me, Master."

"I am simply observing our law."

▲

As soon as he learnt that the attack in Pi-Ramses had failed, Mehy left the main barracks in Thebes and went to the landing stage to meet Paneb's boat. He was worried that Tausert might have granted the Master new powers, or even appointed assistants to help him.

But Paneb was alone when he walked down the gangplank, and he did not have the triumphant look of a man who had just received unexpected honors.

"Did you have a good journey?" asked the general.

"Will you come with me to the prison, Mehy? I may need your support."

"The prison? Why?"

"I must get my son released, and take him back to the village to be tried."

"Your son? There must be a misunderstanding—I'm sure we'll soon clear it up."

"He's the one who caused trouble during the boatmen's festival."

"Ah," said Mehy. "It's a serious case, and the incident caused quite a stir. I'd like to help you, but . . ."

"Tjaty Hori already knows about it."

Mehy looked deeply apologetic. "I hope your son will realize that he did wrong, and will mend his ways."

As they neared the prison, Mehy dared ask the question burning on his lips. "Did you see the queen regent?"

"I had that honor."

"How is Her Majesty?"

"Still reigning."

"I'm reassured to hear it."

▲

As the Master seemed so uninterested in affairs of state, Mehy concluded that the journey to Pi-Ramses had been a failure. No doubt Paneb had presented the regent with some vain request concerning the Place of Truth.

Greatly relieved, the general dealt skillfully with the prison governor and ordered him to hand Aapehti over for transfer to the Place of Truth; the Master's presence reassured the governor.

When Aapehti was brought up from the cell to the governor's office, his spirits seemed undampened by his detention. "There you are at last, Father. I was starting to get impatient."

"The guards will take you to the village. You are to go straight home, and you are not to leave the house for any reason whatsoever."

"You know, I didn't do anything really wrong, and—"

"Do as I have said."

Hearing his father's tone of voice, Aapehti decided he had better postpone the discussion until later.

"I shall need all the details of the charges," Paneb told Mehy.

▲

The Master told Ubekhet, Kenhir, and Hay about his meeting with the queen. "I took the decision without consulting you," he ended, "but I had to give Her Majesty an answer."

"You did the right thing," said Kenhir. "She governs the country and we recognize her as our queen."

Hay was worried. "Shall we be able to produce all the gold needed?"

"It won't be easy," admitted Ubekhet, "because it's a complex process, and if we try to rush it we'll fail."

"Then we mustn't waste any more time."

"First we must convene the court and try Aapehti," said Paneb.

"I have read the evidence," said Kenhir, "and it's overwhelming. Aapehti has no excuse."

"Nevertheless, he belongs to the Brotherhood," Hay reminded him, "and he's a good plasterer. We all did foolish things in our youth."

"We aren't talking about 'foolish things,'" said Kenhir coldly. "We're talking about adultery, violent attacks, and attempted rape. Aapehti is a violent, brutish ruffian, and he mocks our rule of life. Several of the craftsmen's wives have lodged complaints against him. One or two may have enjoyed flirting with him, but most were forced—even cruelly beaten."

Paneb voiced no objection. He said merely, "The court will convene tomorrow morning."

▲

Uabet was in tears. "Why? Why did he do it? His wife adores him, and she'd do anything to make him happy, and yet he goes and mistreats married women. Oh, Paneb, it's like being tortured!" She sought refuge in her husband's arms.

"The gods have wounded you painfully," he told her, "but also they've given you Iuwen, who may be our future Wise Woman."

"You're right. She's as radiant as Ubekhet."

"It is time to leave, Uabet. The case will begin in a few moments."

"I'd rather stay here."

Paneb went to the gateway of the Temple of Ma'at and Hathor, outside which the villagers had gathered. On one side of Aapehti stood Nakht the Strong, on the other was Karo the Impatient.

Paneb faced the crowd and said, "It is my duty, as Master of the Place of Truth, to preside over this court; but the accused is my son, and I might be accused of partiality. On the feather of Ma'at, I swear that there will be none, but does one of you nevertheless wish to take my place?"

No one moved.

"Scribe of the Tomb," he went on, "please read out the charges."

Slowly, Kenhir listed Aapehti's misdeeds and detailed the complaints against him. The young man smiled, certain he'd be treated far more leniently by the village court than he would have been in Thebes, and that he'd win the long legal battle that was about to begin. His membership in the Brotherhood conferred on him a sort of impunity with regard to the outside world.

"The accused shall now defend himself," ordered Paneb.

"It's just idle gossip from females in heat!" protested Aapehti mockingly. "They got what they were looking for, didn't they? Why make such a fuss about it?"

"Does the accused admit the facts?"

"Well, yes, but they all enjoyed it. Women love real men, and fortunately that's what I am."

The villagers were shocked by such arrogance, and there was a heavy, painful silence.

"I shall now pronounce sentence," declared the Master. "The son of Uabet the Pure and Paneb the Ardent, the plasterer Aapehti, has been found guilty of serious violence and of violating the rule of Ma'at, and is no longer worthy to belong to our Brotherhood. He shall therefore be expelled from the Place of Truth. His wife shall have the divorce she wishes, and her husband is named as the guilty party in that matter, too. Aapehti shall never again pass through the gate of the village, and his name shall be expunged from the Journal of the Tomb; it shall be as if he had never existed. No craftsman shall recognize him as a member of either crew. Lastly, his father and mother disown him, and he no longer has the right to call himself their son."

46

The Great Council listened in astonishment to the regent's suggestion.

Setnakhte was the first to react. "But, Majesty, you're asking for an impossibly large amount of gold."

The queen met his eye. "Are you refusing to honor King Saptah's memory?"

"Indeed not, but we'll need our gold to finance a war that many—myself included—believe is inevitable."

"The last work on our dead king's tomb will soon be finished," said Tausert, "and his funerary furniture will be worthy of a great king. But I want him to have gold scepters and crowns, and a large gold prayer-shrine bearing the words of resurrection. Think about my proposal, and we shall speak of it again at the next meeting." She rose to her feet. "I wish to see you privately, Setnakhte."

The old man followed the queen into a small audience chamber, away from indiscreet ears.

"Majesty," he began, "I am strongly opposed to the removal of any gold from our reserves."

"Would you use force to prevent my people gaining access to the Treasury?"

"Majesty—"

"Such action would result in your imprisonment."

"My supporters would react violently. And you wish to avoid a civil war at all costs, don't you?"

"I admit that is true."

"Then give up this plan. For the moment, Egypt must conserve all its stocks of gold."

"I admit that, too. However, do you agree that Saptah's funerary goods should be completed as I have proposed?"

"In principle, yes, but—"

"I shall take nothing from the Treasury," promised Tausert, "but the gold objects will be made, nevertheless. Will you agree to that?"

"If you take nothing from the Treasury, how will you get the gold? By magic?"

"I shall ask the Place of Truth to do what is necessary."

Setnakhte's expression darkened. "Are you planning to deliver gold to the village in secret?"

"You know quite well that that would be impossible."

"So you believe in the legend. Can the Brotherhood really create gold?"

"I dare to hope so."

"What you're really hoping for, Majesty," said Setnakhte, "is to gain time."

"I am hoping to make Saptah's House of Eternity as glorious and powerful as it is required to be, according to our rites and our symbols. If you disagree with that duty—which, I remind you, was considered vital by our ancestors—you must say so before the Great Council."

"How long will the work take?"

"That is for the Master to say."

"He'll tell me, Majesty, you can be sure of that."

▲

Uabet's grief at Aapehti's expulsion was so deep that for several days she could not even speak. The Wise Woman tried to alleviate her suffering by means of herbal remedies, but the best remedy was the attentive presence of little Iuwen, who cared for her mother like an experienced nurse, following Ubekhet's instructions to the letter.

"Where's your father?" asked Uabet, when she could at last speak again.

"He's working," said Iuwen. Her face lit up in a smile of relief. "The Wise Woman said that when you started talking again, you'd start to get better."

"Get better? How can I? Your brother's left us."

"No, he was expelled from the village because he committed crimes."

Uabet did not have the courage to explain to Iuwen that the verdict was the equivalent of a death sentence. Since he was no longer a member of the Brotherhood, Aapehti would be tried for rape like any common criminal, and he would receive a capital sentence.

Uabet had never thought her husband would be so severe. He was the Master and he had had to act as such, not as a father; but Aapehti's mother could not accept what he had done. True, Paneb was not the only one responsible: the court could have reduced the punishment, but no one had come up with any extenuating circumstances. And because Aapehti had left the village insulting the craftsmen and the women he had seduced, no one regretted the severity of his punishment.

A monster . . . yes, Aapehti was a monster, but he was still her son, and she could not forgive Paneb for sending him to his death. If the father had pleaded his son's cause, the jurors would have listened to him.

Iuwen said timidly, "Won't you eat a little bean purée? I made it myself."

Uabet smiled. "I'm not hungry, darling."

"Please try—you will, won't you?"

Uabet gave in. "You're a magician already, Iuwen."

▲

At last a dark night arrived, when the moon was new and there were clouds in the sky. Chisel in hand, the traitor left the village by way of the burial ground so as to avoid Bad Girl, who would be dozing, as usual, beside the main gate.

This was the ideal moment to go to the Valley of the Queens, before Paneb assigned everyone's work the following morning. Aapehti's expulsion had caused the villagers both joy and pain. Joy because the boy, who was "rotten to the core," as Niut put it, would eventually have done serious harm to the Brotherhood; pain because Paneb and his wife were deeply hurt. But everyone admired the way the Master had put aside the fact that Aapehti was his son, in order to safeguard the Place of Truth.

Those who had thought Paneb would be a weak, easily manipulated Master were badly mistaken, thought the traitor. Nothing and no one would make Paneb deviate from his path, and he would be a merciless enemy.

The traitor set off along the path past the shrines of Ptah, patron god of builders, and the goddess of silence, then headed toward the Valley of the Queens. Its guards kept watch over all the Houses of Eternity where queens, princes, and the daughters of kings dwelt. But the traitor knew where the guards were posted and had no difficulty in avoiding them.

Warily, he entered the encampment where the craftsmen stayed when they were working in the valley for a long time. It was made up of little dry-stone houses and workshops for painting and sculpture. The traitor was afraid that one or two craftsmen from the port crew might have decided to sleep here, but the place was deserted.

He knew, from the information his wife had gathered, the location of the princess's small tomb where the golden goose containing the Stone of Light had been placed. The way was clear, but he still moved with great caution, like a hunted animal. And, once again, his caution prevented him from being caught unawares.

Well away from his post, one of the guards was dozing near the tomb. What was the best thing to do? Killing the man was one solution, but if he struggled, and thus alerted his comrades, the traitor was bound to be caught.

While he was searching in vain for some other way, fortune smiled upon him. The guard stretched, spat, and went off to patrol farther away.

This time, the way really did seem clear. But what if this was a new trap? Perhaps the guard had only pretended to go away, the better to lure him into a trap? The traitor cautiously circled the tomb several times, but he saw nothing out of the ordinary.

Feeling more confident, he broke the tomb's dried-mud seal. He pushed open the light wooden door, which would be replaced by one of stout acacia wood once the renovation was complete.

As he hoped, the golden goose had been placed very close to the entrance. It was a magnificent piece, sculpted so perfectly that you would have thought it was alive.

For a moment, the craftsman wished he did not have to damage such a work of art, but there was no alternative. Using his chisel, he removed the goose's head. Inside was a linen-wrapped packet. He would have to open the goose's belly to reach the hidden treasure. He cut the linen cord without difficulty, exposing fine plaques of gold, silver, and copper. These symbolized the celestial metals that would grant favor to the radiant, reborn princess, whom the goose must guard and lead toward the sky.

Treasures worthy of interest, certainly, but not the Stone of Light! Yet another hope dashed. He had been following yet another false trail. The Stone's true hiding place could only be the Temple of Ma'at and Hathor.

Discarding his disappointing booty, the traitor left the tomb and closed the door. He must overcome his disappointment and keep a cool head if he was to leave the Valley of the Queens without being spotted.

47

When he learned of the break-in, Sobek hurried down to the village and asked to see Kenhir urgently. As soon as the old scribe came hobbling out of the main gate, Sobek told him what had happened.

"A theft in the Valley of the Queens?" said Kenhir, aghast.

"Someone must have gone into the tomb, because the seal has been broken."

Kenhir immediately alerted the Master and Hay, and the two crew leaders went straight to the Valley. Together, they took stock of the damage.

"What a strange thief!" exclaimed Hay. "He opened the goose's belly to find out what was in it, but he didn't steal the plaques."

"They were of no interest—he was looking for the Stone of Light."

"Here, in this tomb?"

"He must have assumed that it was hidden in the guard-goose. Did any of your crew sleep at the encampment last night?"

"None that I know of. But I'll soon find out."

▲

Hay sent all the members of the port crew to see first Sobek and then the Master, who both questioned them thoroughly. Their statements, together with the inquiries made inside the village, confirmed that on the night of the theft no one had slept at the encampment.

"My men have been negligent again," lamented Sobek, "and I'm responsible."

"Stop blaming yourself," urged Paneb. "The traitor followed a false lead because he thought we had taken the Stone of Light out of the village. Now that he's realized his mistake, he'll start looking again."

"The men I posted in the Valley of the Queens aren't my best, I admit, but neither are they raw recruits."

"The traitor's unbelievably cunning and wary," the Master consoled him. "Remember, he's eluded all of us for years. I work beside him every day, yet I still don't know who he is."

"How can a man, however skillful, avoid making even the smallest mistake for so long? A demon from the cauldrons of hell must have eaten a craftsman away from inside him and then taken on his appearance."

"That's very possible."

The big Nubian stiffened. "You think so, too?"

"I think people can commit all manner of baseness, but this man has gone beyond all known limits. The Place of Truth initiated him, educated him, fed him, revealed the mysteries to him, enabled him to experience our spirit of Brotherhood. And all he wants to do is destroy it. You're right, Sobek: only a demon could have such a corrupt heart."

▲

The village gatekeeper bowed to the Master. "The Scribe of the Tomb is awaiting you at his house."

There was not a single housewife chatting on her doorstep, not a single child playing . . .

The door of Kenhir's house stood open. Niut had abandoned her broom and her brushes, and was sitting on a stool on the threshold.

"In his office," she murmured.

Kenhir had collapsed into his chair. "It's your son, Paneb.

Uputy brought us a copy of his sentence: slavery for life, in a copper mine in Sinai—and you know what that means. Aapehti appealed to the tjaty's court, but Hori refused to change the sentence. He merely reminded Aapehti that in Egypt the crime of rape carries a harsh penalty."

Paneb did not move. There was a long silence.

Eventually Kenhir said, "As he's no longer a member of the Brotherhood, there's nothing we can do to help him."

"You knew that when I proposed expelling him from the village, and so did everyone else who approved his expulsion."

"I'm not criticizing you in any way, but he's a young man, he might have changed, he—"

"You know he wouldn't."

Kenhir lowered his eyes. "You're right: he wouldn't. But you're going to be very much alone, in the future."

"That's a Master's lot, isn't it?"

"You no longer have a son, but you're growing closer and closer to your spiritual father."

"After lunch," said Paneb, "I shall call a meeting of the two crews at the temple, to assign their next work."

The big man's quiet courage fascinated Kenhir. Paneb the Ardent had had to master many fires in order to channel them into the service of the Great Work. Kenhir had been right when he sensed that the fiery-tempered young creature was exceptional; and—despite everything that made the two men so utterly different—Nefer had chosen wisely in naming Paneb his successor.

▲

When he got home, almost the first thing Paneb saw was a few grains of sand on the floor of the main room. They were scarcely visible, but Uabet normally kept the house so meticulously that they leapt out at him. In all the time they had been married, she had never once neglected her duties like this.

"Are you there, Uabet?" he called.

She emerged from her bedchamber, looking fragile and slender, dressed in the ceremonial robe of a priestess of Hathor.

"Are you going to a ceremony?"

"No. I have asked the Wise Woman to appoint me guardian of the shrines."

"Isn't that too heavy a task for a mother?"

"My son is gone, and my daughter is living at Ubekhet's house, where she is learning the art of healing. I'm leaving this house and I'm leaving you."

He was speechless for a moment, then he stammered, "You want . . . a divorce?"

"I have loved you, in my own way, as much as I could love. But you sent Aapehti to his death, and I can neither forgive you that nor remain your wife. If I stayed with you, I'd end up hating you."

"Have you thought about this carefully?"

"Doesn't what I've just said prove that?"

Paneb knew his wife well enough to know that she would not change her mind. "Grant me one favor, Uabet. Let me be named as the guilty party in the divorce."

She shook her head. "It's better that things be settled justly. Since I'm the one who's leaving, keep this house, which is worthy of the Master of the Brotherhood. I shall live in the one where Aapehti lived. His wife has gone back to Thebes, and the state will pay her a pension. From now on, I shall take care of the upkeep of the village shrines and prepare the offerings. I can think of no better life."

"Uabet—"

"Don't touch me, Paneb. My robe's new, and I don't want it creased."

▲

After several fruitless attempts by friends to bring about a reconciliation, the village court met and Kenhir pronounced the divorce in a calm and dignified atmosphere. Paneb was allocated a cleaning woman, who would also cook for him; Uabet chose to manage on her own. Paneb promised to pay her half his salary and half the revenues from his fields, and, as she was staying in the village, everyone could easily make sure she had all she needed.

All that remained was to determine the fate of Iuwen, who was called before the jury.

"Whose house would you prefer to live in," asked Kenhir in his warmest voice, "your father's or your mother's?"

The little girl thought for a while. "At the moment I have three houses: Daddy's, Mummy's, and Ubekhet's. I'm lucky, aren't I? I'd rather keep all three."

Neither Paneb nor Uabet raised any objection.

"Let's try things that way," agreed Kenhir. "If any difficulties arise, the court will convene again."

"To begin with, I'm going to help Mummy sort her things out. Then I shall help Ubekhet wash the phials." Iuwen took her mother's hand, and they left.

"That little girl never ceases to astonish me," said Kenhir. "She isn't like other children."

"You can't imagine how much she loves to laugh," said Ubekhet, "but when I'm teaching her she opens her mind so completely that the teaching fills her entirely and touches her very heart. Although she's still only a little girl, she already has greater depths than most adults have."

"So she'll be your successor?" ventured Paneb.

"If the gods wish it. But what about you? How are you coping with all this?"

"I'm all right. Perhaps I was wrong not to tell Uabet what I was going to do at Aapehti's trial, but I knew we'd disagree. Without me, and sharing her life more closely with the priestesses of Hathor, she will at least find a kind of happiness."

Ubekhet sensed that Paneb's inner strength had not diminished. On the contrary, the ordeal he had been through had made him become more intensely aware of his office.

Together, the two of them walked slowly toward the temple.

"According to the Ancients," said Paneb, "the greater a

man's abilities, the greater the trials he must face. I must have truly remarkable abilities."

"The way of a Master is both as vast as the universe and as narrow as the path of his own life. Depending on where you look, you will feel either that the temple is being built or else that failures are accumulating."

"In other words, I mustn't feel sorry for myself, even for a second."

"That would be a futile exercise, and anyway you have no talent for it. Besides, you must direct the Brotherhood's work, which plays such a central role in maintaining harmony on our earth. Do you think it would be sensible to waver between these two options?"

Paneb took her hands, and kissed them respectfully.

48

After the body blows the Master had suffered, some craftsmen expected him to be weakened or hesitant. But when he addressed them his voice was as strong as ever and his bearing as authoritative.

"Queen Tausert has ordered us to prepare King Saptah's House of Eternity and its burial furniture for the funeral rites. The starboard crew will leave tomorrow for the Valley of the Kings, to check that the tomb is complete in every last detail, and the port crew will begin making the things needed—Hay has the list of them."

"That won't take us long," commented Karo.

"Saptah's funerary goods are already finished," added the carpenter from the port crew.

"What I have just told you is the official version, which has been given out to the court at Pi-Ramses," explained the Master. "Our real work is going to be much more delicate. We are to create scepters, crowns, and a prayer shrine covered in hieroglyphs."

"Made of what materials?" asked Gau.

"Gold."

"Gold!" echoed Thuty in dismay. "But where are we going to get it from?"

"We shall produce it ourselves," said the Wise Woman, "provided we can obtain the support of our founding ancestor, Amenhotep I. Without him, our efforts would be doomed to failure."

The traitor was jubilant. To make gold, the Master would have to remove the Stone of Light from its hiding place and set up a special workshop, guarded by a number of craftsmen.

He would make sure he was one of them. Then all he would have to do was get rid of one or two colleagues, by whatever means necessary, and steal the Stone.

▲

Amenhotep I was honored at several festivals, the most important of which featured a procession and a memorable banquet. But the one the village was preparing to celebrate was rather different, since each villager was invited to meditate before their founder's statue. For Amenhotep was the supreme judge and, according to the inscription engraved on the plinth of the statue, "He Who Had the Power to See."

As the Wise Woman stood before the statue, the craftsmen held their breath. The Brotherhood's future depended on the ancestor's reaction to her silent prayer. Either they would begin the process of manufacturing magical gold, or they would inform the queen regent that the Place of Truth was giving up the attempt, leaving the way free for Setnakhte.

Ubekhet stood for a long time in meditation, as if explaining to Amenhotep the reasons for this important prayer. When she eventually opened her eyes, the statue had still given no visible sign of approval. Paneb could not help thinking of how distressed Tausert would be when he told her the Brotherhood could not do as she had asked.

But just as Ubekhet was bowing a respectful farewell, the statue nodded, signifying Amenhotep's consent.

▲

The lookout at the First Fort, who was watching the road to the village, almost choked on a piece of flat cake.

"Run and tell Commander Sobek!" he shouted, shaking his off-duty colleague awake. "There are at least a hundred soldiers coming!"

"And you're going to face them single-handed, are you?"

"Well . . . no. I'll run with you."

"But that'll mean leaving the fort unmanned."

"The two of us can't defend it on our own."

The guards were by no means cowards, but the situation was so serious that it demanded Sobek's presence, and getting themselves killed would serve no use at all.

By a stroke of bad luck, the attack had come on the first rest day for more than a month, and the guard was lighter than usual. Fortunately, though, Sobek was in the second fort, checking the state of its brick walls.

"Sir, sir, there's an army out there, with chariots!"

"Block the road with boulders."

His men hurriedly obeyed, and Sobek positioned himself in front of this modest blockade. At the sight of him, the leading chariot slowed down, then came to a halt only a few paces away.

The Nubian recognized Mehy's helmet and breastplate. "Where are you going, General?"

"I've had orders to escort the Master back to Thebes."

"Orders from whom?"

"From Setnakhte himself."

"His orders carry no weight here."

"Are you serious?" demanded Mehy.

"I take orders only from Pharaoh, the Master, and the Scribe of the Tomb."

"You know perfectly well that your men are no match for my soldiers."

"We'll see about that," said Sobek calmly.

"Don't forget that I have to obey orders, too."

"If Setnakhte wants to see the Master, tell him to come to the lay workers' encampment. And if the Master agrees to meet him, there'll be no problem."

"Is that all you can say?"

"No," said Sobek. "I can also give you a warning: if you attack us, we'll defend ourselves."

▲

Setnakhte found it difficult being a guest in Mehy's luxurious home. He could not bear Serketa's childish babbling, and was impervious to her charms. So today he had shut himself away in an office that looked out on to the garden.

"The general has just returned," Mehy's steward informed him.

Warily, the old man made his way to the entrance hall. "Have you returned alone, General?"

"As I predicted, Sobek was unimpressed by the show of armed force."

"So you tamely withdrew?" asked Setnakhte angrily.

"If I'd attacked, Sobek's archers would have fired on my men and there would have been many dead, which would have done untold harm to your reputation."

Setnakhte's anger abated. "That's very true, General. But this Place of Truth seems like an impregnable fortress!"

"That is what successive pharaohs have wanted, ever since its creation."

"Surely the Master won't dare refuse to receive me?"

"Sobek suggests that you go to the lay workers' village. Paneb may meet you there." Mehy suppressed a smile. He sensed that Setnakhte was profoundly humiliated and would make the Brotherhood pay dearly for its arrogance.

"You're governor of the west bank, Mehy. Have you no hold over the Place of Truth?"

"My role is simply to see that no harm comes to it. That's why Sobek's so sure of himself. He knows perfectly well that my soldiers won't attack him."

"Not even if Pharaoh ordered them to?"

"That would be different," agreed the general.

▲

"Tact is not your strong point," Kenhir told Paneb, "but it would be better if you met Setnakhte. Whatever happens, and even if Tausert becomes pharaoh, he'll still be influential. You must think of the Brotherhood's safety at all times, even if you find some things distasteful. And to make sure that everything is done correctly, I shall take your invitation to Setnakhte myself."

"Very well, Kenhir."

The old scribe was relieved. Not only had Paneb not been broken by his divorce, but he was actually gaining in stature by unflinchingly accepting the obligations of his office.

"Setnakhte is a skillful, wily old courtier, and he'll set all kinds of traps for you. Don't talk too much and try to stick to a few simple truths."

"You can rely on me."

Kenhir saw the Master's fierce expression, and wondered if this meeting really was desirable; but offending Setnakhte still further would turn him into an implacable enemy.

"Promise me you will control yourself, Paneb," he said.

"A few simple truths: that is the line I shall follow."

▲

"Are we going to be attacked, Master?" asked Fened, when Paneb met his crew in the main street of the village.

"You seem very worried."

The stonecutter was affronted. "We all have families, so of

course we're worried. Setnakhte's an ambitious man, and he wouldn't think twice about using violence against us."

"I'm worried, too," said Pai. "Why does Setnakhte want to get into the village?"

"To learn our secrets."

"Send him back to Pi-Ramses," advised Karo.

"No, don't do that. It would be better to negotiate with him," urged Renupe.

"Be firm and clear," said Gau.

"That fellow has no business with us," put in Nakht. "Sobek should do his job as usual."

"I shall speak to Setnakhte," said the Master.

"I'm glad to hear it," said Ched approvingly. "I'm sure you won't disappoint him."

49

She was magnificent. Absorbed in her embroidery, she was working passionately. Her long, slender fingers seemed tireless; her posture was as graceful as a dancer's. Whatever she did, she endowed it with beauty and dignity.

"Turquoise."

The beautiful redhead looked up. "Paneb! Shouldn't you be meeting Setnakhte?"

"He hasn't arrived yet."

Turquoise laid down her fabric and needles. "My answer is no, Paneb."

"But I haven't asked you a question yet."

"Don't pretend you weren't going to remind me that you're a free man now. It makes no difference to me whether or not you're divorced. A vow is a vow: I shall never marry."

"I'd hoped—"

"When are you going to give up that hope?"

"What do you think of Uabet's decision?"

"Uabet the Pure is a priestess of Hathor, whose task is to look after the shrines. The rest is not my business."

"And what do you think of my decision about my son?"

"I'm only interested in the Master's decision. And the Brotherhood thought it right."

Filled with desire, Paneb took Turquoise in his arms.

"Haven't you got an important meeting?" she inquired.

"Yes, with you."

▲

On the orders of Beken the Potter, the lay workers had left their village. The only exception was Obed the Blacksmith, who had been given permission to stay in his forge on condition that he did not set foot outside it. Sobek and ten of his men were keeping watch over the area.

Setnakhte was vexed that the Master was not already there. "I am not in the habit of waiting," he told Kenhir.

"He won't be long."

"You should tell him I'm here."

Shaking his head, Kenhir walked slowly toward the great gate. The gatekeeper greeted him, pushed the gate open to let him through, then closed it again.

Although he was by no means a timid man, Setnakhte suddenly felt very alone. He was not at all reassured by the presence of the Nubian guards with their hostile eyes. He was sure that, if the craftsmen attacked, Sobek would not lift a finger to help him. Trying to get away, or simply asking to return to the government buildings, would make him look ridiculous. But Tausert had probably foreseen his reaction and organized a fatal ambush for him. The old man tried hard to reassure himself by thinking of the law of Ma'at, which the regent must respect. But why was there still no sign of the Master?

The more time that passed, the more Setnakhte had to face

facts: on the regent's orders, the Brotherhood was going to kill the last person who could prevent her from taking power. Still, at least he would die on his feet, and eye to eye with the man who was cowardly enough to strike him down.

Nevertheless, when the great gate opened he found that he was trembling.

Paneb the Ardent came toward him; Setnakhte could hardly believe how big he was. The Master was wearing only a workman's leather kilt, and he seemed as indestructible as a mountain. Setnakhte understood why rumor had it that he was capable of knocking down ten men single-handed.

Still under the spell of Turquoise, with whom he had just made love, Paneb greeted his visibly uneasy visitor. "You wanted to see me?"

Setnakhte quickly pulled himself together. "Your welcome is not a very warm one, Master."

"As you must know, the Brotherhood is overloaded with work, and I haven't time for long conversations. Tell me what you want, and I'll try to meet your demands."

"Very well, as you've gone straight to the heart of the matter. The queen regent has ordered you to make several gold objects, but not one ounce of gold will be delivered to you, because we must keep our reserves intact in case war breaks out. Either you cannot obey Queen Tausert, or you're producing the gold yourselves."

"I shall obey the regent."

"Then the legend is true?"

"In certain circumstances, yes."

"What circumstances?"

"That is the secret of the Place of Truth."

"And what if Pharaoh himself ordered you to produce gold continuously, for supply to the Treasury?"

"I would explain that that's impossible. We work only to fashion eternity for the royal soul."

Setnakhte knew the value of the Master's revelations—very

few people had had the chance to hear them. "You could have lied to me, Paneb," he said.

"That is not in my nature."

"Then go on answering me truthfully. How long will it be before King Saptah's funerary goods are ready?"

"About three months."

"That's a very long time."

"The gold shrine is very complex to make, and engraving the hieroglyphs requires great precision—it can't be done quickly."

Setnakhte scowled. "I see. You've taken the queen regent's side. You may live to regret it, Master."

"Why should anyone criticize the Place of Truth for doing what it was founded to do, and its craftsmen for doing their job?"

"Is there no way you could finish the order more quickly?"

"No."

"I suggest you think again," said Setnakhte.

"I have only one thought in my head: to fashion objects of eternity so that King Saptah may act fully in the otherworld."

"You seem to think I'm no more than a low schemer. Your tricks won't stop me ascending to the throne and saving Egypt. And when I've done so, I shall break you."

▲

In the starboard crew painters' workshop, Unesh the Jackal was nervously washing a palette. "I've got a bad feeling about all this," he said.

"It's not the first time the Place of Truth has made gold," retorted Gau, who was working on a preparatory drawing of the gold shrine.

"True," agreed Pai. "But all the same, we're caught between a rock and a boulder. And who is it that's going to be reduced to pulp?"

"The Master knows what he's doing," said Gau.

"But supposing he doesn't?" asked Unesh worriedly.

Nakht came into the workshop. "The meeting's over," he said. "Come on."

The three painters followed him to Kenhir's house; the other craftsmen had gathered outside.

"Paneb's inside, talking to Kenhir," said Thuty.

"That's a bad sign," said Casa. "Setnakhte must have given him an ultimatum."

"Probably just a cheap show of resentment," said Ched.

"I don't think so," objected Karo. "A man whose name is marked by the god Set must by his very nature be dangerous."

"He won't be very dangerous if he has to face the Master," said Ipuy. "Paneb's the one who really possesses the strength of Set."

"The village gate is closed to outsiders as usual," said Didia, "and no old courtier's going to break it down."

"If I had him in front of me now," said Userhat, "I'd rearrange his face for him—then he wouldn't be so haughty. Who does he think he is?"

"I suppose you think Tausert will treat us better?" asked Casa aggressively.

"She is the regent, and that's all there is to it."

"Like Casa, I'm uneasy," confessed Fened, his face solemn.

"I told you," repeated Unesh, "I've got a bad feeling about all this."

The Master came out of Kenhir's house, and the craftsmen crowded round him.

"What did Setnakhte want?" asked Pai impatiently.

"Oh, merely to acquire our secrets and our absolute obedience."

"You didn't . . . you didn't give in to him, did you?" gasped Ipuy.

"What do you think?"

Nakht the Strong smiled broadly. "May I embrace the Master?"

"Gladly—it will make me even more determined to preserve our freedom."

The others all followed Nakht's example, sharing the spirit

of Brotherhood which, above and beyond day-to-day cares, united the craftsmen like the stones of a pyramid.

"Have you designed a special workshop for making the gold?" asked Unesh.

"A House of Gold will be set up in the temple," said Paneb.

"Who's going to guard it?" asked Casa.

"You'll all have more than enough to do, so the guards will be Ebony, Bad Girl, and the priestesses of Hathor."

50

The traitor paced up and down the main room of his house. He was furious. Not only had the Master deviated from custom by not choosing the House of Gold's guardians from among the craftsmen, but he had also sent them home to worship the ancestors, on the very morning when the magical work was beginning. All these precautions meant the traitor could not get anywhere near the Stone of Light. No fewer than four priestesses of Hathor were on guard at the gateway, and four more prevented anyone entering the covered part of the temple.

"I hope you haven't dreamt up some crazy plan," said his wife.

"For the moment, the treasure's out of reach. I'll have to get on with my work, like the others."

"The Master's so suspicious that you'll never be able to steal the Stone."

"Yes I will," said the traitor. "Paneb may not be able to create all the gold we need, in which case he won't stay Master for long. And if he does make enough, he's bound to think the greatest danger is over, so he'll relax the security precautions."

His wife sighed. "Won't you ever give up?"

"I've gone too far to give up—and I know where the Stone's hidden. We'll succeed, I promise."

"I'm afraid. Won't Paneb eventually find out who you are?"

"By then it will be too late, both for him and for the Brotherhood."

▲

"Setnakhte has returned to Thebes," Hori told Queen Tausert. "According to reliable informants, he's far from satisfied. His plan failed, and the Master is keeping his promises."

"I never doubted that he would."

"I did, Majesty. After all, you appointed me to this post to doubt everyone."

"But you've met Paneb," Tausert pointed out.

"My opinion of him does not enter into it. In the battle against a courtier as skillful as Setnakhte, alliances can change at any time."

"You're very pessimistic, Hori."

"No, Majesty, merely realistic."

"Have we lost ground in the last few days?"

"No. In fact, if anything, we've gained some."

"Then why are you so gloomy?"

"Because even if you win, you'll lose."

Tausert approved of Hori's plain speaking. She was glad she had chosen a man from the temple, detached from the realities of this world, a man who would have no truck with flattery.

"That sounds like a riddle. What do you mean?"

"I've studied the members of the court and those close to Setnakhte. His eldest son stands head and shoulders above the common herd, and is the only one who has the stature of a true statesman. He supports his father, who certainly knows very well how talented his son is."

"Do you really think I will bend the knee without a word?"

"I try every day to weaken the influence of Setnakhte's supporters, Majesty, and the results are by no means bad. But I believe the son will soon become far more formidable than his father. Getting rid of Setnakhte would be only a personal victory, not a true one."

His words troubled the regent. "What do you advise me to do?"

"To persevere, if you believe you are right, but to be aware that, whatever the circumstances, what matters is Egypt, not yourself."

▲

The door of the covered temple closed behind the Wise Woman and the Master.

The Master had removed the Stone of Light from its hiding place, and the Scribe of the Tomb had given him the *Book of Accomplishing the Work,* which had fallen from the sky through a window in space and was kept in the Brotherhood's library. It contained both the words needed to drive away evil forces and also the temple-building methods devised by the Ancients.

Ubekhet had brought phials, pots, and vases. Several torches illuminated the chamber where she and the Master were going to try to create gold. She was dressed in a long red robe, Paneb in a white kilt. Slowly they paced round the chamber, halting at each of the four points through which the four different types of light passed: dawning to the east, powerful to the south, accomplished to the west, and secret to the north.

In the center lay the Stone.

"O thou who cannot be enslaved," began the Wise Woman, "O indomitable one, whom no hand can cut or engrave, grant us thy Light."

The stone took on a bright green hue and a soft light began to shine from all its faces. The work could begin.

"Prepare the bed of Osiris," the Wise Woman ordered the Master.

Paneb used five looped crosses, the "keys of life," and ten Set-headed scepters to form a couch, on which he laid a dish containing grains of barley. A dish that was the body of Osiris.

"Now let us open the chest of mysteries."

Standing on either side of the Stone, the Wise Woman and the Master lifted the top part of it, as though it were a lid.

"I know the Light that is inside," said Ubekhet. "I know its secret name. I know that it is at once the Word and the deed."

"I have seen the chest of knowledge," Paneb went on. "I know that it contains the parts of the dismembered body of Osiris, who is at once Egypt and the universe. Only the Light reunites them."

From the Stone, the Wise Woman took a sealed vase. "Here is the blood of Osiris, the mysterious liquid that gives birth to the flood and to all forms of energy. With its aid, matter can be transformed into spirit. Let us fashion the Divine Stone."

From the containers the Wise Woman had brought, Paneb took small quantities of gold, silver, copper, iron, pewter, lead, sapphire, emerald, topaz, hematite, cornelian, lapis lazuli, red jasper, turquoise, and other precious substances. He crushed them and poured them into a cauldron containing bitumen and acacia resin. Twenty-four minerals, corresponding to the twelve hours of the day and the twelve hours of the night, would unite under the effect of the fire, while at the same time their essential qualities would be released.

"Henceforth you are safe from sudden death," said the Wise Woman to the bed of Osiris. "The heavens will not fall, the earth will not crumble."

The long and delicate operation of regulating the fire began. Sometimes it must be stoked up, at others it must be damped down. At the end of the first day, Ubekhet added extract of styrax to the contents of the cauldron. On the second day Paneb filtered the mixture, which then had to rest for two days. When he put it back into the cauldron, he mixed it with terebinth resin and aromatic substances; then he crushed the mixture and wrung it out in a cloth before heating it up again.

At the end of the seventh day, an eye of Horus appeared on the surface of the molten stone in the cauldron.

"We are on the right path," said Ubekhet with relief. "Now

we must separate the mixture into a very fine powder and a resinous layer. Only the blood of Osiris can ensure that we succeed."

Ubekhet broke the seal on the vase she had taken from inside the Stone, and poured a few drops of silvery liquid into the cauldron. Almost instantly, the molten rock separated. Paneb collected the powder from the surface and left the resinous substance in the bottom of the cauldron.

"Spread it out on the dish."

The powder smelt strongly and was incredibly fine. The Master felt like a seedsman sowing a new form of life.

The Wise Woman resealed the vase, put it back inside the Stone, then closed the Stone again. The green glow faded and was replaced by an intense red radiance. She felt dizzy, and swayed on her feet.

Paneb looked at her worriedly. "Ubekhet, are you all right?"

She regained her balance. "Yes. Let us continue."

From the cauldron, Paneb collected a black paste, "the Divine Stone," which would be used only in the House of Gold to coat the most precious statues and endow them with indestructible strength. But this long work would remain pointless and the Divine Stone ineffective until the final phase of the work was carried out successfully.

"We should wait until morning," said Paneb, "and sleep tonight—you're exhausted."

"We can't. Even a moment's inattention would be fatal."

The Wise Woman stretched out her hands above the head of Osiris. "The parts of your body represent the secret forces of the universe; brought back together, they make it live. The potter shall add some of the very first water. May it act upon the raw material and may the heavens bring forth the gold of rebirth."

The Master did as she had instructed.

"May the radiant spirit be born," went on the Wise Woman. "Osiris is life, the one and the many. May the Great Work be accomplished."

Ubekhet and Paneb could do no more. They had followed the Ancients' instructions to the letter, and now they must await the verdict of the matter itself.

In silence, they called upon Nefer the Silent, who, in his flesh and in his spirit, had experienced the transmutation they were trying to repeat.

Osiris remained inert.

Just as Paneb was beginning to fear they had failed, a gold stem emerged from Osiris's heart; it was soon followed by two others, springing from his eyes. And then the entire body came back to life. The god's hair was transformed into turquoise, the top of his head into lapis lazuli, his bones into silver, and his skin into gold.

51

"They're taking a long time," remarked Karo, throwing the dice.

"Making gold isn't as easy as breathing, you know," replied Casa. "My throw."

"You've lost again," said Gau.

"It really isn't my evening."

"You lost yesterday evening as well, and you already owe us a dinner."

"Have you seen Unesh?" asked Userhat. "I've been looking for him for ages."

"He went off toward the temple," replied Karo.

"He's as curious as ever, that one. If he thinks he's going to find anything out before the rest of us do . . . Still, a man can always dream."

"Well, there's no bribing the priestesses of Hathor,"

lamented Ched, who was content to watch the others play. "Anyone would think my charm had stopped working."

"I'm not worried," said Renupe. "The Wise Woman and the Master can do what's needed."

"That may not be enough," said Pai anxiously. "The raw material has never been tamed, so it's free to behave as it likes. There's no guarantee that enough gold will be produced in the time we have."

"Do what we nonplayers do," advised Ched. "Get some sleep."

"I'd probably have a nightmare."

"Why? Isn't your conscience clear?"

"That's got nothing to do with it."

"Stop teasing him, Ched," said Userhat.

"Are you anxious, too?"

"Yes—and irritable with it."

"Steady on," said Karo. "There's no point getting yourselves worked up like this."

Ched started whistling a tune, and Userhat shrugged and poured himself a drink.

Some of the craftsmen were calm, some were impulsive, but they were all on the edge of nervous collapse. Yet another night was beginning, and still the door of the temple remained shut.

▲

The traitor's wife woke him up. "They've come out. Quick, come and see."

Jolted out of a dream in which he had seen himself crowned with gold and wielding Pharaoh's scepters, the traitor asked blearily, "Who are you talking about?"

"The Wise Woman and the Master."

Suddenly wide awake, he dressed hurriedly and ran out of the house. Other craftsmen and several priestesses of Hathor had already assembled before the gateway, which was being guarded by Turquoise, assisted by Ebony and Bad Girl.

"Have they really finished?" asked one of the women.

"Yes, at dawn," said Turquoise.

"And gold was created?"

"They'll tell you themselves."

As she spoke, Paneb and Ubekhet came out through the temple gateway. The Wise Woman was visibly exhausted, and even Paneb looked a bit tired.

"Did you succeed?" asked Fened at once.

"The ancestors looked favorably upon us," replied Ubekhet.

▲

Mehy watched his troops as they trained. The charioteers charged at top speed, making no attempt to avoid the foot soldiers. There were several injuries, and one man was killed, but Mehy was unmoved. The troops must gain battle experience in readiness for the coming war.

Satisfied with what he had seen, Mehy galloped home. He used his horses hard, and it did not worry him that they often collapsed and died when their hearts gave out. They were only animals, after all, and no one but the old sages of Egypt believed that an animal embodied divine power.

As the general was dismounting, his steward ran up to him.

"My lord, your wife . . ." The man was trembling.

"What do you mean, 'my wife'?"

"She flew into a violent rage and broke many precious things. No could stop her, and I—"

"Where is she?"

"In her bedchamber, my lord."

Mehy went into the house. As he walked, his feet crunched on broken vases and pots, more and more of them as he neared Serketa's bedchamber. The shrieks coming from inside were those of a hysterical woman in full cry.

She was hurling jars of expensive ointments at the walls, soiling their delicate paintings. She was leaping about like a grasshopper, and did not even notice that her husband was there. Mehy seized her by the hair and slapped her, so hard that her left cheek split open. Blood spattered her dress, frightening her.

"What . . . ? Who dared . . . ? Is it you, Mehy?"

He grabbed her by the shoulders and shook her until the look in her eyes returned to normal.

"This attack of hysteria is over!"

"Over," she repeated, in the voice of a little girl caught doing something she shouldn't. Then she collapsed onto a pile of cushions.

"Why did you get yourself into this state?"

"I don't know anymore . . . Oh yes, I remember. A letter. A letter from our ally in the Place of Truth. He says the Master and the Wise Woman have made gold. They're all-powerful now, and we can do nothing against them, nothing."

"On the contrary, that's excellent news. Now we know for certain what the Brotherhood is capable of. Its secrets are more vital to us than ever."

"I'm afraid," whimpered Serketa. "People who can perform such miracles will tear us apart like desert vultures."

"Stop talking rubbish. Pour yourself some of your decoction of poppies, and pull yourself together. But start by washing yourself and changing your dress."

Meekly, his wife scuttled into the bathing room.

While he waited for her, Mehy wondered how to deal with this new and dangerous development. The Brotherhood were going to do what the queen wanted. She would gain confidence and pride from her success, and establish herself even more firmly as a woman of power. But it would be only a transient success, which would not deter Setnakhte and his son. In any case, they were too committed to their battle for the throne to submit to Tausert now: to do so would be to sign their own death warrants.

Civil war was inevitable. But which side should he take? Which side offered him the better chance of eventually defeating the victor?

"I'm feeling better, sweet love, much better." Wearing a new dress, freshly perfumed, and with the wound on her cheek soothed with a salve, Serketa seemed once again in control of herself.

"I don't care for people who can't face up to difficulties, my tender quail."

"You're right," she agreed. "But I simply lost my temper. And you can rely on me to fight the Brotherhood until it's destroyed."

▲

After spending the morning teaching Iuwen, who was dedicated to learning the art of healing, Ubekhet relaxed under the persea in Nefer's funerary garden. The tree had grown exceptionally fast, and it now provided a gentle shade. Here, the Wise Woman could feel the presence of her husband, who was alive in the celestial paradise. The persea's heart-shaped leaves gleamed in the sunshine, which made the walls of the village houses shine dazzling white.

Below her, in the village, women were fetching water from the large storage jars in niches in the streets, and taking advantage of the trip to exchange gossip; children were playing with rag balls; and the craftsmen were in their respective workshops. Life was flowing on like the Nile, peaceful, sunny, and majestic. The spirit of the late Master imbued every act of the two crews, and the community's ship continued to sail on the river, which, year after year, swelled with the tears of Isis and deposited black, life-giving earth on its banks.

Why had Ubekhet survived Nefer for so long, if not to ensure that no catastrophe, however grave, could endanger the Place of Truth? Although she no longer participated in its daily joys, she remained their guarantor. Rested now, she set off home.

When she got there, Ebony nuzzled her hand and looked up at her with his bright, confident eyes.

"You're hungry, aren't you?" she said.

The dog licked his lips with a long, pink tongue.

Ubekhet went to the kitchen, where her servingwoman was roasting quails. The smoke from them had long since reached the dog's nostrils and sharpened his hunger. Served up on a bed of chickpeas and accompanied by cubes of bacon, they would satisfy any appetite.

Suddenly there was a loud knocking at the front door. Ubekhet went to answer it, and found Karo's wife on the doorstep.

"Wise Woman, it's an emergency," she said. "My neighbor's little girl has cut her foot badly. Please come—quickly."

"Give Ebony something to eat," Ubekhet told her servingwoman.

"And what about you? When will you eat?"

"When I can," replied the Wise Woman with a smile.

Yes, life went on.

52

"Sit down, Setnakhte," said Hori, "but be brief. I have an extremely busy morning ahead of me."

Since he had taken up office, the tjaty had grown much thinner and his face had become deeply lined. Following Bay's example, he worked day and night, knew every detail of every document, and served the queen's cause with absolute fidelity, to the despair of Tausert's opponents.

"I wish to see the queen."

The tjaty settled himself in his straight-backed chair. "You aren't the only one."

"Don't pretend not to know who I am and why I'm here."

"Indeed I do know."

"And you still dare to bar my way?"

"It is my duty to protect the queen."

"The regent cannot go on hiding behind you, Tjaty," said

Setnakhte. "The time has come for her to give an account of herself."

"You ask a lot, don't you?"

"I've run out of patience, and I want clear answers. Sending me packing would only make things worse."

The tjaty got to his feet. "Then I shall take you to Her Majesty."

"I approve greatly of your attitude, Hori. When I am pharaoh, I shall need a man like you to head my government."

"I am Queen Tausert's to command. If she had to leave power, I should return to the Temple of Amon without the slightest regret."

The tjaty took Setnakhte to the magnificent lake in the center of the palace garden. Sitting in the shade of a sycamore which protected her from the burning sun, the queen seemed absorbed in devising a strategy to win a game of *senet*[4] against an invisible opponent.

"Majesty," said the tjaty, "Setnakhte would like to speak with you."

"Tell him to sit down opposite me and play."

The old courtier obeyed, and Hori withdrew.

Long minutes passed.

"I can see only three possible moves," said Setnakhte eventually, "and none of them will prevent my being defeated rapidly."

"I agree," nodded Tausert.

Refusing to let himself be dazzled by the queen's striking beauty and elegance, Setnakhte said, "King Saptah died one hundred and sixty-five days ago, Majesty, and his mummification lasted only seventy days, in accordance with tradition. You gained extra time in which to provide him with splendid funerary goods, in the hope that the Place of Truth would be able to make gold to create these masterpieces. What is the situation now?"

"Aren't you going to move one of your pieces?"

"This meeting is not a game, Majesty. I must have clear answers."

"I have just received one from the Scribe of the Tomb: the gold shrine chapel dedicated to Saptah is finished." The queen advanced a piece.

"Does that mean you have at last set a date for the funeral rites?"

"Everything is ready, so why delay?"

"Would you be good enough to tell me exactly when, Majesty?"

"In ten days" time."

Bending over the *senet* board, Setnakhte parried Tausert's attack. "When the door of the tomb closes, the period of your regency will be over. And you must announce the name of the new pharaoh to the people."

"I agree," said the queen, destroying his final defense.

"Will you give up power, Majesty?"

"Would that be a sensible thing to do? My late husband devised an ambitious program for building and renovating the sacred buildings, and I intend to carry it through to honor his memory."

Setnakhte stood up, his expression grim. "So you have decided to unleash a civil war!"

"Who can have told you such a terrible thing? Come, let us finish the game."

"I had lost in advance, since you set out the pieces. But the conquest of the throne is a much crueler game, and you are not the only person setting the rules."

"That is true, and I am aware of it, thanks to my tjaty's advice, which prevents me from making a tragic mistake."

Grudgingly, Setnakhte sat down again. "Do you mean you will abdicate power?"

"Because of the beliefs we both hold, neither of us can give up."

"Then you are choosing war!"

"Are you obsessed with the wish to fight? There are other ways of ensuring that irreconcilable attitudes not lead to a devastating war."

"I don't understand."

"I am leaving tomorrow for Thebes, to preside over Saptah's funeral. My reign will begin at the end of the ceremony—and so will yours."

Setnakhte gazed at her in astonishment. "You mean there will be two pharaohs?"

"The office of Pharaoh has always comprised a royal couple. By becoming pharaoh while remaining a woman, I could rule alone, like Hatshepsut; but I do not have the necessary forces. I am therefore suggesting that we reign jointly. If your only goal is Egypt's well-being, you will not refuse."

"Would all decisions have to be joint ones?"

"I shall live in Thebes, and concern myself with the restoration of the temples. You will live in Pi-Ramses, and you will take charge of the country's security. However, if we should be forced into war, you would require my consent."

"You'd never give it."

"I might if your arguments are decisive," said Tausert. "And I rely upon your honesty not to misrepresent the facts."

"What a strange solution."

"Let us think of the interests of the Two Lands, and of nothing else."

"You have just admitted that you're in a weak position, so why should I accept?"

"You are no more capable of reigning alone than I am. I embody a form of legitimacy that you cannot trample on."

Setnakhte stood up and gazed at the lake, with its covering of blue lotus flowers. "I would like to believe in peace as you do, Majesty, but events will not permit me."

"Perhaps you are wrong—pessimists are not always right. When will you give me your answer?"

"Before you leave for Thebes."

As Setnakhte walked away, Tausert made a last move and won the game.

▲

Ebony was playing ball with Iuwen. The dog always guessed which way the little girl was going to throw it, and went leaping after it even before it had left her hand.

Charmer, Paneb's enormous cat, wisely kept out of the way. He sat on the terrace with the little green monkey, which rarely stayed still for more than a few seconds. Bad Girl was dozing in the shade of an awning, waiting for the mixture of barley and spelt that Uabet would soon feed her.

By watching the dog, Iuwen was learning about the world of instincts. Ebony was teaching her to do the right thing at the right time, and about the purity of the act; by sharing time with him, she was becoming more sensitive and gaining more from the Wise Woman's teaching.

Suddenly, his ears pricked. Losing interest in the ball, he raced off toward the main gate of the village.

Userhat's wife saw him pass and realized that something important was about to happen: Ebony was not in the habit of wasting energy. She called to her husband, who hurried off to alert his colleagues. Within a few minutes, the Place of Truth was buzzing with activity, and even Kenhir left his office, where he was writing a new page of his *Key of Dreams.*

"What is all this noise about?" he asked.

"Ebony has gone rushing off to the main gate," replied Renupe.

"And you've disturbed me just because of that dog?"

"The central government must have answered your letter," said Ipuy. "We're sure Ebony senses that Uputy has arrived."

"Go back to your homes and—"

"Uputy's here?" cried Nakht. "Everyone to the main gate!"

"If dogs start laying down the law . . ." muttered Kenhir, but he was carried along by the general surge toward the gate.

Uputy had indeed arrived. He handed a sealed papyrus scroll to Kenhir and said, "A message from the royal palace at Pi-Ramses."

The craftsmen stood aside to let Paneb through.

"Read it," he told Kenhir.

The old scribe broke the seal with a steady hand. After a few minutes, he looked up.

"Queen Tausert will soon be among us to lead King Saptah's funeral rites. Everything must be made ready."

53

Mehy had been informed of the regent's arrival, and had placed his troops on alert. Would he be greeting a disappointed queen or a new pharaoh? His informants in Pi-Ramses had been unable to answer that vital question. All they knew was that Setnakhte and Tausert had talked for a long time, alone, before the regent left for Thebes. But no indiscretion had filtered through, and he would have to wait and see what Tausert said, at the end of Saptah's funeral, to find out whether she was giving up the throne or preparing to start a civil war.

Racked with uncertainty, Mehy went off to hunt in the western desert. Slaughtering his prey would soothe his nerves and give him the clearheadedness he would need so badly when he met the regent. As the man responsible for her safety, he would attempt to extract her final decision from her, and he would then have to decide whether to side with or against her.

If he became Setnakhte's faithful servant, at least for a little while, Mehy would deliver Tausert into his hands—preferably dead, so that she could reveal nothing about his treachery. On the other hand, if he supported Tausert, he would have to persuade her to launch a lightning offensive against Setnakhte, using the weapons Mehy had at his disposal.

Mehy shot several hares, an ibex, and two gazelles, but was

still not satisfied. What outstanding hunter could speak too highly of the pleasure of killing? Master of life and death, the general used his omnipotence against those terrified creatures that failed to escape from him.

Suddenly, he saw a magnificent desert fox, whose bushy tail was striped with white and orange. Sensing that it had been seen, the little creature hid under a flat stone, at the foot of a sand dune.

Mehy smiled. Thinking it had reached safety, the fox had in fact condemned itself to death. Mehy would have no difficulty in moving the stone, enlarging the earth, and reaching his victim deep in its lair. He would shoot it in the throat, before finishing it off with his dagger.

Then something unusual caught his eye: half buried in the sand lay the broken feather of an ostrich. That stupid bird was not rare in these parts, but what interested him was that this particular feather was painted in bright colors. Libyans wore emblems like this in their hair, when they went off to war.

Digging into the sand around the feather, he found the remains of a campfire. So scouts from Libya had dared come this close to Thebes. Mehy knew he ought to go straight to the main barracks and send out patrols, but he had better things to do. Libyans would always, despite their hatred of Egypt, fight for whoever paid the highest price. If Mehy could add some of these unscrupulous men to his array of warriors, it would much increase his chances of victory. True, making contact with them was likely to be tricky, because they were often drunk or drugged, but he already had a plan to avoid any unpleasant consequences in case of failure.

First, though, he must deal with the fox, which probably thought its pathetic ruse had saved its life. It was wrong.

Mehy lifted the rock, and enlarged the entrance hole to the earth, letting in the full blaze of daylight. At the bottom of its hiding place, the little wild creature gazed up at its murderer.

Mehy had seen that look before. It was full of a dignity

and courage that were stronger than fear; it meant nothing to him.

He aimed at the animal's throat and shot, but the arrow landed in the earth, in the very place where the fox had been a second earlier. In angry surprise, Mehy realized that the animal had dug another, deeper burrow, where it had taken refuge after defying him.

In rage, he snapped his bow in two.

▲

"Here she is!" shouted the Nubian lookout at the First Fort; from his position on top of the battlements, he had been watching the road since early morning. He waved his arms to alert the Second Fort's lookout, who waved to the Third Fort's, and so on until the message reached the Fifth Fort.

Sobek emerged from his office. The previous evening the barber had shaved him and cut his hair, and this morning the commander had perfumed his body and put on ceremonial dress. With his harness across his chest and his short sword swinging at his side, he walked out to greet the queen regent.

Mehy had insisted on driving Tausert's chariot himself, but she had remained silent and aloof, and he still knew nothing of her intentions.

Sobek bowed low. "Welcome to the Place of Truth, Majesty."

Both Mehy's soldiers and Sobek's guards were spellbound by the queen's regal bearing. She wore a long, pale green dress, and a gold necklace and bracelets that sparkled in the sunshine.

"Given the circumstances," ventured Mehy, "I must accompany Her Majesty as guarantor of her safety."

"As far as the lay workers' village, yes—but only you, not your troops. Here, I am in charge of our guest's safety. And neither you nor I shall enter the village itself."

"Commander Sobek, this rule cannot—"

"It is the rule of the Place of Truth, General," Tausert reminded him, "and we must all respect it."

Although mortified, Mehy had to obey.

Accompanied by Sobek and Mehy, the queen walked slowly toward the great gate of the village.

"You may return to your chariot," Sobek told Mehy when they reached the gate.

"But I must—"

"The rule, General, remember? Her Majesty herself has just stressed that it must be respected. In any case, she is in no danger here, for she is the village's queen."

"I don't even know how long Her Majesty plans to stay here."

"What does that matter? You and I are servants of the queen regent. When she decides to leave the Place of Truth, I shall ensure that you are informed."

▲

All the villagers had gathered to form a guard of honor, and the youngest children presented a bouquet of lotus flowers to the queen as soon as she took her first steps along the main street.

The craftsmen had put on their ceremonial kilts, and, thanks to Niut's careful attention, even Kenhir looked elegant for once.

The Scribe of the Tomb, the Master, and the leader of the port crew bowed before the queen.

"Majesty," said Kenhir, "this village belongs to you."

"I shall stay in Ramses' palace until the end of the funeral ceremonies," said Tausert. "Is everything ready for the rites?"

"The sarcophagi have been lowered into King Saptah's House of Eternity," replied Paneb. "The gold prayer shrine is finished, and the grave goods are at your disposal."

"So you really have succeeded," said Tausert.

"The gods looked favorably upon us, Majesty, and we followed the teachings of the Ancients as we worked in the House of Gold."

"Tomorrow morning, Saptah's mummy shall be transported to the Valley of the Kings. Only the two crews of craftsmen—no one else at all—will be present at the ritual, and they will place in the tomb the things they have made."

This decision worried the villagers. Surely it must mean that Tausert had lost all power and that her final refuge would be the Place of Truth?

"At the end of the funeral ceremonies," she said solemnly, "I shall be crowned Pharaoh at Karnak, as 'Beloved of Mut,' and 'Daughter of the Divine Light'; at exactly the same time, in Pi-Ramses, Setnakhte will also be crowned. By accepting my suggestion that we share the crown, he has prevented the Two Lands from being plunged into civil war."

Kenhir was utterly dismayed. How could Egypt survive under such conditions?

"My decision will be greeted with surprise," Tausert went on, "but the vital thing was to preserve peace. Setnakhte proved that he cared more about our country's well-being than about his own ambition. In sealing this pact, he has given his word not to act without my agreement. We used to be enemies, but now we have become allies, for the greater good of the kingdom."

The greatness of the queen's soul overwhelmed Paneb. From the tone of her voice, he sensed that she had already detached herself from the material concerns of power, in order to gaze upon other landscapes. But she would remain the inflexible guardian of the pharaonic ideal and might perhaps manage, through her magic alone, to curb the impulses of a monarch who would risk placing his reign under the protection of the most dangerous of all the gods, Set.

"Do you wish to rest, Majesty?" asked Kenhir.

"Later. First I must meditate in the temple."

Preceded by Ebony, two priestesses escorted the queen to the temple while Niut rushed to Ramses' little palace to check that not a single speck of dust defiled the place and that there were fresh flowers everywhere.

On the threshold of the temple stood Ubekhet, the head

priestess of Hathor. "The goddess's dwelling hoped you would come, Majesty."

"We are both widows, you and I, each of us faithful to the only man whom she has ever loved and whose memory never leaves her for a single moment. It is here, and nowhere else, that I perceived the true meaning of love: a total spiritual communion with the way of Ma'at. And the Place of Truth experiences that moment of grace each day. The great Ramses was right: there is nothing more important than preserving its existence."

"I deliver this temple into the hands of its true mistress," said Ubekhet.

"You are the Wise Woman, and you shall continue to celebrate the rites. I have only one request: to gaze upon the Stone of Light."

"You shall see it this very night, Majesty."

"I have at last found the answer to the question that has obsessed me for so long: why you could not find a place for my tomb in the Valley of the Queens. Because, from our first meeting, you knew that sooner or later the Brotherhood must create a House of Eternity for Pharaoh Tausert in the Valley of the Kings. And that moment has now arrived."

54

Pi-Ramses was still recovering from the month-long celebrations following Setnakhte's coronation, but little by little life was returning to normal. So the new pharaoh was not surprised when one morning, soon after dawn, his breakfast was interrupted by Hori, who came bustling in, carrying an armful of scrolls.

The tjaty bowed and said, "I am sorry to disturb you so

early, Majesty, but there are many matters we must discuss, so that I can take the necessary action."

Work had never frightened Setnakhte, so he abandoned his breakfast and sat down opposite the tjaty.

"I have excellent news," Hori continued. "Thebes has celebrated Pharaoh Tausert's coronation enthusiastically, and after King Saptah's funeral she moved into the palace. I have here a list of the large building projects to be undertaken; among them are some in the Delta, which you will no doubt wish to follow closely."

"I thought you were going to resign if I became pharaoh," said Setnakhte.

"As I said, Majesty, I am Queen Tausert's to command. She, too, has been appointed to govern the Two Lands, and I shall therefore continue to serve her—and remind you of your promises."

If the king had given way to the fury of Set, he would gladly have crushed this insolent, unyielding tjaty beneath his heel. But there was no one Setnakhte could trust, except his eldest son—and this man Hori, who was as honest as he was intransigent. The king had considered replacing him, but none of the courtiers he had considered would have made anything like so able a tjaty. It was another sign of Tausert's skill that she had appointed Hori and had foreseen that he would not be dismissed.

Setnakhte put his anger aside and said, "I believe we must work together."

"I am delighted to hear it, Majesty. In that case I shall put problems to you, listen to your solutions, and then ask the opinion of Queen-Pharaoh Tausert, who will undoubtedly try to find solutions agreeable to both of you. With a little goodwill and a lot of patience, everything should work smoothly."

▲

"How are you, Father?" asked Setnakhte's eldest son.

"Worn out and delighted. Worn out because the tjaty doesn't give me a single day's rest. Delighted because he listens to me carefully and doesn't automatically oppose my decisions. But . . ."

"But he's Tausert's eyes and ears in the capital, and he prevents you from doing as you see fit."

"You could not have put it better, my son."

"And that annoys you, so you are planning to put an end to the situation."

"Can you read my thoughts?"

"I know you inside out, and I know that sharing power does not suit you."

"It wouldn't suit anyone."

"What is your solution?"

"Can't you guess?"

"I fear I can, Father. But getting rid of Hori and replacing him with a man of straw would be a grave mistake. He has more than earned the respect in which he is held, and everyone acknowledges how able and skillful he is."

"But he's Tausert's man!"

"What does that matter, since you have sealed a pact with her and you will keep your word? This agreement is a good one, Father. Don't try to break it."

Setnakhte breathed more easily. His son's judgment was exactly what he had hoped it would be, and he would therefore do as he had planned and appoint him commander in chief of the Egyptian armies.

▲

The banquet thrown by Mehy in honor of Tausert, who had just moved into the palace close to Karnak, dazzled even the most world-weary guests. True, the queen-pharaoh spent only a few minutes at the festivities, just long enough to receive homage from the leading citizens of Thebes. But that brief appearance was enough to win them over so completely that they became unconditional admirers.

"What a sublime woman, General," said the mayor, "and what political acumen. I wouldn't be surprised if she succeeded in gradually reducing Setnakhte's authority and regaining the whole of the land."

"You seem to have fallen under our sovereign's spell."

"Who hasn't? A pharaoh who comes to live in Thebes—what an honor for our city! Pi-Ramses loses a little of its glitter because of it. But you don't look very well, Mehy."

"Oh, it's nothing. Just a touch of fatigue."

"You ought to rest more," said the mayor. "Commanding our troops, governing the west bank, working ceaselessly to maintain the province's prosperity: your achievements are truly remarkable! Such devotion to the public good deserves everyone's admiration, but you mustn't neglect your health."

"I'm very well, I assure you."

"Don't worry. All the city's leading citizens have been singing your praises, and I'm sure the queen will confirm you in your offices. I myself spoke enthusiastically to her of your abilities."

"Thank you."

"It was the least I could do. But, Mehy, you must heed my advice and look after yourself."

The general smiled thinly. He looked around. Most of the guests were already drunk. After days of anxiety, wealthy Thebans could at last relax. As Tausert had promised, the new regime would not alter the existing social structure. As soon as the mayor went off to pour his honeyed words into other ears, Mehy left the reception chamber and went to his private rooms.

Serketa soon followed him. She saw at once that his nerves were on edge, and poured him a cup of date wine. Mehy gulped it down; it burned in his throat.

Fatigue! Mehy laughed at the idea, but he felt trapped like one of the creatures he killed so mercilessly. Up to now, he had been the unchallenged master of Thebes, but now he must submit to the will of the queen-pharaoh, who, by all accounts, had no intention of yielding one cubit of her authority to him.

After Saptah's funeral ceremonies, she had left the Place of Truth for the eastern bank, where she had summoned to the great palace audience chamber the ten most important men in Thebes. Naturally, among those men was Mehy.

Tausert's speech had been short and precise: she intended to oversee all areas of activity, including the army. Mehy had had to take her on an immediate inspection of the main barracks, where she had met the senior officers and watched the foot soldiers' and charioteers' training. Profoundly humiliated, he had had to behave like a good, loyal servant of Her Majesty. From now on, she would be issuing the orders and he would have to obey without question.

"I can tell you're thinking about that accursed queen, my sweet love," whispered Serketa, stroking his cheek.

"She is bound to stick her nose into the Treasury records and start controlling what I do. One tiny hitch, and worthless scum like the mayor will start making my life unbearable."

"Assuming I give them the time, my tender lion."

"Don't do anything without my agreement," ordered Mehy.

"Shouldn't we think about killing that tigress?"

The general seized his wife by the waist and pulled her hard against him. "Perhaps we should, my ewe-lamb, perhaps we should—but only when I decide to. Do you understand?"

"Wouldn't it be best to do it sooner rather than later?"

"I hope Tausert's success is only a brief one, designed to dazzle the court, and that she will soon withdraw into a cozy little existence, which I shall ensure she continues. Why shouldn't she come to trust me, as all the others do?"

"Because she is Pharaoh and, what's more, a woman of true power. Beware of her. She's a formidable enemy."

Mehy took the warning seriously. "If necessary, we'll take action before she realizes how I am manipulating Thebes."

Delighted, Serketa began to imagine the delicious moment when she would murder a pharaoh.

"Has Daktair arrived?" asked Mehy.

"He's waiting in your office."

▲

Fat, bearded little Daktair could not keep still. When Mehy appeared, he exploded with rage. "Here you are at last! Why wasn't I invited to the banquet, and why did I have to come in here with a hood over my head?"

"Because this meeting must be kept secret."

Daktair's anger immediately abated: that must mean Mehy had decided to start plotting again. "Do I take it you have need of my services?" he asked.

"I found a Libyan encampment in the western desert."

Daktair turned white. "Libyans! Are they going to attack Thebes?"

"No, they're only scouts. But it's a long time since any Libyans dared come so close."

"I take it you've sent out a detachment of troops to kill them?"

"No," said Mehy. "Tausert is creating me a lot of problems, and I might need some new allies."

"Libyans as your allies? But they're Egypt's hereditary enemies."

"It all depends on the circumstances, my dear Daktair. You are to leave for the desert at once, with some troops who know the area well, and you are to find and capture the scouts."

"Capture them? But the soldiers will kill them."

"My orders will be precise, and you will be there to ensure that they are carried out to the letter: first the prisoners are to be interrogated, then you are to give them a message from me."

Daktair's jaw dropped. "You mean the Libyans will be freed? The troops will never do it."

"Orders are orders. Besides, you'll have your own," and Mehy told Daktair precisely what he expected of him.

"The risks . . ."

"You have no choice, my friend."

At Mehy's icy stare, Daktair's protest died in his throat.

"You had better succeed, Daktair. If you don't, you will regret it."

55

Since matters were so urgent, Paneb had suggested building Tausert's Temple of a Million Years between those of Meneptah and Thutmose IV. The minute he received the queen-pharaoh's agreement, he drew a plan on a leather scroll and gave it to Hay, whose port crew would construct the temple as quickly as possible; the temple was essential if the queen was to have sufficient energy to reign and ward off harmful forces.

The first blocks of stone had been ordered from the quarries as soon as Tausert was crowned, and they soon began to arrive on the site, hewn irregularly to conserve their power; symmetry would have bred uniformity and death.

"Have you mixed the mortar?" Paneb asked Hay.

"We've chosen some excellent gypsum which reacts well to heating, and the joins between the blocks will be narrow." Lovingly, Hay placed his hand on a stone destined for the first course. "This sandstone vibrates harmoniously," he said, "and we shall be able to build thick walls, through which the mineral sap flows freely."

Paneb cut the first groove uniting two blocks of stone forever; Hay filled the groove with a piece of acacia branch. Then Hay shared out the work among the craftsmen of his crew, and each man placed his mark on the stones with which he would be working.

When Paneb heard someone start to whistle a song celebrating the beauty of work, he knew everything would go smoothly.

▲

Beside Paneb, the royal palace guards seemed almost puny. So their captain ordered six men to accompany him and the Master to the huge office where Tausert had spent the morning working with scribes of the irrigation secretariat.

Before receiving Paneb, the queen-pharaoh revived herself

by perfuming her skin and drinking a cup of fresh milk flavored with coriander.

When Paneb was shown into the office, he bowed low before Tausert. "We have begun building your temple, Majesty. The last blocks of sandstone will be delivered before the end of the week, and you will be able to inaugurate the innermost shrine in less than two months. From then on, the shrine will be in use and the ritualists will make offerings there every morning in your name."

"This is wonderful news, Master!"

"The most difficult task is yet to come, Majesty."

"You mean my House of Eternity. Where do you suggest it be built?"

Although not given to anxiety, Paneb felt a certain apprehension as he revealed his plan, for fear of disappointing the queen.

Tausert could not admit it, but she, too, was worried. Whereabouts in the Valley was the Brotherhood planning to create the magic crucible in which her pharaonic soul would be reborn?

"Perhaps, Majesty," said Paneb, "it would be best to show you the site?"

▲

The Nubian guards parted to make way for Tausert and the Master. A pair of peregrine falcons soared overhead as they entered the Valley of the Kings in silence. The heat was intense, the cliffs shining with a harsh light.

Paneb led the way, past the tomb of Ramses the Great. They left Meneptah's tomb on the right and Amenmessu's on the left, took a path that led south, then forked off to the west. The Master did not pause before Saptah's House of Eternity, which was almost opposite Tjaty Bay's. Continuing due south, he halted just before the tombs of Thutmose I and Seti II.

"Majesty, this is the place chosen by the Wise Woman," said Paneb. "Fened the Nose and I agree that it is excellent."

Tausert looked around. "It is at the center of a triangle, of which the base is formed by Bay and Saptah, and the point by my late husband. Is that why you chose it?"

"The rock is pure and responds well to the chisel. We shall be able to cut deeply without too many difficulties."

She touched the cliff face. "Then it shall be here."

"If it pleases Your Majesty."

"This place is magnificent," she said.

Paneb sensed that Tausert needed to meditate, alone, beside the yet-untouched rock where her soul would dwell for eternity. So he walked away and gazed at her, standing motionless in the sun and indifferent to its brutal heat. And the Master knew that the queen-pharaoh and he had been born from the same fire.

Time stood still, and the spirit of the Valley of the Kings entered Tausert's heart, turning a woman and a queen into Pharaoh of Egypt.

"Paneb," she called at last.

He went back toward her.

"When will you begin work?"

"All I have been waiting for is your agreement."

"Show me the plan."

The Master traced it out in the sand. This simple act reminded him of his adolescence and his insatiable desire to draw life and its secrets.

"But you have designed an immense tomb," she said.

"Not only immense, but decorated with paintings of a kind that has never been seen before."

"Isn't it rather overambitious?"

"The Brotherhood's craftsmen are experienced enough to bring it to fruition."

Tausert's beautiful face darkened. "I do not think fate will grant me a long reign. And I long to be beside Seti again."

Paneb was too moved to voice insipid platitudes—which in any case the queen would not have listened to.

"Majesty . . ."

"What is it, Master?"

"The Brotherhood will give of its best, and I shall paint night and day. Not a moment will be lost, and this project will be completed as soon as possible."

Tausert gave a solemn smile. "I trust you, Paneb."

He would have liked to say other words, but the gods would not allow it. All that he could have from this sublime woman was the look in her eyes, a look as pure and as ardent as flame.

▲

Mehy and Serketa gave banquet after banquet, at which they contrived to speak privately with all the most important people in the province. He had established that his prestige was still intact, although the queen-pharaoh's authority was undisputed.

But he knew Tausert would soon identify his supporters and realize that he was using them to maintain his hold on the city of Amon. In exchange for their vows of loyalty, these wretched people had demanded more privileges than Mehy had wanted to grant them.

While he brooded, leaning against a pillar in the reception hall, Serketa was deploying her charms against the keeper of the Treasury archives, a narrow-minded, spineless scribe with a fondness for pretty, inaccessible women. Serketa was a little too plump for his taste, but he was happy to let his eyes wander over her appetizing curves. And when she started speaking in her silly little-girl's voice, he felt strange urges come over him.

Mehy went over to them. "Have you tried this white wine, my dear fellow?" he asked.

"I'm afraid I may already have had rather too much."

"Ah, but we must all make the most of the joys of living," declared the general, generously topping off the scribe's cup.

"Our guest is charming," added Serketa, "and he has such a wonderful sense of humor."

"You flatter me, my lady."

"To be frank, many of our senior officials are not the least bit amusing. You're quite different. I'm sure my husband will soon put a fine promotion your way."

"Indeed, I'm just about to do so," said Mehy. "What would you say to a post as assistant director of the central government of the west bank?"

The scribe was surprised and delighted. "That would be . . . It's . . ."

"At twice the salary, of course.

"I don't know if my skills . . ."

"Don't worry about that. There's just one small condition you need to fulfill: remove from the archives the accounts scrolls on this list, and bring them to me tomorrow morning."

The scribe recoiled. "I can't do that! I—"

"You're so kind," said Serketa, draping herself against him. "You'll do this for us, won't you?"

"You owe your job to me," Mehy reminded him, "and you will owe me your promotion. I can rely on you, can't I?" The menace in the general's voice froze the scribe in his tracks.

"Yes, yes. You can rely on me."

56

The keeper of the archives was so terrified that, the following morning, he was among the first visitors requesting an audience with the governor of the west bank. To avoid arousing his entourage's suspicions by seeming too eager to speak to the scribe, Mehy saw two other visitors first.

When the scribe went into Mehy's office he was sweating, despite the relative cool of the morning.

"Sit down," said the general, closing the door behind him.

"There's no need. I've brought you everything."

"Show me."

The scribe opened a square basket and took out five papyrus scrolls, which Mehy examined one by one. When he had finished, he nodded in satisfaction. If they had fallen into Tausert's hands, she would have realized that, for several years, he had been embezzling public funds. One would, of course, require an excellent knowledge of accounts and the nose of a hunting dog, but it was better not to take any risks.

"I have erased the numbers of these scrolls from the general list," added the archive keeper, whose hands were trembling. "Now it's as if they'd never existed."

"Perfect, my friend."

"And . . . what about my new post?"

"I shall support your candidature at the beginning of next month, and you'll take up your post shortly after that. Allow me to have a few brightly colored Minoan vases delivered to you; I'm sure you'll like them."

"That is too much, really too much!"

"One should always be good to one's friends, shouldn't one? You can be certain you've made the right choice."

▲

With his new salary, the former keeper of the Treasury archives decided, he'd first move house, then set out to woo a good-looking woman who'd be swept off her feet by his charms. After years of poring over accounts, he no longer believed in emotions, but he had complete faith in the irresistible power of money.

His little two-story house stood in a northern district of Thebes. He contemplated it with disgust. How could a man of his notable abilities have put up with so little for so long? The tiny garden, with its two old palm trees, really wasn't worthy of a man of his station. Soon, he'd be luxuriating in the shade of magnificent trees planted beside his own private lake.

A delivery woman arrived, her head humbly bowed. "Precious vases from Minoa, sir. They are for you, aren't they?"

"Absolutely. Put your basket down there on that low table."

Impatient to see the treasures Mehy had sent, the official untied the string, lifted the lid, and bent over the basket. A black viper, enraged by its long confinement, darted out and bit him on the neck.

Panic stricken, the unfortunate man clutched his wound. "Fetch a doctor quickly!"

"There's no point," replied Serketa, whom the scribe now recognized beneath her skillful makeup. "You'll be dead in less than three minutes."

"Help me, I beg you!"

"The general knew that you wouldn't hold your tongue. I shall leave you with the snake, and take back my vases."

Serketa dodged aside from the official, whose desperate struggles only made the venom enter his bloodstream more quickly.

As she observed his brief death throes, the murderess mused that, now the compromising documents had disappeared, Mehy was out of immediate danger. But Tausert would continue her inquiries, and would eventually realize that he ruled Thebes by corruption and threats.

Before the queen could attack him, though, Serketa would kill her.

▲

The craftsmen had gathered in their meeting place, which had been freshly painted, and listened carefully to Paneb's brief address.

Karo was extremely indignant. "You promised to keep to the usual work-timetable and said you wouldn't cancel a single day's holiday. And now you're asking us to work like slaves so that Tausert's House of Eternity can be finished as quickly as possible."

"I don't break my promises," agreed the Master, "and I have no intention of going against your will."

"If we refuse," Pai pointed out, "you won't be able to excavate and decorate the tomb all on your own."

"I shall have to if none of you is willing to make a special effort."

"What's the real reason you're doing this?" asked Ched, a wry smile playing about his lips.

"Since we're talking in the utmost secrecy, you should know that Tausert's reign is likely to be only a short one, and that she expects our Brotherhood to work quickly and well, so that she may have both a Temple of a Million Years and a House of Eternity."

Gau was puzzled. "Why must it be so enormous? Ramses I was on the throne for less than two years, and his tomb is small but no less splendid for that."

"The size of a pharaoh's tomb doesn't depend on the length of his reign," retorted Paneb. "You're all highly experienced, and are masters of your crafts, perfectly well able to build and decorate a tomb of this size."

"Who told you about Tausert's reign being brief?" asked Unesh.

"She did. She'd had a premonition about it."

"And what does the Wise Woman say about all this?" asked Fened.

"Nothing."

"That's a bad sign," said Ipuy.

"Well, I think the Master's plan is exciting," said Nakht. "We've done a lot of work for the outside world over the last few months, and it's time to devote ourselves again to what really matters."

"It would be exciting, wouldn't it, to try to achieve the impossible," ventured Ched. "We had so long to create Saptah's tomb that we had no need to dig deep into our reserves, or ask our hands to give more than they'd ever done before. I haven't Paneb's health and strength, but I shall commit myself to the adventure as wholeheartedly as my strength permits."

"Then there'll be at least two of us," said Didia placidly.

"That's enough talk," cut in Thuty. "Who is against the Master?"

"Bah!" exclaimed Karo. "There's never any point in arguing here. Instead of wasting precious time, let's get ready to leave for the Valley of the Kings."

▲

Relaxed and sated by the murder, Serketa slept until noon. But her feeling of well-being was brutally shattered when she looked into a mirror: to her horror she saw the beginnings of a wrinkle at the corner of her mouth.

Shouting at the top of her voice, she summoned her maid and her hairdresser and told them to bring her creams and ointments. "Hurry, hurry! You mustn't let this hideous thing disfigure me! And summon my doctor at once."

Not until she had been made up to perfection, so that the wrinkle could no longer be seen, did Serketa feel any relief.

Her steward knocked at the door of her bedchamber. "A visitor has been waiting for you since early morning, my lady."

"Who is it?"

"He refuses to tell me his name. I tried to send him away, but he claims he has an important message for you. In the circumstances, what do you wish me to do?"

"What does he look like?"

"He's of average height, stocky, with a round head and black hair."

"Send him to the pavilion and tell him that I'm coming."

The steward had not dared say that, at first glance, the visitor looked a lot like General Mehy. As for Serketa, she was sure he must be Tran-Bel, a dishonest merchant whom her husband had occasionally made use of. She would have no difficulty dealing with him; he had always been putty in her hands.

She checked her makeup again, then went to join her unexpected and unwanted guest. It was indeed Tran-Bel, with his false smile and his hypocritical mannerisms.

"Have you been bitten by a desert horsefly?" she asked coldly. "I did not give you permission to come to my home and disturb me."

"Forgive my effrontery, my lady, but it's a matter of great urgency. No one can hear us, I hope?"

"No one at all."

"Thebes is buzzing with a thousand rumors. It's difficult to sort the truth from the lies, but it's clear Queen Tausert is acting like a true pharaoh and that, as a result, your husband's position has become more . . . fragile. Now, there are strong bonds between us, you and me."

"What makes you think that?"

"Remember, my lady: one of the craftsmen from the Place of Truth is among your very close friends, and I know who he is. That information would be worth its weight in gold to Tausert, wouldn't you say?"

Serketa's eyes blazed.

"Oh," he exclaimed, "I know what you're thinking. This fellow Tran-Bel is becoming tiresome, and my husband and I wouldn't be sorry if he died. Well, don't even think of it: I've taken precautions. Besides, I trust you; and I'm sure General Mehy has a great future."

"What do you want?"

"First, the price of my silence; then, to become a partner in one of your enterprises—one of the best, of course."

Serketa looked at the merchant for a long time. "Very well," she said.

57

Paneb was amazed. "Ill? You say he's ill?"

"Yes, ill," repeated Casa's wife, a belligerent little brunette. "That's how it is, and he must stay at home."

"We're leaving for the Valley of the Kings this morning, and I need every member of the crew."

"Well, you'll just have to manage without Casa. He's asleep, and I'm not waking him up."

"Then I'll do it myself."

"I don't care if you are the Master, I'm not letting you into my house."

"Don't make a fuss, or I might lose my temper."

"If you don't believe me, ask the Wise Woman. She examined Casa, and she said he was too weak to get up."

Paneb took her at her word and strode off to see Ubekhet, whom he found bandaging a little boy's sprained ankle.

"Casa's just malingering," he said accusingly.

"He has a kidney infection, which it will take me a few days to cure," explained the Wise Woman.

"Don't tell me he can't get up and walk to work."

"I'm afraid he can't."

"If you give me free rein, I'll cure him much faster than you will."

"Our rule forbids you to employ a sick man on the site."

Paneb could do nothing but reluctantly give way. He went to Kenhir's house, so the scribe could enter Casa's name in the Journal of the Tomb, together with the reason for his absence from work.

To his surprise, he found Kenhir dressed in a coarse tunic, with his writing materials at the ready.

"What's this, Kenhir? Surely you aren't thinking of climbing up to the pass?"

"Of course I am. You needn't think for a moment that I wouldn't be present at the excavation of a new royal tomb. Let's be on our way."

North Wind, Paneb's donkey, had the honor of leading the procession. As solidly built as his master, he had agreed to carry the Scribe of the Tomb's possessions, and it was he who set the pace for the climb, deploring the fact that the two-footed creatures were so slow and unsure on their feet.

The Master felt a surge of emotion as he stepped back onto the road leading to the pass, where he always felt closer to the heavens. Shrines and stone huts had been built there, and that was where the craftsmen slept during work periods. To preserve the serenity of the place, they were forbidden to light fires or cook food; but the village women brought them excellent meals.

The nights spent under the stars were unforgettable. Paneb sat on the roof of his hut, and gazed wonderingly at the Great Bear, surrounded by the deathless stars. After a while, the Scribe of the Tomb joined him there.

"Can't you sleep, either?" asked Kenhir.

"The day we've just spent, restoring the ancestors' stelae, has left me feeling wide awake. All the time I was thinking of Nefer. His presence here is so strong I can almost touch it."

"Set your mind at rest. You're preserving that presence and making it live on. But have you thought hard about the task you're about to undertake?"

"The fire that's always dwelt within me dictated the plan for Tausert's House of Eternity."

"You haven't changed, Paneb. From the moment I spoke in your favor, at the Court of Admissions, I knew you'd overcome all obstacles; and not even high office has diminished your determination and desire. But be careful. The other craftsmen aren't cast in the same mold."

Kenhir went back into his hut, the only one which boasted three rooms. The first had a bench with a U-shaped seat marked with its owner's name, and jars of fresh water. The second had a stone bed covered with a mat, and the third was an office where the old scribe penned the Journal.

In this modest dwelling, Kenhir forgot his age and his aches and pains, and relived the great days of the Brotherhood, which he had been fortunate enough to share. How right he had been to turn his back on a brilliant but commonplace career, and come to serve the Place of Truth. Where else could he have come so close to the mystery of life? Where else could he have experienced such a spirit of brotherhood, which trials and tribulations only strengthened?

▲

Penbu, the Nubian guarding the equipment store at the entrance to the Valley of the Kings, stood aside and allowed North Wind to pass, for he was the most famous donkey on the west bank. But he looked curiously at the craftsmen.

"There's a man missing," he observed.

"Casa the Rope is ill," explained Kenhir. "He'll join us next week."

The Master called across to Tusa, Penbu's colleague, and told him to guard the entrance to Tausert's tomb as soon as the rock had been pierced. Tusa was armed with a short sword, dagger, bow, arrows, and a slingshot, and had the authority to kill any outsider who tried to enter the site.

With Didia's help, Ched got busy setting up a workshop in a deep crevasse in the rock, using wooden planks to hold pots, crucibles, vases, and cakes of color. A white awning was stretched over the whole, sheltering it from the sun. Given the size of the tomb, both artists and painters were going to need a lot of materials.

Standing before the virgin rock, the Wise Woman handed the Master his golden apron, gold hammer, and gold chisel. When he had removed the first sliver of limestone, he handed it to Fened.

"Perfect," declared Fened.

Paneb wielded his great pickax, then the stonecutters joined in energetically. The other craftsmen gathered up the debris in sturdy willow baskets, and carried it away from the site.

"This rock face is a true joy," exclaimed Nakht. "Anyone would think it had been waiting just for us."

"Save your breath," Karo advised him, "or your arms will get tired."

"And you'd better strike rhythmically," retorted Nakht, "or you'll pull a muscle. What with Casa, that would make two weaklings."

Without a word, Paneb immediately stepped between them. And the tools sang in unison with the rock.

▲

Serketa massaged her husband's back as he lay beside the lotus pool in their garden.

"We must kill Tran-Bel at once," decided Mehy. "Am I right in thinking that the mission won't displease you, my sweet love?"

"It will amuse me very much. But it's too soon, my tender lion."

"You want to give that little Syrian rat another chance?"

"We can still use him."

"I've nothing more to fear from Tausert, so why should I bother with a treacherous little creature like that?"

"Precisely because he has that fine quality. We shan't find a better ally to execute the little plan I've dreamt up."

Intrigued, Mehy rolled over on to his back and looked up at her. "Tran-Bel an ally? You're losing your mind. All that matters to him is making a profit."

Serketa ran her index finger slowly over his broad chest. "Exactly, my crocodile, exactly. And because of that charming weakness, the little rat won't suspect a thing. In fact, he'll be so delighted that he'll forget all about taking precautions."

"You're arousing my curiosity. Are you becoming a strategist?"

"That's for you to judge."

As Serketa outlined her plan, Mehy's mouth almost watered

with pleasure. Not only was the idea an excellent one, but it would also give them a decisive advantage over the Brotherhood.

▲

Paneb had not dreamt that the project would move forward so quickly. But the craftsmen's enthusiasm and precision had opened wide the rock, and work on the descending passageway was going unusually quickly.

Once his kidney infection was cured, Casa had rejoined his comrades and demonstrated that he was as hardworking as ever.

In the artists' workshop, the designs were taking shape; and the sculptors had also set to work eagerly, with no need for prompting by the Master.

Kenhir felt great joy, a joy more profound than anything he had ever experienced. With his vision and the strength of his personal magic, Paneb the Ardent had given new inspiration to the crew, whose energy and talents seemed inexhaustible.

Each evening at the settlement on the pass was a happy one. The craftsmen rejoiced in the work they had done, talked of what they would do the next day, and argued over small details of their craft until the Master intervened. Tausert's House of Eternity seemed to have taken complete control of the crew, and even Ched, normally so distant, had grown passionate about decorating this new Great Work.

Nourished by this thirst for creation, Paneb never felt tired; he slept only two hours a night, and derived his strength for the next day from gazing up at the stars.

Always the first to rise, the Master knelt before a stele engraved by one of his predecessors, and spoke the ritual words of greeting to the reborn sun before waking the heavier sleepers.

Kenhir stood up with difficulty. "These follies aren't for men of my age," he said. "But what wonderful times we're living in."

"They do indeed seem so," said Paneb.

"Only 'seem'? Ah, you're thinking about the traitor, aren't you?"

"And about Nefer's murder, as I do every morning."

"I fear there may be no more to say about that."

The Master's gaze narrowed. "Someone's climbing the path to the pass."

"Are you sure?"

"I think it's a woman."

58

Paneb was right: it was a woman. As she came closer, he recognized the slender form of Uabet the Pure.

She wasn't carrying a basket of food, so he worried she might have climbed all the way up to the pass to argue with him over a private grievance.

However, she soon set him straight. "I've brought you an urgent message from Pi-Ramses. Uputy was most insistent, so I thought it best that you and Kenhir should get it as soon as possible."

"Thank you," said Paneb.

"I'll go back now."

Kenhir read the message, which was from the tjaty.

"Surely it should have passed through the hands of Queen Tausert?" said Paneb in astonishment.

The old scribe was very annoyed. "It's an order from Setnakhte: he requires us to excavate his House of Eternity in the Valley of the Kings."

"Thebes doesn't come under his authority."

"Setnakhte is a pharaoh," Kenhir reminded him, "and his demands are legitimate. We must obey."

"Two tombs at once? That's impossible! I'm already asking the craftsmen to give more than their best."

"We'll just have to find a way."

"There can be no question of working more slowly on Tausert's tomb. Go and negotiate with Setnakhte, Kenhir. I'm sure you'll persuade him to be patient."

"Don't overestimate what I can do. According to the tjaty, the king's in a hurry and knows exactly where he wants his House of Eternity to be: in the center of the Valley, close to the pharaohs he most reveres, Ramses I, Seti I, and Ramses II."

"But it's for the Brotherhood to suggest a site, one that takes account of the terrain. No other king has ever tried to dictate where his tomb should be—the choice has always been left to us."

"Will you at least consider his suggestion?" asked Kenhir, who felt trapped between two boulders of equal size.

"The craftsmen are tired. It's time to go back to the village at the pass."

▲

The meeting was stormy; but the village was sacred, under the invisible protection of Nefer and the ancestors, and each man spoke with dignity.

Userhat summed up the situation. "It's simple. Two pharaohs are reigning at the same time, both want their own tomb, and we can only create one. As we've already begun Tausert's, and as she lives at Thebes, I'd say the argument's settled."

"No, it isn't," objected Unesh. "Our rule obliges us to obey an order from Pharaoh, especially if it concerns his House of Eternity."

"Can you split yourself in two, and work in two places at the same time?" inquired Thuty sarcastically. "If so, we'd all love to see it."

"Setnakhte will make us pay dearly if we refuse," said Renupe anxiously.

"It's up to Queen Tausert to sort it out with him," declared Karo.

"Isn't it the Scribe of the Tomb's job to get us out of difficult situations like this?" asked Pai.

"We must close ranks and not let ourselves be set at odds," advised Ched.

"Then there's only one solution," announced the Master. "We must satisfy both pharaohs' demands."

"And how on earth will we manage that?" demanded Ipuy.

"First by granting you three rest days. Then by appointing a smaller crew, which will begin excavating a tomb for Setnakhte in the center of the Valley."

"Will you be in the small crew?" asked Didia.

"No, I shall be busy with the main site."

"Then who will?"

"Nakht, Fened, and Ipuy. I'll give them a copy of the map of the Valley, and they'll work according to that."

As Paneb spoke, the traitor suddenly thought of a plan. It would mean running the minimum risk in return for the maximum advantage, starting with the inevitable dismissal of the Master. Once he was out of the way, the Brotherhood would be shaken to its foundations and its defenses weakened.

And then the Stone of Light would be within his grasp.

▲

At dead of night, watched closely by Bad Girl and Ebony, Kenhir slid open the three bolts on the strong room door. Apart from the Master, he was the only person who knew how the mechanism worked.

"Everything all right?" asked Paneb.

"There's no sign that anyone's tried to break in."

With the aid of a torch, the old scribe moved the exceptionally fine copper chisels, then untied the thick string round an ebony box. Anxiously he lifted the lid: the treasure was still safe. Delicately, Kenhir unrolled the papyrus on which was drawn the map of the Valley showing the tombs' locations.

"I'll copy the part that concerns us," said Paneb, "and give it to Fened tomorrow morning."

While the Master drew the plan with a steady hand,

Kenhir listened carefully. But neither the guard-goose nor the dog showed any sign of unease.

Nothing untoward had happened by the time Kenhir closed the strong room door again. The village was sleeping peacefully.

"I don't like this," said the Master.

"Were you expecting the shadow-eater to attack?"

"No, I mean Setnakhte's demands."

"You found the right solution, and everyone's accepted it."

"The right solution . . . I'm not so sure about that."

"What are you afraid of?" asked Kenhir.

"I wish I knew. Come on, let's go home and get some sleep."

▲

Kilts strewn all over the floor, dirty pots in an untidy kitchen, a wreck of a bed: Fened's house had been sorely neglected since his divorce some time before, because the stonecutter paid little attention to domestic chores.

Paneb shook him. "Wake up, Fened."

"What . . . ? Oh, it's you. But this is a rest day."

"Here's the map you're to use, once I've struck the first blow with my pickax."

"Before I study it, I need to open my eyes properly."

"Some help in the house wouldn't go amiss."

"No, no more women in my house! I'll do the sweeping myself."

"If you promise you will."

"A Servant of the Place of Truth always keeps his word," Fened reminded him as he got up. "But tell me, why are you trusting me to take such a responsibility?"

"Because circumstances mean I can't do it myself. But don't worry: if anything goes wrong, the responsibility will still be mine."

"All right. I'll wash and dress, and then we'd better get back to the Valley."

▲

Daktair was worried sick—literally. Because of his queasiness and the flux in his bowels, he'd had to go off on his own several times, which meant that the soldiers had to slow down their march. They resented the presence of a mere scribe wholly unused to expeditions like this, but, as General Mehy himself had ordered them to obey Daktair without question, the soldiers' commander had told them to keep their mouths shut.

"Still no trace of the Libyans?" asked Daktair, placing a hot stone on his belly to calm the spasms.

"As a matter of fact there is—and you should think about it."

"About what, Commander?"

"Things could well turn nasty. Libyans are more dangerous than wild animals, and there's likely to be fierce fighting. A man like you isn't prepared for it."

Daktair puffed up like a toad. "General Mehy has entrusted me with a mission, and I'm going to carry it out, whatever the risks. I'm the leader of this expedition, not you. And I remind you that I want the Libyans alive."

"It's obvious you know nothing about either the terrain or the game we're hunting."

"I was told that this raiding party was made up of Thebes's best desert troops. Well, prove it."

The officer was stung by the challenge. "Yes, we are the best—and we'll be glad to prove it."

"That's exactly what I'm hoping for. When will we make contact with the Libyans?"

"Within two days at most. They're beginning to go round in circles and they're leaving tracks. That means they're tired and that they've no specific orders. They may be cunning, but they won't escape us."

59

The leader of the Libyan scouts had an extra toe on each foot. This had earned him both the nickname Six-Toes and a reputation as a lawless demon. He knew every cubit of the desert; he also knew that, if he was to survive in such a hostile environment, he must never relax his guard, not even when he was asleep.

Twenty times, as he approached western Thebes, he had eluded Egyptian patrols made up of warriors as formidable as himself. He felt almost invulnerable, and longed to make Pharaoh's subjects pay dearly for the humiliations they had inflicted on his people. It was too soon to plan a massive attack on the rich city of Amon, which was well defended; first he must locate the forward guard posts, so that the attack could be properly planned.

"May we light a fire, sir?" asked his right-hand man.

"In the shelter of that little hillock over there. Use yesterday's embers."

"That won't be easy."

"What do you mean?"

"We left them at yesterday's camp."

Six-Toes dealt the man a resounding slap. "I ordered you to bring them!"

The scout pulled out a knife. "Nobody treats me like that!"

"You stupid idiot! To the Egyptian patrols a sign like that's—"

An arrow buried itself in the ground between the two men; and a harsh voice stopped them in their tracks.

"You scouts are our prisoners. If you try to resist or run away, you'll be killed."

Torture, then summary execution: that was what awaited them. Six-Toes would gladly have hurled himself into the fray but the patrol was too close. One false move, and he'd be bristling with arrows.

"Tie them up," ordered Daktair.

The ropes dug into the scouts' flesh, and they grimaced with pain.

Daktair turned his attention to Six-Toes, whose arrogance showed him to be the leader.

"What is your name, and what are your orders?" he demanded.

The Libyan spat, covering Daktair's beard with saliva; the scribe wiped it away with the back of his hand.

"Let me deal with that dirty cur," said the commander.

"There's to be no violence."

"But you don't know who you're up against."

"This ruffian's called Six-Toes," said one of the guards, looking at the Libyan's feet. "They say he's one of their best scouts—a prize well worth capturing."

"I wish to talk to him alone," said Daktair.

"Be careful," warned the officer before he walked away.

Six-Toes stared at Daktair in surprise. "You're not a soldier."

"No, I'm a negotiator."

"If you've invented a new form of torture, get on with it. In any case, I shan't tell you anything."

"General Mehy wishes to meet one of your leaders, in the greatest secrecy."

"Don't try to make a fool of me!"

"The meeting is to take place at dead of night, in three new moons, near the abandoned well at the end of the Wadi of the Gazelles."

"Do you really think we'll fall for a crude trick like that?"

"The general will come with only a few soldiers, not with his army—you can check that easily. Your leader must do the same, or there'll be no meeting. And believe me, you've got a lot to lose, because the general intends to treat his future allies very generously."

"His future allies?" repeated Six-Toes incredulously.

"There's something Mehy wishes you to do, and he'll pay very highly."

For a fraction of a second, greed overcame incredulity. "You're lying!"

"I shall release you and your men, so that the message can be passed on."

"Let us go? I don't believe you."

Daktair walked over to the soldiers. "Untie the Libyans and let them go."

The commander started as though bitten by a horsefly. "That's out of the question! All these criminals must be put to death."

"Didn't you understand me, Commander?"

"Understand what?"

"This handful of scouts doesn't interest General Mehy," said Daktair quietly. "He wants to get his hands on their leaders, and only a well-planned ambush will enable him to do that. What's more, you'll play an important part in that ambush."

▲

"I like it and yet I don't like it," concluded Fened the Nose.

"Could you be a little clearer?"

"The rock is welcoming, the limestone is of good quality, but the site's like a woman nothing can satisfy."

"You're still thinking about your divorce," scoffed Ipuy. "Forget your wife once and for all, and you'll see that life's worth living."

Fened stuck his chest out. "I've never confused my personal problems with my professional duties. You're nicknamed 'the Examiner,' so you ought to know that."

"Woman trouble ruins the steadiest of hands," opined Nakht.

"Instead of inventing pointless proverbs, why don't you

pick up your mallet and your chisel? That way, we might make some progress."

"There are those who talk, and those who work," observed Ipuy, wiping his big pickax.

"You're missing Tausert's tomb," said Fened.

Ipuy laid down his pickax and stared hard at his colleague. "The world of humans is divided into two categories: imbeciles and the rest. And I'm afraid you may belong to the first category. In choosing the three of us to do this exploratory work, the Master honored us with his trust, and I am particularly proud of that."

"Did you just call me an imbecile?" demanded Fened.

"It's not time to break off for lunch yet," cut in Nakht. "You can finish arguing later."

He continued to excavate the passageway, and his two companions joined in, watching each other out of the corners of their eyes.

"A little more to the right," said Fened, who was following the Master's plan scrupulously.

"That's odd," said Nakht.

"What is?"

"The rock's resonance is different here."

"Let me listen." Fened used the broad chisel. "You're right. Anyone would swear it has no depth."

"Take another look at your map."

"We can't have made a mistake. We're heading in the right direction."

"Then let's carry on."

The three men set to work again, with still more energy. Although they might not be able to rival their colleagues, who were making astonishing progress on Tausert's tomb, they would show them that a small crew could achieve a great deal.

Nakht swung his pickax again, but this time the point sank into the rock so deeply that he lost his balance and let go of the handle.

"What's got into you?" asked Ipuy irritably. "I bet you've been drinking behind our backs."

Sheepishly, Nakht got to his feet. "Don't talk rubbish," he snapped. "I've never come across a snag like that before. This place must be cursed—it's the only explanation."

Ipuy bent over the crack Nakht had opened up. "No, there's no sign of evil spells. All you've done is open up a hole into a sort of cave."

Fened held a torch over the hole. "Let's enlarge it."

Nakht did not need to be asked twice. With strenuous effort, he managed to open up a hole big enough for Ipuy to slide through.

"What can you see?" asked Fened.

"Another passageway," said Ipuy. "I'll have to climb."

"Be careful."

"Don't worry, I'll be fine."

Ipuy was gone for only a few minutes, but it seemed like an eternity.

When he returned, he was ashen-faced. "It's unbelievable. We've just broken through into King Amenmessu's tomb!"

60

"It must be serious," Ched told Paneb. "The crew excavating Setnakhte's tomb are asking for you."

The Master climbed back up to the daylight. "What's the problem, Fened?"

"It's more of a disaster than a problem. We followed your plan, and broke right through into Amenmessu's House of Eternity."

"That's impossible!"

"But it's the truth," lamented Ipuy.

Paneb went straight over to the site; he saw that Ipuy had not exaggerated.

"What are we to do?" demanded Nakht, visibly shaken.

"Seal up the passageway you've excavated."

"Are we abandoning the site?"

"There's nothing else we can do."

"I didn't like it," Fened reminded him. "I didn't like it at all."

"You can protest later," said Nakht. "For now, we're sealing up that passageway."

▲

The crew set off back to the pass in heavy silence. Paneb led the way, and the others had difficulty keeping up with him. When he got there he stood gazing at the setting sun as if nothing else existed. The craftsmen ate their evening meal without a word. Only Kenhir dared go near Paneb, who was gazing down the mountain, his shadow stretching far below him.

"I must write the Journal of the Tomb," said Kenhir quietly.

"What's stopping you?"

"The whole crew has been told about that terrible accident, and I'm obliged to put it in writing."

"Carry out your duties," said Paneb.

"Unfortunately, that won't be the end of it."

"What else will happen?"

"The Master isn't above the Brotherhood's laws—quite the reverse, in fact. Because it's such a serious matter, I must convene the court."

Paneb turned to face him. "You want to put me on trial?"

"Either the court will acquit you, and you'll continue to direct the Brotherhood's work, or you'll be found guilty of this error and will have to resign."

A very long silence followed the Scribe of the Tomb's words.

"I shan't appear before the court," said Paneb, "because I already know what their verdict will be. I alone am responsible, so I alone am guilty."

Their attention caught by the Master's strong voice, the craftsmen had stopped eating and were straining to hear what he was saying.

"Don't take that attitude," urged Kenhir. "You know everyone holds you in the highest esteem."

"An esteem that will lead to my dismissal. You're living in a land of sunlight, but you can't bear its brilliance. We're cast in different molds, you and I. What you seek is your comfort, your safety; you won't let the light of high summer flood into your heart. Tomorrow, you must return to the village and elect another Master."

All the craftsmen got to their feet.

"What are you going to do?" asked Kenhir anxiously.

"I shall go to breathe the air of the Peak of the West and burn myself in its fire."

The Master's expression was so grim that no one dared argue. But when he left the settlement, Nakht went after him.

"Master, you'll never get back alive from up there."

"What does that matter? I'm banished from the Brotherhood."

"But the court hasn't delivered its verdict yet."

"My fault is worse than a crime, and no true craftsman would try to say anything else. So I shall ask the Peak of the West for justice."

The rest of the crew had caught up with them and were listening anxiously.

"If it finds Paneb innocent," said Thuty hopefully, "he'll remain our crew leader and Master."

Kenhir's head hung low. He knew very well that the Peak had never in the past granted forgiveness to a guilty man. It would have been better for Paneb to appear before the

"Assembly of the Set Square and the Right-angle," which would have recognized his good faith.

But Paneb was not a man for half measures; having once been Master, he would not become a simple craftsman again. By confronting the Peak's all-consuming fire, he wanted to be purified of his misdeed by the Divine powers themselves, and to continue to create Tausert's House of Eternity, in which he had been planning to express all his craft.

As Scribe of the Tomb, Kenhir could not deal leniently with a Master, whatever his qualities might be, for the work to be accomplished came before the man. That had been the Place of Truth's law since its foundation, and if it weren't applied the Brotherhood would perish. Paneb's popularity meant the craftsmen would hate Kenhir for being so unbending, but there was nothing else he could do. By insisting on applying the law, he was protecting the entire village.

"I suppose we're to kick our heels at home while we await the Peak's judgment?" suggested Unesh caustically.

"Unless Kenhir decides to take charge himself," replied Casa drily.

The old scribe ignored the taunt. With the aid of his stick, he began the descent. His bones ached, and he did not even feel like admiring the wonderful view that had so often enraptured him. Henceforth, he would be regarded as Paneb's persecutor, and in the end he'd probably have to retire and live outside the village—though he'd never stop loving it. At least he'd die with a clear conscience, knowing he'd met his obligations as Scribe of the Tomb, the most thankless job of all. But he couldn't stop wondering why a painter as experienced as Paneb had made such an elementary mistake in copying the map.

▲

Turquoise went to see Kenhir, but Niut refused to let her into his office.

"Is it true," asked Turquoise, "that the Scribe of the Tomb has sent Paneb to his death?"

"Of course not. It was Paneb himself who decided to climb the Peak—no one made him do it."

"But Kenhir wanted to drag him before the court."

"That was his duty," said Niut firmly, "because of the seriousness of the Master's error—I said exactly the same thing to Uabet. No craftsman or priestess of Hathor would ever criticize the thoroughness of our rule. My husband simply applied it, and we ought to congratulate him on doing so."

"Why's he hiding away like this?"

"Because he's worn out and depressed. Do you think he was happy about Paneb's decision? There's no point tormenting him; he's only done his duty."

Impressed by Niut's staunchness, Turquoise withdrew and set off for the Wise Woman's house. She had never imagined that Paneb might die; she could feel the warmth of his desire as clearly as though he were holding her in his arms and had never left her.

Since their first, passionate encounter, the intensity of their lovemaking had never dimmed, and Turquoise had never taken another lover. She remained a free woman, free to charm anyone who pleased her, but since becoming Paneb's mistress she had never desired another man. To think that she could be so deeply in love. Once a young rebel, and now raised to the rank of Master of the Brotherhood, Paneb radiated a strange magic, and she did not yet know all its secrets. No, she did not want to lose him.

The Wise Woman was deep in conversation with Iuwen, who was asking for news of her father.

"Is it true that he has gone into the mountains all on his own?"

"Yes," said Ubekhet.

"Does he want to reach the top and see the goddess?"

"That's right."

Knowing the Wise Woman would never lie to her, the little girl became thoughtful. "Very well," she said eventually. "I shall go and read the scroll about diseases of the lungs," and she went into Ubekhet's library.

"She doesn't realize how serious the situation is," said Turquoise.

"Yes, she does."

"But she seems so calm, so unworried."

"She knows both the Peak and her father."

"Let me go up, too, so that I can help Paneb."

"It's too late," said Ubekhet. "He must face the Peak's judgment alone."

▲

"At least drink a little vegetable broth," Niut urged Kenhir, who was huddled in a low chair.

"I'm not hungry or thirsty."

"Not eating and worrying yourself sick won't bring Paneb back."

"The whole village hates me."

"What does that matter, if you're at peace with yourself?"

" 'At peace!' That's easy to say."

Niut frowned. "Why are you punishing yourself? What do you think you've done wrong?"

"I don't know, but I feel that I've missed some important detail. Give me a little wine."

"Do you think that will clear your mind?"

"One never knows."

Niut gave him just enough wine to cover the bottom of a cup.

As he drained it, Kenhir at last realized what it was that he'd missed.

"I can't walk—my legs hurt too much. Go and fetch Fened at once. Tell him to bring me the map Paneb drew."

61

As he climbed toward the Peak of the West, Paneb remembered Ched's warning: "Life inevitably faces us with ordeals that make us fall a long way; and the fall will be harder for you than for other men. Always remember the victory over the dragon of darkness."

Did the sun-scorched mountain really hide a monster he must fight? His thoughts went back to the fall that had just lost him the office of Master, into which he had put his heart and soul. He was always ready to fight the most daunting enemies, but that loss had caught him unawares and he had been beaten before the fight began.

The priestesses of Hathor said that no one should climb the Peak without offering flowers to the goddess of the West, to appease her anger; but Paneb's hands were empty and the only thing he could offer her was a rage fit to shake the surrounding hills.

He must not reach the shrine at the summit at dawn or dusk; only the full light of noon would offer a valid judgment. So he waited until the sun was at its height before climbing the Peak, which was at once the Place of Truth's protector and a pitiless flame that would destroy the unwary and the vain.

When he reached the shrine, Paneb raised his fist, and shouted, "You who love silence so well, answer me! Since you are the incarnation of Ma'at, mistress of the sky, of births and transformations, tell me if you judge me worthy to lead the Brotherhood of your servants. Is the fault I committed so serious that it prevents me from creating Pharaoh Tausert's House of Eternity?"

At first, there was nothing but silence: an implacable silence, so heavy that even Paneb's shoulders almost gave way beneath its weight. But he held firm and questioned the goddess again, with the same fervor.

And the mountain moved. It was not an earth tremor but a very slow, almost dancelike swaying, and yet it made him stagger.

"So you speak at last. Don't hesitate. Speak louder, so that I may hear your verdict clearly!"

Paneb had just regained his balance when the rocks at the summit split open, and red light blazed out. He cried out in pain, clutching at his eyes, but managed to keep his footing.

When he opened his eyes again, he was blind. "You want to stop me painting because you are a cruel goddess," he roared. "Have I forgotten how to tell good from evil? Have I taken a false oath, or sullied the name of Ptah, the god of builders? Because I rebel against your silence, you try to destroy me by humiliating me, but you will fail. May the lion within you devour me, and may the furious wind bear me away!"

▲

Kenhir's voice was unsteady. "There has been a terrible mistake—no, a piece of sordid dishonesty. Paneb did nothing wrong. Look at the map, Ubekhet. Look at it closely."

The Wise Woman examined it carefully. "Paneb didn't draw this line," she said, pointing.

Kenhir was jubilant. "Exactly! The traitor stole the Master's drawing from Fened's house, made a corrupted copy, and left the copy for Fened to use. That's why the disaster happened. If I hadn't looked at the map again, I'd still think Paneb was responsible."

"Have you asked Fened about it?"

"Of course. He says it would have been easy to steal the original map and leave the copy in its place. Fened the shadow-eater, twisted enough to commit a misdeed and present himself as the victim? No, that's absurd."

"I'm going to find the Master," decided Ubekhet.

"If the Peak had spared him, he'd have been back a long time ago."

Kenhir was probably right, and the traitor's ruse had indeed killed the Master, but Ubekhet refused to give up hope. As she set out on the path to the Peak, a small hand slipped into hers.

"If you're going to find Daddy, I'm coming with you."

Ubekhet hesitated for a long time, but Iuwen's face was so determined that she agreed. The child, she thought, was strong enough to bear it if, as seemed likely, the worst had happened.

They climbed slowly. A few paces from the summit, they found the Master sitting on a rock, gazing at the Peak.

"Daddy!" Iuwen ran into his arms and snuggled against his chest.

"The arm of the Peak struck me," he explained, "and I felt its breath after it had made me see its power. It gave me new eyes at the very moment when darkness overcame me in the full light of day. Open your ears, Iuwen: the Peak will be generous if you know how to talk to it."

Ubekhet embraced him. "We know you did nothing wrong, Paneb. The traitor stole the map you drew, and replaced it with an altered copy. He hoped the stonecutters would make a fatal mistake and that you'd be held responsible."

Holding his daughter tightly, Paneb drew himself up to his full height. "Does that mean I'm confirmed in all my offices?"

"The goddess has judged you innocent and the Brotherhood's court will confirm her judgment. Your ordeal has enabled you to know the Peak's fire, which from now on will give life to your hands and your works."

▲

When the traitor met Turquoise in the main street of the village, he was amazed to see her looking so happy.

"What is there to be happy about?" he asked.

"Paneb's back."

"A priestess of Hathor told me the Peak wounded him seriously. Is that true?"

"Quite the opposite: it found him innocent. The Wise Woman's taken the Master to Sekhmet's shrine so that he can pay her homage, and tomorrow we're having a banquet in his honor. If you knew how happy I am!"

"That's obvious, Turquoise, that's obvious. I'm happy, too—very happy that Paneb has survived his ordeal."

"His heart's like a huge cauldron containing many more masterpieces—and we shall soon see them, thanks to the Peak."

More radiantly beautiful than ever, she hurried off to the shrine. The traitor trailed dejectedly back to his house.

His wife looked up from her cooking pot of pork with lentils. The moment she saw his face she knew what had happened. "Paneb's safe and sound, isn't he?"

"The mountain spared him."

"He isn't like other men. He's protected by Set."

"People thought Nefer was protected by the gods, too, but I killed him easily enough. Mere superstition isn't going to stop me."

"I'm getting more and more afraid."

"Stop sniveling. We're not going to give up the fortune waiting for us outside. Forget about being afraid, and think of a large, beautiful house, with plenty of servants, and lands which our peasants will cultivate for us. Paneb's only a man. I shall kill him just as I killed Nefer, I shall seize the Stone of Light, and we shall get what we've always wanted."

There was a knock at the door.

Terrified, the traitor's wife flattened herself against a wall. "They've identified you and are coming for us!"

Anxiously, the traitor opened the door a little way and looked out.

Niut the Lively was standing on the doorstep. "The Scribe of the Tomb has summoned all the members of the starboard crew to his house."

"I'll come straight away."

Niut went off to tell another craftsman.

"Don't go," pleaded his wife. "It's a trap, I know it is. Kenhir will arrest you in front of all your colleagues."

The traitor was torn. If his wife was right, all they could

do was run away at once. But how had he been found out? Besides, even though Sekhmet hadn't killed Paneb, it was still true that he'd made a mistake by using the false map, and that his mistake had caused a disaster that made him unworthy to be Master. The traitor would be sure to remind Kenhir of that fact, so that Paneb would be condemned.

"Let's leave the village now!" urged his wife.

"No," decided the traitor. "I'm going to Kenhir's house."

▲

All the members of the starboard crew gathered round while Paneb examined Fened's map closely.

"This is a forgery," he said at last, "and there are three ways I can prove it. First, this isn't the ink I used to make the original copy; second, the lines are a different width; and lastly, if you compare this papyrus with the piece in Kenhir's stores, you'll see they're different."

"I confirm all three points," declared Kenhir. "There is therefore no need to convene the court, because the Master has done nothing wrong."

All the craftsmen were relieved and delighted; and Karo was the first to congratulate Paneb.

Ched turned to Fened. "I think you've got some explaining to do, don't you?"

62

Fened was frightened. "Explaining? What about?"

"It's simple," replied Ched. "Either someone stole the map the Master drew and replaced it with a forgery, or else you dreamt up this plot yourself."

"Me, do something like that? You're mad!" The stonecutter quailed under the craftsmen's accusing stares. "You're wrong, I tell you. I'm innocent!"

"Come with me," ordered Paneb.

"Where are you taking me?"

"If you're guilty your punishment will be severe, but if you're innocent you have nothing to fear."

Realizing there was no escape, Fened followed Paneb, who led him to one of the shrines Uabet tended.

The priestess stood aside to allow the two men to enter a dimly lit vaulted room. Between the statues of Amenhotep I and his mother stood the Wise Woman, holding a statuette of Ma'at. She raised the statuette high, and said, "As you stand before eternal righteousness and our holy patrons, do you swear, on the life of Pharaoh and of the Master, that your heart and hands are clean?"

Fened knelt down, his eyes fixed on Ma'at. "I swear it."

Paneb raised him to his feet. "Let me embrace you."

▲

The news Tausert had had from the tjaty was hardly cheering. Acting on reports gathered by his son, whose honesty everyone respected, Setnakhte was stepping up his preparations for war. Political upheavals in the hinterland beyond Canaan and Syria were making Egypt look more and more tempting, and, as the diplomats' efforts had achieved little or nothing, an invasion looked increasingly likely.

Fortunately, though, there had been no serious incidents in the protectorates, so Setnakhte had not yet demanded the queen-pharaoh's approval of a preemptive attack. And Tjaty Hori was continuing to ensure Egypt's prosperity.

Tausert loved Thebes. Here, she experienced a peace that seemed beyond her reach in Pi-Ramses. She often went to Karnak, celebrated rituals in the great Temple of Amon, and spent all-too-brief hours in the palace garden.

The queen-pharaoh was leaving her office after a meeting

with the superintendent of the grain stores when her private secretary presented her with an unexpected request.

"The Master of the Place of Truth wishes to see Your Majesty as a matter of urgency."

Tausert felt suddenly dizzy, and for a moment she swayed.

"Majesty," said the scribe in alarm, "are you all right?"

"Yes, yes, don't worry."

"I'll send the Master away so you can rest."

"No, I'll see him. Bring him to me in the garden."

Tausert had never felt so exhausted. She barely managed to walk out of the palace into the garden and sit down in the shade of a tall sycamore. Wearily, she closed her eyes and thought of her late husband, who each night appeared to her more clearly in her dreams. From time to time, when she was listening to administrators' reports, she was surprised at how detached she felt, as if the exercise of power no longer interested her; but she put it down to tiredness.

Sensing that someone was near, Tausert opened her eyes. Paneb was standing before her in the full blaze of the sun.

"What is the urgent matter that brings you here, Master?"

"You know that King Setnakhte has ordered me to excavate his House of Eternity in the Valley of the Kings."

"Yes, of course I know. What is urgent about it?"

"The Brotherhood cannot carry out his order."

Tausert stiffened. "What am I to understand by that?"

"That the crews of the Place of Truth are fully occupied in building your Temple of a Million Years and your House of Eternity. We cannot take on any additional work."

"Surely you are obliged to obey an order from Pharaoh?"

"Not when the order is absurd and there's an obvious and better solution."

"And what is that solution?"

"It will surprise you, Majesty, and I will need your unqualified approval. The tomb I have designed is vast, so, since we have two pharaohs reigning at the same time, why not link them for ever?"

"Are you—can you be?—suggesting that I welcome Setnakhte into my House of Eternity?"

"Yes, if you are the first to rejoin the Divine Light. If not, it is King Setnakhte who will welcome you."

Tausert was shocked. "I am indeed surprised, Master. Do you really think I will accept it?"

"Yes, Majesty, because I am speaking of a work in which personal quarrels and temporal matters have no place. Pharaoh's spirit will live for ever in your House of Eternity."

The tomb of Tausert and Setnakhte . . . The queen closed her eyes again, to conjure up this strange image.

"Upon the name of Ma'at, Majesty, I swear that I shall toil unstintingly to make your House of Eternity the most beautiful in the Valley of the Kings. Through my paintings, I shall convey everything the Brotherhood has taught me and everything I have discovered during my years of work. Your face will shine out among the goddesses, and the magical colors will ensure that it can never fade."

If she had been younger and had had more vitality, Tausert would have rejected Paneb's suggestion. But, knowing that she would never again leave Thebes and that the Master was sincere, she gave in.

"I accept, but I am not the only person involved. Setnakhte is sure to refuse."

"Can you not persuade him, Majesty?"

"I am the very last person who should try."

"If you permit," said Paneb, "I'll do it. I'll leave for the capital at once, and request an audience with him."

"My secretary will give you a letter to him, but I fear you are bound to fail."

"I prefer to be hopeful, Majesty."

"What if Setnakhte refuses even to contemplate the idea?"

"Whatever happens, I shall devote myself to your House of Eternity."

▲

"Carry on like that," the Master told the stonecutters, who were making their way through the rock at a remarkable rate.

"This is the best work we've ever done," exclaimed Nakht. "I've never worked so eagerly. It's as if this place had been hoping for us to come—we haven't met the slightest difficulty."

"Yes, but you haven't got rheumatism," objected Karo.

"I've got a pain in my backbone," complained Casa.

"Lean your back against me," ordered Paneb.

He set the point of his breastbone against the painful place, wrapped his strong arms round Casa, and squeezed hard, as if trying to suffocate him.

"Breathe right out."

As Casa's lungs emptied, Paneb squeezed even harder, and everyone heard a crack.

"That feels much better," said Casa, once he had been freed.

"Anyone else need a doctor?" asked the Master.

"No," replied Kenhir, from his seat in the shade of the cliff face.

"Ched and Gau will ensure that my plans are carried out, and you must check everything carefully, Kenhir."

The Scribe of the Tomb stood up and leant on his walking stick. "This is a dangerous journey you're making, Paneb."

"Don't worry, I'll come back."

"Pi-Ramses is more dangerous than a nest of vipers. Setnakhte regards you as one of Tausert's main supporters, and he's not forgiven you for that. I am worried that he'll turn down your proposal and take you prisoner."

"He cannot by himself force a new Master on the Place of Truth. And I am counting on you to ensure that our rule is observed."

"If you'd only listen to an experienced man's advice for once, you wouldn't go."

"If I don't meet Setnakhte, how can I make him agree that a shared tomb is necessary?"

▲

Turquoise stood before the great gate of the village, her russet hair hidden by a magnificent black wig and her eyes delicately accentuated with makeup.

Paneb halted, his bag on his shoulder. "Are you against my going?" he asked.

"No one could stop you going, not even the woman who loves you."

He gazed at her with such intensity that she shivered.

"Go, Master, and do as your office requires, even if it destroys you. If you don't, I shall no longer love you."

63

Setnakhte usually got up early, but today he had been forced to remain in bed by appalling pains in his lower back, which his doctor could ease only with the aid of a strong decoction of poppies. Shortly before noon, the king allowed himself to be examined.

"Well, Doctor?" he said impatiently.

"I'd like to be able to tell you that this is just an ordinary backache, but I am not in the habit of lying. Do you want the truth?"

"Yes—and all of it. Don't keep anything back."

"As you wish, Majesty. The truth is simple: you are old and your vital organs are worn out. You have more energy than most men, so you have managed to forget that fact up to now, but your defiance cannot last. Of course, you can take strengthening medicines, but they will have only limited effect and can do no more than delay the final outcome."

"You mean death?"

"You must prepare yourself for it, Majesty."

"How long?"

"If you lived more than a year, it would be almost a miracle. I strongly recommend that you reduce your workload immediately, and take as much rest as possible. Otherwise my forecast will be much too hopeful."

"Thank you for being so frank," said Setnakhte.

"One more, and rather happier, thing: we have many drugs that can ensure you feel no pain. And I shall of course be at your disposal, day and night."

▲

Despite his lack of appetite, Setnakhte had forced himself to eat some lamb chops and a salad. His back was less painful, thanks to the doctor's drugs, and he had a half-hour meeting with Hori before his private secretary brought in the confidential messages.

"A letter from Queen Tausert, Majesty. The Master of the Place of Truth brought it."

"Paneb the Ardent? Are you sure?"

"He is a giant of a man, a good head taller than the captain of your personal guard."

"Then it is indeed Paneb. But why has he come all this way to bring me a letter?"

Intrigued, Setnakhte read the message, which was a simple letter of recommendation, asking him to receive the Master as soon as possible.

"How many meetings have I this afternoon?" he asked.

"Four, Majesty: the overseer of the army's weapons—"

"Postpone them until tomorrow, and send Paneb in."

Setnakhte rinsed out his mouth with a mixture of water and natron, and sat down on a chair whose back was decorated with "power" scepters symbolically linked with Set. Alas, now that he at last exercised power, his divine protector had abandoned him.

Like Seti II, Setnakhte had taken a risk in choosing to be a servant of Set, for only Seti I, father of Ramses the Great, had been able to master that celestial fire. Seti's reign had been one of the most magnificent in Egypt's long history; no one should have tried to follow in his footsteps.

Paneb was shown in; he bowed low before the king.

"According to Tausert's letter, Master, you wish to consult me urgently."

"The site you chose for your tomb is unsuitable, Majesty."

"Ah. So you wish to suggest another?"

"Exactly."

"And you came all this way to talk to me about it."

"Yes, Majesty, because of its extremely unusual nature."

Setnakhte was concerned. "It is still in the Valley of the Kings, isn't it?"

His somber voice rock-steady, Paneb said, "I think the vast tomb currently being built could house both our pharaohs."

"The same tomb for myself and Tausert . . . ?"

"The queen has agreed."

Setnakhte could not hide his astonishment. "Are you sure of that?"

"Absolutely sure, Majesty."

"Tausert and Setnakhte, linked for all eternity . . . And you are asking for my agreement?"

"It is my most heartfelt hope."

The old man would have liked to stand up, take the air, call a meeting of his advisers, but he no longer had the strength. A few days earlier, he would have hurled insults at Paneb for daring to defy him like this. But today, everything was different, so different . . .

"Is the work far advanced?"

"We're making rapid progress," confirmed Paneb. "Do you wish me to submit my plans to you?"

"That will not be necessary; your skills are well known. I also accept your proposal, Master, but I have one demand to make of you: hurry."

▲

Accompanied by the detachment of desert troops that had captured the Libyan scouts, Mehy set off to the nocturnal meeting he had arranged with them.

Although partly reassured by the general's presence, the men were unhappy about venturing into the desert in the middle of the night. Apart from its many venomous snakes, it was filled with evil spirits that could not be killed by even the most battle-hardened warrior.

There was only one consolation: the Libyans and other sand travelers must be as frightened as they were.

"There aren't enough of us," said the commander of the detachment.

"This meeting must remain absolutely secret," Mehy reminded him.

"Yes, sir, but you're taking too big a risk."

"Capturing a Libyan chieftain is very difficult—you know that as well as I do. Whatever the risk, the chance is too good to miss. Besides, I'm glad to have a chance to prove that I don't spend my entire life in an office. Can you imagine how delighted the queen will be when we bring the rebel back to her?"

"He'd be a fine catch," agreed the commander.

As soon as they reached the Wadi of the Gazelles, the soldiers switched to single file and became doubly alert. The commander, who took the lead, carried a long forked staff, and the man at the rear carried a heavy huntsman's pouch Mehy had given him.

When they came in sight of the abandoned well, the commander became restive. "Before we go any farther, General," he said, "let me send one of my men to check the area."

"There's no need. The Libyans will be there."

"Unless we take precautions, they'll simply kill us like rats in a trap."

"Don't worry, Commander. They won't do anything until they've seen what we're offering them."

Mehy's calm did nothing to reassure the soldiers, who shared their commander's views.

When the party was only a few paces from the well, the Libyans emerged from hiding. There were eight of them; they took up position in a semicircle and brandished their pikes.

"Don't move," Mehy ordered his men. He stepped forward. "I asked to meet a tribal chief. Has he had the courage to come?"

It was Six-Toes's turn to step forward. "I am not merely a scout. I am also the chief of a fearless tribe. And what about you? Are you really General Mehy, commander of the Theban army?"

"I am."

"Why do you want to meet me?"

"Recently you've been coming very close to our territory."

"One day the whole of Egypt will belong to us."

"In the meantime, I have a business proposition to put to you."

Six-Toes was as astonished as the Egyptian soldiers. "I do not involve myself in trade."

"If you go on attacking our caravans, I shall send my troops to find and kill you; you'd have no chance of escaping. But I've something much better to offer you." He gestured to the man with the pouch to come forward, and told him, "Open it and spread out the contents on the ground."

Six-Toes could not believe his eyes: the dim moonlight must be playing tricks on him.

"It's exactly what you think it is," said Mehy. "Feel free to handle it."

The Libyan knelt down. It was gold, several small ingots of gold, worth a small fortune! He raised questioning eyes to Mehy. "What do you want in return?"

"An end to your attacks in the Theban region, and a Libyan raiding party that I can contact whenever I wish and that will obey me without question."

"Do you think I'm a fool? How could I trust a general in Pharaoh's pay?"

With lightning speed, Mehy unsheathed his dagger and slit the throats of the commander and the man who had carried the gold.

"Kill the others!" he ordered the Libyans.

Two spears were instantly plunged into the third man's chest. The fourth was wounded in the shoulder, and tried to run away. Mehy snatched up a spear that had landed in the sand, and took careful aim: the spear struck the man in the back, killing him outright.

"If you trust me, you'll get much more gold than this," Mehy told Six-Toes, who was lost for words.

64

Daktair had got even fatter. He could never resist the little snacks his Egyptian cook prepared, and the more worried he was, the more he ate. That morning he was so anxious that he'd devoured a knuckle of pork, some soft cheese, and several bunches of grapes, and he was still hungry.

He, the brilliant inventor, had allowed his comfortable life to lull him into inaction, when he should have been fighting the long-outworn superstitions that prevented Egypt from accepting new ideas and methods.

The man responsible for his failure had a name: Mehy. That damned general had tempted Daktair with promises of a dazzling future, but those promises had been broken. Mehy had failed to acquire the Stone of Light, and his determination to seize supreme power was nothing but an illusion. Still, at least the lying general should be dead by now, killed by the

Libyans in the desert—that meeting proved he'd lost his mind.

"My lord, shall I comb and perfume your beard?" asked his servant.

"Hurry up. I must leave."

Daktair would not go to his workshop, where his inventions lay neglected after being rejected by the temples. No, he would go to the royal palace to ask for news of Mehy. Either the general's body would have been brought back, or he would have disappeared. And if, by some misfortune, Mehy had returned wounded or even unharmed, Daktair decided, he would denounce him to Queen-Pharaoh Tausert, telling her everything he knew about the man's wickedness. He would explain that he himself had been threatened and manipulated, and that his only concern was for the truth. That way he would have his revenge on the madman who had caused his downfall.

Daktair had just finished dressing when his steward announced a visitor: "General Mehy is in your reception room. He says he's in a hurry."

Daktair paled. The only thing he could do was try to escape by way of the garden. But the general would soon realize what was happening, and Daktair would be captured before he could cross to the west bank and reach the palace.

And yet . . . Surely Mehy wouldn't dare kill him in his own house? The servants would accuse the general of the crime, and their statements would earn him the death penalty. No, Daktair had nothing to fear so long as he didn't leave his house. And if Mehy so much as raised a finger to threaten him, he'd call for help.

His stomach in knots, he went to the reception room.

His visitor stopped pacing up and down and snapped, "You kept me waiting long enough."

"General, it really is you!"

"Did you think I'd died in the desert?"

"It was a very dangerous venture, and I—"

"Don't worry, my faithful friend, I'm indestructible. Everything went splendidly. I now have a Libyan raiding party at my disposal—and before long it's going to be very useful."

"What did the troops make of the meeting?"

Mehy stared straight at him. "They're dead, naturally."

"You don't mean . . . ?"

"There's only one way of being dead, my dear Daktair, and I couldn't have any witnesses to the meeting left alive."

Daktair swallowed with difficulty.

"But you're different," said Mehy smoothly. "You're an ally."

"You can be sure of that, General."

"I have some good news for you. Queen Tausert has canceled her audiences because her health has suddenly worsened. She can no longer study documents and steer the ship of state. That means I'm master of Thebes again, and the Place of Truth has lost its main supporter. What better time to deal it its death blow?"

"That's marvelous."

"However, I need a particular weapon, my very dear friend, and you're going to get it for me."

▲

Although he was in complete charge of Mehy's huge house in Middle Egypt, Imuni had still not come to terms with his expulsion from the Place of Truth. It was he, not someone else, who should be running the village—and he had documents to prove it.

Now that he had recovered from his long period of depression, Imuni was finally going on the attack. Using detailed legal arguments, he would have the village court's decision overturned, have Kenhir dismissed, and ensure that he, Imuni, was appointed Scribe of the Tomb. Then he would expel Paneb and install himself as Master of the Brotherhood.

Of course, there was still the Wise Woman, and he had no hold over her. He would need the local court's agreement to abolish that office. Well, it was just a matter of being patient.

Imuni warmly greeted the mayor of Thebes's assistant, an accomplished man who was well versed in all the complexities of Egypt's laws.

"Thank you for taking the time to study my case and coming to see me."

"I am very fond of this region," said the scribe, "and your case interests me."

Imuni tensed."What do you think of my legal argument?"

"It has its points, but it won't be enough to defeat your opponents."

"Then I've no chance!"

"I didn't say that," replied the scribe. "But your best course of action is to find and exploit a legal technicality, and above all not to go into the matter in depth. In view of the unique nature of the village's court, you'd be refused permission to bring a case against it."

"But the Brotherhood treated me unjustly! They didn't recognize my worth, they ignored my skills and refused me the post I was entitled to."

"That may be, my friend, but I'm viewing this from a strictly legal point of view, and your statements will have no validity."

Imuni calmed down. "You mentioned a technicality. Have you found one?"

"I think so. The Brotherhood's religious function means it must observe a strict calendar of sacred festivals and holidays. According to that calendar, your expulsion was pronounced on an unfavorable day. That put you in danger, and you are therefore entitled to reparation—in other words to be readmitted. Once you are inside, you can submit your official application to lead the Place of Truth."

"Will Queen-Pharaoh Tausert agree to my doing that?"

"Her health is failing. It will almost certainly be Setnakhte who makes the decision."

For the first time since he had been hounded from the village, Imuni smiled.

▲

Turquoise lay naked on the terrace of her house, bathed in the strong noon sunshine. Beside her was a long-necked vase of ointment made from "stable" oil, acacia flowers, and melted fat; the ointment perfumed the skin and gently colored it brown to protect it from the sun.

Turquoise took a little on her fingertips and rubbed it over her breasts. Paneb sat beside her, drinking in the delicious spectacle.

"Will you put some on my back?" she asked.

She turned onto her belly, and Paneb smoothed ointment gently into her skin, unleashing waves of pleasure to which she abandoned herself utterly. When he bent down and kissed her neck, she could no longer resist her desire. She pulled him down on top of her, and they made love passionately. The sun was their accomplice, lavishing burning caresses on them and feeding their desire.

Afterward they lay peacefully side by side.

"Do you still refuse to marry me?" asked Paneb.

"More than ever. It would be mad to exchange a lover like you for a commonplace husband! Besides, breaking my vow would bring misfortune to both of us. Put that thought out of your head once and for all, and think about the speech you must make to the two crews."

On his return from Pi-Ramses, Paneb had briefly told Ubekhet, Kenhir, and Hay that Tausert and Setnakhte had accepted his suggestion, and then visited Turquoise, whose welcome had been everything he could have hoped. Now the craftsmen, who saw him more and more as a hero who could overcome the worst difficulties, were waiting to hear the details.

"I hate making speeches," grumbled Paneb. "The way's clear now, so all we have to do is work hard and make the tomb of Tausert and Setnakhte beautiful beyond compare."

"You aren't in competition with your predecessors," said Turquoise.

The comment stung him like a whiplash. "No, but I am with myself—if I weren't, I'd be content with what I've already done. For this tomb, I shall demand that my hands give everything they haven't already given."

65

For twenty hours, Paneb toiled to produce a matchless blue pigment, carefully controlling the fire beneath the crucible so that the ingredients were reduced to powder. This he then crushed, moistened, and formed into round cakes, which would be dissolved little by little, as required. Then, using pistachio seeds, he prepared the fine varnish he would need to fix the paintings.

When they entered Tausert and Setnakhte's House of Eternity, the craftsmen sensed that their work was taking a crucial step forward.

Even Ched's heart was in his mouth. "Is the light bright enough for you, Master?" he asked.

Thirty triple-wicked lamps had been carefully arranged so that they flooded the sloping passageway with intense light.

"It's excellent. Have we got enough spare wicks?"

"Kenhir has allocated us an entire chestful."

The Master carried out a final check on the walls. The limestone had been covered well with a fine layer of plaster, forming an ideal surface for the brush.

"This work is marvelous," he pronounced.

"The detailed plans are ready," said Ched, "and we're ready to draw the grid."

"That won't be necessary."

Ched's eyes widened. "Not necessary? You're not going to use a grid? But it gives you the correct proportions."

"Either they live in my hand, or I shall fail."

"You're taking an enormous risk!"

"I know," said Paneb. "The vision of this House of Eternity has haunted me for many nights. I see each of its figures, I feel their intensity, the intensity of the signs of power that radiate light in the darkness. When we close the entrance of the tomb, a ritual will be set in motion, and the gods will speak. In painting them and giving life to their Word, I want to be worthy of the Place of Truth."

His solemn voice echoed in what was, as yet, only an inanimate, empty space. And all the members of the starboard crew, who had thought they knew the Master well, suddenly realized that he was greater even than they had imagined.

"Nefer the Silent has been reborn in his spiritual son," murmured Didia.

"In effect, it's still the same Master leading the Brotherhood," added Thuty.

Paneb stood silent and motionless for a long time before the wall. Then he said, "It's time for you to leave and rest at the pass. I shall spend the night here."

As soon as the craftsmen had left the Valley, he set to work. Like the dying sun, which entered the darkness to be regenerated during the twelve ritual hours, he was left alone with his emerging work, facing the ordeal of the silent tomb.

▲

When they returned to the site, the crew found the Master sitting beside the entrance to the tomb, his eyes half closed. The sun was already high in the sky.

"May I go in?" asked Ched.

Paneb nodded.

Followed by his colleagues, Ched entered the passageway, which was still lit by the waning lamps. On the walls, they discovered the fantastical figures of the gatekeepers of the underworld, brandishing their knives. Paneb had turned these fearsome beings into masterpieces, whose living colors touched the soul and awoke it to unseen realities.

"What incredible precision of form and detail," exclaimed Gau. "And he's done it without using a grid."

"If we didn't know the incantations needed to pacify these creatures, I would be really frightened," confessed Pai.

"The fire of the Peak has given life to Paneb's hands," said Unesh.

The craftsmen lapsed into silence, unable to take their eyes off these pitiless guardians, the guarantors of righteousness.

Paneb soon rejoined them. "To work," he ordered.

"Shouldn't you sleep for a while?" suggested Renupe.

"Kenhir would accuse me of laziness. Let's carry on excavating and prepare new colors."

▲

As usual, the banquet given by Mehy and Serketa was a great success. Among the wealthy and distinguished guests was the head doctor at the royal palace, upon whom Serketa, dressed in a gown that made the most of her generous cleavage, had been lavishing special attention.

Mehy refilled the doctor's cup with red wine from Khargeh and said, "The whole province is singing your praises, Doctor. Everyone says you're exceptionally skilled."

"You flatter me, General."

"Not at all, my dear fellow. After all, your colleagues' jealousy is the best possible proof of your success."

"Have they been criticizing me?" asked the doctor, taken aback.

"I loathe envious people, and I have discouraged them."

"How can I thank you, General?"

"Fortunately, I enjoy perfect health. But if I have the slightest problem, I shall call for you."

"I'd be honored. But tell me, General, these criticisms, did they put my position at risk?"

"A great many doctors would love to take your place and enjoy the considerable benefits attached to it. But don't worry. I'm your staunchest supporter, and my opinion carries some weight in Thebes."

"I'm fully aware of that, General, and you may consider me in your debt."

Mehy led his guest into the garden, far from the din of the great reception room, where the many guests were enjoying the delicious dishes.

"You know I have a deep affection for our queen, who lights up Thebes with her presence," said the general quietly, "and I must confess that all these contradictory rumors about her health are making me extremely anxious. Some say it's merely a brief, trifling indisposition, others that she has a serious, perhaps incurable, illness. I haven't been able to speak with Her Majesty for three weeks now. Several decisions await her attention, and I no longer know what to think."

The doctor was embarrassed. "I understand your position, but I regret . . ."

"I admire your honesty and discretion, Doctor; but bear in mind that this concerns an affair of state. Her Majesty appointed me to ensure the safety of the city and the province, and without precise instructions my task is proving difficult. That's why I ventured to speak to you."

Deeply troubled, the doctor bit his lip. "General, if I tell you the truth, may I have your word that you will say not a word to anyone?"

"I repeat: this is a matter of state. You may certainly rely on my silence—and my support."

"Which I am going to need," said the doctor.

"Are things even more serious than I thought?"

"The queen has an incurable disorder of the blood, General. When my colleagues realize I've failed, they'll accuse me of incompetence and I shall be dismissed, even though I've done everything any doctor could possibly do."

"Do you mean to say our beloved sovereign is dying?"

"Her case is indeed desperate."

"That's terrible news! But you were right to confide in me, and, as I said, I shall protect you."

"General, I don't know what to say, and—"

"Go and try to enjoy yourself a little, my friend."

Mehy smiled as he watched the doctor walk away. As soon as Tausert was dead, he'd dismiss the useless creature and send him off to rot in some small town in Nubia. The important thing was that soon his only adversary would be old Setnakhte.

The head steward came up to him, bowed, and handed him a sealed scroll. "An urgent message from Pi-Ramses, my lord."

From across the room, Serketa saw her husband move to one side to read the report; she knew it would be from one of his loyal officers, who often sent him confidential information.

As he read, Mehy's face turned purple; she hurried over to him.

"This is incredible," he snarled, "incredible! Paneb has been to Pi-Ramses and had a meeting with Setnakhte, and only now do I hear about it! We could have arranged an ambush, intercepted Paneb, the—"

Mehy opened his mouth very wide, and gasped for air. Dropping the scroll, he clutched his chest.

"What's the matter, my sweet love?" asked Serketa anxiously.

"A terrible pain . . . It hurts, I . . ."

The steward caught him as his legs gave way beneath him.

"A doctor, quickly!" screamed Serketa. "The general's having a seizure of the heart!"

66

The craftsmen had donned their ceremonial clothes, and gathered to greet Queen-Pharaoh Tausert when she arrived to dedicate her Temple of a Million Years. The ceremony ought to have begun at dawn, but they were still waiting, and the sun would soon reach its zenith, bathing the small but exquisite building in light. Overhead, ibis and pink flamingos soared in a clear blue sky.

"Are we going to have to spend the whole day here?" grumbled Karo.

"Yes, if need be," retorted Renupe.

"You don't suffer from the heat like I do," protested Gau.

"Now that you come to mention it . . ."

"We could ask permission to have a drink," suggested Casa.

Sitting in the shade on a stool, the Scribe of the Tomb, who had overseen the preparations for the ceremony, had become more and more worried as time passed.

"I don't think Tausert's coming," Paneb murmured in Kenhir's ear.

"She may just have been delayed."

"You know she hasn't."

"The ceremony hasn't been postponed. We must be patient a little longer."

"Yes, but how much longer?" asked Paneb. "The craftsmen are already hungry and thirsty."

The old scribe got to his feet with difficulty and spoke with the priest whose task was to make offerings each day to the queen's *ka.* The priest agreed to go to the palace to find out what was happening.

Just as he was leaving the site, he met a delegation from the capital. After a brief conversation, he came back to Kenhir.

"Her Majesty has been detained," he announced. "We are to begin the rites without her."

"Shouldn't we postpone them?" asked Paneb.

"Her Majesty's orders are explicit."

The Brotherhood headed for the shrine. The Wise Woman would bring it to life and make its power shine forth; but would that be enough to restore the queen's health?

▲

Mehy's house was not the usual hive of activity. The cook did not know which dishes to cook, and no one dared ask Serketa for instructions, for she was in a state of nervous agitation close to madness.

Eventually, the door of Mehy's bedchamber opened and the head doctor of the palace appeared.

Serketa pounced on him. "Well, Doctor?"

"Your husband will live."

"Is his heart badly damaged?

"I don't think so—this was simply a warning. But he must work less hard in future, and take more rest. I've prescribed him remedies that will set him back on his feet, provided he doesn't overexert himself."

Without a word of thanks to him, Serketa rushed into the bedchamber. She was afraid she might find her husband too weak to continue on his path to power. If so, it would be a pity the doctor had saved him, and she would have to rid herself of the useless burden.

But Mehy was on his feet, his complexion pink, eating a plate of figs.

"How are you feeling, my sweet love?" asked his wife.

"Perfectly well—and very hungry. Don't worry, my heart is as strong as granite, and a moment's tiredness isn't going to slow me down."

Serketa said in her little-girl voice, "Would you like to prove it?"

Mehy kneaded her breasts. "You'll never have a more virile

man than me, but there's something urgent I must see to. I need gold for the Libyan raiding party, and it's arriving today from Nubia."

"Don't you have to deliver it to the temple at Karnak?"

"Of course I do, and I shan't fail in my duties."

"But then how . . . ?"

"Our friend Daktair has a fertile mind. He'll help me solve this little problem."

▲

Under the command of General Mehy himself, the soldiers delivered the gold and silver ingots to the temple Treasury; they were to be used to decorate the temple. The high priest received the general for a few moments, and congratulated him on the precautions he had taken; since he had been supervising the transport of these most precious materials, there had been not one theft.

As usual, a goldsmith from Karnak checked the purity of the metals. Ordinarily, an elderly craftsman, close to retirement, carried out this task, which took only a short time because the Egyptian officials working in Nubia had never sent poor-quality gold or silver to Thebes. But on this particular morning, the usual inspector was ill and his place was taken by a young goldsmith renowned for his meticulousness.

He spent a long time examining each ingot before marking it "good."

"Come and have lunch," said one of his colleagues. "You've been working for more than five hours without a break."

"I'm coming. Ah, just a moment."

"Hurry up. I'm hungry."

"No, it can't be . . ."

"What's the matter?"

"The head goldsmith must be told."

"We can't disturb him now."

"Never mind lunch. This is serious."

▲

The Scribe of the Tomb was in discussion with the Master when Niut interrupted them.

"The head goldsmith from Karnak is asking for you at the main gate."

The two men looked at each other in surprise. The goldsmith seldom left the city of Amon, and he was not known as an ardent defender of the Place of Truth.

Paneb helped Kenhir to his feet and handed him his walking stick.

"You must consult the Wise Woman again," said Niut, "and take your medicines properly. Otherwise age will really start to take its toll on you."

Deciding not to begin an argument he was bound to lose, Kenhir hurried out of the house.

▲

The head goldsmith seemed as supercilious as ever, but Paneb could detect anxiety beneath the arrogance, and the man was clearly reluctant to reveal exactly why he had come.

"No one must overhear our conversation," he said nervously.

"We'll sit down over there, at the foot of that hill," decided Paneb. "We won't be disturbed there."

Kenhir looked on with amusement. This haughty man probably needed to ask a favor of the Brotherhood, which was why he was having such trouble getting the words out.

"We have a problem," confessed the goldsmith.

"A dishonest craftsman?" suggested Kenhir.

"No, of course not. A delivery of dubious gold and silver."

"From Nubia?"

"Yes."

"That's impossible," exclaimed Kenhir. "The inspectors are absolutely ruthless about checking the quality."

"I agree, and that's what we've always found. But this time there is some doubt, and I should like . . . a second opinion."

"So you want to consult our goldsmith, Thuty the Learned."

"If you can persuade him to do it—he and I have no great liking for each other."

Indeed, when Thuty had briefly worked at Karnak for the Brotherhood, he had been glad to leave, because he had loathed having to obey a petty-minded official who was less skilled than himself.

"Thuty must make his own decision," said Kenhir, not without a certain satisfaction. "The Master will put your request to him, but I cannot promise anything."

Like Kenhir, Paneb had no wish to bow the knee before their guest, but he had a feeling that the head goldsmith was an instrument of fate, and that he must take heed of such a sign.

▲

Thuty had been consulting the Wise Woman, who had succeeded in unblocking the channels in his liver and freed him from a stubborn headache. He was on his way home, and looking forward to a hearty lunch, when he bumped into the Master.

"Thuty, I need your expertise."

"No problem. What about?"

"Some gold and silver ingots."

"I've checked ours, and they're all of the highest quality."

"These belong to the temple at Karnak—their head goldsmith brought them."

Thuty's temper flared. "That self-important, useless little tyrant? He can manage without me!"

"Coming to us was a big humiliation for him."

"Not big enough! Let him climb every mountain path on his knees, and then we'll see."

"I'm asking for your help, Thuty."

"As Master, you mean?"

"Exactly."

"That's different. And I won't have to talk to that miserable idiot?"

"No, you won't. I'll act as go-between."

▲

"All the gold ingots looked perfect to us," said the head goldsmith shakily, "all except this one."

Thuty felt its weight, scratched it with a miniature chisel, and laid it against his heart. "There's some silver in it, which is normal. If you've had me brought here on a fool's errand, I'm leaving."

"No, please don't go," begged the head goldsmith. "We agree with what you said, and I reprimanded our young inspector, who has a tendency to be overzealous. On the other hand, with regard to this silver ingot, I fear that his assessment—"

"Say no more," commanded Thuty.

This time, he was not satisfied with the results of his examination. "I must go back to my workshop."

He returned an hour later, and looked his former superior in the eye. "What does your young inspector think?"

"He thinks there's something strange about it, and he's reluctant to stamp it 'good.' "

"And he's right. You ought to promote him at once, because he has a true feel for metal. The ingot was made by a highly skilled forger, using a very cunning trick—I think I'm one of the few who know about it. Soft white pewter is washed four times, producing what looks exactly like high-grade silver. It would deceive almost any inspector, no matter how skilled and experienced."

The head goldsmith fainted.

While he was being revived by the Wise Woman, Kenhir sent an urgent message to Sobek. As soon as the goldsmith could walk, he, Kenhir, Paneb, and Thuty went to the Fifth Fort, where Sobek was awaiting them in his office.

Kenhir told the commander what had happened. "Someone reliable must be sent to the mine this silver came from," he said. "It's important that it's done without alerting the officials at Karnak, because one of them may be involved in the fraud."

"How can you possibly think such a thing?" exclaimed the head goldsmith indignantly.

"Stop cackling like an old goose," advised Kenhir. "Either there's a plot involving the mine and Karnak, or else the ingots delivered by the mine are of the correct quality."

"In that case," said Paneb, "the ingot must have been stolen and replaced by a substitute while the metals were being transported."

"Then we must check the conditions of transport and question those responsible," said Sobek.

"I agree," said Kenhir. "So you must leave immediately with Thuty and two of your men. And don't come back until you have the answer."

67

The silent temple was bathed in faint light.

"Awaken in peace, O Divine power," intoned the Master.

Taking the statuette of Ma'at from the innermost shrine, Paneb anointed it with perfume, decorated it, dressed it, and offered it subtle essences of foods. By so doing, he renewed the pact between the Brotherhood and the Divine universe, at the dawn of a new creation.

After speaking the words of knowledge, Paneb offered the Brotherhood's protector a gold statuette one cubit tall, fashioned with the aid of the Stone of Light. Then, deeply moved by what he had just experienced, he removed all traces of his footsteps and closed the doors to the innermost shrine.

Outside, the newborn sun's light blazed out as it emerged from the Peak of the East. Ubekhet was waiting for him, her sweet smile as radiant as the sun.

"I shall never get used to this," Paneb confessed as they left the temple. "How can a human being encounter Ma'at without dying instantly?"

"It is your office as Master that communes with the goddess," said Ubekhet. "If that did not happen, righteousness would vanish from this earth and abandon it to countless forms of evil. Let us strengthen the presence of Ma'at in this world, and so make it fit for us to live in."

There were few people about in the village, because Paneb had granted a rest day so that everyone could go and buy what was needed to prepare for the great Festival of Ptah.

▲

While his wife was buying fabrics in the lively, colorful market, the traitor pretended to be interested in an herb seller's wares. The woman's face had been skillfully made up to alter her appearance, and was partly hidden by a heavy, coarse wig.

"I received your coded message," whispered the traitor.

"Have you made any progress?" asked Serketa.

"I think I know where the Stone's hidden, but it's very difficult to get at, and I don't want to take any risks."

"Behave just as normal. We'll soon be able to help you more directly."

"What are you planning to do?"

"You'll see. At the moment, we have a problem."

"Is it to do with me?" asked the traitor anxiously.

"No, don't worry. But I need information that only you can provide and that will enable me to solve the problem."

The traitor told Serketa what she wanted to know.

▲

Turquoise applied makeup from a shell lined with mother-of-pearl, and dressed her hair with pins and a fine-toothed wooden comb. She applied a perfume Paneb had bought from the workshop at the temple in Karnak; it took fifty days to make, and its blend of scents made her even more alluring.

Then she donned the long red gown of a priestess of Hathor, and a necklace of pearls set in cornelian, alternating with pendants shaped like pomegranates.

When she left her house and went toward the temple, even the sharpest-tongued village women were struck dumb with admiration. At forty-seven, Turquoise was still a dazzlingly beautiful woman.

She was not the last person to arrive at the temple gateway: Casa's wife had had to change her dress at the last moment because one of the straps had broken.

"Ipuy the Examiner and Uabet the Pure have organized the festival," announced the Master. "They will describe its different stages; as usual, the first will be homage to Ptah."

Userhat the Lion unveiled an impressive statue of the god wearing a white robe from which his hands emerged, holding the "stability" pillar and the "power" scepter. With one voice, the craftsmen sang a chorus to the harmony of creation, after which some of the priestesses of Hathor made music on their lyres, flutes, and harps.

"The festival has begun well," said Karo, "but we're all worried about Thuty. Shouldn't he be back from Nubia by now?"

"Considering how much metal he must inspect," said Paneb, "there's no need to be alarmed. And don't forget that Sobek's there to protect him."

Reassured, the craftsmen eagerly prepared for the first banquet.

▲

As evening fell, Bad Girl sounded the alarm; Ebony at once followed suit. Someone was approaching the village.

"Nakht, go and see who it is," ordered the Master.

Nakht ran to the great gate. He came back a few minutes later, with a beaming smile. "It's Thuty. He's waiting for you in Sobek's office."

Paneb took the Wise Woman and the Scribe of the Tomb with him to the Fifth Fort. When they went into Sobek's office, they found Thuty and Sobek both looking very pleased with themselves.

"You wanted answers," said Sobek, "and we've found them. The miners weren't very pleased to see us, but as soon as I said I was from the Place of Truth, their attitude changed. I was able to inspect the ingots, and Sobek questioned the inspectors. Everything was as it should be."

"What did you do then?" asked Paneb. "Did you question the men who transported the ingots?"

"Yes, we did. They're soldiers, under the direct authority of the governor of Nubia. Their commander was adamant that none of them was involved in the fraud—in fact, he insisted on coming back with us, to take an oath before Ma'at and write a sworn deposition. If you want to talk to him, he's at the Second Fort."

So the goose and the dog had been right: they had indeed sensed an unusual presence.

"To whom did he hand over his consignment?" asked Paneb.

"To General Mehy himself," replied Sobek. "And one detail puzzled him: instead of delivering it to Karnak straightaway, the general stored it for a whole day in a warehouse on the west bank. What's more, according to one of the guards, Mehy was seen going into the warehouse with Daktair, the head of the central workshop."

"And Daktair knows a great deal about metals," Thuty put in.

"So," said Sobek, "I believe that Mehy ordered his accomplice Daktair to forge a silver ingot, and then they carried out the substitution together."

"Which may mean Mehy needed the real ingot to use as a large bribe," suggested Paneb.

"The traffic has probably been going on for a long time," Sobek continued. "Mehy's a thief and a crook, who buys people in order to maintain his grip on Thebes."

"Yes, but unfortunately," Paneb pointed out, "we've no proof."

"Isn't all this circumstantial evidence enough? I've written a detailed report; added to which there are the statements from all the witnesses we questioned."

"Everything points to Mehy," agreed Kenhir. "And let's not forget his last attempt to discredit the Master."

"Or the many times we've distrusted him," added Sobek. "It's quite likely that he's committed other crimes besides common theft. He must be brought to trial and made to confess. When he's stripped of his privileges and has to face his judges, he'll be revealed for what he really is: a coward."

"Yes," said Kenhir, "but his high rank means that the only person who can order his arrest is Queen-Pharaoh Tausert."

"I'll go to the palace tomorrow morning," promised Paneb, "and tell her everything we've discovered. Even if she's bedridden, she'll know what to do."

For the first time in many years, Sobek felt a certain pleasure in being alive. At long last, Mehy was going to be brought to book.

▲

By using all his persistence and powers of persuasion, Paneb had overcome all but one of the obstacles blocking his way to the queen. The last one, though, was formidable: the head doctor of the palace, who had forbidden anyone to enter Tausert's bedchamber.

"What I must tell the queen is of the utmost importance," argued Paneb.

"She cannot receive you," said the doctor.

"This concerns the safety of Thebes," stated the Master. "Let me speak to her, Doctor, or you'll be responsible for a terrible disaster."

"I couldn't help you, even if I wanted to," lamented the doctor.

"Why not?"

"Her Majesty has lapsed into unconsciousness. She will not wake again."

68

"There's a letter for you," announced Niut.

Kenhir looked up from his restorative breakfast of fresh milk, dried fish, figs, and hot bread fresh from the oven. "Read it to me," he said.

When he heard what it said, he almost choked. "Go and fetch Paneb."

Paneb was just as astounded. "This is an attempt to provoke us," he declared.

"But what if the informer's telling the truth? In situations like this, there's often someone who cracks, for fear of the consequences."

"What do you suggest we do?"

"The simplest thing. And perhaps at last we'll find out who it is that's persecuting us."

▲

While he waited for Serketa to arrive at his warehouse, Tran-Bel gloomily checked his accounts. His profits had plummeted since the traitor at the Place of Truth stopped supplying him with choice items. No longer could he have each one copied many times, and then sell the copies as original and unique.

Although he was adept at cheating his many customers, Tran-Bel was becoming disenchanted. His only expertise lay in figures, so he did not know the first thing about making a fine piece of furniture, and the few ideas he had come up with had all been failures. Profit was his sole obsession, and he nurtured it like a precious child; so, to restore his finances as quickly as possible, he had decided to blackmail Mehy and his wife.

At last Serketa arrived; she wore her usual heavy disguise.

Tran-Bel said, "I was getting impatient, my lady, and I was beginning to wonder if you really do mean to involve me in your grand plans."

"In the grandest of all, my friend."

Tran-Bel rolled up the papyrus he'd been checking. "Are you serious about this?"

"As serious as anyone can be. Fate has obliged us to be allies, so why not join forces?"

"What is this plan?"

"Once I've spoken, there'll be no way back for you, and we must act together, without second thoughts. Do you agree?"

"Very well, my lady."

"After long years of searching, we have at last located the tomb of Amenhotep I, the founder of the Place of Truth. And we're going to rob it of its priceless treasures."

"But how will you get into the Valley of the Kings?"

Serketa smiled contemptuously. "The craftsmen's trick was to make people believe that the tomb lies in the forbidden Valley. But we now know that it doesn't."

"And you know where it really is?"

"Yes, and we're going to rob it tomorrow night. If you like, you can join the expedition."

"I want more than that. I want to organize it myself, using men chosen by me."

Serketa hesitated. "I may have difficulty persuading my husband—"

"Those are my conditions, and they won't change. Where is the tomb?"

"Meet me at the foot of the hill of Thoth after sunset, and I'll give you a map. I'll wait there for you, so we can share out the booty."

"Very well, but come alone."

▲

Accompanied by his three longest-serving employees, who were just as excited as he was by the prospect of fabulous wealth, Tran-Bell surveyed the area. It was isolated, and seemed perfect for hiding such an important tomb.

The lookout saw Serketa coming; as agreed, she was alone.

"Have you got the map?" demanded Tran-Bel, his nerves on edge.

"Here it is." She handed him a leather case bound with thick cord.

He untied the cord with some difficulty, and slid out a papyrus scroll, which he examined by the light of the moon. "The tomb isn't far from here—just behind the second hill, toward the west."

"Have you brought the necessary tools to dig your way down to the entrance?"

"Of course, and it'll be easy to force a way in."

"Do it quickly."

Tran-Bel and his men ran toward their goal, confident of success. He was already planning to allocate himself the largest share of the loot.

As soon as they were out of sight, Serketa hurried away. Tran-Bel might have written a letter denouncing the general, but he had made a serious mistake in sending it to the deputy tjaty, one of Mehy's staunchest supporters. In exchange for destroying the letter, the official had been lavishly paid.

And Tran-Bel was no longer a threat; he was a useful pawn in the game in which Mehy pitted himself against the Brotherhood.

▲

"Here it is," whispered Tran-Bel. "Let's start digging."

The spades tore up the ground eagerly, and the four men uncovered a flight of steps.

The merchant's eyes bulged as the sealed door of a tomb appeared. "We're rich, my lads!"

Tran-Bel was about to break the seals with his pickax when Sobek's thunderous voice froze the thieves to the spot.

"You have been caught desecrating a tomb," shouted the big Nubian. "Don't try to run away, or my men will kill you."

Everyone knew that such a serious crime was punishable by death, and that no judge would show mercy. One of the thieves tried to escape by running toward the desert. An arrow caught him in the neck and he fell to the ground, dead.

"Stand still, the rest of you," advised Sobek, "or you'll get the same."

So, thought Sobek, rubbing his hands in satisfaction, the letter Kenhir had received, signed with the name of one of Tran-Bel's employees, had been the truth. With Kenhir's agreement, Sobek had decided to try to catch the culprits red-handed, and he had done just that.

"I am Tran-Bel, a well-known and honorable merchant. Don't touch me!"

"It's a little late to be afraid, my lad," said Sobek. "Tie them all up."

"I . . . It's not me . . . It's . . ." Suddenly, a terrible fire ripped through Tran-Bel's belly. His features distorted with pain, he stretched out his arms toward Sobek, then fell face-down on the ground.

"We didn't touch him, sir," said an astonished guard.

A putrid stench began to rise from the corpse. Serketa had chosen a poison with a delayed action, which would prevent the songbird revealing anything to the forces of law—whom Kenhir was sure to have alerted after reading the letter she had written.

Just as she planned, Tran-Bel had untied the poison-impregnated string, then dropped it in the sand. From that moment, he had had no more than half an hour to live—just long enough to reach the door of the tomb and then drop conveniently dead.

▲

Kenhir was perplexed. "So it was Tran-Bel who wanted to destroy the Place of Truth."

"Not at all," replied Sobek. "He was only a small fish in the Nile."

The Wise Woman and the Master agreed.

"The incident was simply a diversion," Sobek went on. "We mustn't slacken our grip on Mehy. Tran-Bel was poisoned, and there's no one more skilled in that deadly art than Daktair, who's head of the main workshop in Thebes and whom we know to be a friend of the general."

"You may well be right, but you've no evidence, have you?" said Kenhir.

"My instinct tells me Mehy will soon be cornered," insisted the Nubian.

"I agree," said the Wise Woman calmly, "and that makes him all the more dangerous."

"Tausert can't order his arrest," said Kenhir sadly, "so what are we going to do?"

"We must tell King Setnakhte," advised Paneb.

"Without any formal proof?"

"I'll take the responsibility."

"Be careful," warned Sobek. "If Mehy thinks he's being attacked, he'll react violently."

"But he'd never dare use his troops to attack us," said Kenhir. "No Theban soldiers would obey such an insane order."

"All the same, I shall take extra precautions," promised Sobek.

"There is one other consideration," Paneb pointed out. "It's more than likely that the traitor will try to help him from inside the village."

69

Kenhir was dictating to Niut a long report for King Setnakhte, detailing the Place of Truth's suspicions about Mehy, when they were interrupted by Hay.

"Uputy's here, Kenhir," he said, "and he's asking to see you."

"I'm busy. Can't it wait?"

"He says it's very important."

"Am I never to be left in peace?" grumbled the old man. "First this interminable report, which mustn't contain a single mistake, and then I have to leave for the Valley of the Kings. People have no respect for old age anymore."

"It's hard work that keeps you so healthy," observed Niut.

Leaning heavily on his stick, the old scribe made his way as fast as he could to the lay workers' camp. The messenger's insistence had aroused his curiosity.

"Did you know that Imuni's back in Thebes?" asked Uputy, after he'd greeted Kenhir.

"In Thebes? That little snake?"

"I'm afraid so; and he insisted on giving me this personally." He handed Kenhir a papyrus scroll. "It's a lawsuit: he hopes his expulsion from the Brotherhood will be annulled. He's got the support of one of the mayor's assistants, who's a very clever lawyer, and he's convinced the court will order his immediate reinstatement. He even thinks he'll become Master."

Kenhir read the scroll immediately.

"Is it serious?" asked Uputy anxiously.

"It's nothing but legal quibbles, but yes, we must take it seriously."

"But that little rat won't win, will he?"

"We'll fight with all our strength," Kenhir promised. "But let's put Imuni out of our thoughts for a moment. I have a most important mission for you."

Uputy drew himself up with great dignity. "I'm at your service."

"In a few days, I shall give you a message to be delivered to King Setnakhte, and you must take it to Pi-Ramses yourself."

"That's a great honor. But I'll have to tell my superiors where I'm going."

"Be very careful," Kenhir warned him.

"I'll take the boat reserved for urgent messages. Nothing will go wrong."

▲

Daktair was gulping down an enormous portion of goose in cumin sauce when Mehy burst into the room.

"Move yourself, Daktair."

The fat man almost choked. "Move? W-where to?"

"You are leaving for Gebel Zeit with my assistant and five of my servants who know how to hold their tongues."

"But it'll be an exhausting journey."

"You know the place and you know what you must bring me back. And be quick about it."

"Perhaps I'm not the man for the job and—"

"Oh yes you are, Daktair. You are indeed. In fact, you're the only man who can carry out this delicate mission with complete discretion. As soon as you get back, we shall make our move. You should be delighted: you've been wanting me to take decisive action for ages."

▲

While the two crews worked to finish Tausert's vast tomb, Sobek was busy setting up a new lookout system for the village. Increasingly certain that an armed attack would come, he had a feeling Mehy's men would not take the official road, which was closely watched, but another. So he had stationed men along tracks and paths where they would not be expected.

With great delight, he had gone back over every piece of evidence he had gathered about Mehy, together with all the new information. Armed with an investigation order signed by Kenhir and countersigned by the deputy tjaty, who had not dared refuse Kenhir's request, Sobek had been authorized to search the official records of Thebes for information about transfers within and between the various forces of guards. His search had uncovered crucial evidence, and he was eager to get back to the village and show everything to Kenhir and Paneb.

Some time ago, there had been an attempt to transfer Sobek from the Place of Truth to the river guards. Among the proposals turned down by the tjaty was a document showing that the man behind the attempt had been none other than

Mehy. Sobek knew that Mehy, if he had succeeded, would have been able to appoint a puppet in Sobek's place, thus depriving the Place of Truth of all real protection. He would also have been able to prevent Sobek from making inquiries into the murder many years before of one of his Nubian guards—a murder that Sobek was sure Mehy himself had committed.

His heart pounding, Sobek crossed the Nile by ferryboat, then spurred on his horse to reach the village as quickly as possible.

As soon as they were informed of his return, the Master, the Scribe of the Tomb, and the Wise Woman hurried to Sobek's office.

He told them quickly of his discoveries. "I no longer have any doubt at all about Mehy's guilt," he concluded, "and King Setnakhte will be equally convinced. Mehy is a murderer. He killed anyone who got in his way or who might have denounced him—even his own wife's father, Governor Abry."

"The man you describe is an absolute monster!" said Kenhir.

"There's worse," Sobek went on. "Here's the anonymous letter accusing Nefer of murdering my man, and here's the letter from Mehy arranging my transfer. Compare them."

"The writing's identical," noted Paneb.

Ubekhet turned pale.

"Mehy tried to make us believe Nefer's murderer was a lay worker," Sobek reminded them. "Why should he do that, if not to protect the traitor in the Brotherhood? The traitor is working for Mehy, not for himself, and Mehy's only goal is to destroy the Place of Truth and steal its treasures."

There was a long silence.

The Wise Woman closed her eyes. Eventually, she said, "Sobek is right."

"I'll kill him with my bare hands!" promised Paneb.

"It is not for you to mete out justice," said Kenhir sternly. "I shall add all this information to my report, and Setnakhte will certainly order Mehy's arrest."

▲

Mehy had spent the morning hunting birds with his throwing stick in the papyrus forest, but with little success. He went home in an extremely bad mood and, once again, took out his rage on his household.

Serketa was stretched out beside the lake. Her radiant smile reassured him. "Our little problem has been solved," she said.

"Tran-Bel is dead?"

"Have I ever failed, my tender darling? Look, an officer brought you this report."

The general read it with satisfaction. "Just as you planned, Sobek lay in wait, and caught Tran-Bel and his men red-handed. Tran-Bel and another man are dead, and the other two looters have been arrested and thrown into prison."

"Sobek and the Place of Truth can no longer be in any doubt: their worst enemy is dead. So they will lower their guard and—"

There was a discreet cough from a few paces away. Mehy's head steward bowed and said, "Your private secretary is asking for you, my lord."

"Tell him to join me in my audience chamber," ordered Mehy.

▲

The secretary looked worried. "I have alarming news, General."

"About what?"

"With the palace's agreement, Commander Sobek is carrying out an extensive investigation into your affairs. He has taken away the document proving that you requested his transfer, many years ago."

"That is indeed annoying."

"And he may have discovered other things, too."

"Why are you so worried?"

"Because Uputy is soon to leave for Pi-Ramses on a special mission: he's to take an important message to King Setnakhte."

"Have you any idea what it will say?"

"No, but I fear it may be about you, General."

"Tell me immediately if you find out anything new."

Mehy dismissed the man and returned to his wife. "A new problem, my sweet."

Still stretched out, she opened greedy eyes. "Is someone else trying to harm you?"

"Sobek still hasn't given up. I'll take care of him myself as soon as Daktair gets back. In the meantime, you're to deal with Uputy."

"That won't be difficult."

"The message he'll be carrying must not reach Setnakhte. You must replace it with another, which will be found on his corpse and taken straight to the king. In it, I shall denounce Paneb and the Brotherhood as dangerous plotters against our beloved monarch."

"What a delicious idea," purred Serketa.

70

Savagely beaten by Mehy for knocking over a cup of wine, the little Nubian serving girl fled to the stables in tears; the head steward searched for her in vain.

She made up her mind to leave this place where she was so badly treated. And unlike the other servants, who were terrified of the general, she would have the courage to tell the truth. She had heard about the officer who protected the craftsmen's village, a fellow Nubian who was known to be incorruptible. She would tell him everything.

As soon as the coast was clear, she slipped out of the stables, made her way cautiously out of Mehy's estate, and crept across the fields to the edge of the desert, where a peasant woman told her the way. Ignoring her tiredness, the girl walked all the way to the First Fort.

When she got there, a Nubian guard stopped her. "Just where do you think you're going, my girl?"

"To see your commander."

"Oh yes? And what might that be about?"

"I want to lodge a complaint against General Mehy."

The guard ought to have burst out laughing, but something about the girl made him take her seriously. "I'll tell him. Wait here."

When she was shown into Sobek's office, she was at first daunted by his sheer size. But she overcame her fears, for she was determined to see this through to the end.

Sobek gave her a piercing look. "You want to talk to me about Mehy?"

"He's beaten me many times—look."

She showed him her arms, and Sobek saw that they were badly scarred.

"That's a very serious offense, serious enough to earn him a prison sentence."

"Good!"

"He's a powerful man. Will you have the courage to face him before the court and repeat your accusation?"

"Ten times over, if need be."

"Very well. Then I'll take your statement, and we'll go together to a judge to register your complaint." Sobek smiled. Even before the pharaoh had examined the evidence sent to him by Kenhir, Mehy would be locked away.

"He's not the only one who deserves to be punished," added the serving girl.

"Really? Who else does?"

"His wife—she's a madwoman! She flies into terrible rages, she rolls about on the ground, she eats for hours on end, or screams at the top of her voice. He calms her down by making love to her like a rutting animal. And she's always getting dressed up in peculiar clothes."

"What do you mean?"

"She is incredibly rich, yet she hides a peasant woman's clothes in a chest, and horrible, coarse wigs, too, and I've seen her go out dressed like a pauper."

Sobek recalled that a peasant woman had been suspected of murder. . . . Could the murderess have been none other than Serketa, carrying out Mehy's dirty work?

"Once," the girl went on, "a little scribe came to see them, and they talked about you and the Place of Truth. He had a syrupy voice and a face like a rat."

"Can you remember his name?"

"Imuni, I think."

So Imuni really was the traitor! The Brotherhood had rid itself of him, but Sobek knew he must take action without a moment's delay to prevent the evil couple from doing yet more harm.

"You must stay here for the moment," he said. "My men will see that you have food and drink, and you'll be protected."

The girl stood on tiptoe and kissed him on the cheek.

More moved than he let himself appear, Sobek ran to the village gate. As soon as Kenhir emerged, Sobek told him about the girl's revelations.

"This time, the general is lost," said Kenhir. "It's a pity Uputy has already left for Pi-Ramses, or I could have added these accusations to my report. But never mind. I can always do it later."

"Already left?" said Sobek, aghast. "But he's in mortal danger! He'll never be suspicious of a peasant woman."

▲

Uputy had put on his best clothes, polished the heavy Staff of Thoth, the symbol of his office, and slipped the Scribe of the Tomb's report into his white leather pouch.

On the road to the landing stage he saw a peasant woman lying at the foot of an old tamarisk, writhing in pain; her face was partially hidden by a coarse wig. Uputy ought not to have stopped, but he could not let her suffer like that. Besides, the boat would not leave without him.

He went over to her and asked gently, "What's the matter?"

"I think I've broken my leg," moaned Serketa plaintively.

"I'll go and fetch help."

"No, no, I'm afraid to stay here on my own. Help me stand up."

"That's not a good idea—you may make things worse."

"I beg of you, help me."

Serketa's plan was both simple and effective. When the messenger stretched out his hand to her, she would use the dagger hidden under her tunic and stab him in the heart. But in order to distract him, and to ensure a good angle of attack, she tried to support herself on the Staff of Thoth.

"Don't touch that!" exclaimed Uputy indignantly, stepping briskly back.

Serketa was on her feet now, dagger in hand.

"You're mad!" said Uputy with conviction.

With a scream of rage, Serketa rushed at him.

Realizing that the precious message was in danger, Uputy did not hesitate. He used the Staff of Thoth as a club and smashed the woman's skull. Her face dripping blood and her eyes rolling up in her head, Serketa clutched the hilt of her dagger and swayed from side to side. Then she collapsed in a heap, dead.

"Thoth, god of knowledge and of the sacred words, does not allow people to attack messengers," declared Uputy by way of a funeral oration.

▲

Hathor was there, wearing a blue wig crowned with a red sun, out of which sprang a red and black cobra. So was Ptah, in his tight-fitting tunic of dazzling white, enfolded by the wings of Ma'at. Osiris wore a gold necklace and a red cape, and was seated on his throne, facing a great lotus flower on which his four sons stood. And there were countless other gods and goddesses, whom Paneb had painted with incomparable genius.

Now he was putting the finishing touches to his most remarkable work: Tausert's immense sarcophagus chamber. Its pillars were decorated with elegant figures, the base courses with the various pieces of funerary equipment, and the great wall with a giant scene depicting magical transmutation and the preparation of the new sun. Above a gigantic ram with green and red wings, two men, accompanied by bird-souls, held up a red sun disk fashioned by a black scarab beetle; and an infant sun was developing in the bosom of the universe, protected by the sky-goddess, Nut, who would send it forth into the light of dawn.

Although Paneb had used an enormous number of lamps, Kenhir had not scolded him once; and Uabet the Pure had worked especially hard to produce the wicks. Uniting powerful work and delicate execution, Paneb had both lit up the tomb with bright colors and created the powerful symbols that would keep Tausert's soul at the very heart of eternity.

Paneb was determined to win the battle against death, which prowled around the queen-pharaoh, and he had not allowed himself a moment's rest.

The familiar sound of Kenhir's walking stick striking the steps echoed along the descending passageway. Dazzled, the old scribe halted on the threshold of the chamber.

"Who are you really, Paneb, to have created such marvels?"

"No more nor less than a Servant of the Place of Truth."

"During my long life I have admired very few people, and I ought not to admit this to you, but I thank the gods for permitting me to see these paintings."

"We shall vanquish death once again."

Kenhir sighed. "I wish I could stand here and look at the paintings for hours, but worldly matters demand our attention. Sobek is waiting for us at the entrance to the Valley. Something serious has happened."

▲

"Uputy has killed Serketa, General Mehy's wife," Sobek told them when they joined him. "She was disguised as a peasant woman and tried to stab him. She was carrying a letter signed by Mehy, accusing the Brotherhood of plotting against Pharaoh—I'm sure she was going to substitute that letter for Kenhir's report. I went to the general's house and to his offices on the west bank, but he wasn't there."

"He's probably hiding in the main barracks at Thebes, on the eastern bank," suggested Kenhir.

"Yes, I think you're right. And unfortunately I haven't the authority to arrest him."

"I'll add these vital details to my report at once, and you must give them to Uputy."

"He's been given an armed escort, and he awaits your order to leave. There's another piece of good news: thanks to the testimony of a serving girl who came to see me to lodge a complaint about having been beaten by Mehy, we now know the name of the traitor: former Assistant Scribe Imuni."

"Imuni, Nefer's murderer?" stammered Kenhir. "How could he possibly have committed such an appalling crime?"

Paneb said nothing; he seemed unruffled by the news.

"I suggest that you go back to the village and arm yourselves," said Sobek earnestly. "I'm afraid that the general, like any wild animal at bay, may well become more vicious than ever."

71

Mehy stood in his office in the Theban barracks, where he had taken refuge as soon as he heard of Serketa's death, and scowled at the army officer in front of him.

The officer was not happy—it was never wise to cross

General Mehy—but he delivered his bad news unflinchingly. "The Place of Truth is under the direct authority of Pharaoh. Without an explicit order from His Majesty, no Theban soldier would ever attack the village or spill the blood of a member of the Brotherhood."

Mehy had expected as much; and he knew Setnakhte would not give such an order. He hastened to reassure the officer. "We must take pride in our men's loyalty," he boasted. "It will ensure that Egypt remains a great power. Soon, we shall carry out an exercise using our new weapons. Have them deposited in the first storehouse."

The officer bowed and left the office.

Mehy's scowl deepened. He was safe for the time being, but when Setnakhte's royal decree reached Karnak he was bound to be arrested.

The Place of Truth had not won yet, though. Through violence, Mehy would yet achieve victory.

▲

Only one day later than Mehy had planned, Daktair reached the barracks. He was as exhausted by the forced march as the general's assistant and the five servants.

"Have you got what I need?" demanded Mehy.

"Yes, General. Plenty of stone-oil," said Daktair.

"And you've checked its properties?"

"You won't be disappointed, I assure you."

Mehy smiled. "Then all we have to do is take the weapons from the first storehouse and join the Libyans, who are hiding in a ruined fort in the desert."

The barracks gatekeeper was astonished to see Mehy himself, his assistant, and a group of civilians loading swords, spears, bows, and arrows onto donkeys and leaving the barracks in great haste, but it was not for a simple soldier to pass comment.

▲

Six-Toes had a connoisseur's appreciation of the razor sharp swords, lightweight spears, and exceptionally hard arrowheads.

"Our best weapons," said Mehy, "and these aren't all—we also have something completely new. We shall use it to destroy the Place of Truth, after we've killed the Nubian guards."

"Where is it?"

"In those jars."

The Libyan opened one. "But it's just greasy, stinking oil."

"It has remarkable qualities, as my friend Daktair is about to demonstrate."

Daktair spread a little of the oil on one of the chests that had been used to transport the weapons and, with the aid of a flint, set it alight. The intensity of the flames and the speed with which they spread astonished Six-Toes and his men.

"With this oil," said Mehy, "we can burn anything, even stone."

He picked up the jar and poured its contents over Daktair.

"General, what are you doing?"

"You like trying new things, don't you? Let's see how you like this," and he flung the burning remains of the chest at Daktair.

Daktair caught fire instantly. He ran off into the desert, his terrible screams chilling the Libyans' blood, then at last collapsed, reduced to a blackened corpse.

"That's how the Servants of the Place of Truth will die," gloated Mehy. "Now, Six-Toes, deal with my assistant and those stupid servants. I want to wipe out all traces of the past."

Only Mehy's assistant tried to put up a fight, but a dagger soon slit his throat.

"This oil is nothing in comparison with the fabulous treasure we are going to capture," declared the general. "With its aid, I shall lead Libya to total victory."

▲

Just when everything seemed quiet and peaceful, Charmer's hair stood on end, Ebony growled, Bad Girl ran up and down the main street, flapping her wings, and the gatekeeper pounded on the gate.

Led by Paneb and the Wise Woman, the craftsmen hurried to the gate, where they found Sobek impatiently awaiting them.

"One of my lookouts has spotted about thirty armed men coming this way," he said. "I've alerted my superiors, but no one will take any responsibility in Mehy's absence."

"We aren't soldiers, and we don't know how to fight," said Pai, fear in his voice.

"May the silent grow ferocious if the sacred places are threatened, for God will not permit any man to rebel against the temple," intoned Ubekhet, quoting one of the ancient sages. "If and when necessary, I shall call upon my allies in the Peak of the West."

Kenhir ordered the swords, spears, and daggers manufactured by Obed the blacksmith to be taken out of the strong room, and told the craftsmen, "Given the gravity of the situation, I authorize you to use these weapons."

"The port crew will come with me," said Paneb. "The starboard crew will stay in the village to protect the women and children."

Sobek was about to protest, but then he suddenly understood the reason behind Paneb's decision. The Master believed that the traitor was not Imuni but someone still in the village, one of the starboard crew. If the traitor was given a weapon, he'd try to murder Paneb during the fighting.

Paneb drew Hay to one side, and said quietly, "I have total confidence in you, Hay. Stay close to the Wise Woman. Protect her and obey her, whatever she asks of you."

"You have my word on it."

Though he hid his feelings, Paneb was still worried. If the traitor tried to damage the village from inside, would Ubekhet detect his wickedness in time, and would Hay and the starboard crew be able to kill him?

"Come with me," said Sobek. "I'll tell you what you must do."

Paneb decided to use only one weapon: the great pickax marked by celestial fire. Who better to give him the strength to win than Set, god of storms?

▲

Mehy had avoided the usual road to the village and chosen an obscure track where, he was sure, Sobek would not have posted any lookouts. The Libyans would kill the Nubian guards, and the general would plunge his sword into the belly of their commander, ensuring that he suffered a slow, painful death.

And then would come the massacre—not one villager would be left alive. The Libyans would seize the gold the craftsmen had made, Mehy would capture the Stone of Light, and then he'd cover everything with stone-oil so that the fire destroyed every last brick of the Place of Truth.

The raiding party was moving along the edges of the fields when the Libyan at the front collapsed, an arrow through his throat. By the time Mehy had established where it had been fired from, four more of his men were down.

"Over there—the little mound!" shouted Six-Toes, and he ran to attack it.

Mehy had a grim premonition that all was lost. How could they be attacked here, so far from the village, in a place that should have been unguarded? Several more Libyans fell, and he realized that the attack was turning into a disaster. He tried to make off through the fields, but three craftsmen cut off his retreat. He swerved and headed for the hills, in the hope of outrunning and outclimbing his pursuers.

He caught up with Six-Toes and his men, who were fighting ferociously and trying to save the situation. Two Nubians were dead, and several others had been wounded. The battle swayed back and forth, and the Libyans seemed to be getting the upper hand: two craftsmen were on the point of being killed.

Suddenly, as if by magic, several cobras appeared out of the ground. They struck at the Libyans and bit them on the legs.

"The Wise Woman's allies!" shouted Paneb. "With them here, we've nothing to fear!"

Stubbornly, Six-Toes attacked the furious Sobek and tried to stab him in the side, but Sobek was too swift for him and plunged his sword into the Libyan's chest.

The craftsmen stopped fighting, for the cobras were taking care of the last of the Libyans.

"Carry the wounded to the village," ordered Paneb. "Ubekhet will care for them."

The attack had been violent but brief, and calm soon returned to the sun-drenched hills. Not a single member of the Libyan raiding party was left alive.

"Sir," reported one of Sobek's men glumly, "we can't find General Mehy's body."

"That coward!" sneered the commander. "He took to his heels and ran for the mountains. But he won't get away."

The Master, who had been in the thick of the fight, was leaning against a rock, getting his breath back.

"Paneb, look out!" yelled Sobek.

Lunging out from his hiding place behind the rock, Mehy drove a double-bladed dagger into Paneb's back.

As though it were nothing but an insect bite, Paneb swung round without a sound.

Mehy went as white as a sheet. "That's impossible! You should be dead!"

"All your accursed life, you've done nothing but strike from behind, out of the shadows. I act in the full light of day, looking my opponent in the eye."

As he had promised Ubekhet, Paneb lifted high his great pickax and brought it down with all his strength, plunging the point deep into Mehy's skull.

72

At last Ubekhet emerged from her house.

"Well?" asked Kenhir, and all the villagers waited in great anxiety for her answer.

"Paneb's alive. But he's very seriously wounded, and he'll have to rest for a long time."

The big man appeared behind her, his chest heavily bandaged and his face gray with pain. "I'll rest later," he said. "What we've just learnt from Uputy means we've got urgent work to do. We must take the sarcophagus to the Valley at once."

"You're mad," protested Hay. "Didn't you hear what Ubekhet said?"

"Come along. We're leaving right now."

Uputy had delivered two messages, reporting the deaths of Tausert and Setnakhte. The two pharaohs would be buried in the same House of Eternity, the period of mourning had begun, and Egypt must choose a new king.

The traitor was jubilant. During the fighting he had not tried anything, and with Serketa and Mehy both dead he no longer had anyone to fear. During the coming troubled times, he'd find an opportunity to steal the Stone of Light and leave the village. And then the Stone would be his and his alone.

No one could denounce him now, and Nefer's murder would go unsolved.

▲

Once he was alone with Ubekhet in Tausert's tomb, Paneb brushed the last touch of blue onto the headdress of Ma'at, the goddess he had chosen to paint last of all. He traced two broken lines, symbolizing the life-giving fluid she gave to those faithful to her.

Marveling at Ma'at's sublime face, Ubekhet knew that the

Master had at last attained serenity of heart and absolute beauty of form. Paneb had worked on seven Houses of Eternity during his career, and he had become one of Ma'at's most remarkable servants.

The Wise Woman seemed bathed in clear golden light. "Let us now bring the sarcophagus to life," she said.

At the prow of the granite ship in which Tausert's soul would sail through the celestial paradise lay the Stone of Light. Ubekhet knelt down, her hands raised in a sign of worship, and spoke the words of power.

"Here, in this House of Gold where the Widow brings Osiris back to life, the mysterious work of transmutation takes place. The Sky-mother stretches out upon the body of light and lifts the spirit to its place among the immortal stars. You lead our sovereign along the beautiful paths of the afterlife, and now I give you eyes, that you may see."

A soft yet intense light shone out from the stone, enveloping the sarcophagus. It was no longer simply carved stone and wood, for it had become "the Giver of Life."

"The Stone's energy is exhausted," announced the Wise Woman. "Take it and set it next to the great wall."

Paneb picked up the stone block; it seemed weightless in his hands.

"Gaze upon the scarab beetle, Paneb; gaze upon it with all your might."

He concentrated hard. Suddenly, all the suns he had painted with magic material began to emit beams of light, which focused on the stone and entered it. The Stone of Light's energy was replenished.

"What we make makes us," said Ubekhet, "and our greatest secret is the exchange of Light. For as long as we know how to paint living suns, the Stone will continue to shine."

▲

Kenhir was in a dreadful state. First, he was worried about Paneb's health, for the Master had taken insane risks by returning to the Valley of the Kings; second, he kept asking himself which craftsman could possibly have killed, lied, and feigned brotherhood for so many years?

He ran through them all in his mind, over and over again, but although each man undoubtedly had his weaknesses, such evil seemed unthinkable. No, not one of them, whatever his faults, could be a monster like Mehy.

And yet Kenhir had agreed to the plan suggested by the Wise Woman and the Master to identify the traitor.

▲

As the sun set, the procession of craftsmen halted before the Temple of Ma'at and Hathor.

"Our present work is finished," declared Paneb. For once he sounded tired—and indeed he was exhausted from struggling against the pain. "Now we are free from the threat that has hung over us."

"But supposing the new pharaoh's hostile to us?" asked Ipuy.

"Setnakhte's eldest son will soon be proclaimed king," revealed Kenhir, "and he has made his intentions clear. He will attend the funeral ceremonies for his father and Tausert, and he has assured me by messenger that the Place of Truth will remain one of the country's most important places."

This excellent news was greeted with joyful cheering.

Paneb cheered with the rest, but Nakht saw him sway and quickly gave him an arm to lean on.

"We all need rest," admitted the Master, and his voice was weak.

"You most of all," said Ipuy.

The craftsmen dispersed, but the traitor did not go home. Instead, he followed Paneb, who staggered off to the temple.

The traitor hid in a corner, from where he saw the big man pick up a cube-shaped object hidden under a cloth and hoist it onto his shoulder. Followed by Kenhir, who kept turning to look behind him, Paneb set off along the path to the main burial ground.

So, he was indeed carrying the Stone of Light, and the traitor was at last going to find out its hiding place!

When Paneb and Kenhir entered the courtyard in front of the old scribe's tomb, the traitor thought he was about to be disappointed yet again; then he saw Paneb climb onto a platform where a small pointed pyramid had been built. The Master took off the cloth, and for a moment the Stone lit up the darkness before he laid it deep in a chamber at the base of the structure.

Of course! The pyramid, symbol of the first ray of Light that had created the universe. The perfect hiding place. Like the other villagers, the traitor had often looked at Kenhir's tomb, but he had never suspected a thing.

Paneb and Kenhir went back down the hill toward the village.

Now the traitor knew.

▲

"You really ought not to get up," Ubekhet told Paneb.

"You know I must. My work isn't finished yet."

Not all the Wise Woman's magic would make him rest, so she simply smoothed healing ointment over the deep wound, replaced the honey-soaked bandage, and gave him something to reduce the pain. With a wound like that, she knew, no one but Paneb could have put one foot in front of the other.

When he got up, he was careful not to disturb Charmer, who, sensing that his master was ill, had slept on the bed.

"Will you let me help you?"

That voice . . . It was Turquoise's voice, wasn't it? Turquoise, here in his house!

"Is it really you?" he asked in amazement.

"I'm making you a proper breakfast. You must get your strength back."

▲

The Nubian guards were delighted. At last the permanent state of alert had been lifted. They were returning to routine duties and had been granted leave. Moreover, Kenhir had given them food, clothes, and precious ointments to thank them for their heroism.

All that remained was to learn the name of the new pharaoh, but the rumors emerging from the capital were worrying. Setnakhte's eldest son had the support of the Great Council as well as the common people, and would therefore probably defeat the various factions in the capital. But they were anxious to know what coronation name he would adopt, because that would reveal the form his reign would take.

"Light duties today once the water delivery is done," said Sobek. "The craftsmen and the lay workers are having a holiday, and so are you."

Once the donkeys had left, the village did not wake up as it usually did. After the whirlwind that had nearly swept it away, it was treating itself to a lazy morning in bed, though Uabet the Pure and two other priestesses had honored the ancestors on everyone's behalf.

The traitor knew this was the moment he had been waiting for.

73

Once his work was done, Paneb had collapsed, and for long, agonizing hours he hovered between life and death. Turquoise had not left his bedside once during all that time; without her magic he would not have survived.

Now, at last, the Wise Woman pronounced the outlook much more favorable. "This is an illness I know and can cure."

Paneb took Turquoise's hand. "Why don't you stay here with me? I'm a free man now."

"Have you forgotten my vow? If I broke it, I wouldn't deserve your love."

"I have the authority to release you from that vow," said Ubekhet.

Paneb held Turquoise's hand more tightly. "No one, especially not a priestess of Hathor, can oppose the Wise Woman's decision," he said enthusiastically.

Turquoise did not answer, but he saw from her smile, and the new brightness in her eyes, that he was at last going to spend every night with the love of his life.

There was a brief commotion outside, and Kenhir burst into the room; he looked years younger.

"Two pieces of good news! I've finished my *Key of Dreams* at last, and Niut's going to make several copies of it. People may criticize my literary work if they wish, but at least it will be passed down to future generations."

"And what's the second piece of news?" asked Ubekhet.

"Ah, the second! It's just as important, I have to say. We've been told the new pharaoh's name." Everyone hung on his words. "He's to be called Ramses, the third of that name."

Paneb jumped to his feet. "Ramses! Ramses reigns again!"

A loud bark caught everyone's attention. Ebony was standing in the doorway, his eyes bright and his tail wagging furiously.

"Then there's only one more problem to solve," said the Master.

▲

Of course, the traitor was taking a big risk. But Sobek's guards were keeping only a light watch, the villagers were dozing, and he would never have a better opportunity to seize the Stone of Light. Afterward, he would escape along a road that ran parallel to the Valley of the Queens, together with his wife, who was keeping watch at the little western gate.

He reached the burial ground and sneaked between the tombs until he reached Kenhir's tomb, the pyramid on its narrow platform looming over it.

Sharp claws suddenly raked across his hand. "Charmer! Get away from me, you filthy creature!"

Yowling, the fur on his back arched into spikes like a dragon's, the enormous cat drew back reluctantly. Dodging the traitor's fist, he jumped up onto a low wall.

Ignoring his wounded hand, the traitor removed the Stone from its hiding place. It was heavy, but he was strong enough to carry it to the nearest farm, where he could hire a donkey. He wrapped his treasure in a length of linen and hurried back down the path to the village, drunk with a twisted joy.

▲

Paneb had seen everything.

So that was the traitor. The very man who had dared stand up in the Brotherhood's meetinghouse and declare, "You cannot take the poison out of the crocodile, the snake, or the evil man." The craftsman who had constantly urged Aapehti to do evil. The artist who had falsified documents to mislead the Master and throw blame upon his companions.

That was the man who had murdered Nefer the Silent. A man whom the Wise Woman had cared for and whom his brothers had loved. A cold man with an unattractive face, a big nose, and a flabby body. A man who had constantly lied as he acted out his devilish part.

A man called Gau the Precise.

▲

When the traitor reached the village's western gate, the person awaiting him was not his wife but the Master himself.

"Your accomplice has been arrested, Gau. What are you carrying that is so precious?"

"Just some personal belongings."

"Don't you mean the Stone of Light?"

"Nonsense!"

"Why did you murder Nefer?"

Gau smiled contemptuously. "I was the only man worthy to be Master, so it was better that he should die. And how right I was to make an ally of General Mehy. He's made me rich and powerful."

"You cowardly, hypocritical, greedy criminal," roared Paneb. "The monster that waits beside the scales of judgment—waits to devour the sons of darkness—will have a real feast."

Gau took a step back. "You wouldn't dare kill me. Ma'at forbids you!"

"How dare you speak the name of the goddess of righteousness?"

Gau was terrified by the big man's rage—he was going to break his skull! There was only one way out: the path up to the Peak.

He fled up the slope, clutching the Stone of Light. When he felt his hand begin to burn, at first he thought it was just the scratch Charmer had given him; but the pain grew and grew, until it was almost unbearable and he had to put the Stone down. But the pain became even more intense, as if both his hands had been plunged into fire.

Suddenly, his eyes misted over. The rocks all around seemed to swell until they lost all consistency and were lost in a thick fog, although the morning sun reigned in a clear blue sky.

"What's happening to me?" whimpered Gau the Precise. "I . . . I'm going blind."

When he put his hands to his eyes, they, too, began to burn. With a cry of terror, desperate to escape the torture, he staggered on up the path as fast as he could.

A royal cobra, incarnation of the goddess of silence, appeared before him, poised to strike. It sank its fangs into his neck.

▲

Nakht and Didia opened the main gate of the village to allow Ramses III to enter. His noble bearing made a great impression on everyone present.

Paneb's chest was still heavily bandaged, but he managed to bow before the supreme Master of the Place of Truth.

"Your privileges are to be maintained," declared the new pharaoh, "and the Great Works I plan will require the initiation of more young craftsmen who have heard the call. Take this task in hand, Master."

A woman approached Pharaoh; her poise and nobility were such that he recognized her instantly as the Brotherhood's spiritual mother. She offered the king a branch from the persea tree that shaded the tomb of Nefer the Silent, who would be present forever among his brethren.

As he gazed at the Wise Woman, Ramses understood a great truth. Only here, in the Place of Truth, could mankind continue to be shown the path that led toward the Light.

ENDNOTES

1. This description is based on a recent scientific study of the eyes of the famous "Louvre scribe," which demonstrated the remarkable knowledge that ancient Egyptian doctors had about the structure of the eye.
2. The *Akh-menu* at Karnak, whose ruins can still be admired.
3. Recent analyses have proved that the Egyptians used cobalt blue as a pigment three thousand years before its discovery in the West.
4. Ancestor of our game of chess.

CHRISTIAN JACQ is the author of the bestselling five-volume Ramses series, which sold eleven million copies in twenty-nine countries. He has a doctorate in Egyptian studies from the Sorbonne in France. He founded, and now heads, the Ramses Institute, which is dedicated to preserving the endangered archaeological sites of Egypt.